To J___,

Best Wishes,

Mark Bowden

Go Navy!
_____

December
2013

Also by the Author

Victory Road
2011 Winner, Gold Medal Award, Military Writers
Society of America

The Texas Gun Club
2010 Winner, Gold Medal Award, Military Writers
Society of America

Praise for *The Texas Gun Club*

"*The Texas Gun Club* is an excellent WWII war novel—realistic, well-plotted, many actual events.... [It] describes the successes and failures of command and battle: friendly fire, poor communications, death, destruction, courage, and valor. It has found a place on my bookshelf ... I am looking forward to the author's promised next novel in the series [*Victory Road*]."

— Lee Boyland, Reviewer
Military Writers Society of America (January 2010)

"*The Texas Gun Club* is a well-written account of a very real critical World War II battle. Only the characters are fictional. Careful attention to detail in weapons and equipment, as well as period 'soldier slang,' brings [characters] to life as real people who we might have known back in 1939.... *The Texas Gun Club* highlights one great tragic truth of warfare: because of personal turbulence and logistic screw-ups, and despite unit lineage that may go back to the Revolution, we almost always fight the first battle with ad hoc organizations. The Salerno landing found the 36th Texas Division executing a difficult maneuver (establishing a lodgment on a distant defended shore) against an experienced, welled commander (Field Marshal Kesslring), with precious little time and space to sort it out and get it right. A good read for those who would lead."

— MG Don Daniel, USA (Ret.)
Former Commander, 49th Armored Division, TXARNG

"*The Texas Gun Club* is an absolutely superb book. The characters are incredibly realistic, as is the action and the story line of the two cousins dovetailing through history. That it will be a series is refreshing, and I look forward to reading the next excerpt.... For a Navy guy, Commander Bowlin has a great handle on the Army. Time for him to get back to the next installment."

— BG Jack Grubbs, USA (Ret.) PhD, PE
Author of *The Dryline* and *Bad Intentions*

For God and Country

For God and Country

A Texas Gun Club Novel

Commander Mark Bowlin, USN (Ret.)

For God and Country
A Texas Gun Club Novel

The Small Press
16250 Knoll Trail Drive, Suite 205
Dallas, Texas 75248
www.BBSmallPress.com
(972) 381-0009

ISBN 978-1-612547-97-8
Library of Congress Control Number 2011944107

Printed in the United States of America
10 9 8 7 6 5 4 3 2 1

Author contact information:
Commander Mark Bowlin, USN (Ret.)

For God and Country is dedicated to Alex Bowlin.

Acknowledgments

First and foremost, I need to thank Susan and Alex for their support during the writing of *For God and Country*. Many generous people offered technical advice, editorial suggestions, names, and help in a multitude of ways. I'd like to thank my primary readers, Stan Bowlin and CDR Bob Rose, USN (Ret.); as well as CAPT Doug Grossmann, USN; CAPT Scott Kawamoto, USNR (who taught me how to roister long ago); CAPT Valerie Ormond, USN (Ret.); CAPT Doug Peabody, USN; Lt Col Frank Chawk III, USMC; CDR Mark Gerschoffer, USN; CDR Rob "Two-Bit" Hoar; Lt Cdr Robert Hawkins, MBE, RN; LCDR Craig Ozaki, USN (Ret.); Capt Fin Jones, USMC (Ret.); the Reverend Mike Allen, PhD; Gary BGE Beams; Michele Di Lonardo; Toni Bernardi Rose; Cynthia Stillar-Wang and her team at The Small Press; and Bob Wranosky.

Rome Hwy 6

Cassino

Liri River

Sant' Angelo

Gustav Line

Rapido River

Garigliano River

46th Division (Br)

143rd Inf Crossing

141st Inf Crossing

Mt Trocchio

Victory Road

San Pietro

Rapido River
Crossing
Pfc. Ed Kulis
Jan. '44

N

Chapter One

January 23, 1944
1100 Hours
Mount Trocchio, Italy

Murder.

It was just a word, but it ran endlessly through the officer's thoughts.

Murder.

What was done to them was nothing short of murder. They had been led like lambs to the slaughter, and then they had been murdered. Hundreds of Texans dead. Thousands of Texans to languish for years in a German prisoner of war camp. Many more forever wounded in body and mind. And for what?

Murder.

They were all dead. His friends, his cousin. Dead.

Murder.

A crime that cried out for vengeance. *No. For justice.*

The tall officer unconsciously wiped away a silent tear before it could freeze to his face. He was uncomfortable—the rocks of the castle ruins were cold and unyielding against his damaged body—but he didn't move. The mountain left him exposed to the harsh winter day, but he had thought that perhaps from its peak he could see some signs of life on the battlefield. He thought that, maybe, he could see his cousin. If he had even a suggestion or hint that his cousin was still alive, there was not a force in nature that could stop him from crossing the freezing river again and bringing him home. But he saw nothing.

A temporary truce had been arranged and the short peace had already come and gone as American and German medics had worked through the battlefield together. The war was back on, but the battlefield remained silent. There would be no further attacks across the river today—there was no one left to send over.

The officer scanned the battlefield again through the scope—he had taken a sniper rifle with the unlikely expectation that he would be able to help those on the other side. He saw nothing and sighed. His sigh turned to a groan, and the groan gave way to a single, broken sob of despair. They were all gone.

He took a deep breath and decided it was time to leave. He couldn't help anyone here, but he was needed down in the valley. The company, the battalion, the regiment . . . the division . . . would have to be rebuilt. There was work to be done.

As he was turning to leave, movement in the corner of his eye caught his attention. It was a staff car. *Another general come to assess the carnage*, he thought bitterly. The car moved slowly, the driver not wanting to rock the vehicle as he drove across the cratered road.

The officer brought the rifle up to his cheek and looked at the car and its emerging occupant through the scope. Through the distance, he saw a tall, arrogant-looking officer emerge from the car. Even without the distant glint of silver stars, he knew who the officer was. He shivered first, and then his whole body began to tremble with a building rage and hatred.

More than the German grenadiers, more than the enemy artillery or their spotters in the brooding abbey on the mountain, more than the swift freezing river or the mud or the minefields, the man in his crosshairs was responsible for the slaughter of his friends and family.

Murder.

Chapter Two

Four Weeks Earlier

December 25, 1943
1300 Hours
Mount Sammucro, Italy

The battlefield was quiet for the first time in nearly six weeks, when the first of the Allied offensives had begun against the series of German winter lines. It wasn't entirely quiet—distant artillery boomed out from time to time, and an occasional rifle shot could be heard, as could the sounds of hundreds of thousands of men in the mountains and valleys of central Italy—but as battlefields went, it was deadly silent.

A cold wind from the northwest kept everyone's head down and three officers huddled in the lee of a collection of rocks—the location of fierce fighting only that morning.

First Lieutenant Sam Taft had a broad smile on his face as he handed a flask of T. W. Samuel's bourbon to his cousin, Captain Perkin Berger.

"You're sure?" Sam asked.

"I am," Perkin replied with a smile in return.

"So it's over?"

"Yep. It's over. The great battle of San Pietro, which no one will ever hear about again, is over. Finished. *Fertig. Finito.*" Perkin took a long pull on the flask and handed it to his battalion commander, Major Bill Spaulding.

Spaulding also took a long pull on the flask, then handed it back to Sam nearly half-empty. Following the shot of bourbon with a wad of tobacco into his cheek, Spaulding said, "The scouts are reporting the Kraut positions on this pile of rocks have been abandoned. Completely abandoned: weapons, equipment, wounded. Everything. Looks like they've finally withdrawn to the Gustav Line, and our work here is about wrapped up. I'm thinkin' no more counterattacks . . . So I reckon we're in defense while the army figures out the next step. Maybe we go into reserve for a while."

"Thank God!" Sam said, and he smiled again as everyone nodded in agreement.

As the other two officers remained reclined against mountain rocks, Sam was inspired to stand up, and in a deep, carrying voice, he began to sing:

God rest ye merry, gentlemen,
Let nothing you dismay,
For Jesus Christ our Savior
Was born on Christmas Day,
To save us all from Satan's power
When we were gone astray.
O tidings of comfort and joy,
Comfort and joy,
O tidings of comfort and joy.

Several nearby soldiers grinned when Sam started the second verse, then forgot the words and began to hum. Coming to his rescue, Major Spaulding stood up, grasped Sam's shoulder, and enthusiastically finished the song by himself in his raspy smoker's voice. Perkin didn't sing, but instead directed the impromptu concert from his seat on the ground with a vaguely incoherent wave of his hands and a contented smile on his face. It was Christmas Day, after all, and the bourbon was beginning to have an effect, but the holiday spirit was less influential than the realization that a battle had been won—a terrible, nearly Pyrrhic victory, but a victory nonetheless.

Sam and Bill sat down again, and Sam surveyed his small group with deep affection. It was one of the few occasions that Sam enjoyed being a soldier, and it was due entirely to the company he was keeping at that moment in time.

Bill Spaulding had been his friend and comrade for over three years; there was no soldier whose judgment he trusted more. The vision before Sam wasn't that of a recruiting-poster soldier, though. Spaulding's uniform was filthy. One leg of his trousers was torn at the thigh, showing a dingy nonregulation union suit, and Spaulding's leggings were covered in mud, as was his pitifully inadequate jacket. A dented helmet covered an unshaved face, which bore the still-raw scars of a terrible artillery wound from only months before. That he looked as good as he did was a testament to the skills of the two medics who had feverishly sewn his face together again in the midst of the ferocious barrage. To Sam, the major was a soldier's soldier and the iconic picture of a combat veteran.

Sam's cousin, Perkin, looked little better than Major Spaulding. Perkin was closer to Sam than anyone but Sam's wife, Margaret. They had been raised almost as brothers along the Gulf Coast of South Texas, and they still regarded each other as such years later and far away on the distant shores of Italy. Despite his relaxed smile, Perkin looked desperately tired to Sam, but then so did everyone else.

Sam studied his cousin for a moment. His uniform was slightly cleaner than either Sam's or Spaulding's, but not by much. His three-quarter shoes and leggings had been recently replaced by a pair of highly coveted jump boots—the original owner had been killed at Salerno and the boots had been used as trading currency until they found their way to Perkin, who had paid a premium price in cash and cigarettes. As Sam looked at his cousin's normally handsome face on this Christmas Day, he saw it was smudged with dirt and bore fading yellow and blue bruises that were accentuated by deep circles under his eyes. He also bore scars on his face—less extensive than Spaulding's but more recent.

Without saying so, Sam reflected that he had seen hobos during the Depression who looked in better shape than his cousin. Seeing something unexpected, Sam leaned forward and with his fingertips pushed Perkin's helmet back slightly on his cousin's head. To his cousin's annoyance, Sam exclaimed gleefully, "Gray hair! Bill, look at this! He's got gray hair!"

The major leaned forward as well and studiously examined his friend's hair. He nodded with an amused grin, "I'll be goddamned, Perk! You got a dozen or so of 'em and you ain't even thirty yet."

Perkin removed his helmet and ran his hands through his hair. As he looked at his hands to see if any of the gray had rubbed off, he said, "It's a sign I'm overworked. You ought to give me some time off. But look close—if they're movin' some, maybe they ain't gray hairs. I think I got cooties. I've been scratchin' up a storm." He grinned as the other two officers wiped their hands subconsciously on their coat fronts.

Spaulding snorted slightly and said, "Your personal hygiene's the least of my worries. Half the battalion's lousy and the other half's got trench foot. And using Aggie math, the third half's got the clap. Had the clap—but I suppose we'll have to deal with it again after we get some R&R."

"Any idea when that might be?" Sam asked.

"Nope. May be awhile. I was hopin' that we'll get the chance to come off the line for a spell but I don't know who relieves us. We're in sore need of replacements and they'll need to be trained before we move forward again. I gotta think that someone else gets the point this time, but I don't know who," Spaulding repeated.

The three officers nodded. They were all of the same mind: it was someone else's turn.

2100 Hours
1st Battalion Headquarters, NW of San Pietro, Italy

As soon as the determination was made that the Germans had completely withdrawn to the Gustav Line, truckloads of food were brought forward to the provisional battalion headquarters. From there, a small mule train carried tin buckets of once-hot turkey and mashed potatoes to the troops still on Mount Sammucro. In contravention of orders, pockets of soldiers tentatively started small fires in the lee of boulders. When the Germans didn't respond with artillery fire, but with campfires of their own, the Texans enjoyed their Christmas dinners with light and warmth. Presents were exchanged between buddies, dry socks and cigarette lighters being the most frequently shared gifts.

Chaplains held Christmas services where they could. Most of the division had been inactive that morning—

only the 1st Battalion of the 141st Infantry Regiment had
been in combat*—and many of the chaplains had held
services for their units in the morning and then moved
up the trails to tend to those pickets still on the mountain.
Hymns could be heard through the darkness, and a mix of
celebratory red and green flares in the distance reinforced
that the German Army was taking the night off as well.

Perkin and Major Spaulding had spent the remainder
of their afternoon working off the nearly imperceptible
effects of Sam's bourbon by walking from outpost to
outpost on the mountainside before beginning a perilous
descent of Mount Sammucro in the twilight. The two
officers had done it many times before in the preceding
week, but it was still a challenge to manage the sharp rocks
and mountain scree in the dim light. Between the exercise
and the cold damp mountain air, by the time Perkin and
Spaulding arrived at the headquarters, they were both
absolutely famished and ready for a small Christmas
celebration.

It was a hurried affair, as there had only been time
to set up a mess tent with folding tables and chairs in
the shadow of the mountain. Kerosene lanterns gave the
tent light and an artificial sense of warmth. A pine sapling
had been cut by Spaulding's soldiers and decorated with
tinfoil strips. It was placed ceremoniously on the head
table with its base wrapped in camouflage netting. No
presents graced the tiny tree, but on that night it seemed
that no other trappings of civilization were needed.

In addition to the battalion staff, Major Spaulding
had invited his four company commanders, one platoon

---

* The 36th Division, like most US infantry divisions in WWII, had
approximately 15,000 soldiers of whom about a third were infantrymen. The
36th had three regimental combat teams (141st, 142nd, 143rd) formed around
three rifle battalions (plus numerous other units), which in turn were comprised
of three rifle companies and a heavy weapons company. Each company had
three rifle platoons and a weapons platoon. On paper, a full-strength company
was 187 soldiers.

leader, a noncommissioned officer, and a junior enlisted soldier from each company to share his Christmas dinner. Most of the invited officers had already eaten with their own troops before making their way to the battalion HQ, but as hunger had been ever-present over the past month, they were confident of making it through a second dinner with their commanding officer without much distress.

The Able Company commander, Captain Ronald Ebbins, and First Lieutenant Sam Taft were the last of the company grade officers to arrive. Ebbins looked furtively around, as if he felt uncomfortable in the presence of soldiers. He nodded briefly to Major Spaulding, who was engaged in a tactical discussion with a buck sergeant from B Company, and found a seat with the commander of C Company—a roundheaded, quiet officer named Wilson.

Sam was carrying his gas mask bag, which Perkin suspected held one or more bottles of bourbon but no gas mask. Perkin watched as Sam moved through his friends wishing them a merry Christmas and then headed off to find the senior NCO among the cooks. Perkin grinned to himself, as he knew what was on Sam's mind.

Five minutes later, Sam rejoined the dinner guests. Perkin watched as Sam's eyes sought out Ebbins and then Perkin. Sam moved along the edge of the tent, avoiding interaction with his company commander, until he reached Perkin.

"Hey, Bear!"

"Hey, yourself. When's chow? I'm starving." Sam eased himself into a seat across the table from his cousin. "Damn, my legs are sore. How was your stroll across the mountain this afternoon with Bill?"

"Not bad. I think the companies are all set and we can defend Mount Sammy if we have to, but I don't think we will."

"Good."

Sam seemed unsettled to his cousin, and his eyes drifted toward Ebbins, who had now joined several officers by a makeshift bar. Perkin nodded toward them. "You wanna join 'em?"

"Given my druthers, no. Let's just have a drink here." Sam motioned to an orphaned Italian boy from San Pietro—a newly hired, unofficial employee of Uncle Sam—and the boy brought over a bottle of wine and two glasses.

"Having problems with Captain Courageous?"

Sam stared at his cousin for a moment, and then laughed. "I swear. You can read me like a book. You know, it's funny you should say that." He shook his head, and said in a low voice, "Don't repeat this . . . I ain't sure but I'm afraid he's a little gun-shy. You know . . . on the line." Sam had lowered his voice. He despised gossip and didn't want to spread rumors of cowardice, but talking to Perkin was different.

"What happened?"

"Well, about 0830 we were cleaning up the last of the grenadiers—the wounded ones who were covering the German withdrawal. My platoon was on the northwest slope, and Beams's platoon was on my right. Frank McCarter in reserve. At first, we were moving slowly 'cause we were drawin' some rifle fire and some artillery, so we moved up close to their fellas and they quit the heavy stuff. We took out an MG-42 nest that was mostly just makin' noise, because the gunner had bandages over his eye and couldn't see too well and his loader was in worse shape. We start chuckin' grenades at 'em and they surrendered faster than a Frenchman in springtime. So we punch through 'em, and then about a hundred yards up, we see a squad hop up and start running down the trails. Kenton and his boys set off after 'em and we find ourselves almost running down the mountain in pursuit of them and some others who were decamping. They weren't shootin' anymore. Just runnin.' There's some mortar rounds comin' down near us, but it's just smoke to cover the withdrawal. Anyways, Ebbins gets on the radio and screams at me to stop and return to his position."

"Really? Why?"

"I gather he thought the Krauts were gonna counterattack again to cover their withdrawal. He was about seven hundred yards behind us at this point, so I figured he couldn't see what was goin' on. I told him that we had 'em on the run and to let me finish 'em up, but he insisted."

Perkin looked puzzled. "Let me get this straight. He thought they were going to counterattack up the mountain to cover their withdrawal from the mountain? That don't make much sense."

"No, it don't. I tried to explain that to him when we got back but he wasn't thinkin' real clear. He said I exceeded my orders, so I explained that our orders were to clear the last of the German defenders off Mount Sammy, which is what we did. When I said that, he told me I was insubordinate."

"What?"

"Yeah. So I told him to write me up if he really felt that way, and he began to backtrack some. I don't reckon anything will come outta that, but Jesus, Perk, he was all white and shakin' and I don't think it was anger at me for doin' my job."

Sam had a troubled look on his face that Perkin seldom saw. He knew that given Sam's history with Ebbins, he wouldn't say anything up the chain of command, lest he be accused of pursuing a personal agenda. Perkin had no such qualms.

"You should have said something to Bill earlier. Let me talk to him; maybe he can calm Ebbins down some."

Sam shook his head. "No."

"The battalion commander needs to know that one of his company commanders isn't up to the job, don't you think?"

Sam shook his head, "If it gets to that point, I'll say something myself. But let's not forget this is his first time in real action. It takes some gettin' used to." He shook his head again. "I'd rather help Ebbins work through this myself."

Perkin was about to protest again when they were interrupted by the mess sergeant who leaned over Sam's shoulder and said in an East Texas accent, "We got two dozen eggs, four cups of sugar, and a gallon of cream." The sergeant handed a scrap of paper to Sam. "But I cain't read your instructions. What's next, sir?"

Sam spoke in low tones so that only the sergeant and Perkin could hear. "Ya gotta separate the eggs. In the yolks, whip in about two-thirds of the sugar. Then add the two quarts of bourbon, slowly working it in. Then, in another bowl, whip the whites and the remaining sugar together just like for a meringue. Then combine the two bowls, and then fold, fold mind you, the cream into the eggs. It's the best damn nog you'll ever have. Promise. Now hurry along so it's done by the end of dinner."

The wine turned out to be a decent Sangiovese, and the cousins toasted one another and their friends and family back home. They were joined at their little table by a platoon leader from Dog Company who was in an exceptionally jovial mood after having lived through his first battle and, being a former teetotaler, having drunk his first three glasses of wine.

The battalion cooks had done them proud. Even with the battlefield conditions, the occasional freezing rain, and the short notice, they served roasted turkey, mashed potatoes and gravy, fresh rolls, stewed cauliflower, and buttermilk pie. It was certainly the best meal that either Sam or Perkin had eaten for weeks, and in the nature of hungry men, the assembled soldiers all swore that it was best food they had ever eaten.

Toward the end of the dinner, as Sam was finishing his third piece of pie, two battalion cooks carefully carried in a huge glass punch bowl filled with Sam's eggnog. The bowl had been liberated from a destroyed home in San Pietro, and the red faces and wide smiles of the cooks suggested that they had liberated some of Sam's bourbon as well.

They carried it up to the front table where Spaulding and the company commanders sat on one side of a long table facing the remaining guests. The mess sergeant leaned over and whispered to Major Spaulding while his men filled paper coffee cups with the eggnog and passed them out to the assembled soldiers.

Major Spaulding accepted a cup of the eggnog, tentatively sniffed at the beverage, and then turned the cup upside down. The eggnog didn't move. Seemingly coming to a decision, the battalion commander stood up, and in the gradually ensuing silence, he indicated that his guests were to keep their seats.

"Gentlemen, may I have your attention please? I'd like to thank y'all for comin' here tonight. I know that everyone is tired and looking forward to gettin' back to your companies and havin' a quiet night's sleep, so I won't keep y'all here long. Please charge your glasses with the remainder of the wine, before we advance to our next objective . . . this . . . uh . . . curious eggnog, which smells promising even if it melted my nose hairs."

Spaulding watched as the men filled their cups—a mixture of wine glasses and canteen cups—and then said as he stubbed out a cigarette in his plate, "Please stand. I'm gonna teach you an old Able Company tradition: the

Texas Roister. As in war, do as I say, when I say it, and y'all may live through the experience." When the soldiers were all standing with full cups, he continued, "The Texas Roister is a time-honored tradition which our historian, Captain Professor Berger, assures me was the last act of the defenders at the Alamo."

Perkin looked at Sam and grinned. He had made that up two years before while drunk at an Able Company party at Camp Bowie.

"And as we are the 1st Battalion of the famous Alamo Regiment, it's only fittin' that we should carry on the tradition."

Sam rolled his eyes back at Perkin and whispered across the table, "I think the fumes from the eggnog got to him. Bill ain't normally this long-winded."

"We're gonna do four toasts, but we only drink at the end. And it all goes down. OK, gents, hold your cups out like this." Spaulding demonstrated by holding his cup out with his wrist bent outward at a right angle. When everyone complied, he said in a firm voice, "To God!"

Led by Perkin and Sam, the soldiers seconded the toast, "To God!"

They watched as Spaulding then did a curious thing: instead of taking a drink, he brought the glass of wine up to his ear, held it there for a moment as if he were listening to the wine's stories, and then he brought the glass back down in front of him still held at the awkward angle. Following Sam and Perkin's lead, the others did likewise.

"To Country!"

"To Country!" This time the deep voices toasted in unison, and the movement of the glasses to ear and back was much more fluid.

"To Texas!"

"To Texas!" Enthusiasm was in their voices, and grins of anticipation were now seen throughout the audience.

"Gentlemen, our next stop is Rome. It's a damn hard road gettin' there, but, 'On to Rome!'"

"On to Rome!"

"Now, boys, do what I do!" With a loud rolling "Roiiiiiisssssster!" Spaulding downed his drink in a single swallow and slammed his empty glass on the table. With evident satisfaction, Spaulding watched as the soldiers followed his lead with a stretched-out "roister" of their own.

Applause, laughter, and cheers followed; the soldiers who hadn't had much cause lately for applause, laughs, or cheers quickly moved their attention to uncovering the mysteries of Sam's eggnog, and amid a boisterous dissonance of carols and roister-practicing, the Christmas celebration resumed anew.

Chapter Three

December 27, 1943
1000 Hours
CINC Southwest Headquarters, Monte Soratte,
Italy

Major Douglas Grossmann sat alone at a conference table in a mahogany-paneled room, where two months before he had received the most depressing news possible: orders to establish a spy network in the Naples–Caserta–Cassino area of operations and infiltrate the American high command. On paper, it sounded challenging but doable. He was more American than German after all, and he had done it before at Salerno. But in practice, it would be more than challenging. At Salerno, the Allies were disorganized, but by the time they took Naples and continued their march north along the Italian peninsula, they had networks of their own. Intelligence collection networks of spies and collaborators. Counterintelligence networks manned by hard men—professionals who played the great game to win. He had thought it a death sentence.

Then a disagreeable prick of a colonel had told Grossmann that good men were dying by the millions on the Eastern Front. All German soldiers were expected to do their part, including dying if necessary, and he was asked, "What makes you special?"

That's the kind of question that a soldier might have an answer to, but can't really articulate to an unpleasant superior officer, so Grossmann had taken his orders, fulfilled his mission as best he could, and come back to the German lines. But it hadn't been without cost. Now he was sitting in that same room, waiting for the same disagreeable prick of a colonel, in order to find out the consequences of his last mission and perhaps learn something of his next assignment.

Grossmann had been given a week off and now it was time to get back to the war. He was ready. Christmas had been spent alone in a small apartment that he kept near the Piazza Navona. He had been tempted to put on civilian clothes and cross the river to go mingle with the crowd at Saint Peter's Square, but he decided to stay in bed and sleep instead. He was a deeply, deeply lapsed Lutheran in any case, and had no desire to participate in a Catholic ceremony simply because he was lonely.

That was the crux of the problem—the source of his discontent. Major Grossmann was lonely. His comrade and good friend, Captain Mark Gerschoffer, had been killed at San Pietro by an American captain named Berger, and his own source with access to the American camp reported that the Texan had tortured his friend for information before executing him.

His source, Antoniette Bernardi, was the one person he would have liked to spent Christmas with, but she had gone with her family to a villa they owned in the north of

Italy to spend the Christmas season skiing. Grossmann had to call in several favors to get the necessary passes and arrange the rail transport, but Bernardi had earned it all. She was Germany's premier agent in Italy.

She was an amazingly dangerous woman. Grossmann knew that she lied fluently and manipulated men like puppets. She was beautiful, hypnotic, and a dedicated fascist, and in the words of his predecessor at the Rome station, she had "a heart as cold as a witch's caress." He knew all of these things and more. She unnerved him, yet he still desired her. He knew that if she were to seduce him—it would never be the other way around—she would own a majority of his soul, which would never be returned. Intellectually, he knew that to become Bernardi's lover was akin to signing a Faustian pact with the devil, but like Faust, he dallied with the notion that losing his soul might be worth it. He certainly would never really control events in this world again. He had sighed on that Christmas morning and wondered if she had been there with him, at that moment, whether he would have signed the pact. He probably would have, he reflected.

This Monday, however, was a different day. It was time to leave the self-pity, the loneliness, and the unrequited desire behind and focus on work. But what was he to do, and what was the High Command's plan for their German-American intelligence officer?

He had been told his last mission was a success even if he personally did not see it as such. Grossmann had penetrated the Fifth Army headquarters on so many occasions that he knew the Italian workers in the canteen by name, and Bernardi's work had been nothing short of spectacular. She was singularly successful in convincing Allied officers to demonstrate their worth to her by discussing units, locations, and destinations over a bottle of wine or in bed, and she had provided time-sensitive information on Allied operations that had been used to great effect in delaying the Anglo-American advance up the peninsula. Her greatest coup was the discovery of a stockpile of American mustard gas aboard a liberty ship in the Italian port of Bari. Weeks later, the Allies were still cleaning up the mess from the Luftwaffe bombing of the *John Harvey*.

All good things come to an end, however. Grossmann's ring was broken up, although he didn't know exactly how. When Gerschoffer had been taken prisoner and reportedly executed by Captain Berger, Grossmann suspected that his cover was blown. He certainly wasn't inclined to wait around and find out. Grossmann hurriedly collected Antoniette Bernardi from Caserta, and they made their escape, via Naples and Mondragone, to the sea. In a contract Camorra boat, one with a rich history of smuggling cigarettes, people, and narcotics, Grossmann and Bernardi successfully made a nighttime transit to Gaeta in German-occupied Italy.

Grossmann had been told to take some time off before reporting to work again. He would have liked to return to Germany to see his father in Darmstadt, but ironically, he wasn't sure he would be able to arrange the necessary transportation for himself. So he stayed in Rome and thought.

He had spent one evening with the wife of an Italian officer—an unfortunate soldier captured in Russia—but she was becoming resentful of the German occupation and carped incessantly about the hardships she had to endure. When he had left her flat the next morning he had tossed some lire on her entryway table in respect of happier memories, and he knew he wouldn't see her again.

As for other carnal pursuits, it seemed that the remaining Italian ladies of his acquaintance had recently found either God or patriotism—their motivation made no difference to Grossmann as they were no longer sleeping with German officers. The lack of other available women had driven his thoughts back to Bernardi, and from there he alternately found himself wishing for her return or a transfer back to Paris. Perhaps that would be the best of all possible worlds: nightclubs and French women and fine wines and no Antoniette.

In his meeting with his Abwehr superiors this morning, he thought he might press the argument that he should return to Paris. The Allied landings in France were only a matter of time, and his services would be needed there. Too many Americans would be flooding into France and the Low Countries for him to be personally identified in that theater. It would be safer there.

Grossmann had been waiting twenty minutes past the appointed time of the meeting before the colonel arrived. The delay made him both anxious and irritable. Taking the counsel of his fears, he began to worry that he was in trouble—that despite the initial praise, he would be blamed for Gerschoffer's death and the subsequent collapse of his network. *Christ*, he thought, *they're going to send me to the Russian front.*

That was the preeminent thought on his mind as the door finally opened and in strode the disagreeable colonel. Grossmann leapt to his feet, offered a crisp salute, and was waved to his seat by his superior as the colonel hanged his overcoat and hat on a rack in the corner of the room.

"Major Grossmann." The Abwehr colonel studied Grossmann for a moment before continuing. "You seemed to have survived your ordeal. I recall you were upset with the prospect that you might not."

Grossmann decided there was no sufficient answer, so he said nothing.

After an uncomfortable moment of silence where the colonel merely stared at Grossmann, the colonel said,

"Captain Gerschoffer did not. Survive, that is. Explain why you lived and he did not." The colonel pulled out a pack of American cigarettes from his breast pocket and lit one using an American Zippo lighter with a painted image of Betty Boop. He did not offer a cigarette to Grossmann.

"Well, sir. We were operating in different areas. As you know, I was in the American encampment at Caserta, and Captain Gerschoffer was providing support to my mission as well as serving as a conduit to corps headquarters in Cassino. At the time of Gerschoffer's death, we were respectively in the midst of two opposing armies and separated by forty kilometers . . . I guess I don't understand the nature of your question." Grossmann understood exactly the nature of the question. The colonel wished to make him uncomfortable and defensive.

"Yes, I see that. Just answer the questions, Major. How did Captain Gerschoffer die?"

"As I noted in my report, sir. It appears that he came into contact with an American intelligence officer of the 36th Division named Berger in San Pietro. My source said that Berger kidnapped Gerschoffer from San Pietro, tortured him, interrogated him, and then executed him before escaping back to American lines."

"It was this same Berger, was it not, who captured your team in Pisciotta?"

"I think so, sir, but I don't know for sure."

"And Captain Gerschoffer had taken the responsibility of ordering that team to Pisciotta?"

"Yes, sir. To arrest the Irish priest."

"Yes, now I remember. Back to Gerschoffer's death. Where is your source now . . . the Roman whore?" The colonel lit another cigarette from the butt of his first.

"She's in the Lake Como region of Italy. In Sondrio."

"Yes. On the Swiss border, correct?"

"Yes, sir."

"And you arranged her travel?"

"Yes, sir. For her and her parents. I got the passes through the provost's office. They were authorized."

"Quite." Abruptly the colonel asked, "Did you know that your whore and your Neanderthal captain were lovers?" The colonel smiled a nasty smile and waited for Grossmann's answer, but he didn't have to. The look of genuine shock on Grossmann's face was sufficient.

"No, sir. I wasn't aware of that. I had warned—"

"Have *you* taken her as a lover?"

"No, sir." Grossmann stared at the colonel and asked, "What are you getting at?"

"We knew you hadn't. Just a few more questions, Major. Where was Captain Gerschoffer from?"

"His family moved quite a bit, sir. I understand they're in the East now—in Posen. That's where I sent the letter to his family." It had been difficult—those letters always were, but this was particularly hard.

"Not Germany, Major, where was he from in the States?"

"He wasn't born in the States, sir. He was born in the Fatherland."

The colonel sighed in exasperation. "Do I need to ask the question in English so you can understand?"

"He was from Georgia, sir. In the South. But he was a German patriot who—"

The Abwehr colonel interrupted again. "You were saying Georgia's in the South, correct?"

"Yes, sir. It's in the areas called the Old South and the Deep South. They're not exactly the same. You see—"

"Is Texas also in the South?"

"Yes, sir, but not completely in the cultural sense. Texas is unique because it's so large. It's bigger than prewar France and it's part southern, part western, part Mexican, part cowboy, part redneck, part roughneck . . . and all loudmouth as far as my experience goes."

"Indeed. They both fought for the Confederacy in their Civil War?"

"Yes, sir. Why?"

"Does . . . I mean, *did* Captain Gerschoffer speak in a Southern accent?"

Grossmann nodded. He wasn't sure where the conversation was heading, but it inevitably wasn't going to be down a good road.

"Are the accents the same?"

"No, sir. Texas has several regional accents but they're similar to a Georgian tone in many respects. The two state accents would be distinct to a Southerner but maybe not to a Northerner. It's the difference between a Philadelphia accent and a New York accent: they'd know the difference even if no one else did."

The colonel smiled again—a brief, cynical smile showing tobacco-stained yellow teeth. It was a singularly disagreeable smile, Grossmann thought.

"I don't care about Philadelphia, Major. Do you think the Southerners still have an affinity to one another?"

"Yes, sir. Absolutely. Can you tell me why you're asking this?"

"Yes, of course. Did it occur to you that Gerschoffer's not dead? That perhaps he defected to his fellow Southerners with the connivance of his lover, the Roman whore, who's now poised to flee to Switzerland—with your assistance? That as we are speaking, your particular friend is being feted and debriefed by American intelligence about our military dispositions, about Abwehr operations, the state of the Fatherland, and the Führer? Answering questions about . . . you?"

1015 Hours
141st Infantry Regiment Headquarters, San Pietro, Italy

The regiment had commandeered a small house on the edge of San Pietro. It was one of the few remaining houses left standing in the unfortunate village. A week before, all the roads and walkways through the village were nearly impassable, as the buildings had collapsed from the shelling and assault of the town. Now, defined trails led back to the church and a few standing homes, but in truth, San Pietro was all but destroyed and little more than a ghost town.

The residents of San Pietro had been trucked away by the Italian authorities to displaced-persons camps, but many had already returned. Perkin had talked to many villagers, some of whom he had met in the caves before the assault, and they were still in shock and denial about their misfortune. Women sat in the rubble of their former homes and cried; children looked through the ruins searching for toys or food; the men were gone. They had been taken away by the Germans to build their defenses on the Gustav Line.

Perkin leaned against the wall of the house and watched as one of his soldiers sat on a slab of stone and played a game of jacks with a girl from the village. He recognized the girl, Stefania Frattini. She had confidently led him by the hand through the passages of the caves into the village only a few weeks before. Then she had been starving and diminished, and in the dark, she looked as though she were eight or nine years old. Fed, washed, and in daylight, she seemed older—maybe thirteen or so—but she still seemed small for her age. Conversely, watching Private Edwin Kulis on the ground playing the child's game, he somehow seemed younger to the captain than the calm, bookish killer that he knew. What the captain didn't know was that Kulis was much younger—he had fraudulently enlisted at fifteen and had just turned seventeen during the Battle of Salerno.

"Hello, Stefania Frattini!" Perkin waved from his wall.

"*Ciao*, Perkin Berger!" She turned to Private Kulis and ordered, "Don't cheat!" and then ran over to hug the tall Texan.

"You're looking as pretty as a peach today, Stefania. How are your mama and grandfather?

"Good, good. How is *Cugino Orso*?" Stefania had met Sam once and she had thought that if she lived to be a hundred, she would never again meet a man so large.

"Cousin Bear's fine. Just this morning, I watched him eat a whole ham and two dozen eggs for breakfast." He winced as soon as the words were out. The Frattinis didn't have much to eat, and he wished he hadn't made a joke about food.

No harm was done. Her eyes widened slightly, "Really? No. You kid. You have the locket? Can I see the picture again?"

The locket had been a present from Perkin's Italian girlfriend, Gianina—an art restorer at the Neapolitan National Gallery. On the morning of her death in the terrorist bombing of the Naples Post Office, she had given Perkin a large rectangular locket. When he opened it, he saw a miniature depiction of Saint Michael subduing Satan. She had painted it onto a small ceramic tile and filed it to fit within the locket. Saint Michael, Gianina had told him, was the patron saint of soldiers and would protect Perkin. But the source of Stefania's fascination was not just that Saint Michael was also a patron saint of San Pietro, nor the widely held belief among the ladies of the town that Perkin had been sent to San Pietro to do Saint Michael's bidding—it was the face that was painted on Saint Michael's muscular body. Gianina had crafted a remarkable depiction of Private Edwin Kulis, even down to his army-issued glasses.

"That's the man I plan to marry," she said simply.

Somewhat alarmed, Perkin muttered under his breath, "Be careful you don't catch something." Private Kulis had lost his virginity in an Italian brothel and had never looked back.

"I'm sorry, I didn't hear you."

"I said you'll be quite a catch someday. Does he know?" Perkin grinned as he looked over at his soldier, who was practicing his skills at jacks.

"Oh, no. I won't tell him until I'm sixteen," she said in a businesslike tone. "Mama won't let me kiss a boy until then, and I can't get married until I'm seventeen. The war will be over I'm sure, and then I can go to America."

"Don't you think he'll be a little old for you? By the time you're old enough to date, he'll be, I don't know, in his mid-twenties."

"That doesn't matter in Italia. Besides, he's only a few years older than me. He's maybe sixteen or seventeen at the most."

"No, Stefania. He's twenty-two. Did he tell ya he's a teenager?" Perkin's alarm was beginning to mount again at the prospect that his rifleman was hustling a very young teenager.

Stefania faced Perkin and rolled her eyes, her hands on her hips. "*Capitano*. We haven't discussed these things other than agreeing to be pen pals. He knows nothing about nothing. But I can tell you as an Italian woman, I know how old he is!"

"Is that a fact? I didn't know that Italian women were so perspicacious." He grinned again, relieved.

Stefania wagged her finger at him, "You should not use words I don't know. But if it means we are smart, we are. I tell many things just by looking at people."

"Really? What do you see in Eddie?" He nodded his head toward Private Kulis.

"He's small like me, and has good teeth, and he's very, very smart. Like me."

"I don't reckon you have to be the Oracle of Delphi to divine those things. What else do you see?"

"I think he's very calm, and he's very comfortable in his skin. Nothing bothers him, he likes to be a soldier, and I think he will want to stay one when the war is finished. I'll have to give that some thought, though, because I don't know about being a soldier's wife. One last thing . . . I think he looks up to you."

"That's because I'm taller, honey, but thank you. What about Cousin Bear, what do you see there?"

"That's easy. His heart is bigger than he is. Who else?"

"Why, me, of course."

"Oh, my friend . . . you are very hard to see, but you are funny, smart, and . . . *allora* . . . troubled, I think."

1020 Hours
CINC Southwest Headquarters, Monte Soratte, Italy

Major Grossmann was stunned. What the colonel was proposing was unthinkable, but he only had Bernardi's word to go on. Mark Gerschoffer would not have turned sides, of that he was certain. Not unless it was true that he was Bernardi's lover and she directed him to do so. Her influence on men was formidable.

"Sir, do you have any evidence that Captain Gerschoffer did as you imply?" he asked of the colonel.

"Evidence? No . . . what evidence do you think might apply?"

"I don't know, sir. Why do you think the situation is anything other than what I described in my report—that Captain Gerschoffer was killed after being captured?"

The colonel smiled again, and Major Grossmann found himself wishing that the colonel would quit doing so. The senior Abwehr officer coughed harshly and then said, "Because I don't trust you. I don't trust your whore, and I don't trust Gerschoffer. Or didn't, perhaps I should say." The colonel used his fingers to delineate his point. "Let's see. We don't have a body. We haven't seen a corpse. There's no collaborating intelligence from the American camp. Your whore is perfectly poised to defect to Switzerland, and, well, I've always wondered about your allegiance. It's Occam's razor. My hypothesis is simpler and more logical than your own, which is, to wit, that an American intelligence officer infiltrated a heavily fortified city and kidnapped one of *our* two German-American intelligence officers—a savage brute of a man—tortured him, and executed him. What do you say to that?"

"I can't express what I'd like to say, Colonel. Other than noting you're wrong about Mark, and about me, I haven't a goddamned thing to say." Grossmann began to feel nauseous. This morning was going worse than he imagined it possibly could. What was next? Orders to the Eastern Front? An interrogation?

The colonel shook his head and looked at his wrist-watch. "Ach, Major, you're still stuck in your American uniform. You need to embrace your Aryan side for a moment and follow orders, which are to explain to your superior why he's wrong. I'll give you thirty seconds to convince me, or I'll turn this situation over to the Gestapo for more, uh . . . well, let's call it objective resolution. Go!"

Grossmann glared as the colonel glanced again at his watch. "Don't bother, Colonel. It won't take that long. You didn't question our allegiance when we provided the operational intelligence that delayed the American advance, nor when we discovered the American stockpile of mustard gas in Bari. You never questioned my allegiance when I uncovered ties between British intelligence and the Vatican, nor when I planted the time bombs in Naples. There's no basis to question it now. I am devoted to the Fatherland. I've killed for it, and I'm prepared to die for it. What more do you want?"

The colonel leaned back in his chair and studied Grossmann again as if he were fascinated with his subordinate. "I don't know, Major. Something's not quite right with you. Well, anyway, what is that American phrase? 'No sense beating a horse to death'? Suffice it to say, I'm not convinced—I think you'll turn the first time things get tough on you." He paused, lit another cigarette, and stared in silence for a full minute at Grossmann before continuing, "*I* think you'll turn, but that doesn't really matter. Admiral Canaris doesn't, which is truly good news for you, I suspect. *He* thinks your work has been exceptional. Maybe they have different standards in the navy, I don't know. Oh, here's a little present from the admiral." He pulled a small rectangular box from his leather briefcase and slid it across the table to Grossmann. When Grossmann opened the box, it revealed an Iron Cross. "The admiral thought that perhaps we might do more for you, say, maybe some more leave or even a mention of your name to the Führer . . . but I convinced him this was quite sufficient." Switching to English and then to Latin, the colonel continued, "He said to tell you as I gave you this, and I quote, '*Audaces fortuna iuvat.*' Unquote."

Fortune favors the bold. Grossmann stared mutely at the box for a moment. It was his first award of the Iron Cross, a medal that he had coveted greatly since the war began. The manner in which it was awarded, though, left him a little dismayed.

"Thank the admiral for me, please, sir."

"Yes, of course. No pithy Latin or Greek phrase for him in return? No? Well, good luck then."

Grossmann looked the colonel in the eyes, saw that the other officer was enjoying his discomfiture and confusion, and struggled to achieve a neutral tone. "Good luck with what?"

"Your next assignment, of course. The admiral and I had quite a discussion about this. I thought that you should try to infiltrate the American staff again, but he thought that perhaps the risk would be too high. Maybe a little cooling-off period and we shall try again. Wouldn't want you to suffer the same fate as your friend, would we? That's a rhetorical question. No need to answer. So here's the summation of your future, if you can call it that. You are relieved of responsibility to the Rome Abwehr station immediately. That's been de facto for some weeks in any case as you've seemed to have lost all your Yankee doodles—to one man, I might note. You are to be a semi-independent agent, answerable only to the admiral and me. I insisted on that, by the way. Here is a letter specifying that you are on orders from Admiral Canaris and requesting the assistance of other Axis units as required." The colonel handed over an envelope and waited until Grossmann read through its contents. "If your whore doesn't sleep her way into Switzerland, you may retain her services on an as-needed basis; the Abwehr will pay her fee and expenses, of course. Now, to the assignment at hand: the admiral wants you to resume your work on the Vatican."

At this, Grossmann sat up a little straighter in his chair. Finally, the meeting was turning around. This was good news and he forgot about both the Eastern Front and Paris. He was familiar with the problem as his office had done the initial investigations and analyses. Over the course of the past year, and with Bernardi's help, he had

turned a priest in the Vatican Curia into an unwilling source
of information for the Third Reich. Through the priest's
information, Grossmann was able to develop an accurate
model of the internal workings of Vatican politics. More
importantly, in his opinion, he uncovered indications that
a renegade group within the Vatican, led by Monsignor
Hugh O'Flaherty, had established a considerable network
to assist escaped Allied prisoners of war and downed pilots
in avoiding capture by the Germans. It was Grossmann's
contention that O'Flaherty's network was acting as a front
for British intelligence, although he had never been able
to document the connection other than establishing that
a fellow Irish priest in the Vatican had a brother in British
Army Intelligence.

"You have two objectives, Major. You are to ascertain
whether the Vatican is assisting escaping Allies. We are
particularly interested in any connection to a foreign
intelligence service. That your suspected network may
have the blessing of His Holiness is of intense interest,
of course, although such information would ultimately be
immaterial in the Führer's decision to demarche or depose
the Pope."

"Really? I would think—"

"No need to exert yourself, Major," the colonel
interrupted. "The Führer will do that for you, and he will
do what he feels necessary to achieve the greater end. He
does not require our justification, but we will provide it in
any case, of course."

"OK, what about the SS?"

"The SS? Oh, yes. As they seem to have taken over
the Vatican as their own personal project, that might
pose a problem. Hmm . . . what to do about the SS?
Let's see . . . Oh, here we go . . ." He stared disdainfully
at Major Grossmann, and then said as if he were talking
to a small child, "Let's not tell them, Major."

Ignoring the sarcasm, Grossmann pressed on. "And if they learn about our operation, whatever that might be?"

The colonel smiled a humorlessly. "Perhaps you can pretend to be General Wolff's son again. Maybe that will help. But . . . perhaps it would be better to not come to their attention. So here's your second objective. If you can confirm the existence of such an Allied network, you are to follow it to its logical and physical end. Penetrate the escape network and identify the personalities, transshipment points, safe houses, collaborators, et cetera, all the way back to Allied lines. When you are done, the Abwehr, not the SS, will expose the Vatican to the Führer, and we will shut down the Allied operation. Discretely and permanently."

1025 Hours
141st Infantry Regiment Headquarters, San Pietro, Italy

Perkin pushed himself away from the farmhouse and said good-bye to Stefania. His meeting was about to start. He called out to Private Kulis to stand by in case he was needed, then walked around the corner of the building toward the front door.

Two soldiers who had been milling about in front of the farmhouse door saluted. Perkin automatically returned their salute, and as he glanced at the soldiers' faces, he involuntarily exclaimed, "Jesus Christ!"

"No, sir." One of the two second lieutenants responded, "Hiroshi Ozaki."

Perkin laughed. "Thanks for clearin' that up for me, Lieutenant. Y'all took me by surprise—I thought for a second we must've fought around the world. But," Perkin looked around, "at second glance, it appears we're in the same shitty valley we've been in for weeks."

He offered a hand to the two lieutenants, then asked, "Y'all in the 100th, uh, Hiroshi?"

"Yes, sir. This is Scott Kawamoto, and usually Haole boys call me Craig, not Hiroshi." He indicated the other soldier, who looked curiously at Perkin as if he were trying to divine what the tall Texan would do next.

"And what brings you here? Ain't y'all attached to the 34th?"

Kawamoto spoke for the first time. "Yes, sir. I understand the Texas Division is coming off the line, and the 34th is relieving you. We don't know if the 100th is moving or not, but we were sent to look over the terrain and get a head start on a turnover just in case."

Perkin smiled widely and said, "That's the best damn news I've heard all day. I gotta run, but it's nice meetin' you fellas. I'll see ya around."

Perkin walked into the small farmhouse, leaving the two Nisei soldiers behind. An orderly sitting at the door waved him to what was once a small living room. Today the furniture had been pushed aside to make room for a large map easel, and a dining table that had been set against a wall held stacked helmets, jackets, and weapons.

Colonel Robert Wranosky, Lieutenant Colonel Alvin Miller, and Major Bill Spaulding were standing by the map easel and as Perkin entered the room, Wranosky pointed to a coffee pot resting on a potbellied stove.

While Perkin was filling a tin cup with steaming hot coffee, he overheard Major Spaulding ask Colonel Miller, "So, no more than a week or so? That's what you're saying to me?" Miller was the division's G2—the senior intelligence officer of the 36th.

"I can't see it takin' much longer than that. Depends on what the Limeys can wring outta him. Oh, hey, Perkin."

Seeing Perkin with a cup of coffee in his hand, Colonel Wranosky said, "I meant for you to get me one, Professor. How're things?"

"Another day in paradise, sir. How're you these days?"

"Couldn't be better. I take cream and sugar," the thickset Alabaman said with a grin.

"Yes, sir. Would you like a back rub too?" Perkin exaggeratedly rolled his eyes, grinned, poured another cup of coffee, and added cream and sugar. As he was bringing it back to the regimental commander, he pretended to sneeze in the coffee and as he was handing the cup to Wranosky, he said, "Just like you like it, sir."

"Thank you, Captain. The same level of quality control I've come to expect from you." Wranosky was clearly in a good mood. "Perkin, Fifth Army has a good deal for you. You don't deserve it, a' course, but you're gettin' one anyway. I've talked to Bill, and we're also gonna extend it to Sam as well."

"Sir, I can't go home on a war bond tour now," Perkin said modestly. "Our work ain't done here!"

"You know, sometimes I wonder what standards they have at the University of Texas that they saw fit to give you a PhD." Wranosky shook his head in mock sadness.

"I traded 'em five box tops for it, sir. Same way I got my army commission."

"And they both got the short end of the stick. No, the G2 at army wants you to go with their naval intelligence bubba to Eighth Army and brief them on what you know about this German intelligence officer and his outfit. Although I told 'em that Fifth Army might likely not survive without you, they indicated they were willing to accept the risk."

"Gutsy move, sir." Turning to Major Spaulding, Perkin asked, "Does that put you in a bind, sir?"

"No. We received notification this morning that we're coming off the line by Thursday. Sergeant Taylor can manage your affairs here for the battalion for a few days, and if you want to take Privates Kulis and Fratelli for drivers that's fine as well. The British expect officers to have a batman, but y'all have to share those boys."

"Great. And what about Sam?"

Colonel Wranosky answered, "He goes too. Just for fun. General Walker's arranged for a hotel in Naples for our officers to use for R&R, and Sam is at the top of the list of my boys to go, but Bill here says Sam's not keen on Naples. So he can go with you and spend New Year's celebrating with the British. Trust me. It'll be a good time."

"Thank you very much, sir. I got to admit, I'm looking forward to it." Perkin was indeed pleased. There hadn't been much time spent with Sam since the division went back on the line in mid-November. "What about uniforms? Orders?"

Spaulding replied, "We're cuttin' orders for you boys and the colonel wants Captain Finley-Jones to accompany you. He'll grease the skids for you with their intel folks, and Colonel Miller has already done some of that. You'll carry your weapons, of course, but y'all shouldn't need them. We're arranging to get you a hot shower and deloused before you go, and I've directed the quartermaster to draw clean combat uniforms and your service uniforms out of storage. The British can be kind of formal so you might want to get the stains outta your tie."

Colonel Wranosky reached into his pocket and handed four three-inch pins to Perkin. "These are for your service uniforms."

"What's this, sir?" Perkin asked. He held one up to the light and looked it over—an infantry-blue rectangular box overlaid with a small metal musket and an oak leaf wreath.

"It's the new Combat Infantryman's Badge—it was authorized by the War Department about the time we started operations against San Pietro. A friend of mine on General Marshall's staff sent me out a box of them for occasions like this before they were even authorized. There are two badges for infantrymen—the expert and the combat. As the name implies, this is for infantry soldiers—officers and men—who've been in combat. It helps people know who you are and where you've been, which is a dogface in shit up to his neck. You'll wear it right above your service ribbons over your left pocket. Make sure they're shined up before you talk to any Limeys."

"Yes, sir. I thought the smell and the flat feet were all anyone needed to identify a rifleman, but thank you." Perkin was oddly touched by the small piece of metal. It seemed the army's infantry was getting little glory or recognition in the war—Marines and aviators seemed to have the best public relations—and this little recognition mattered greatly to the captain.

The meeting broke up, and Perkin and Spaulding were heading out when the regimental commander called them back. "I almost forgot. Do y'all have any objections to workin' with Jap soldiers?"

The two officers looked at each other and shrugged. "Not if they're fightin' on our side," Spaulding replied.

"I didn't think you would. Them boys outside want a look at our positions. Give 'em a staff ride and point out the salient features of our geography and defenses. Three, four hours, tops."

"Sir?" Perkin asked. "I thought the 100th had Caucasian officers. Both of those lieutenants are Orientals."

"You noticed that too, Professor?" Wranosky said dryly. "Well, that's the way it was when the battalion was sent over. These boys have battlefield commissions. About half their white officers are dead or gone, and the battalion's promotin' up through the ranks. I'd bet that Ozaki was a corporal a month ago." Wranosky pointed his finger at Spaulding, then Perkin. "Don't let their size fool you. These sons-a-bitches are tough and may just save your ass someday. Make sure they get a fair shake."

1725 Hours
Mount Lungo, Italy

The wider reception to lieutenants Ozaki and Kawamoto left no such impression that the Nisei officers would get a fair shake. Reactions from some of the Texas officers they encountered during their staff ride had ranged from muttering to shaking of the heads. A friend of Perkin's, a lieutenant from Atlanta, Texas, ignored their outstretched hands and just glared down at the two lieutenants with his hands on his hips. Captain Ronald Ebbins's loud pronouncement to a gaggle of fellow officers at lunch still had Perkin fuming: "Jap officers? Next thing you know, you'll be taking orders from niggers and Mexicans. I'll be damned if I will!"

Perkin had started to get up from his seat to confront Ebbins but stopped when Lieutenant Kawamoto quietly said, "Let it be, sir. We've heard this before. We're big boys, and anyway, words won't change his mind."

"I wasn't gonna talk to him," Perkin growled, but he sat back down. He tried to dismiss Ebbins from his mind, but it gnawed at him for the rest of the day.

Major Spaulding decided to use the staff ride for the Nisei officers as a training opportunity for all his new replacement officers in the battalion, so he pulled a heavy truck from the motor pool and loaded up a collection of second and first lieutenants. Perkin and Spaulding sat in the back of the truck with the other officers, and they headed south from San Pietro onto Victory Road. As they drove, Spaulding took a precarious stand on the bed of the truck and pointed out the salient features of the battle:

"To our immediate right is Monte Lungo. Our battalion engaged the 29th Panzer Grenadiers there on the first of December. We split our battalion between Lungo and this little spur coming off this here hill—driver, stay on the road, goddamn it! Not all these minefields have been cleared."

The drive to the southern end of the Mignano Gap and back took several hours and the discussion was technical and animated, with Spaulding doing most of the narration. Perkin was impressed with some of the new officers who asked pertinent questions and quickly seemed to grasp the difficulties of mountain fighting and the operational stresses of fighting in such a confining battlefield.

The two Nisei officers shared their insights in mountain fighting from their experience with the 34th Division—fellow guardsmen from the Dakotas, Nebraska, Iowa, and Minnesota. Particularly chilling was Lieutenant Ozaki's description of a bayonet battle on the mountaintops where he explained how they had held against counterattack after counterattack.

His account of their battle and Perkin's description of the taking of the westernmost mountaintops by the 1st Special Service Force and the 142nd Infantry Regiment left some of the other officers looking nervous and confused—they sat wide-eyed in the back of the truck saying nothing, or when asked questions by Spaulding didn't seem to understand his questions. Perkin felt a lot of sympathy for these young men, who in some cases had been in replacement camps in Africa or Sicily less than two weeks before. The casualties of the Italian campaign were higher than expected, and many of the officers simply hadn't had the opportunity to get their bearings in this strange land before being thrust into leadership responsibilities. *Welcome to the army, boys*, Perkin had thought.

This dichotomy was on Major Spaulding's mind when the truck brought them back to San Pietro. As they disembarked from the truck, Spaulding said to Perkin, "I'm glad that we're comin' off the line for a while. Some of these boys are ready to go, but most of 'em ain't. We'll have to capitalize on whatever downtime we get to train these fellas up."

"Yep. I was thinkin' it'd be helpful to know whether we're going straight up this valley or gonna be back in the mountains. Any idea when we'll find out?"

"Nope. The optimist in me thinks the army will give us a couple months or so to get sorted out again, but the pessimist in me says we won't get more than a few weeks. And you know, since I've been in the army, that optimist ain't been right once. Having said that, I don't want you and Sam to rush back on our account. Take a week. Send word if you want more time. We've got you covered here at battalion, and I want to see if Ebbins can organize his movement off the line and execute a training plan without Sam there to do it for him. As far as I can see, Sam is the company commander in all but name. The good news is that Ebbins relies on him for everything. Of course, the bad news is that Ebbins relies on him for everything. The worst news is that every time Ebbins overrides Sam, Ronald's wrong." As if to accentuate his point, Spaulding spit a long stream of tobacco juice onto one of the few remaining bushes in the valley, then looked up at the lonely bell tower of San Pietro's destroyed church. "Just like these youngsters here, I need to get him standin' on his own two feet."

Perkin nodded and contemplated sharing Sam's conversation about Ebbins being gun-shy, but said nothing. They were beginning to rejoin the group of officers when a very angry Private Kulis came running up to Perkin.

"Sir, may I talk to you for a moment?"

Perkin nodded, and broke off from Major Spaulding. "What's up?"

"Sir, I was watchin' the Jap officers' jeep like you told me, and a couple of the new guys in Able Company told me that you were lookin' for me here in the town. But when I got up here, y'all weren't done with your staff ride yet, so I went back down and them sons-a-bitches had let the air outta two of the Japs' tires. I'm awful sorry. And sir, I shouldn't say nothin' but . . ."

"Go on." Perkin was looking at the private with interest. In several engagements where he had personally witnessed Kulis under fire, the soldier had never even broken a sweat. He was the coolest killer he had ever met, but the diminutive rifleman's face was almost black with anger.

"I saw Cap'n Ebbins lookin' that jeep over just fifteen minutes before them jokers showed up. I reckon he put the idea in their heads."

"Oh. Well. You let me deal with that. Did they cut the tires, or just let the air out?"

"They let the air out," Kulis fumed.

"OK. Here's what ya do: get down to the battalion motor pool and see Sergeant Ochoa—you know, the Ochoa from Gregory, not the one from Falfurrias. Tell him to get a compressor over there on the double and get those tires pumped up. Tell him this is a favor for me and there's a pack of smokes in it for him if he gets it done in less than twenty-five minutes—we've got another half hour here."

When Perkin rejoined the group a minute later, his battalion commander looked at him curiously and asked, "What's goin' on?"

"Oh, nothing to worry about." Turning and addressing the group, Perkin said, "Over here, the Germans had 40mm anti-air artillery that they also used against advancing ground forces. You can see how well they sight down the valley toward Mignano. Now, if you look at the nearby craters and the wreckage of their triple-A pieces, you get a sense of our own accuracy with artillery and the effectiveness of our munitions . . ."

Chapter Four

December 28, 1943
1100 Hours
Highway 6, North of Caserta, Italy

The Italian countryside bore the evidence of fighting, although the respective armies had passed by nearly two months before. Little stone farmhouses and villages were destroyed from the intense combat as the Fifth Army pushed the Germans to the winter line, and stone walls that had marked smallholdings and town boundaries since the day of the Roman Empire had been crushed by the tracks of armored vehicles. Cemeteries marked the tragedy with newly dug graves.

While the British liaison officer, Captain Waller Finley-Jones, slept uncomfortably in the back of the jeep, Sam took it all in with deep sorrow. He had no particular love for the Italian people, but most of his exposure to the nation came with his few interactions with the Neapolitans—and Naples was in a very rough state these days. If he had been given the choice of staying with the platoon and working, or going to Naples on R&R, he likely would have chosen the work.

Although he didn't know the country Italians, the rancher in him shared in their loss. Little farms of water buffalo, cattle, and swine had been stripped of their livestock, barns had been shelled, and the orchards, olive groves, and vineyards had been scarred by the passing of the warriors. Mile after mile of burned-out buildings, destroyed tanks, and dismantled trucks marked their passage, and Sam felt himself wishing he'd stayed with the company.

As Perkin drove, Sam pointed out the features of the land—the rock of the mountains, the fertile soil of the valley, the trees, and the few animals that he saw. But even that experience was ruined by the army. They were stuck in a southbound convoy of trucks headed to the port cities of Naples and Salerno—the trucks that would bring back food and ammunition for General Clark's polyglot army. The trucks moved at a snail's pace—or at least, so it seemed to the impatient soldiers—and the sight of the unshaven and weary soldiers in the trucks also struck Sam as sad.

Whenever Perkin got the chance to pass, he pushed the jeep to its limits and seemingly flew past the heavy transporters and the ubiquitous two-and-a-half-ton trucks. He had long ago lost the other jeep, which contained Privates Kulis and Fratelli. They knew where they were to rendezvous in Caserta, so Perkin didn't seem to worry, but Sam was concerned that they would have trouble finding each other on the palace compound.

In truth, Perkin looked the happiest that Sam had seen him since Gianina's death six weeks before. Sam had initially thought that it was the release from responsibility that was the source of his happiness—the knowledge that the fight on the winter line was not his burden for a week or more. But the more Sam studied his cousin, the more he began to recognize an old look: Perkin had done something ornery, and he was chomping at the bit to tell Sam about it.

"What'd you do?" Sam asked.

"What?"

"What'd you do?" he repeated. "You got that look." He had to raise his voice as they passed a line of field ambulances.

Perkin looked innocently at his cousin. "What look's that?"

"It's the same look as when you set off the smoke bombs in the school on graduation day. I know that look. What'd you do?"

Perkin laughed out loud—a good, strong laugh. It was infectious, and Sam began to grin in anticipation.

Sam asked again, "What? Was it Ebbins?"

Perkin's grin widened. He nodded.

"Did ya get him back for screwing with the Japs?"

"Uh-huh."

Sam felt a momentary pang of alarm, then decided he didn't care what happened to Ebbins. "What'd you do? Cut the brake lines on his jeep?"

Perkin slammed his fist down on the steering wheel. "Damn!" he cried out in mock anger. "I didn't think of that!"

"Come on," Sam protested.

"OK. I was showin' off my combat infantryman's badge this morning to B. G. E. Beams, and Ronnnn-allld walks by and wants to know what it is. So I tell him about it, and I could see he's interested, so I made sure he knew he's eligible. You could almost see the weight coming off his shoulders, cause he ain't done any actual fighting, but this is tangible proof for back home that he was there. Know what I mean?"

Sam nodded. "Oh yeah, I know what you mean."

"Anyway, as we both know that the only thing Ronnnn-allld likes more than undeserved laurels is money, so I'm showin' it off and playin' it up, and when he ain't lookin' I wink at B. G. E. And then I tell Ebbins, 'Of course, you could always take the cash option.' Without missin' a beat, B. G. E. says, 'That's what I'm gonna do. I need the money.' So Ebbins goes, 'Whaddya mean cash option?' and I tell him you get a choice of $500 cash or the CIB in recognition of your services. All you gotta do is get approval from the regimental commander."

Sam started laughing, "Oh no . . . you didn't. Besides, he's not that gullible."

"Oh, the hell he ain't. Greed trumps all, you know. Besides, Beams played it up real straight: he told him, 'You gotta let the commander know before the awards ceremony,' which he heard was comin' up as soon as we were off the line. I swear, Ebbins was almost running over to Colonel Wranosky's headquarters to ask for his money. When he left, Beams told me, 'B. G. E. stands for Beams Gigged Ebbins,' and then he fell over laughing. I swear his platoon'll get the point for the rest of the war, but I don't think he cares."

The thought of Ebbins explaining to the explosive Wranosky that he would prefer money to the Combat Infantryman's Badge made Sam double over with laughter. "He'll get his head taken off!"

"Who? Beams or Ebbins?"

"They both will. Wranosky will shit all over Ebbins, and then it'll flow downhill onto Beams. But he's an old Aggie too. He can take it." Sam laughed again. He was beginning to enjoy the drive.

"I hadn't known that until he said he gigged Ebbins. Was he there with you?"

"Naw. He was there before me, and he left to join the Houston PD after they cancelled his major during his sophomore year."

"Really? What was that?"

Struggling to remember the word exactly, Sam replied, "Phrenology . . . or something like that. But he said it helped him a lot in his job in Houston."

"I don't doubt it. So, he's gotta be in his thirties, then."

"Yeah . . . I'd reckon so. Pretty old to be a platoon leader."

"I don't know how he gets up in the morning. So, let me tell you about the history of that town we just went through. Although we're in the ancient land of the Samnites, who fought several wars with the Roman Republic in the fourth century BC, the interesting thing about Capua was its sacking by Mohammedans in the ninth century AD. You see . . ."

1145 Hours
Fifth Army Headquarters, Caserta, Italy

Sam's freshly restored good mood continued for the rest of the drive despite Perkin's history lesson about the sacking of Capua. Saracens were less interesting to Sam than the emerging sun and the warming temperature, and although the wind through the jeep was brisk, Sam found himself beginning to relax. He was on vacation.

Even the drive onto the Fifth Army compound didn't bring him back to the darkness of earlier. Sam disliked the army, in particular the unnecessary rules and regulations and pomp that accompanied all of the army save the frontline units. As they drove up Sam woke Captain Finley-Jones, and they all straightened their ties and garrison caps to regulation standards. MPs were reportedly stopping even officers for not wearing ties, and the offending soldier was fined on the spot. Sam was sure that money went straight into the MP's pocket.

The Italian palace, a holdover from when the Bourbons reigned in this part of Italy, was the most magnificent structure that Sam had ever seen. Mostly constructed in the eighteenth century, the palace itself had well over a thousand rooms, while the palace grounds boasted numerous gardens and other equally beautiful buildings over its thousands of acres. It was known as the "Little Versailles," but Sam saw nothing about it that qualified as little. As a wealthy man in his own right, Sam was stunned at the opulence of Caserta.

An MP passed them through the barricade after checking their orders, and they were directed to an outlying building serving as a mess hall on the palace grounds. They didn't know when they'd get another hot meal, so they headed for lunch first. While they drove along a magnificent avenue lined with tall trees, Sam took in the beauty of Caserta and then suddenly laughed out load as Ebbins had crept into his thoughts again.

As Sam had borne the brunt of most of Perkin's practical jokes over his lifetime, he was delighted at the thought of Ebbins being brought up short by Colonel Wranosky. He had no particular opinions one way or the other about the Nisei officers, but his innate sense of fairness and a long-standing antipathy toward Ebbins had led him to high expectations of an eventual revenge by Perkin when he learned of the incident the night before. His cousin hadn't disappointed, and Sam chuckled again.

He was even happier when they arrived at the mess hall. A triumphant pair of privates greeted the crestfallen Perkin, and a gloating Private Kulis crowed, "We took a back road. Ha–ha! I told Vince we'd beat y'all here!"

1230 Hours
Fifth Army Headquarters, Caserta, Italy

While Captain Finley-Jones sought out the senior British officer on the Fifth Army staff and Sam and Private Fratelli staked out a table and a coffee pot, Perkin and Private Kulis went to track down Lieutenant Commander Jimmy Cardosi.

Cardosi was a naval intelligence officer who'd been in Italy since before the landings on Sicily the previous July. He had helped prepare the battlefield for the landing forces on that island and then moved to the mainland in anticipation of the landings at Salerno. Working sometimes on his own, sometimes with the Office of Strategic Services, sometimes with his British counterparts, and almost always with the Neapolitan mob, he helped to once again shape the battlefield. He had walked through Italy dressed as an itinerant laborer looking for field work. He got a good feel for the population's weariness of war and the fascists, their fear of the Germans, and the unlikelihood of any meaningful opposition from the Italians to the Allied landings. Cardosi's reports, sent back to Allied planners through contacts in the OSS, helped drive the decision to land at Paestum and Salerno, even though he personally preferred the beaches at Formia and Gaeta.

As soon as it was clear that the landing force had permanently established its lodgment at Salerno, Cardosi was moved onward to Naples. It was there he reached his limits, watching impotently as the Germans systematically took their revenge on the city. Industry was looted or destroyed; the port was savaged as ships were sunk in the channel and the valuable cranes destroyed; the people were terrorized and forced into labor battalions. It was the most wanton violence Cardosi had ever witnessed against a civilian population.

When the Allies finally took Naples, they found a city population that was on the verge of starvation and living among disease and filth. They also found a lieutenant commander in desperate need of some relaxation and time away from the war. After two weeks' leave on the island of Capri, he was assigned to the Fifth Army as a naval intelligence liaison officer to General Clark's staff, a job that the recovering officer found to be extremely boring. So he looked for other ways to help out, and one of the passing assignments that he received was the investigation into the German terror bombings in Naples.

It was a puzzle that slowly came together during the month of November. His growing list of contacts in the Camorra, prompted by gold bullion and the word of an Italian-American capo in a New York prison, began to report on rumors of a German intelligence team that specifically targeted Americans. This German team was reportedly responsible for planting time bombs in areas where American soldiers were likely to congregate: Italian army bases, bus depots, museums, and the Naples post office.

It was during the San Pietro operation that LCDR Cardosi came to Perkin's attention, and together they began to complete the puzzle. But Perkin had other duties to attend to, and Cardosi had been left to finish the analysis on his own. His briefing to Perkin and Kulis showed that his time had not been wasted.

"Since I saw you last, Captain, I submitted an inter-rogation request on the soldiers that you guys captured at Pisciotta. They had been shipped to a prisoner camp in Palacios, Texas—"

"Hey, Palacios is just north of where Sam and I are from."

Cardosi nodded. "You have to love life's little ironies, don't you? So those fellows were sent to Camp, uh, Hulen in Palacios, where they were working out on the economy for local farmers: picking hayseeds or cotton balls or whatever you rednecks do down there. The CIC sent over some interrogators, and these guys talked without much, um, persuasion. It seems they'd rather talk and continue to work and almost live outside the wire than to spend the remainder of the war in solitary.

"This is what we've learned. They all worked at a separate Abwehr command in Rome. The commanding officer is our buddy, Major Douglas Grossmann, and his deputy was Captain Mark Gerschoffer. We knew all that already. Grossmann had an American mother, killed in a bombing raid, and a German father. His upbringing was primarily American, and he went to high school in Coronado, California. Now, take a gander at this."

Cardosi pulled a large photograph from a folder and passed it over to Perkin. "Naval intelligence made a copy of this from his high school yearbook. Is this the guy you saw in Ogliastro?"

Perkin studied the photograph intently and tried to recall that day. He had stopped in the village looking for Able Company and chatted briefly with a man fitting Grossmann's description and wearing the uniform of a major in the US Army. The student in the picture looked intelligently at the camera. *A nice looking kid*, Perkin thought, *but a choirboy can grow up to be a killer too.*

"It's him. A lot younger, but definitely him. That's damn good work!" Perkin was impressed. A lot of effort had gone into this investigation—this photo had to have been flown to Europe.

"Thanks. The Office of Naval Intelligence has made this a priority at my request. There's more. His soldiers believe that he came back to Germany for college, and one of them thought he graduated in 1935 or '36 with a degree in either language or linguistics. One of his soldiers non-concurred and said the major graduated with a degree in the classics. If they hadn't said he was a womanizer, I'd have marked him as a homo. Either way, they agreed he went to the University of Heidelberg. After graduation, he went directly into Hitler's expanding army as a junior intelligence officer.

"The interrogation reports indicate that after the war began, he served in France and was posted to Italy after Pearl Harbor. He's never been directly in combat, only support activities. As I said, he's described as a lady's man, a good leader who takes care of his troops, a moderate to heavy drinker, a smoker. Fluent in English, German, French, and Italian, and—get this—Latin. Proficient in Spanish and Romanian. He was trained in Berlin to speak English with multiple accents, including West Coast and East Coast American, English upper class—what they call Etonian—and Welsh blue collar. I have a list of aliases that he's used—my favorite is Neville Drinkwater, which is what he favors when he impersonates an Englishman. Physically, he's exactly as you described him. Blond hair, blue eyes, slight build—uh, about 1.7 meters tall or about 5 feet 7 inches, and about 65 kilograms, which is just shy of 145 pounds."

"Any thoughts on how he regards the United States? Does he have divided loyalties?" Private Kulis spoke for the first time.

"That's a damn good question, shipmate. That's why I asked it myself. They didn't know. The whole group had either spent extensive time in the US or had American parents like Grossmann and Gerschoffer. They all claimed to have been deeply upset with the war against us, but they may have been blowing smoke up our asses. Hard to say. But there's a possibility we may be able to turn him, if that's what you're thinking."

"Yes, sir. I'd reckon the trick would be . . . how do we make contact with him?"

Turning the German intelligence officer may have been on Kulis's mind, but as Perkin sat there listening to the discussion, he thought, *I have other plans for Major Grossmann.*

1630 Hours
San Lupo, Italy

The Eighth Army was engaged in combat operations on the other side of Italy in a town called Ortona, on the Adriatic Sea. As the crow would fly, it was less than one hundred miles across the peninsula from Caserta, but crow miles were irrelevant in Italian navigation. Even if crows could make it across the Abruzzi Mountains—the highest range in the Apennines—in winter, the small party of soldiers couldn't. Even in jeeps.

They decided to stay on the main highways and started south with the intention of heading to a point almost even with Naples and then across the peninsula to Foggia. From Foggia, they would turn north again and reach the Eighth Army along the coast. It was fine in theory. In practice, the plan was found lacking.

No sooner had the two jeeps gotten on the highway than their progress slowed to a crawl again; out of boredom Sam even stepped out of his jeep and walked alongside the jeep carrying Cardosi, Finley-Jones, and Fratelli. It was more military traffic clogging the road. Still, they pressed on. Once they turned inward, they decided, the traffic would abate and they could make up for lost time on what Cardosi called the athwartship highway. It was another plan doomed to failure.

Less than five miles south of Caserta, they were pulled off the highway by MPs who were restricting the road to priority supply traffic. They could pull off the side of the road and wait for the supply trucks to pass, which would go on until past dark, or they could find another route. Besides, they were told, the Luftwaffe was making both day and night raids on the Fifth Army supply lines, and in the considered opinion of the MP corporal, they were better off away from that main line of communication.

It seemed like sound advice, so they turned around, and after a quick retreat, they took a narrow but paved road up into the foothills of the Abruzzi. Sitting in the jeep in a small village called San Lupo, Perkin did a rough calculation and figured that over the course of the past two hours, they had only advanced toward their objective some fifty or sixty kilometers.

"We've gone maybe thirty or thirty-five miles, but we got at most another half hour of daylight. What are your orders, sir?" he asked of Lieutenant Commander Cardosi.

"We're on no specific time line. I had planned a little slop into our schedule, and Eighth Army isn't expecting us until the day after tomorrow, anyway." He eyed two pretty Italian women who were looking curiously at the Americans. "Maybe we see what San Lupo has in the way of lodging."

As the other men got out of the jeeps and stretched, Cardosi walked over to the two ladies and immediately engaged in an animated conversation that lasted a full five minutes before he returned shaking his head.

"No hotel for another fifteen miles or so. They're sisters and they offered to let us stay at some villagers' homes, which would probably be just fine. But they had a condition."

"What's that?" Captain Finley-Jones asked.

"They want Sam to stay with them."

Sam was only paying half attention when the sisters' demand sank in. He sat down abruptly in the jeep. "What do they want?" he asked, alarmed.

Cardosi repeated the condition with a grin. "I'm guessing a six-foot-five American to share for the evening . . . no kidding, shipmate. That's what they said."

"But I'm married!" Sam protested, and to Perkin's great amusement, Sam began to blush.

"I mentioned that. I'm not sure they care."

"I'll stay with 'em," Kulis volunteered.

"Me too," said Fratelli, looking hopefully at the sisters.

"Sorry, you guys. It's Lieutenant Taft or nothing." Cardosi looked at Sam expectantly.

"Sam, maybe they just want to cook you dinner or something. You know, mother you a little bit. I wouldn't worry about it." Perkin said, grinning at his cousin's discomfort.

One of the sisters pointed at Sam, then at herself as she put a slight gyration in her hips. The other sister mockingly blew a kiss at Sam.

"My mother never did that," observed Private Kulis. "You know, I don't speak much Italian, but I understood that, and it ain't what the cap'n said."

Finley-Jones laughed. "What do you Americans say? Take one for the team? Old boy . . . I must say in case you haven't realized it . . . this is your chance to take two."

2005 Hours
Santa Croce del Sannio, Italy

The lobby of the hotel was cold and drafty, as there were no guests staying at the inn before the arrival of the Americans. Displaced persons frequently passed through Santa Croce, but if they didn't have lire, dollars, or pounds sterling, they didn't stay in rooms—although the hotelier would sometimes let them sleep in the hotel's garage if the weather was unpleasant. Three months before, Reichmarks were accepted, but no longer.

The region had seen some fierce fighting between the Germans and the Eighth Army, although Santa Croce had been spared the destruction that had come to other nearby towns. Since an American hospital unit attached to Eighth Army had left Santa Croce the month before, the town had returned to the dull state that characterized mountain life in southern Italy, and which had led to a steady and constant migration to the United States for over a hundred years.

As soon as paying guests arrived—and they paid in advance—things picked up rapidly at the hotel. The hotelier and his son quickly got a blazing fire going in what Perkin believed was the largest fireplace he'd ever seen, and hotelier's wife had pulled several soft and heavy chairs into a semicircle before the fire.

The hotel didn't have a restaurant of its own, but the hotelier's brother-in-law had a nice restaurant across the street. The six soldiers had requested—and tipped heavily—to have food brought from the restaurant so they wouldn't have to leave the comfort of the chairs and the fireplace. This naturally led to a fierce argument between the hotelier and his brother-in-law. Such things were not done; they *must* eat at the restaurant, the brother-in-law insisted. He was so evidently hoping that the curiosity of American soldiers might bring in some additional customers that the hotelier knew he would not relent until the tip was shared. Eventually, about a third of the money exchanged hands, and the restaurateur was so pleased that he resolved to prepare a special dish, and would the Americans please be patient?

They would, of course, but they were hungry now. More money left the Americans' pockets and made their way across the street to the restaurant, and soon plates of cheese, bread, olives, pickled vegetables, and salami were sent over and placed on a large coffee table. The hotel did have a bar, and several bottles of wine were opened for the Americans.

The hotelier spoke no English but he initially gathered that a massive soldier had displeased his companions. Fascinated, the hotelier watched as all of the soldiers castigated the large man, and he held his breath as twice the massive man stood up in disgust to leave, only to be coaxed back to his chair by another tall man. Americans, he had been told, love to drink and fight, and he was concerned that their apparent disapprobation of the large man might lead to an altercation, but as he watched longer, he realized that the large man was simply being teased. The hotelier relaxed as the tall, black-haired soldier eventually got the big man to smile sheepishly, and then they both began to laugh.

"I'm sorry to let you boys down. I simply couldn't do what was being asked of me, and I deeply appreciate your . . . what's that word, Perk? Lucent?"

"I don't know, lurid, maybe? Oh, uh . . . lucid?"

"Yeah, that's it. Waller, I deeply appreciate your lucid arguments that I should've slept with the DiRenzo sisters for my own physical well-being. You're right. I've been feeling right poorly lately, and as you said, no doubt some fornication would brace me up quite nicely. Yes, Private Kulis, I know that it would have brought great credit to the regiment, and I'm prepared to answer to Colonel Wranosky when we return should the subject arise. Commander, I'm sure the navy issues Italian sisters to ensigns upon commissioning like you said, but as I say every day, to my great regret, I'm a soldier. Private Fratelli, thank you for offering, well, insisting, that you step in for me when it was evident that I let the team down. I'm sorry the DiRenzo girls suddenly had other plans. Uh . . . let's see . . . who have I left out?"

"Me!" Perkin said.

Sam laughed and looked around the circle of his friends, "Yes. It's hard to imagine, gentlemen, but my cousin stood up for me. Why, I don't know, but he did. Hard to say which is was more shocking: the DiRenzo girls' behavior or that, but this has been a night of firsts, I can tell you."

Perkin snorted, "That's the thanks I get? And why? I'll tell ya why. Couple reasons. First, Maggie made me promise to protect you from the DiRenzo girls—or girls like 'em in any case—although I told her no one would be interested in you. I guess I was wrong—I certainly didn't suspect a two-fer, that's for sure. And second, I helped get ya outta that because I know you couldn't navigate through a situation like that without embarrassing either yourself or the regiment—most likely both. You don't appreciate the subtleties of delicate social situations like I do." Perkin looked pensive for a moment, then nodded sagely. "Yes, it was just better this way."

Sam rolled his eyes. "You remember the Three-Minute Vertical Berger Plan? That situation was proof you couldn't handle somethin' like this, but I could."

Captain Finley-Jones jumped in, "The Three-Minute Vertical Berger Plan? What the devil's that?"

Perkin started to explain, but Sam held his hand up like a king holding court.

"Silence, boy. This is my story. When Perk and I were home for the summer during our freshman year at college, our grandparents were traveling and Perk decided to throw a little party. Old Perkin has this beautiful old home on the bluff overlooking Corpus Bay, and . . ." Sam's face grew sad for a moment as he got homesick, then the thought passed. "And Perk invited everyone he knew—including about ten girls that he'd dated in the past or was currently seeing. I think he was gamin' the numbers . . . you know, invite ten in the hopes that one shows up. Since all ten knew that I was gonna be there, and they were just using Perk to get to me, all ten RSVP'd. So Studley here panics and goes into crisis mode 'cause if the girls get the notion that he's not only datin' more than one of them, but maybe all of them, well shoot, Perk might as well join the priesthood for the summer. As usual, he comes runnin' to his older cousin—"

"By a week!" Perkin interjects.

"And don't that just put a burr under his saddle? Anyways, he comes runnin' to me for guidance, and I devise the Three-Minute Vertical Berger Plan—"

"You did not!"

"An ingenuous plan so breathtaking in its simplicity that I contemplated copyrightin' the whole process and selling it to Charles Atlas. The key, as I saw it, was for Perkin not to sit down with any one girl all night long. He had to mingle. He could walk a girl out to a car or maybe down the block, but no holding hands or nothin' forward like that. Laying down on one of the blankets with a girl was out of the question. In short, he had to remain vertical for the entire night."

"And the three minutes, sir?" This was Private Fratelli's first foray into the officers' conversation.

"Ah, yes. He could only talk for three minutes before he "had" to get someone a drink or talk to this fella or somethin' like that. As long as he was a host and in constant motion and supremely upright, he'd be fine."

Perkin was preparing to tell his side of the story, which was that Sam's only contribution to the Three-Minute Vertical Berger Plan was to call Perkin a dumbass for inviting all the girls in the first place, when the food finally arrived.

The owner of the restaurant, his sole waiter, and his two oldest teenage daughters brought over a large soup tureen and bowls for the soldiers on a metal cart that seemed to have four independent wheels, which caused it to go sideways when pushed through the lobby. As one daughter placed a cloth napkin into the lap of each soldier, the restaurateur watched as the other daughter carefully ladled a steaming, thick, orange-colored soup into the bowls. The waiter then ceremoniously handed a bowl and a spoon to each soldier.

"My lord, this is good!" exclaimed Sam. "What is this?"

Lieutenant Commander Cardosi spoke to the restaurateur, who answered and then bowed slightly to Sam. Cardosi then asked another question.

"It's pumpkin soup—a house specialty. I asked him what the *secondo*, the next course, would be, but he said it's a surprise."

"I hope it's as good as this," said Perkin.

It was. Fifteen minutes later, the owner, his daughters, and the waiter returned. Sliced and buttered potatoes were carefully ladled onto the plates next to a meat dish, and they all stood by proudly to watch the soldiers' first bites.

"That smells lovely," said Finley-Jones. "What is it? Porcetta?"

"It smells like it," Cardosi concurred. But as he took a bite, a slow smile spread across his face. "But it's not. My grandmother used to make this. Any guesses?"

After pork, the guesses ranged from chicken to duck to goat but it was Private Kulis who had the right answer. "It ain't pork, sir." Kulis said with a wondrous look on his face. "It's rabbit."

"Rabbit?" Fratelli was surprised. "Are you sure?"

"I ate so much rabbit and squirrel during the Depression, I can't be wrong. But I ain't ever had it like this. Please tell him this is a damn sight better than my mom's stewed rabbit, sir."

The restaurateur beamed, bowed to an enthusiastic round of applause, and then they left the soldiers to their dinner.

**2345 Hours
Santa Croce del Sannio, Italy**

The dishes were cleared and the young enlisted soldiers departed to pursue what Private Kulis called the Three-Minute Horizontal Kulis Plan. Cigars were passed around and the hotelier had sold them a bottle of kruskovac—fiery pear brandy from Croatia. The fire was dying down, and the men simply enjoyed the warmth and comfort of a building and a fire more than they could possibly have ever imagined.

No one wanted to talk about the war, but inevitably, that's where the conversation led. The peculiarities of old comrades from the Texas Division were discussed and, when necessary, explained to the British Army officer and the American naval officer. Finley-Jones reciprocated with a story of a fellow Welsh Guardsman in Tunisia who, upon walking into an operations briefing and seeing a chart pinned to the wall, wanted to know what the fuss was about casual ties.

"Casual ties?" asked Sam.

"Yes, casual ties," said the Welsh officer with a smile.

"I don't get it either, I guess."

"The chart was a posting of casualties, not casual ties. Poor Captain Williams was exhausted, the old sod, and even when it was pointed out to him, he had a hard time reading it straight."

Sam wrote the word out with his finger in the air, and then started laughing—a deep belly laugh that momentarily awakened the hotelier who had fallen asleep at the front desk.

"Speaking of reading," Finley-Jones went on, "I understand that silly bugger Ebbins can't read a compass. You need to watch him closely, Sam."

"Oh ... Waller, I know, but let's not ruin a nice evening by bringing up Ebbins."

"Fair enough, Sam." Finley-Jones obviously wanted to say more on the subject of Captain Ebbins, but he let it pass.

"Gentlemen, I'm getting ready to hit my rack, but I want to ask you fellows: What's next? Where do you guys head now?" Lieutenant Commander Cardosi slewed his gaze to the remaining brandy and, belying his statement about turning in, poured himself another glass.

Perkin answered, "Well, we have to breach the Gustav Line. So there's only one way to go and that's north."

"I know. I've looked at the charts, uh, maps. I guess I mean, any idea what role you'll have? How it'll be done?"

"I don't know, Jimmy." Perkin spoke softly, seriously. "There's a couple different ways to crack this problem, I suppose. Preferably, we'll get up in the mountains like we were in San Pietro and keep pushing, pushing, until we work around them. Once we roll up their flanks in the mountains above the abbey at Cassino, their position on the line in the valley will be untenable. The second option is a full-scale push across the Rapido River: most of the Fifth Army in assault from the Tyrrhenian Sea to the Abruzzi, with the armored divisions in reserve and ready to exploit whatever gap the infantry divisions make. That would be costly, but probably quicker. Once we breach the Gustav Line, it's just a matter of days or weeks until we get to Rome."

"So it has to be the whole army, not just a division?"

Perkin shivered. "A single division? No. It'd be slaughtered. There's a German corps in prepared defense on the Gustav Line in the Liri Valley alone. You'd be sending two regiments, with the third in reserve, against . . . I don't know . . . two or three veteran German divisions. And they'd have to effect a river crossing in order to do it. It would be like one of those forlorn hopes of ancient warfare."

"What's that?"

Finley-Jones answered, "Well, it's not really ancient—except to an American. A forlorn hope is an assault force sent in against overwhelming odds to breach a defense. Rather like the storm troopers of the day. The assault force has traditionally been volunteers with the promise of promotion or advancement as the reward for successfully surviving. During the Peninsular War, Wellington used one at the Battle of Badajoz in 1812 in order to the end the siege there. Most of the forlorn hope was killed, along with another four thousand or more troops. It was a terrible affair."

Perkin spoke again, "It's the river crossing that has me worried. My daddy was killed at our victory on the Marne in '18. His division, the 3rd, was in defense, and the Germans kept sending wave after wave of assault troops to force a crossing of the river. They were slaughtered by our own General Walker, no less—just like any single division trying to cross the Rapido will be. That's why it's imperative to have either a patient campaign up in the mountains or an assault across a broad front. Make the defenders spread their forces out, or it'll be a repeat of the Marne. But this time, it'll be us sucking hind tit."

Chapter Five

December 29, 1943
0945 Hours
Campobasso, Italy

It had taken the group longer to get on the road than they had desired. The two younger soldiers had to be pulled from their beds by Sam and Perkin, much to the chagrin and embarrassment of the restaurateur's daughters. Kulis, in particular, remained in such bad shape from the previous night's debauchery that Perkin had decided it would be a safer course of action to drive himself.

While Sam and Perkin saw to the red-eyed and hungover privates, Finley-Jones and Cardosi saw to breakfast. A small café sold them a dozen cornetti—Italian croissants stuffed with butter and jam—and filled all the canteens with an indescribably black, viscous coffee.

Perkin would have liked to have spent a little more time in the picturesque village, but it was beginning to snow, and in any case, he didn't want to deal with an angry father on behalf of his troops. Consequently, the officers unceremoniously dumped the privates into the backs of the jeeps, and the party made a hasty departure from Santa Croce del Sannio.

The going was slow because of the accumulating snow and the winding roads through the Abruzzi foothills, but it wasn't long before they began to see indications of recent combat. Coming around one bend, the party was surprised when the landscape changed dramatically. Gone were the trees and brush, replaced by a burned and scarred hillside. Tree stumps indicated heavy artillery shelling, and two burned-out German halftracks had already begun to rust in a roadside ditch.

It was an unnerving transition, Perkin thought. One side of a hill was an idyllic winter scene. Around the bend was death and destruction. Except for the sleeping privates, the soldiers all instinctively checked their weapons, and Sam sat his Garand across his lap. Even more eerie was the absence of animals—no birds, or deer, or even rabbits. It was if the passing combat had taken all life on the hill for eternity. The remainder of the drive to the next town of any size, Campobasso, was a repetition of the same phenomena. The little highway wove through pristine mountain forest, followed by the devastation of war.

Perkin was almost relieved when Campobasso came into view. It was considerably larger than Santa Croce, but as they approached the town, it was apparent that the war had not passed Campobasso. Reminiscent of San Pietro, shattered and collapsed buildings could be seen from a distance.

A large Canadian Red Ensign and a manned roadblock greeted them as they rolled up to the town. Two soldiers in British-looking uniforms approached Perkin and Sam's jeep, which was in the lead. The soldiers at the checkpoint offered a British salute upon recognizing officers in the jeep, but when they asked for orders, the accents were clearly North American.

"Where are you headed, sir?" a lance corporal asked of Perkin.

"We're on our way to Eighth Army headquarters." Perkin replied.

"Who's that?" the lance corporal asked, indicating the sleeping Private Kulis.

"Our driver."

The soldier laughed. "Excellent. Been on a bit of a bender? He smells like he's had a few for the king."

Perkin nodded, "He had some for the king, some for Roosevelt, and a few for Uncle Joe just to make sure he drank to all our allies."

The Canadian soldier laughed again. "God bless him. A word of advice, sir. Get him tidied up or the English MPs in the rear will write him up; they never pass up the chance to chivvy the Yanks. Don't try and cut the corner to Vasto—most of the bridges remain out, and there's a Kiwi roadblock to the north that you should avoid. They're searching traffic looking for contraband booze, which they're not authorized to do because it's not contraband, but they do it anyway." His face darkened—he obviously had strong feelings on the issue. "It just goes straight into their own goddamned mess. Stay on this road until you get to the coast, sir, and expect a slowdown at Termoli, and then just follow the signs from there."

Perkin thanked the soldiers and returned their salute as the jeeps passed through the roadblock, and then took in the horrors of Campobasso. A much larger town than San Pietro, it had suffered somewhat less than total destruction, but the damage and loss of homes and businesses still shocked the soldiers who had yet to harden to the worst of the vicissitudes of war.

1115 Hours
Vasto, Italy

The little procession had cleared numerous checkpoints, and they were without question in Eighth Army
territory. The vehicles that they passed were a mix of
Imperial equipment and American Lend-Lease, many
carrying the scars of recent combat. The soldiers reflected an army as multinational as their own Fifth
Army. Canadian, Indian, New Zealander, and British
divisions comprised the heart of the Eighth Army, but
other nationalities were also represented. Finley-Jones
pointed out several small Asian soldiers that he called
Gurkhas—"Splendid fellows," he said. "Absolute brutes
in battle."

The Canadian soldier was correct: there had been
little traffic on the road to the coast, but it picked up
dramatically as supplies raced to the front from whatever
Italian ports on the Adriatic remained functional. All
along the coastal road, Perkin and Sam saw the signs of
recent combat, and Sam remarked to his cousin that he
imagined it was what Georgia looked like after Sherman's
army swept through—buildings had been leveled on the
streets to provide effective roadblocks; stores and hospitals
had been looted by retreating German troops; and ancient
stone bridges had been dropped into numerous streams
and rivers. The soldiers from the Fifth Army held their
breath as they passed over makeshift pontoon bridges and
the amazing Bailey Bridges.

When they reached the coastal highway, traffic
slowed again. Kulis, after being tidied up, fell asleep once
more. Perkin looked at his cousin, who seemed deep in
thought.

"Somethin' on your mind? You ain't said much this
morning."

Sam looked around to see if Kulis was asleep, and then nodded. "After you and the boys turned in last night, I got around to reading Maggie's letter. It'd been burning a hole in my pocket since mail call yesterday morning, but I wanted to, you know, read it in private."

"Is there somethin' goin' on back home?"

Sam sighed, "I don't belong here, Perk. I should be at home. With Maggie. It's unfair to ask her to run that big ranch by herself. Unfair to wait for me all these years—we might not get home until '47 or '48, and we ain't hardly doin' anything here on the continent. We're just now gettin' started, and look how long the Great War took." He looked hard off into the distance at a pasture that was bereft of animals.

Perkin felt his cousin's mood shift from self-pity to anger. "I don't believe that, Sam. Once the second front's begun in earnest, we'll be home before you know it. I heard there's more than a million dogfaces headed to England for the cross-channel landing. As soon as we get 'em across, the war's as good as over. Hell, you've seen how well we've done here, and it ain't like Italy's made for modern warfare. I'm telling ya, we'll meet the Soviets in Warsaw and have a hell of a party, and I promise it'll be long before '48."

"It don't matter if we're home by Christmas. This goddamned war is taking too long. It's unfair for her to put up with all that crap."

"Bear, what did Maggie say to set you off so?"

Sam hesitated, then said, "She was at our bank in Corpus to settle on a parcel of land that she bought over by Gum Hollow—"

"That's a bit from the ranch, ain't it?"

"Yeah, that's OK. It's some pretty property that abuts the back bay—we can go giggin' for flounder there when we're home."

"Oh Lord, I can't think of anything I'd rather do," Perkin said sincerely. "Except maybe trout fishin' in the front bay. So what's the problem at the bank?"

"Well, she was waitin' for her appointment, and she overheard two men talking. She looks over and one of 'em was old man Ebbins. Ronald's dad."

"Uh-oh."

"Yeah, and he started to braggin' to this other fella about how much money he's made off the war—"

"He didn't!"

"He did, and it gets worse. He keeps braggin' and then tells this other man that he hopes the war goes on forever."

Perkin was disgusted. It was not that he didn't know some people back home were profiting from the war, it was the unforgivable thought that a man with a son in a fighting unit in a theater of the war would voice such a sentiment.

"I hope Maggie gave him a piece of her mind."

Sam's frown disappeared and a proud grin spread slowly across his face. He reached over and slapped Perkin's thigh with the back of his hand. "My girl did better than that. First she punched him in the face and knocked the old man down. Then she sat on his chest and slapped the hell outta him until the bank guard came and pulled her off. When Ebbins got to his feet, you know what that son-of-a-bitch did? He told the guard to hold her so he could hit her back. The guard wasn't gonna do that, of course, but he was gonna have her arrested, until it came out what Ebbins said. Turns out the guard's an old Marine and lost a son at Guadalcanal and has another boy missing in action from Makin Island. So the guard hollers out, 'What the hell?'—although Maggie wrote 'heck'—and he draws his nightstick and breaks old Ebbins's collarbone faster than you can snap your fingers. I guess he was fixin' to kill the old man, but the bank president stopped him first."

"By God, that woman's got some starch!" Perkin slapped his hand down on the steering wheel. "It does my heart good to hear stories like that!"

"Yeah, and believe me, that's just her gentle side. But you know the Ebbins family ain't likely to let that pass. I think that he would've pressed charges against her, except he'd either get laughed outta Texas for gettin' beat up by a girl, or rode out on a rail for what he said. He tried to press charges against the guard, but the guard claimed he was defendin' Maggie, so I suspect that's that. Maggie says it likely won't go nowhere. But all of that aside, I'm still worried about what Ebbins might try. Maggie wrote that she thinks some Mexican fella's taken to followin' her, and someone put sugar in her gas tank one day in town. *My* gas tank—it was my pickup, goddamn it! She made it to Gregory before it died on her, and she had to have the engine stripped completely down and cleaned—I don't doubt that old Ebbins is up it to all."

"Oh, Sam." Perkin looked at his cousin with concern. "You gotta be just sick. You want me to write Pop?"

"He already knows. I am worried, but . . . well, Ebbins also got that guard fired from his job at the bank. So it looks like I now got a new employee—a former Marine who knows nothing about cattle, but always carries a Colt .45 that he brought home from Belleau Wood. Between her sharp tongue and that old Marine Gunny, I guess it's Ebbins that ought to watch out!"

1645 Hours
Eighth Army Headquarters, Vasto, Italy

"Good afternoon, gentlemen. I'm Captain Perkin Berger, the intelligence officer of the 1st Battalion, 141st Infantry, 36th Division. The classification of this briefing is secret. I would like to state up front that this is the work of Lieutenant Commander Jimmy Cardosi of the United States Navy. Commander Cardosi was, until about an hour ago, serving as the naval intelligence liaison to the Fifth Army. When we arrived this afternoon, he found a set of orders awaiting him, and he's now rejoining the combined fleet."

Perkin kept his thoughts about Cardosi's orders to himself, but they could only mean one thing: the Allied Command was preparing for another amphibious landing in Italy. That was Cardosi's specialty—intelligence collection prior to a landing. *Maybe a shot at Rome is in the works*, he thought. *Or perhaps even a landing in northern Italy to cut Kesselring's supply lines.*

Cardosi had been apologetic, but Perkin could see the excitement in his face. As he made his good-byes, he pulled Perkin aside and said, "I know that if you get the chance, you'll deal with this son-of-a-bitch. All I'm asking is to make one round from me." Cardosi had looked around, and then lowered his voice. "I shouldn't say anything, but based on what we talked about last night, I'm not so sure that Fifth Army's thought through the next step for you guys. I hope I misunderstood the planners, but I think they've got you rednecks slated for the river. You keep your head down, Perkin, and I'll look you up in Rome."

He handed over his briefcase with photos and notes, shook Perkin's hand and returned his salute. An awaiting navy jeep whisked Cardosi away. The total elapsed time from when they checked in with the US Navy liaison officer at Eighth Army to Cardosi's departure back to the fleet was less than ten minutes.

Private Kulis and Perkin were in a darkened room in front of several officers, British and American, assigned to the Eighth Army staff. When they had arrived at the briefing room, Kulis had a crash course from a British NCO on how to work a slide projector while Perkin prepared his thoughts. The senior officer present was a British colonel from the Eighth Army staff named Scrope—an intelligence officer who looked younger than Perkin. As the briefing went on, essentially a recitation of Cardosi's update from two days before, the British officer took copious notes. He nodded frequently, but swore intensely when Grossmann's culpability in the Bari bombing was brought up.

"Damn him, and damn that fool colonel of yours! That whole bloody affair caught us flat-footed, you know. We didn't know about the mustard gas aboard your freighter in the harbor, and because of that, many of our doctors didn't know what they were treating. The gas saturated the clothing of the victims, including an untold number of British sailors, and when the doctors and nurses handled them, they picked up traces of the agent as well. Poor buggers."

Perkin nodded uncomfortably. He didn't want to be in the position of defending the American stockpile of the poison gas, nor the actions of the colonel who had disclosed the information to Grossmann's agent, Antoniette Bernardi.

Perkin continued. He told the assembled officers what he knew of Grossmann's background—where he went to school in California, what was known of his family, his major at college.

"Where did you say he went to university?" The questioner was a man with an English accent that Perkin hadn't noticed before. Two men wearing civilian clothes were sitting in the back of the room in a dark corner not reached by the light of the slide projector. One of the men, a small gray-haired man wearing a crumpled suit, stood.

Perkin stared into the darkness for a moment, then answered, "I didn't say, sir. I was about to mention that he went to the University of Heidelberg."

"That makes sense, doesn't it? Heidelberg isn't far from Darmstadt. Were you aware that Heidelberg is a fanatical pro-Nazi university?" The small man stood and walked forward until he was in the edge of the shadows.

"No, sir, I wasn't."

"Yes. The Nazis took over the university in the middle part of the last decade and released those that had, well, democratic sympathies. They even made redundant a few old monarchists. Naturally, they were replaced by professors of a National Socialist bent, and the student body underwent a strict indoctrination into Nazism. In past centuries, Heidelberg was known for the fighting fraternities. Today, for feeding the officer corps of the SS."

"Thank you, sir. I didn't know that. I would note, however, that interrogations of the soldiers that we captured in Pisciotta indicated that while Grossmann considered himself to be a German patriot, he was also apolitical."

The small civilian spoke again, "Thank you, Dr. Berger, that's worth knowing. Please continue."

Perkin stared briefly back into the shadows and then shared with the audience the remainder of what he knew about Grossmann, Bernardi, and Gerschoffer.

The small man stood and spoke again, "Would you please detail your encounter with Captain Gerschoffer for us?"

Perkin nodded and took a deep breath. This was not a subject he wanted to discuss. "Yes, sir. I was conducting a reconnaissance of the village of San Pietro, and I had acquired a German uniform. During my reconnaissance in the village, I met Gerschoffer by chance and we struck up a conversation. I realized at that point that I was talking to one of the men responsible for the terror bombings in Naples. He thought I was a panzer grenadier, so he offered to give me a ride back to my unit. I accepted, and when we were out of San Pietro, I produced a weapon and interrogated him. He told me of Grossmann's unit of *Auslandsdeutsche*, and of Bernardi, although he wouldn't give me her name, and of the penetration of the Fifth Army staff and the mustard gas at Bari."

A British major spoke, his tone incredulous: "Am I to understand you put on a German uniform and simply strolled through the village?"

"Yes, sir. Something like that."

"Is your German that good?"

Perkin's audience sat forward in their seats, and he felt a trickle of sweat run down his back. For one of the few times in his life, he did not relish the attention.

"No, sir. I had, um, been wounded . . ." Perkin indicated the scars and bruises on his face. "And my face was pretty heavily bandaged. I couldn't hardly move my lips . . . he didn't question it."

"Good God, man!" the British officer exclaimed. "They would have executed you!"

"It was one of those 'it seemed like a good idea at the time' experiences, sir. Now, if we could move on to the issue of—"

"Pardon me, Dr. Berger. How did you induce Gerschoffer to speak and what ultimately happened to him? Is he available for further interrogation?" Perkin was interrupted by the small man in the back.

A long silence. "He's not. As I was saying, maybe we should move on to the issue of Grossmann's training . . ." Perkin had brief flashback where he was sitting in a bloody car with Gerschoffer, the German officer pleading for his life—a plea that was answered with a scream of hatred and revenge as Perkin pulled the trigger on his Colt.

Perkin stopped for a glass of water and was glad to see his hand wasn't trembling. He composed himself, the small man took his seat again, and the briefing continued without further questions. When Perkin finished, his audience filed out, and while Private Kulis was putting away the slides and pictures, Perkin was joined by the British colonel and the two civilians.

"Professor Berger—" the small man began.

"Excuse me, sir. I've not been on a faculty. I haven't earned that title, and quite honestly, I am surprised to hear it from you, as I don't believe I mentioned my degree. In any case, Perkin works just fine, or you can call me Captain if you prefer."

"OK, Perkin." It was the taller of the two civilians speaking. Also gray-haired, he was lean and fit, and spoke in an American accent. "My name is George Hill. My colleague is Charles Ackernley. We work in a combined counterintelligence task force on special issues on behalf of General Alexander. I'm on loan to the War Department from the FBI, and Mr. Ackernley worked for the Special Branch of the Metropolitan Police."

"You're cops?"

"Police? No. Not anymore," Ackernly said. "We're detectives from previous lives. We have investigative skills that most soldiers don't have. Colonel Scrope," he nodded to the British officer, "asked us to listen in, to see if we can help."

"You see, Captain . . ." Scrope said, and then turned to the listening Kulis. "Private, would you step outside for a moment?"

Kulis looked to Perkin and, at Perkin's nod, left the room.

Scrope continued, "Major Grossmann's outfit has come to our—meaning British—attention before—and you were present when he did. When we learned of your, ah, intervention on behalf of Father Riley, and Riley told us through his brother of the events and of the American-accented German soldiers, we put out inquiries to our network in Rome. We learned enough to sketch a picture, figuratively speaking, of his Abwehr office in Rome. All of this was coming together for us about as time-coincident as it did for Fifth Army. I must say, old boy, that I'm truly grateful for your presence here today, as well as for your excellent briefing. It helps us to complete our profile, and adds many more pieces to the puzzle. We are deeply indebted for the photographs by the by, and I can assure you, they'll be put to good use in short order."

Perkin looked at the group and sized up the men before him. There was something going on, but he couldn't put his finger on it. He paused for a moment, then asked, "What have you learned that we don't know, and what is your interest in me?"

Scrope didn't answer. He looked at the American civilian, Mr. Hill, who said, "As for you, Perkin, you naturally came to our attention at Pisciotta. Were you really going to execute those soldiers before the priest arrived?" He stopped speaking and an understanding smile flitted across his face. "Don't look so alarmed. But I should tell you that through our counterparts at Fifth Army, we've had a look at your file and read your after-action reports from both Salerno and San Pietro. In addition to your reconnaissance at San Pietro, we were particularly impressed with your handling of the affair at the monastery. You're a decorated combat soldier; you seem to have a knack at being at the right place at the right time; and you don't seem to shy away from . . . well, hard work. We have a common interest in Major Grossmann, and we'd like to pay him back for the trouble he caused from Naples to Bari—and when we get the opportunity to do so, we'll do so in spades.

If we can count on your support, we'd like it. Now, to the heart of your question, and why we're talking to you now: we think we know what Major Grossmann will do next!"

1730 Hours
Eighth Army Headquarters, Vasto, Italy

Sam stared disbelievingly at Captain Waller Finley-Jones. "And why in God's name would I want to do that?"

"Sam, as you chaps said long ago, we've seen the elephant. But for all the hard fighting that we've done, it's been a slog on the beaches and in the mountains and the valleys. I'm saying we should get a close look at the street fight that's going on now and take the lessons learned back to the division."

"Yeah, I understood the words the first time, Waller. We sometimes even speak the same language. I just wanna know why I would want to." Sam shook his head. He had no desire to go to the front lines to see urban warfare up close, no matter how altruistic the motives might be, but he knew that Perkin would be enthusiastic as soon as he heard of it. If Perk was going, he would feel honor-bound to go as well.

"Rome, Sam. Rome. Once we breach the Gustav Line, there's nothing between us and Rome. No spring line, no summer line. Just open valley. But when we get to Rome, if the Germans don't have the humanity to make it an open city, it'll be our Stalingrad. There'll be fights for every street, every row house, every piazza, stone by stone, yard by yard. It's what's happening just ten miles from here in Ortona. The Canadians are fighting the German's 1st Paras, and it's a laboratory of modern warfare. We should go see that laboratory for ourselves."

"I ain't a scientist, damn it, I'm a cowboy."

"Oh, don't be such an old bones, Sam. We won't go into action, just observe it. And think through what I've said—even if we give Rome a miss, there's a thousand hamlets, villages, towns and cities between here and Berlin."

"What's a hamlet?"

"It's a small village."

Sam shook his head, "Why wouldn't we just shell the damn thing?"

"I think you're missing the point, Sam."

"No, Waller, I think *you're* missin' the damn point. This is my vacation, remember?"

Finley-Jones smiled at his friend. He knew that although Sam was grousing, he would come around. "It's too cold to sit on the bloody beach, isn't it? Come on, we'll wake up, get some bangers and chook, and then just go have a look see."

"What the hell's bangers and chook? I already told ya, you ain't gettin' me in a whorehouse."

Finley-Jones smirked, "Pity. No, bangers are sausages, although a little blander than those ones stuffed with hot peppers that you gave me. I shan't forget that, and I will enjoy my revenge someday!"

The memory of Finley-Jones eating jalapeno-stuffed sausages drew a laugh from Sam. He asked, "Ain't my fault your food's tasteless. Why do you call 'em bangers?"

"They have a rather unfortunate tendency to explode."

"Oh. That's swell. Exploding sausages and chook—which is what? A detonatin' biscuit?" Sam picked up his Garand and began to break it down for cleaning.

"I keep telling you, real biscuits are what you might call cookies; your biscuits are rather unimaginative scones; and chook . . . well, chook are army eggs." Powdered eggs to be exact, but Finley-Jones thought he'd leave that out.

"Army eggs? You mean the green ones?"

"Only if properly cooked in copper pots, you know. What do you say?"

"I'm cleanin' my rifle, ain't I?"

1745 Hours
Eighth Army Headquarters, Vasto, Italy

A British orderly brought in two pots of tea and a tray of ham and butter sandwiches at the request of Colonel Scrope. Perkin sent Kulis to find the rest of their party and tell them to go ahead and find something to eat, and that he would track them down later.

"So, y'all think you know what Grossmann's going to do next? Have any thoughts then on where he might be?"

"We do," said Ackernly. He seemed to be collecting his thoughts as he absentmindedly put two teaspoons of sugar into an empty cup and then poured a little milk onto the sugar. Only after he had stirred the two together did he add the steaming tea.

Scrope spoke while the civilian tended to his tea. "Captain Berger, what we're going to tell you is classified most secret. Sorry, top secret—old habits die hard. I can't stress enough that this information needs to be closely guarded, and that unauthorized disclosure of what we're going to tell you could severely compromise the Vatican and His Majesty's Government." Scrope had an intense look on his face, and to emphasize his point, he said again slowly, "Compromise His Majesty's Government."

"I understand, sir. Does this have something to do with Father Riley?"

Ackernly raised his hand as if to indicate he wanted to tell the story. He took a sip of tea first, and in a quiet voice he said, "Yes and no, young man. Riley is involved, but it goes much farther than a low-level priest. Have you ever heard of Monsignor Hugh O'Flaherty?"

"No, sir."

"O'Flaherty is one of Riley's fellow Irishmen in the Vatican. Another Jesuit. Whereas Riley was in the Jesuit Curia before being stranded in southern Italy, O'Flaherty is assigned to the Vatican Curia. If you're not familiar with how they run things in God's little acre, the Roman Curia are the administrative offices of the Church. They help develop, promulgate, and administer Church policy, and O'Flaherty is considered a fast-track chap. Brilliant, overly Irish, and a scratch golfer of all things."

"Overly Irish?" Perkin asked.

"Well, yes, despite his good deeds which I'll detail momentarily, he's not a fan of the British Empire. He is, what one could say, that truly rare beast—a good, devout, fearless man. But a man who grew up in the shadow of the Irish Civil War and partition, and the Black and Tans. I don't think he'd cross the street to help King George."

"So, what's his connection to Grossmann?"

"I'll get to that . . . O'Flaherty was arrested by British forces in Southern Ireland in '21, but was released without any further action. It appears to have been a case of being in the wrong place at the wrong time. He graduated from Mungret College in Limerick and was ordained in '25. Most of his time as a priest has been spent at the Vatican, although he has traveled extensively and he was assigned to what was essentially a diplomatic mission for a year in Haiti and the Dominican Republic. He also completed a mission in Palestine and, significantly, spent two years, '36 to '38, in Czechoslovakia."

"So he's had the opportunity to view the jackboots firsthand."

"Exactly. Beginning during the North Africa campaigns, O'Flaherty began to visit the prisoner of war camps here in Italy, serving as an English interpreter to another Vatican official. He was always friendly to all the lads, including the English ones, and he would bring back names of the fellows he met and broadcast them over the Vatican radio. It was a great help to many families whose boys were reported as missing in action, when in fact they were prisoners of the Italians. When some of them later escaped in the confusion following your landing in September, they made it to Rome and sought out O'Flaherty. He put some of them up in his apartment—in the German College no less—and others were sent into sympathetic Italian homes. It appears that his sympathies were not just to the Allied boys but to anti-fascist Italians, Jews, and, well, anyone needing protection from the Germans."

"How did he come to your attention?" Perkin was intrigued by the story of the Irish monsignor and was wondering how this would affect him.

"A couple of different ways, actually. Believe it or not, both of our countries still maintain a diplomatic mission to the Holy See. Although O'Flaherty is not working with us by any means, he lets our chap at the Vatican know who he's got under his wing, and they pass him funds to help finance the operation. Also, we've had a handful of men trickle back to our lines from Rome, and they've told us of the help that they've received from the monsignor. That's how we know—"

Hill, the American official, interrupted, "There may have been just a trickle back to us, but we think O'Flaherty has more than a thousand of our boys—of every flavor imaginable—tucked away in the Vatican or helpful Italian households. And when I say every flavor, that's what I mean: Yanks, Brits, Diggers, Kiwis, Canucks, Yarpies, Rhodies—and soldiers from a hundred points in the British Empire that you and I never heard of before.

Think of the footprint of a thousand Allied soldiers. So ..."

"So," Perkin said, finishing Hill's thought, "if there are that many looking to get out, and they're using the Church as a conduit, they've now come to the German's attention."

"Yes!" said Ackernly. "Therein lies the rub. O'Flaherty's come not only to our attention, but that of Jerry as well, and I imagine the SS and the Gestapo are preparing to bugger him like a choirboy. I can't tell you how much I admire this man whom I've never met, so I would feel dreadful were that to occur."

Perkin thought for a moment. "Are you positive that he's come to the Germans' attention?"

Colonel Scrope looked at the others, and when Ackernly nodded, Scrope answered, "Yes. Can't discuss sources, but we're sure."

"Do you have a feel for when the Gestapo might move against him?" Perkin felt his excitement mount, and he wondered, *What's my role in this?*

Scrope answered again. "No. We're getting a sense that there may be a power struggle among German intelligence agencies on this issue—specifically the Abwehr and the Gestapo. We're not sure. We believe that the SS is conducting this train, and we have further reason to believe that they have prepared contingency plans to depose the Pope and occupy the Papal territory. We've even heard of plans to establish an Anti-Pope in Lichtenstein. But ... we also have indications that a move against the Vatican is being held in abeyance."

Ackernly nodded and said, "If that's the case, what would you suppose that they are waiting for, young man?"

Perkin considered the question. "Well, it may be that the cost of doing it would be too severe, that it'd cause too many perturbations, specifically among the Austro-

German Catholic population, or in, say, Vichy France or Hungary or Croatia or neutral Ireland—that the plan's not postponed, but in fact shelved indefinitely. No sense inflaming all of Catholicism over a thousand POWs. Or perhaps they're waiting to see if there is a change in the fortunes of war—a turnabout on the Eastern Front. A postponement of the channel crossing. Maybe a stalemate or even a victory here in Italy. Maybe if the war shifts back in their favor, who cares what the world of Catholicism thinks?" Perkin saw Ackernly lift his eyebrows and shrug. Perkin thought he knew what Ackernly was thinking and he continued, "On the other hand, when's Hitler *ever* given two hoots about what anybody thinks of him? Maybe he just wants an airtight case against the Vatican before he moves first?"

"I think that's a triple twenty, Captain Berger." Scrope had a pleased yet serious look about him.

Ackernly asked another question of Perkin. "Do you see how this comes together now?"

"Yes, sir, I think so . . . The Germans will use Grossmann to penetrate O'Flaherty's network—posing as an American or British soldier. He can spend time in the Vatican halls learning O'Flaherty's mysteries, and that information will then be used to build Hitler's case against the Pope."

"Indeed," Scrope said. "Grossmann will use his unique capabilities to infiltrate O'Flaherty's network. The information that he gathers may be used to either construct a false case positing a relationship between the Pope and Allied Intelligence, or be used as a justification for abandoning the Concordat. Remember that this is a man who we believe burned the Reichstag in order to declare emergency powers, and who certainly staged a flimsy pretext for war against Poland. This is not beyond Hitler. Regardless, the best case is that the Pope is hopelessly compromised, and the worst case is that Pius XII's reign ends in a concentration camp, and Hitler loots Vatican City three ways to Sunday!"

Perkin nodded seriously. It was plausible. "OK. We're in agreement about this, so what does this have to do with me?"

"Well, let's work through the next steps together, young man." Ackernly may have been a policeman, but he seemed more like a teacher to Perkin. "What would you do?"

"I'd go to Rome and kill Grossmann." Judging by the reactions Perkin saw on the faces of the three men around him, he wasn't sure that was the preferred course of action. While Hill nodded in silent approval, Scrope had an amused look about him, and Ackernly was openly skeptical.

Ackernly spoke, "Just like that?"

"Well, you gotta find him first, but yes, sir. Just like that. If O'Flaherty has an underground railroad to get escaped prisoners out of Italy, then it can work in the other direction. Look, I'm just a battalion intel officer and I've only been that for a few weeks . . . I don't know about these things, but surely the OSS or MI6 have people in Rome. Why not use them? Or their transportation?"

"It's not that simple, young man. Grossmann may be getting close to penetrating Vatican City, in which case, it's too late. British or American intelligence needs to get to him outside the walls of God's little acre. We can't run the risk of establishing any linkage between us and the Pope, and while we'd like to get to him in Rome, unfortunately, our people there are few and are not the sort of chaps that specialize in the type of work you suggest. Besides, they don't know what Grossmann looks like."

Perkin rapped his knuckles on the table and said, "Well, I do. Send me, and if I get the chance, I'll kill him for God and country—in Saint Peter's Basilica, if necessary." Perkin hardly thought about the words as he spoke them, but they were the truth. The unspoken words were, "I'll kill him for myself." Perkin had a burning desire to avenge the murder of Gianina, and he would be willing to take extraordinary chances to exact it.

"I'm afraid that's out the question, Perkin," Hill said. "You don't have the training or the language skills for this. No," he raised a hand to forestall a protest from Perkin, "you have demonstrated amazing talent and determination, but this isn't for you."

"I don't get it, gentlemen," Perkin said, shaking his head. "Y'all don't have the bubbas in Rome to do it. You're unwilling to let me do it. So what is your plan, and please, Mr. Ackernly, let's not play the didactic game again."

Scrope and Hill smiled as Ackernly said, "I apologize, Dr. Berger—my wife says that's a very annoying habit. Well, here's what we'd like from you. Enjoy your stay with Eighth Army until after the New Year's, and then we have a small favor to ask of you."

Chapter Six

December 30, 1943
1120 Hours
Ortono, Italy

The six soldiers moved down the shattered street, careful to avoid the rubble and debris of the destroyed homes. It was only safe to walk where the cobblestones were visible or where recent tracks indicated a tank or other vehicle had moved through. The retreating 1st Parachute Division of the German Army had demolished buildings into the streets, and then booby-trapped the debris.

The Germans had not been the only force of destruction in the unfortunate port town of Ortona. They had been pursued relentlessly by the Seaforth Highlanders and the Loyal Edmontons of the 1st Canadian Division, and as Captain Finley-Jones had presciently described it to Sam the previous day, it was a fight that raged block by block, street by street, and house by house.

As they walked into the village, a road sign proclaimed that Ortona was a West Canadian town. Sam's father had taken him and Perkin on a vacation through the Canadian Rockies to the Pacific coast once. He didn't remember it looking like this. Sam was struck by the incongruous nature of the destruction, and as he followed their Canadian guide, he reflected how it was odd that some houses seemed whole, while the adjoining row house had gaping holes through its stone walls. Some row houses had collapsed roofs, while the red tile on others seemed unscathed.

Their guide was not unscathed. He was a sergeant from the Seaforth Highlanders named Walter Tevis—a young rifleman whose broken right arm was encased in a cast and rested in a dirty sling. He had been wounded a week before when a row house he was in collapsed upon him. Sergeant Tevis explained that he was unsure whether the crew who had fired the tank rounds that brought down the house was still alive, but he said he wanted to thank them. The day that he spent trapped under the rubble had given him the best sleep he'd had since early December.

Before they left that morning, Sam and his party had been told at the Canadian headquarters that engineers had heard Tevis and his squad mates calling for help and had carefully dug them out. Tevis had refused evacuation and treatment until he had been ordered to a field hospital by another sergeant who was in command of what remained of his company. Tevis had been placed on light duty at the divisional headquarters and had been delighted to get out of the office to give the American party a mini-staff ride of their own.

"Too damn many wogs over there, sir," he confided to Sam. "Hate to be thought one of them."

"Wogs?" Sam had heard the British use of the term, but he hadn't seen any foreigners at the Canadian divisional headquarters.

"Wogs are them With-Out-Guns."

It seemed that contempt for the rear echelon personnel was universal in armies, although division wasn't entirely rear echelon in Sam's opinion. Sam's heart warmed to the Canadian soldier as he told them that he'd been in combat since the July landings in Sicily, and that he'd been promoted twice in the field since then.

"We're facing the 1st Paras now. They're pretty serious soldiers, but we beat the hell out of them here. There weren't a lot of prisoners taken on either side."

Sam wasn't surprised. The town looked like a larger version of San Pietro. Once picturesque, now a shattered shell of a village, it would be a long time before Ortona recovered. But it wasn't total devastation like San Pietro. There remained habitable houses, and Sam was sure that Ortona would not be abandoned.

Sam watched as Perkin joined a collection of German prisoners and engaged one of them in conversation. The soldier that Perkin talked to first seemed friendly enough, but a battered corporal leaned over and hissed at the soldier to shut his mouth. The corporal looked at Perkin and said in English, his voice dripping in venom, "Americans? You should have got here sooner. We would have gutted you bastards too."

Perkin laughed as he replied, "Anytime, partner. My division is about eighty miles that way." He pointed west. "Look for the Lone Star flag. It's hard to miss—it's the one heading up the peninsula toward the Reich. Oh . . . I'm sorry. So is yours. Enjoy prison, asshole."

The German prisoner started to retort but was rapped hard on the back of his head with the butt of a rifle by one of the soldiers guarding the captured men. The guard snarled at the paratrooper in a North English accent, "Shut your trap, you daft bugger! You're talking to an officer." The German glared at his captor but said nothing further.

As the soldiers were being led away, Perkin walked alongside the British soldier.

"Hello, Private. You're not of the Canadian Division?"

"No, sir. Private Kettle, from Lancashire. I'm a linesman with the 78th Division. I was sent over to help these blokes out with their bloody prisoners. It's not that they collected many Jerries, it's just there's not many Canucks left to guard them."

1215 Hours
Orvieto, Italy

It was unlike any other building he'd seen in his life. Having traveled through North America and Europe, Major Grossmann had seen hundreds of churches and cathedrals, but never before had he seen one like the cathedral in Orvieto.

The front facade was Gothic, he decided, although perhaps there was a touch of the renaissance in it as well. He thought he could sit there and admire the cathedral all day. It was an undertaking that could only have been completed in centuries. *Amazing—hundreds of years to build a church.* The outer walls of the church were equally unique. Alternating strips of dark gray stone and white stone gave the cathedral the air of some giant stone prisoner's uniform.

Grossmann was sitting on the steps of a closed *gelateria* across the small piazza from the church. It was too cold for ice cream these days, and none of the Italians had money for such luxuries in any case. He watched as people scurried by—housewives dressed in winter black carrying their meager bag of groceries, and men holding onto their hats lest they blow away in the wind.

Grossmann himself was chilled to the bone, but he had a role to play. Although he considered himself something of a film aficionado, he had never heard of Strasberg or method acting, yet he found himself doing exactly that. He wanted to get into the role of a downed American pilot as thoroughly as possible, and he thought, as he sat there, about how such a man would approach the priest in the cathedral.

He had begun preparations for this role immediately after he left the company of the disagreeable colonel. Grossmann was already north of Rome, so he thought that he would attempt to penetrate the network like an American would. Not necessarily at the Vatican, not straight at the problem, but work it from the flanks at a smaller church—take his time and take it all in, that was his mission. But while the cathedral was definitely smaller than Saint Peter's, it was not small—and it was captivatingly beautiful.

The night before, Grossmann had been driven by an Abwehr driver to the outskirts of the hilltop village of Monterubiaglio, where he had immediately turned about in the dark and started walking toward the highway leading to Orvieto. He had chosen Monterubiaglio because an American bomber had a perfect emergency landing in the garlic fields nearby a few days before, nearly taking out an anti-aircraft battery in its landing. The crew had been swiftly captured, and the whole incident was known to by the locals yet was unobserved. If asked, he would say that he was part of that crew.

An American uniform and parachute had been hidden under a tree by an Abwehr team near the village, but not hidden so well that it wouldn't catch the eye of any number of locals passing by. He was wearing ill-fitting farmer's clothing along with American-issued underwear and socks and regulation boots. He had also taken a set of one of the officers' dog tags—a man who generally matched his own description—and Grossmann hoped that he would never run into a squadron mate of the downed flier. Grossmann had started his journey without an overcoat and was thoroughly chilled by the time a farmer had given him a ride in a horse-drawn cart.

Although the farmer's eyes had widened when Grossmann spoke in what he called Tarzan Italian, the farmer didn't ask questions. When he dropped Grossmann off a mile up the road, Grossmann had the farmer's heavy sweater, the farmer had an American A-11 wristwatch, and Grossmann had been told in slow basic Italian to go to the church in Orvieto—the priest there was a good man, maybe he could help.

Grossmann had wanted to stay off the main thoroughfares to avoid questioning by German soldiers and Italian police, so he chose to walk down unpaved country roads. As he did so, he thought about the farmer's advice, and was amused that even the peasants knew where to go.

He was picked up by another farmer driving a dilapidated truck with brakes so questionable that even the Germans had passed on the opportunity to requisition the vehicle. This farmer took Grossmann to within a mile of a German roadblock on the highway and as he dropped Grossmann off, the farmer pointed out a path used by the locals to skirt past the prying eyes of the occupiers. It was a dirt trail that had several cutbacks up the ancient volcanic hillside leading to Orvieto. Grossmann passed several Italians along the path but they generally kept their heads down in the biting wind. Besides, it was best not to pay too much attention to strangers these days.

That might have applied to peasants, but it certainly didn't apply to policemen or the military. Sitting on the steps of the gelateria, Grossmann thought that he'd best move before too long. He didn't look Italian—he was too fair for this part of Italy—and he was beginning to shake again from the cold and inactivity.

He stood and stretched. The long walk of the morning and the cold were making him stiff. Grossmann casually strolled across the piazza, and after marveling again at the architecture and the art of the facade, he entered the church.

1215 Hours
Ortona, Italy

The further the soldiers advanced into Ortona, the worse the destruction became. Bodies were beginning to be collected, and the pungent smell of the decaying bodies—some of which had been lying in the street for over a week—was nearly overwhelming.

"It don't matter, does it, Bear? How many times you smell it? It still turns your stomach." Perkin wrinkled his nose in disgust.

Sam nodded grimly. He'd always hated the smell. As a boy, it'd been his chore to handle the workhorses to drag dead cattle off to a hollow on the ranch, and it was the one memory of home that brought him no pleasure.

Private Kulis watched the exchange between the two cousins, and perceptively interrupted, "Sir? Can I see your new toy again?"

Sam's face instantly lit up, the smell of death forgotten, and he handed it over to Private Kulis, taking Kulis's M-1 Garand in exchange. It was a Johnson M1941 semi-automatic rifle—a weapon that Sam had coveted for years—and a present from the departed Lieutenant Commander Cardosi.

That morning an American chief petty officer had delivered the rifle wrapped in brown paper and tied up with twine. The old gunner's mate had passed it over along with an ammunition pouch full of loaded stripper clips to a very surprised Sam with the words, "I was told to tell you, 'Use it well, redneck.' Sorry sir, those were the commander's words."

It had been spied the night before when Cardosi checked into the navy's small administrative office at Foggia airfield—he had been turning in the M-1 carbine that he had drawn before their trip across Italy. The M1941 had been used in combat in the Pacific by a Marine in the early part of the war and later turned over to a ship's company as surplus. The rifle and the ship eventually found their way to the Mediterranean, and the rifle had been brought to Termoli to issue to naval personnel assigned ashore. The chief accepted the carbine, two packs of cigarettes, and twenty dollars in exchange, and a smudged signature reassigning the weapon completed the transaction along with an extra ten bucks paid in advance for the delivery. As the chief was heading back to his jeep, he called out, "It's zeroed to 300 yards, L. T. I did it myself, and it's a damn fine rifle!"

Kulis looked it over again with an envious look on his face, "Oh, it sure is sweet, sir. It's got to be about the sharpest lookin' rifle I've seen. Can I fire it when we get the chance?"

"Maybe we can stop somewhere in the country on our way back, and *I'll* zero it in. I don't trust some squid to do it for me."

Kulis passed the rifle over to Private Fratelli who likewise made admiring comments about Sam's new rifle. After being further passed to Sergeant Tevis, then to Finley-Jones and Perkin, Sam finally got the Johnson back. Sam wasn't the type who needed the approval of others to boost his own self-worth, but a little friendly jealously never hurt to pick up a man's spirits.

He was consequently a much happier man by the time they came to a large roadblock of rubble. Although a lane had been cleared around the rubble, Sergeant Tevis led them into a house.

"I wanted to show you what we did here. Ortona's been a fight that's been conducted from one house to the next. The Jerries have been masters at holding a house until forced out, then after we've moved on, they reinfiltrate with snipers and sometimes heavy weapons. When we started this fight, we found that we would have to take the same one of these row houses two or more times. No one likes to bleed for the same ground twice, so we had to figure out a better way, and here it is. Follow me."

Tevis led the soldiers up the stairs of the row house. Blast marks and bullet holes covered the walls and the floors of the upper landing, and a dark stain indicated the loss of a lot of blood, although no body was in the upstairs.

"Although these houses all look different from the outsides, on the inside they're largely the same. You got a landing, two to four bedrooms, and maybe a privy, although that may be downstairs as well. Note that there are no closets like we might have back home, just wardrobes, which made this easier."

Captain Finley-Jones interrupted, "Taxes here are based on rooms and improvements to homes. To a bloody tax assessor, closets count as rooms; therefore, they charge more in taxes. Many of these homes look ramshackle on the outside but are quite livable on the inside. Same reason. The poor buggers are just trying to get out of taxes."

Tevis smiled his first smile of the day. "Thank you, sir. I'd wondered about that. So, two bedrooms, no closets. Then we'd come in on the ground floor and Jerry'd retreat upstairs. Then they'd throw potato mashers at us until we either blew the outside wall in on top of them with a tank, or they just ran out of ammunition. They usually would try to surrender at that point."

"Try to?" Fratelli asked with a grin.

"They'd try. Not a lot of quarter given here. So we figured there had to be a better way. We found that if we took one house and got upstairs, all we had to do was blow a hole in one of these bedroom walls in this house through to the adjoining house, which would stun the Jerries, then we'd toss grenades at *them*. Made it a much more even fight. Come here and take a look at this, but for God's sake, don't touch a damn thing. As I told you earlier, the Germans booby-trapped everything: doors, beds, light switches, shaving mugs, dolls, pictures—everything. Sometimes with big charges that bring down a wall or a ceiling, but mostly just small charges that blind a fellow or take off his hand."

Sergeant Tevis led them to a bedroom to the right of the landing. It had a gaping hole in its outer wall leading to another family's home.

"I blew this wall out. In that home—mind your step, sir—I put a chair up against the wall. Put some plastic explosives, what we call a beehive, on it. Set a fifteen-second fuse and then ducked across the hall to the other room there." He pointed to a distant room across a dark hall. "When the charge blows, you come running across with grenades. Two grenades, then a team with Tommy guns like yours, sir, comes in and finishes the work. We call it mouseholing." Sergeant Tevis led them back across the first home and showed them a hole leading to the home on the left. "See? We've mouseholed down this whole damn street."

Sam and Perkin ducked through the hole first, their boots crunching on the rubble of stone, bricks, mortar and plaster on the floor. In the dim light afforded by the gray sky through the room's single window, they noted the damage done by the grenade blasts and the bullet holes pocking the walls. There was no blood in this room, however.

When Perkin commented on the fact, Sergeant Tevis pointed across this house and its landing to another room on the far side of the landing. "They were in the other side, sir. Sometimes we got 'em, and sometimes we didn't. Sometimes we found 'em hiding, but mostly they fought until we killed 'em."

1245 Hours
Orvieto, Italy

Grossmann had entered the church awkwardly, uncertain what to do. It had occurred to him that perhaps he should dip his fingers in the holy water by the door and cross himself, as he had seen others do in a Catholic church before, but he wasn't sure of proper way to do it. Church life had never been part of his upbringing. In spite of himself, Grossmann felt uneasy in the cathedral. The sense of awe carefully designed into medieval cathedrals usually touched his sense of appreciation for the men and women of past centuries who had built these monuments to their God, but today, it left him feeling unworthy—as though the church knew his ulterior motives were impure.

He dismissed the feeling as superstition. As he stepped further into the cathedral, his old appreciation came back to him. Those builders of the past certainly knew the effects on the common man of the towering vaulted ceilings, the grotesque carvings, the mysterious statues and reliefs, the beautiful, meaningful stained glass windows, and the frightening crypts of the cathedrals.

Grossmann considered himself neither common nor spiritual, yet the cathedrals had the same effect on him.

The inside was even more striking than the exterior. The same gray-and-white striped pattern dominated the nave, which was narrower than Grossmann expected. Highly polished floors had intricate inlays, and giant striped columns with carved capitals held up the clerestory with its great vaulted windows high above his head. From the entrance through a bronze door within a much larger bronze door, Grossmann could see murals in the distance, and even though the day was dark and gray, and the light coming from the windows of the clerestory was dim, this house of God seemed to have a golden glow.

Grossmann passed by two older Italian women who were walking out of the church. They stared briefly at him and he offered a winning smile in exchange. The women looked away quickly, wrapped themselves tightly with their shawls, and headed out into the brisk day. He walked to the walls of the nave and soaked in the architecture and the art. It was beautiful. *There is no other word for it,* Grossmann thought.

Grossmann also realized with a bit of a start that he didn't come to this church as a tourist. He didn't have the luxury of strolling around admiring the frescoes. An American pilot wouldn't be doing so. Yet Grossmann looked around the large church and saw no priest to approach, so he continued to walk along the perimeter walls to the right of the nave until he came to the transept, the cross aisle of the cathedral. He turned outward and walked only a short distance before he was stopped by a wrought iron gate. As Grossmann looked back into the chapel behind the gates he saw that the walls were covered with frescoes, and he had an overwhelming urge to see the art for himself. Unconsciously, he reached for the handle to the gate.

"Can I help you, signore?" a deep Italian voice spoke from behind Grossmann.

The speaker was a priest, dressed in an ordinary black cassock. A large man with a pale face and black eyes, the priest was unsmiling.

"Uh . . . yes, Father. Do you, uh, do you speak English?" Grossmann spoke in a low voice. He was surprised to find himself suddenly nervous.

"No." The priest's visage was unchanged. He did not appear surprised by the question, but despite his previous words, neither did he appear willing to be helpful.

"Uh, is there someone here who does?" Grossmann let some of his nervousness show.

"No English," the priest said again.

"Well, you're a helpful son-of-a-bitch aren't you?" Grossmann said to the priest, whose eyes hardened. "Ahh, I thought so. You speak English!"

"What do you want?" the priest hissed in a low voice—his English quite understandable.

"I need help, Father. I was shot down, and I need food, a place to stay, and transportation out of here." Grossmann's put a hint of desperation in his voice.

"The Church is not involved. We cannot be involved, and we cannot help you with a place to stay or transportation. This is a place of worship, not a lodge for combatants." The priest opened the gate to the chapel and led Grossmann in. "Sit here. Make no sound. I'll bring you some food. Then you must leave."

Grossmann found a chair in the chapel and turned it to study the frescoes on the wall. They were incredible, but he found that he couldn't concentrate on the art in the chapel. This was an unexpected turn of events, he thought. He honestly hadn't anticipated being turned away by a priest, and he sat there thinking of alternative plans.

He could always leave the cathedral, walk down to the highway, and then identify himself to German military forces. He could then relocate to another village or even to Rome and try again. That would pose no particular problems, but he hated the thought of being mocked for his failure by the disagreeable colonel.

Maybe he wasn't being forceful enough. Maybe he should threaten the priest or perhaps cause a disturbance in the church. On the other hand, maybe he wasn't supplicating enough, he thought cynically. Perhaps he should be on his knees and praying when the priest came back.

There was another option. He had passed several cave entrances along the path he took coming into the town. He could ride out a cold and uncomfortable night in a cave and then walk to the next village. Perhaps pick up some intelligence about the network from well-meaning locals like the farmer that morning. *Not that he'd known much,* Grossmann said dryly to himself.

Grossmann postponed a decision for the moment and turned his attention to the large empty chapel. This room also seemed to emit a golden glow—the walls were covered in frescoes and portraits, but the empty space on the walls and the trim were gilded. It was a tall room, and Grossmann estimated that the height of the room was maybe fifteen or more meters to the top of the vaulted ceilings. At slightly above eye level were portraits, and the captions on the art read Dante, Virgil, Homer, Empedocles, Lucian, Horace, Ovid, and Orpheus. As a student of the ancients, Grossmann approved of the choices, even as he doubted the accuracy of the likenesses. Above the level of the portraits were the huge frescoes, and as near as Grossmann could discern, the subject of the frescoes were the apocalypse. He shivered as he studied the paintings depicting the Antichrist and the end of the world, the damnation of the sinners and the resurrection of the faithful, and the call of the elect to heaven. With all of the death and violence surrounding him, the possibility crossed his mind that perhaps the apocalypse was near. *It's a good thing I don't believe in this superstition,* he thought. *It'd be pretty damned depressing thinking this awaits me.*

He jumped as a voice behind him said, "They are mostly by Luca Signorelli—late fifteenth and early sixteenth century." The priest had reentered the chapel with a brown cloth bag in his hand.

Grossmann shrugged, "Sorry, Father. I'm unfamiliar with him. This room is amazing."

"Signorelli did one of the frescoes in the Sistine Chapel. Yes. This chapel is amazing. As is the other chapel across the aisle. It's the *Cappella del Corporale* from the miracle of Bolsena."

Grossmann had no idea what the miracle of Bolsena was. Not wanting to display any further ignorance, he said nothing, just nodded.

The priest didn't seem to care whether Grossmann comprehended or not. He handed the bag over to Grossman, which when opened revealed a half loaf of bread, a small hard sausage, and a wedge of hard cheese. "You must leave. Catholic soldiers of the occupiers come here to pray."

Grossmann allowed the desperation to return to his voice, "Father? Do you mean to just kick me out? Isn't there something that you can do? Get me in touch with people that can take me south—get me to Rome?"

"No. You must leave," the priest repeated. "The Church will not get involved in your war."

Grossmann found himself getting angry—an illogical sentiment but the irony escaped him for the moment. "Well, thanks for the banquet, Father. If I do get picked up by the Nazis, I'll be sure to mention your name."

The priest shrugged, turned, and walked away leaving a stunned Grossmann standing alone in the beautiful chapel.

1400 Hours
Ortona, Italy

The staff ride was coming to an end. They had walked several miles through the shattered town and were approaching its northern limits. There had been gunfire throughout the day's walk but always in the distance. It was getting noticeably louder the further north they went.

Sergeant Tevis had given them a good appreciation of the hard realities of urban warfare. Every home was a defensible position—and the Germans had made excellent use of the cover and concealment afforded by the destruction. Snipers had flooded the town, as had engineers bringing mines and booby traps. German withdrawals were always covered by counterattacks, many of which were then exploited if the opportunities looked good.

The German Army had vastly more experience in this kind of warfare than the Canadians, and lessons learned from Stalingrad had been leveraged in the fight at Ortona. The Canadians for their part had proven up to the challenge. The Highlanders and Edmontons were shown to be tough, resilient, and innovative, and interrogations of German prisoners indicated a respect for the Canucks and their fighting abilities. The interrogations also indicated that the Germans were puzzled over the Eighth Army decision to assault Ortona directly in the manner that they did. But the Germans were ordered to defend every inch of the town, and they did so to the best of their considerable ability.

Sergeant Tevis walked the group through many of the row homes, and they became quite familiar with additional mouseholing techniques as Sergeant Tevis was rightly proud of the Canadian innovation. From several second floor balconies, he showed them the burned out hulks of tanks—both Canadian Shermans and German Panzer IVs. In one of these apartments, Tevis showed them a tube that was similar to a bazooka launcher. It was the new German antitank weapon, which prisoners were calling the "*Panzerfaust*."

"I gather it's based loosely on your bazooka, which they've seen in Russia, Africa, and now Italy. It's got a heavy shaped-charge warhead—I'm guessing at least a pound or more—that's fired with a black-powder propellant. Biggest problem with it as far as I've heard is that it's a short-range weapon. Maybe thirty or forty yards at most. Now, here in Ortona, that doesn't matter. Jerry'll hide behind a wall like this, wait for a tank to pass by, and then step onto the balcony and fire into the tank from above or into the rear armor. Then they drop the tube and run off."

"So infantry has to stay up with the armor?" Perkin asked.

"Yes, sir. We turned the tables on 'em a couple times and hit their Mark IVs with PIATs from above. They worked OK, too." Sergeant Tevis turned to Captain Finley-Jones, "Sir, I'm not a fellow that complains, but their panzerfaust is a better weapon, excepting in range. I've not seen a bazooka, so I can't say anything about that, but this is lighter and easier to fire than the PIAT, so more fellows can carry them into battle. I'm not one for predictions, but these panzerfausts are going to make things pretty difficult for us if they produce them in any number."

Finley-Jones nodded, "Yes, Sergeant. I daresay this isn't the first time Jerry's built a better weapon than us. Likely won't be the last. How were they using their armor?"

"Every way you can think of, sir. They would use them as mobile artillery, antitank, antipersonnel. Sometimes main guns, sometimes coax machine guns. They got very good at bringing down these row houses with tanks. That's what happened to me, I think. We were in an end house and firing from an upper window, and a tank comes around the corner down the street. We didn't see it until it until the turret was turning to sight us in. It fired a round, not at us in the window, but at the base of the house. At the foundation's corner. That put us in the mood to leave, and we were running for the mouse hole when it blew out the other corner. The whole house collapsed before we could get out." Tevis's jaw tightened at the memory. "Sometimes if they've got the right angle, they can take out two corners with one shot. Sometimes they have to blow out each corner to collapse the house. You know, it's a damn queer feeling to have the floor fall out from under you!"

A sudden burst of machine gunfire erupted. By the sound, the soldiers judged it was very close—and it was German in origin. To a man they all hit the floor, even though there was no indication they were being fired at directly.

Without hesitating, Private Kulis crawled to a window, peeked out, and quickly withdrew his head. He reached up, undid the latch, and pushed the window open with the butt of his rifle.

"Sir." This was addressed to Perkin. "This apartment is on a *T* in the street." Kulis used his hands to illustrate. "We're at the cross of the *T,* and down the end of the street that runs perpendicular to us is a big house or a villa. There's something goin' on down there." He looked over the windowsill again, and didn't move this time during another burst of machine gunfire.

"It's about 180 yards or so that way," he pointed north with his entire hand. Suddenly, he moved quickly to a crouching position, whipped his Garand up to his cheek, and fired three rounds through the window down the street. The noise from the rifle in the confined space was deafening, and without dropping his rifle, he said loudly, "There was Krauts moving up the street, sir. I just dropped one. I think they're trying to either reinforce that house or cover while they evacuate."

Captain Finley-Jones was the senior officer, and without thinking, he took command. "Fratelli, you and me to the rooftop. Perk, you and Sam find a window on the other side of the stairs. Kulis, stay where you are." He looked at the unarmed Sergeant Tevis and quickly handed him the American Colt .45 that he carried. "Cover the stairs."

1405 Hours
Orvieto, Italy

Grossmann walked around the town of Orvieta thinking of the reaction of the cathedral priest and his refusal to help. Although not much of a Good Samaritan himself, Grossmann decided the priest's actions were remarkably un-Christian. Maybe he should have asked for sanctuary like some medieval knight. *Does it still work that way?* he wondered.

It was only after he climbed onto one of the city walls and ate some of the priest's food that the irony of his anger hit him. He was angry with the priest for doing exactly what was in the interests of the Third Reich. *If only all priests felt the same way*, he thought as he laughed at himself. Then the thought sunk in.

Cursing his stupidity, Grossmann stood on the wall and stretched to his tiptoes. The grand cathedral dominated the Orvieto skyline, but less than five hundred yards away, Grossmann saw a spire rising above the rooftops, although not nearly as high as the cathedral. Off in the distance he saw another one, and then maybe one more beyond that.

The farmer had told him to talk to the priest at the church—*la chiesa*—not *la duomo*—the cathedral. He had naturally assumed that the network to the Vatican stemmed from the dioceses. But what if it came from the roots of the Church, the small parish priests? It was worth a look, and if it didn't pan out, he would find a German unit outside of town and bed down for the night.

No time like the present, he thought, and Grossmann returned what remained of the sausage and cheese to the bag and dropped down from the wall. Despite the gray skies, Orvieto was a beautiful town and he thought that maybe after the war had stabilized some and he was done with this mission, he could come see more it.

The town itself was built upon the remnant of an ancient volcano, where the hardened magma had remained long after the slopes of the volcano had eroded into dust. It gave the town the air of a medieval fortress overlooking the lowlands below, and as the old rock spire of the church came into view, the whimsical thought of being a medieval baron was flitting through Grossmann's mind. Grossmann's daydreams strayed to the promising rights and privileges of being a feudal lord and then to princesses, fair maidens, and peasant girls. Consequently, he was not wholly attentive when he rounded the final corner and saw a two-man German patrol taking a cigarette break in front of the church.

Grossmann instinctively turned about, but he had taken only a single step when he heard the inevitable command: "Halt!"

"Come here." It was a corporal who spoke at least rudimentary Italian.

Grossmann walked slowly over to the two German soldiers, his mind trying to determine how to best handle the situation. He looked around the street and the small piazza, and the few Italians that he saw scurried away from the church as quickly as possible. Maybe a few words quietly would make the German patrol move along.

"Papers!"

That posed a problem for Grossmann. He had left his letter from the Abwehr high command behind in case he was searched during this mission, and he had not stolen or acquired Italian papers. It was something that he was hoping to avoid.

Under a poster glued to the stone wall of an apartment proclaiming German friendship for Italy, the two soldiers looked at Grossmann with suspicion. It had been their experience that Italians quickly handed identification cards over while praying for a smooth encounter with the German patrols. Otherwise, they would be turned over to the state police of Mussolini's rump Italian Social Republic.

"Corporal," Grossmann spoke in German in a low hushed voice. "I'm an Abwehr officer. Major Grossmann. I need for you move along and clear this area. Now."

Grossmann almost sighed with relief when he looked into the face of the corporal and saw intelligent brown eyes looking back at him with interest.

"Is there anything we can do for you, Herr Major?" The soldier spoke in equally hushed tones.

"No. Wait . . ." Over the shoulder of the private, a teenager who was watching the exchange with some bewilderment, Grossmann saw a priest leaning on a cane emerge from the old stone church. The priest stopped in the doorway and was observing Grossmann and the two soldiers intently. Grossmann leaned slightly to his right and using the private to obscure his face from the priest's view, he ordered, "Rough me up a little. Then go. Now. Now!"

After a second's hesitation, the corporal slipped his rifle off his shoulder and handed it to the private. He grabbed Grossmann by the sweater, pulled him close, and screamed in his face, "Next time I ask you for your papers, you'd better have them! Now stay out of my way for the rest of the day!"

The corporal threw Grossmann to the ground, angrily grabbed his rifle from the private, and snarled at his confused comrade, "What are you looking at? Let's go."

Grossmann lay on the street watching the German patrol march off, their boots thumping on the cobblestones. *I wish I had a handful of soldiers as quick as that corporal,* he thought. He stood up and after waiting until the Germans disappeared from view, he walked over to the priest and said in what he hoped was American-accented Italian, "Father, could I talk to you for a moment? In private?"

The priest, an old man, stared at Grossmann and shook his head no, but as he was shaking his head, he said in a quiet voice, "Meet me at the back of the church in five minutes." He turned, walked back into the church, the closing door clanging shut behind him.

1405 Hours
Ortona, Italy

Perkin and Sam rushed toward the bedrooms on the other side of the landing. That would give them a view of the large house slightly better than Private Kulis's. The door was shut, and Sam stopped short of the door on the landing.

"Has this house been cleared?" he asked of Perkin.

"I don't know. I'll kick it open," Sam said. "Stay back!"

Sam leaned far back and kicked the door hard above a decorative glass doorknob. The force of Sam's kick nearly tore the door from its hinges, and as it slammed hard back into the bedroom wall, a small dark metal object dropped with a heavy thud and rolled under the bed.

"Grenade!" Sam shouted, and as he and Perkin both flung themselves to either side of the doorway, he thought he heard the call echoed. Two seconds later, the grenade exploded with a loud, sharp crack and wood and metal fragments screamed through the doorway—just as Captain Finley-Jones and Private Fratelli came running down the stairs. One or two seconds after the first grenade exploded, the second grenade exploded on the upstairs patio.

"Bloody hell!" screamed Finley-Jones as he dropped to the ground writhing in pain. "Get my boot off! Get the goddamned thing off!"

Sam watched for a brief moment as Perkin pulled his knife and cut through the laces of Finley-Jones' boot, and then Sam crouched low and went into the bedroom. He was breathing hard from the excitement, and his heart was pounding. In a day chock-full of amazing things to see, the spectacle of seemingly thousands of small white feathers drifting through the smoke in the room, and blown about by the cold biting wind coming through the shattered window, surprised him more than he would have suspected.

It was largely quiet outside. The German machine gun had been silent now for several minutes, and Sam wondered if they were holding fire for a reason or if they had evacuated their positions.

His heart quieted, and his breathing slowed down as the feathers continued to whirl about the room. Sam looked out the window and saw a small squad of Canadian soldiers moving cautiously down the street, bent over low and ready to dart into one of the houses if necessary.

"Hey, y'all!" Sam called out. "What's up?"

A Canadian soldier crouched in a doorway and called back, "We trapped some of the bastards in that house there. They shot the boy we sent up with a white flag to ask 'em to surrender. We're gonna take care of 'em right and proper. Can you provide covering fire from there?"

"Yes. We're gettin' a BAR onto the roof right now."

"Excellent! Hey, are you fellows Yanks?" The Canadian soldier squinted and stared at Sam in the window.

"Texans," Sam corrected laconically. "Let me know when you're ready."

"Cowboys, eh? Well, don't shoot us, for God's sake. We're running in under your fire. Stand by!"

Sam turned and saw Finley-Jones crawling into the room dragging Perkin's Thompson. Perkin must have gone to the rooftop with Finley-Jones' American M-1 Garand. In a voice loud enough to carry to the roof, Sam called out, "We're givin' cover. Shoot the windows out, they're running in under our fire! Stand by for my command!" He looked at Finley-Jones, whose face was white and pinched with pain. "What happened to you, Waller?"

"A fragment from one of the grenades cut clean through my boot and took my big toe right off."

"Good God. Do you want morphine?" As Sam was talking, he began to drop the elevation on the sights of his Johnson. He really wished that he'd had the opportunity to fire and zero in this rifle. He hated to trust someone else's judgment. He finished that, then laid out several stripper clips of .30 caliber ammunition.

"Yes, desperately. Just not for a toe. They'd laugh me out of the regiment, but by God it hurts. What rotten luck."

Sam called out to the soldiers in the house. "I'm gonna fire. I need to zero in this rifle." He heard Perkin shout, "Go ahead," and he sighted in on the doorknob to the house. Sam flipped off the safety, took a breath, let it out, and gently squeezed the trigger. The Johnson roared as it fired, and through the smoke and the haze, Sam saw the front door swing open to the villa, only to be slammed shut from inside. The doorknob was gone. He'd never doubt another gunner's mate again.

"Hey! What are you shooting at?" The Canadian soldier called up to Sam.

"I was zeroing my new rifle."

The Canadian was looking up at Sam with worry evident on his face, and Sam knew exactly what was on his mind—*What kind of idiot goes into battle with a rifle he's never fired?*

"I thought we were sightseeing today," Sam groused to himself by way of answer to the imaginary question.

"Well, you'd better get your rifle ready. Our engineers are almost set." The Highlander was shaking his head in disgust.

"I'm done," Sam said. No sooner had he said the words when he thought: *Engineers?*

1420 Hours
Ortona, Italy

The Canadian soldiers were in place and Sam was just waiting for the assault to begin. For the life of him, he couldn't understand what the Highlanders' intent was. If he had been in command, he would have ordered an artillery strike on the house or brought up mortars. Reduce the building from a distance and kill anyone who ran. It would have resulted in the destruction of the home, but it would have been more economical in the lives of his soldiers. He shook his head and anxiously awaited the start of the assault.

He didn't have much longer to wait. The soldier who had been his interlocutor looked at his watch, raised his arm as the seconds counted down, then dropped it with the cry, "Now!"

In his deep booming voice, Sam called out, "Fire!" and the small American contingent at the battle of Ortona opened fire to the man. Sam could hear the sharp barks of the rifles and the short bursts of Fratelli's Browning Automatic Rifle.

Canadian riflemen opened fire at the same time, and the remaining windows of the home shattered, as the door and the adjacent walls were instantly shredded. Four men ran hard underneath the rifle fire. They weren't carrying rifles. Instead, they were carrying satchel charges, and Sam realized what they intended to do: they were going to blow up the house with the Germans in it.

One of the Canadian engineers fell and lay unmoving. Sam didn't know who fired the shot that killed the engineer, but he was amazed that any soldier within the house managed to survive long enough at a window to get off a shot. It was the last shot heard from the German defenders.

Sam kept firing at the windows and when he fired eight rounds, his mental counter waited for the ping of the automatic ejection of the en bloc clip of the Garand, but it didn't happen. The Johnson had an internal rotary magazine that held two more rounds than the M-1. Sam fired his two remaining rounds, then fumbled with inserting the two five-round stripper clips and reloading the rifle. As he reloaded the M1941, he remarked to Captain Finley-Jones how awkward the process seemed compared to the Garand. He would have to spend some time on the range and refamiliarize himself with the weapon. The thought also ran through his mind that perhaps he could arrange to just quietly ship the weapon home to the ranch.

When the engineers got close to the house, they ducked down below the level of the windows and crawled to the corners. The three remaining engineers set their charges, and two of them ran back underneath the cover of friendly fire. One engineer, however, sprinted to the fallen soldier, grabbed his charge, set the fuse, and flung the satchel toward the house. He picked his fallen comrade up, and with his dead friend over his shoulder, he walked steadily to his lines without another glance at the German-held villa.

Once the team was back in Canadian held buildings, the fire dropped off, and a Highlander officer made it formal by giving the order to cease-fire. The door to the villa opened, and a white towel was waved through the doorway. A German soldier tentatively walked onto the front step waving the white flag before him. The German was promptly shot by several of the Highlanders, and he dropped straight down onto the step. Sam didn't fire, but he approved of the Canadians' actions. *You pays your pennies, you takes your chances*, he thought.

When they came, the explosions were staggered. The two charges at the back of the building went off first and were only separated by a few seconds—sharp cracks of explosions that left billowing clouds of white smoke. The third satchel went off over half a minute later at the left front corner of the villa, and still the house stood, although a large chunk of the building had been blown away. A dazed German soldier walked to the gaping hole in the house and stared at it stupidly through the dust as though he were drunk. A Canadian sergeant shouted at everyone to hold their fire—he wanted to see if the fourth charge brought down the house on the soldier.

It did. Fifteen seconds later, the final charge blew and with a groan, the upper floor of the house slid forward and the villa collapsed like a house of cards amid a chorus of jeers from the Highlanders. The once beautiful home was reduced to a flat pile of rubble—the last skirmish in the battle for Ortona.

1455 Hours
Ortona, Italy

Perkin and Sam weaved precariously among the rubble as they carried Finley-Jones by an arm around each of their necks to an aid station. Upon further examination, his big toe wasn't entirely removed by the grenade fragment, but Perkin doubted whether it could be saved. Perkin was impressed with how well Finley-Jones was taking what he called "a little setback," but the Welsh officer wasn't much help in moving over the uneven streets.

The other soldiers were carrying the weapons and Private Kulis staggered under the heavy weight of another new acquisition. It was a 1918 Mauser antitank rifle, which Perkin had found next to a dead German soldier on the rooftop patio. It was the largest man-portable rifle the Americans had ever seen, and they were determined to carry it and its heavy ammunition back to the 36th with them as a souvenir acquired during the day of sightseeing.

Finley-Jones had seen the antitank Mauser before in North Africa, and between small gasps of pain, he told the rest of the party what he knew of the weapon.

"Jerry came out with these at the end of the Great War, and they were pretty effective at cutting through the thin armor of the day. But they've been obsolescent in that role since the thirties, although if you get behind a tank with it, you might be able to put a round through the engine block."

"What d'ya think they were using it for here, sir?" asked Private Kulis.

"They may have wanted to try it against the top armor of a Sherman, which would explain why we found it on the rooftop. But my guess is that while the Canucks were mouseholing their way across Ortona, the Germans would shoot at them from the rooftop through the walls of the house across the street. It's got a 13mm round—about the same as your .50 caliber—so I reckon it would cut through the brick and mortar of these houses right smartly. Might even go through a bunker, who knows?"

"I can't wait to fire it!" Kulis said. Several passing Highlanders grinned at the sight of the diminutive rifleman carrying the massive weapon.

"Better let Lieutenant Bear fire it first," Perkin said with a smile. "It's as tall as you are. Literally. The recoil on that beast might just break your shoulder."

"I don't mind, sir. I just wanna shoot it."

The aid station had several ambulances standing by, but their services had been mercifully underutilized over the past twenty-four hours. Finley-Jones was loaded onto a stretcher and placed on one of the racks in the ambulance. The driver offered to carry the remaining soldiers to a bend in the road before the hospital, but explained as he was not allowed to give combatants transportation, he would have to drop them off unseen.

Sergeant Tevis declined the ambulance ride, saying that he didn't plan to ride in one until needed, although he gratefully accepted two packs of cigarettes from Perkin and Sam.

"I told you fellows not to touch anything," he lectured with a knowing grin. "It's OK. I know you officers just can't help yourselves sometimes. Good luck to you gentlemen." Tevis offered an awkward left-handed salute and then headed back to the headquarters—with Finley-Jones's forgotten .45 in his pocket and a smile on his face.

1550 Hours
Orvieto, Italy

The old priest had let Grossmann in through the back of the church and led him to the church office, where he collapsed wearily into an incongruously new leather-bound chair. This church was a stark contrast to the Orvieto Cathedral. The Church of San Giovenale predated the cathedral by several hundred years, and where the cathedral's opulence was appropriate to house the miracle of Bolsena and the occasional presence of the Pope, the Church of San Giovenale was built for quiet worship—it had done so day after day and year after year for a millennium. There were no gilded walls, no ornate capitals, no admiring portraits of ancient philosophers— just battered pews and the brown stone and ancient arches that held up this house of God against a thousand years of war, pestilence, and unstable geology. There were no well-maintained frescoes by Signorelli who had worked in the Sistine Chapel—the art on the walls of the Church of San Giovenale were votive frescoes that were as cracked, chipped, and faded as its priest sitting before Major Grossmann.

In the dim light of the office, the priest looked up at Grossmann with interest, who noted that the priest's age did not disguise his alert eyes. Grossmann warned himself to be careful around the old man.

"Do you speak English, Father?" Grossmann asked.

"I'm afraid I do not, my son. Are you English?" The old man was obviously uncomfortable, and Grossmann thought his presence frightened the old man. Then it occurred to him that the priest was in pain.

"No, Father. I'm an American. Is . . . is there something I can do for you? Would you like a cushion or something for your back?"

"No, thank you. It's not my back but my hip—I fell and broke it two years ago, and there's not much that can be done for me. Well, maybe a glass of wine would help us both." The priest pointed to a decanter of wine on a marble covered sideboard. While Grossmann poured two glasses of a thin red wine, the priest continued, "I suppose the question is, what can I do for you? Or maybe we should start with introductions. I'm Father Giuseppe Girelli."

"I'm glad to meet you, Father. I'm First Lieutenant Douglas Peabody. Everyone calls me Doug. We were shot down two days ago, and I got separated from my crew. I'm trying to get back to my lines in the south."

"How do you come to speak Italian so well? I believe I hear a Roman inflection."

"My mother is Italian. My father is all American— meaning nothing in particular." Grossmann had been hoping to avoid using his Italian skills but the priest had seen him speaking with the German soldiers in Italian.

"You must favor your father, then. You don't look Italian." The priest finished his wine and signaled for Grossmann to refill his glass.

"My mother is very fair, Father." By way of explanation, he added, "She's from Bolzano. Not even born in Italy but in the old Hapsburg Empire. She always thought I should learn the language, so she spoke it to me as a kid, and then I studied it in college. I never thought about it, but my professor was from Rome. My mom also taught me some German, and she even tried to teach me Magyar, but that's a hard one."

The old priest nodded. "It certainly is. Well, I'm glad she taught you Italian. You speak it well. Where are you from in America?"

"Point Loma, California, Father . . . on the West Coast. Have you ever been there? To the United States?"

"No, but I've been to Rome. That's far enough for me. Tell me, young man, what can I do for you?"

Grossmann looked the priest in the eye; he asked an honest question, so Grossmann would give him an honest answer. "I was hoping to have your help, Father. Whatever you can give me—I need to get back to Allied lines."

"Where are those lines these days?" Father Girelli motioned for Grossmann to put the wine decanter on the table, and he filled his own glass.

"Well, sir, it's moving, but draw a line between Formia and Ortona and that's roughly it. Do you know how to do it? To get me back there?"

"God will find a way, young man. Trust in Him."

2000 Hours
Orvieto, Italy

Whether it was in God's plan for Major Grossmann to make it back to Allied lines remained unclear to Grossmann, but he felt comfortable that he was on the right track for the evening at a minimum.

The church maintained a small apartment adjacent to the church grounds for the use of the priest, and one of the pastor's parishioners had prepared dinner for Father Girelli and his guest. It was a simple meal of pasta covered with olive oil, crushed tomatoes, garlic, and spicy peppers, but Grossmann had been so hungry from being cold that it seemed quite extravagant.

Father Girelli continued to drink wine, and when the decanter was empty, he simply decanted another bottle of the same uninteresting thin red wine, to Grossmann's amusement. Yet, despite the voluminous amount drunk by the old priest, it seemed to have no effect on his faculties. As Grossmann discovered, Girelli was very sharp despite his outward appearances.

Although not particularly well traveled, Girelli had a voracious appetite to learn about other countries, and he was keenly interested in politics and world affairs. His understanding of the war matched that of Grossmann's, and despite stringent Axis controls on information, Girelli seemed to be extremely well informed. The Vatican radio and the BBC kept him educated quite nicely in their Italian broadcasts, he said.

"Aren't you afraid that the Krauts will catch you with a radio and have you imprisoned?"

"It's illegal to have a transmitter, not a receiver. Besides, look at me, young man . . . how can an old man like me be a threat to the Germans, or to that fool Mussolini, either? I'm not worried."

Grossmann himself listened to the BBC, and he was in agreement with Father Girelli that the reporting was basically sound and reliable, although he had caught the BBC dishing out what he considered to be misinformation on many occasions. Still, it was more reliable than the German war reports known as the *Wehrmachtbericht*—which Grossmann had thought of as fairly reliable in the days of victory after victory. Now it seemed there was less good news to report.

"Your navy and Marines are doing quite well in the Pacific it seems to me, although it certainly seemed to have begun poorly for them. So is the Royal Navy.

Did you hear that they sunk the *Scharnhorst* three days ago?"

Grossmann was stunned. He had seen the battle cruiser depart port in Kiel before the war, and he been extremely impressed with the size and awesome power of the ship. It was not the same blow as the sinking of *Bismarck* two years before, but it still stung.

His shock must have been visible. "What's the matter, Douglas? I would have thought this to be delightful news."

Cursing himself for his weakness, Grossmann put a sad smile on his face and said, "It is, Father. It is. It . . . well, I lost a brother on the *Hornet* when she went down at Midway. I wanted to fly, and he wanted to be in the navy. I get a little sad every time I hear about a ship being sunk—even a German one I guess—because it makes me think of Don. How did the British get the, what was the ship? The *Scharnhorst*?"

"I'm very sorry about your brother. Yes, the *Scharnhorst*. The English caught it out to sea—evidently on a raiding mission against a convoy to Murmansk. The BBC reported that it was sunk by other ships."

"Any survivors?" Grossmann asked. He remembered that the ship had a complement of nearly 2,000 men.

"Only thirty-six. Maybe it went down like the *Hood* in '41."

"Maybe. Or more likely they died of hypothermia. Most men can only live for a few minutes in water that cold. What else have you heard?" Grossmann shivered involuntarily at the thought.

"That there's a great battle taking place in Ortona. But you probably already know that, and that the Soviets continue to push the Germans out of the Ukraine. All in all, it sounds like the war is going better for the Allies. You must know more of this than I, what do you think? Will we win in '44?"

"I don't know, Father," Grossmann answered truthfully. "But I think that it all hinges on two things—at least here in Europe. If we land successfully in France, Germany is doomed. And if they can't contain the Bolsheviks in the east, then the Germans are truly doomed."

"Bolsheviks? So you are opposed to communism?" The priest looked at Grossmann with some interest.

"Absolutely. Americans hate communists." The priest's interest was noted by Grossmann, who was looking for a way to change the subject. He didn't want to get into a political debate with Father Girelli.

"Have some more wine, Douglas. Hatred isn't the right emotion. They should be pitied. They are godless and will never know salvation. It's the same with the Nazis and the fascists. They have abandoned God." In the first sign that perhaps the wine was getting to Father Girelli, his face began to turn red and his voice trembled with emotion.

"What about those who join the Nazi Party in order to get ahead in a country like that? What do you think happens to them on judgment day?" Grossmann was a German nationalist, but he had never been an ardent believer in Nazism. But to be competitive in the army and whatever might come afterward, he had joined the Nazi Party while at Heidelberg. There was little choice in Hitler's Germany.

"If they helped promote that malignancy, if they helped bring about this greatest of all human tragedies, I think they will have much to answer for, don't you?"

2000 Hours
Vasto, Italy

As hotels went, the Adriatica Hotel in Vasto wasn't

much. It had been built in a previous century, although which one wasn't clear to Sam and Perkin. The bedrooms were small with two single beds each, but the cousins' shared room at least had a small balcony overlooking the Vasto Gulf of the Adriatic Sea. The bathrooms were down the hall, the elevator had quit working in 1937, and carrying Captain Finley-Jones up the three flights of stairs had been a chore.

The field hospital had wanted to keep him overnight, but he wanted to return to the hotel, and the hospital had no empty cots in any case. When they found out he had a hotel room, the hospital released him with the proviso that he not exert himself and that he return daily to have his bandages changed and sutures checked. His wound had resulted in an amputation of most of the big toe on his right foot, and it throbbed terribly. He promised his doctor that he would not exert himself and would go straight to bed; five minutes later, he promised his nurse that he'd meet her at the hotel bar at 2015.

"You need to hurry up and get ready or our dates will be gone in the blink of an eye," Perkin continued to admonish his cousin. "And don't give me your 'I'm married' speech again, and 'I can't talk to another woman until the war's over' nonsense. Waller and I have dates for tonight, and those nurses are bringin' along a third wheel 'cause we got one and they took pity on you." As Perkin brushed his teeth, he said, "I think you can take a deep breath and relax. She's most likely ugly, and moreover, she's bound to find you repulsive in any case. Your chastity's safe in my hands."

"I can't tell you how much comfort your words give me," said Sam dryly. He was actually ready and waiting for Perkin to finish. Sam knew Perkin's ritual, and combing his hair would come last. "I think those were Maggie's last words to me: 'I'm glad your chastity's in Perkin's hands.'"

Perkin grinned at his cousin and said, "I don't doubt it. Her last words to me were, 'Bring him home, Perkin.' But her unspoken words were, 'Bring him home less dull and uninterestin' than he is now.' I shudder every time I think of how much work I have ahead of me."

"Well, ain't this typical then? You got work to do, and you're passin' on that to chase a skirt."

"Unlike you, I can do more than one thing at a time. You 'bout ready?" Perkin adjusted his tie in the mirror and winced at the vivid scars and fading bruises on his face.

"I've been ready. Let's go. We need to pick up Waller if we're going to get there on time."

Perkin grinned again as Sam caught his own unintentional wordplay, and his resulting deep booming laugh made the old windows of the Adriatica Hotel rattle.

2300 Hours
Vasto, Italy

Sam's companion for the evening was neither ugly nor repulsed. She was, however, the tallest woman that he'd ever met, which is why the dates of the other men thought that they should bring her along—Sam was the tallest man they'd ever met.

Her name was Sylvia Midgley, and she was a captain. In addition to being tall, Sylvia had brown hair and brown eyes, a formidable bosom, and striking patrician features. She came from the English countryside and was married to an English army officer currently serving in Burma. She had been a prewar nurse and joined the army nursing corps to beat the boredom and do her part. As she told Sam, she hoped to run across her husband someday in the service before the war was over, but she thought they had a "bloody long distance to cover."

Over the course of several whiskies, Sam and Sylvia found that they were kindred spirits. She said her home was in the Cotswolds near the village of Bourton-on-the-Water, which Sam approvingly misunderstood to be Bourbon and Water. The Cotswolds, she explained, were English thoroughbred country, and she said that her father maintained a large stable of horses that he raced at Cheltenham.

She and Sam talked about country life and horses, while Perkin and his date danced to the music of a small Italian band crammed into a corner of the bar. After a few drinks interacted with his pain medication, Finley-Jones found that he could dance after a fashion with his cane and heavily bandaged foot providing a pivot for his other questionable moves. Sam asked Sylvia to dance, not because he wanted to but out of politeness, and the Texan was extremely relieved when she declined. As she was so tall she had seldom been asked to dance, she explained, "except by short men who wished to plant their faces in my cleavage."

"You can't blame 'em for trying. How tall are you?" Sam asked.

"Almost six feet three inches. How about you?"

"Six four and some change. You're as tall as Perkin, I think. Is your Michael tall?" Michael was the name of Sylvia's husband.

"Oh, no. He's average height for an Englishman—maybe five foot seven or eight. It doesn't matter, though. He's the only man I met who didn't care that I towered over him. What a lovely man," she sighed. "What's the story of your cousin?"

"Perkin . . . well, he's unique. He's the smartest bubba in Texas, and it turns out he's a bit of a soldier as well—kind of a killer egghead. We grew up together—sometimes at his house in town, sometimes on my ranch. He's pretty good on a horse as well, but he doesn't have the passion for it like I do. He'd rather spend the day sailing on the bay or fishing than ride a horse—although I gotta admit that I wouldn't mind doing either of those right now."

"What's he like personally? I mean, is he going to be nice to Helen?"

Sam looked to where Perkin and his date, Helen, were dancing closely to a slow, sentimental song. "Oh gosh, yes," Sam said. "He's a gentleman."

"Will he try to get her into bed?" Sylvia asked directly to a startled Sam.

"Lord, what a question! I don't even know how to answer that," Sam said.

Sam's evident shock amused Sylvia and she said with a wicked grin, "With the truth, Bear." She had already learned Sam's nickname from Perkin. "Will he?"

"Well, I don't know. Uh, hmm, I hope so . . . I mean, she's a beautiful girl, and he could tolerate a little affection." Sam was puzzled by the question. "Why do you ask?"

"The saying in England these days is that there are only three problems with you Yanks: you're overpaid, oversexed, and over here. I was just wondering how oversexed you chaps really are."

Sam laughed. He'd heard the joke before about American soldiers in Britain. "I'm all American and I haven't made a pass at you, have I?"

"No, and I don't expect you to, either. You're the real deal, Sam—a true gentleman who's in love with his wife. Anyone could see that from Land's End to John O'Groats. I was just wondering about Perkin."

"I said he's a gentleman, but I didn't say nothin' about him bein' blind. I'm not blind either . . ." He nodded toward the dancing couple, and they both watched as Perkin and Helen moved even closer to each other, swayed a little slower, and Sam grinned when Helen put her head on his shoulder and pulled Perkin in tighter with her arm. "And I can see that he'll try . . . and succeed."

"Want to make it interesting? I've got a quid that says he gets nowhere . . . shot down in flames." She laughed with the friendly challenge in her eyes.

"Good lord! Are all English girls as . . . as . . . what's the word I'm looking for?"

"Brazen? Bold?"

"No, I was thinking of scary." Sam looked at the dancers again. "How much is a quid?"

2330 Hours
Orvieto, Italy

They had stayed up drinking late at night, the blackout curtains obscuring the dim light from Father Girelli's kerosene lantern—electricity was sporadic in peacetime, now it was even more so. Major Grossmann had tried to moderate his drinking as much as possible, but the priest was a good host, and when they switched to brandy later in the evening, the quality of the spirits improved dramatically.

Grossmann lay on the floor of Girelli's small living room in a bedroll put together by the priest. He could hear the priest snoring in the bedroom, but that wasn't what was keeping Grossmann awake. He was trying to sort through what the priest had told him about the network—that he had helped smuggle escaped prisoners of war to Rome before, and that he had a fairly foolproof method worked out. Grossmann saw plenty of room for error in the plan, but thought it was certainly workable for him. That wasn't it, either. There was something in the back of his mind that disturbed him about the evening that he couldn't quite pin down.

It wasn't the priest's thoughts on the morality of the war or about Nazism—he had reconciled his own thoughts on those subjects long ago. Nor was it the priest's evident satisfaction that Germany was finally losing the war—an objective man, he was becoming reconciled to that thought as well. There was something else that bothered him—a misstep that he had made, perhaps. *What was wrong?* Grossmann shrugged to himself and thought that perhaps his mind would be clearer in the morning. He rolled over on the hard stone floor, and having compartmented his worry for the time being, Major Grossmann quickly fell asleep.

Chapter Seven

It was coming to the end of another year, and looking back on it, Major Douglas Grossmann reflected that it had not been a good year. His country was on the ropes, even if its leadership would not admit to such heresy. In the past twelve months, the Americans and the British had defeated the famed *Afrika Korps*, successfully landed on both Sicily and the continent, and were slowly grinding their way to Rome and beyond. If the Allies were not defeated in the inevitable cross-channel landing, the war was surely lost.

It might be anyway, he thought. The Soviets, who were so close to defeat themselves only two years ago, had now pushed the once invincible Wehrmacht back almost to the borders of the Reich. The failures at Stalingrad and Kursk put to bed the notion of any *lebensraum* in the east for the Reich and at best signaled a long struggle between the Führer and Stalin. At worst, well, the worst was unthinkable to Grossmann.

The Americans and the British on one hand; the Soviets on the other. *It was the old adage that Erasmus recorded,* he thought: *Incidit in scyllam, cupiens vitare charybdim—he runs on Scylla, wishing to avoid Charybdis.* Germany's odyssey had indeed been strange and wonderful. Now it threatened to become a nightmare.

He still hadn't resolved his disquiet from the night before—even as he was preparing to leave Orvieto. The nagging sense that he had done something wrong remained, yet the priest seemed to have no questions whatsoever about his authenticity. As Grossmann waited for the priest to awaken, he returned to his musings about the year and a passage from Leviticus came to mind—a passage that seemed an appropriate complement to both Homer and Erasmus: "And I will set my face against you, and ye shall be slain before your enemies; they that hate you shall reign over you; and ye shall flee when none pursueth you."

He had come across the passage once while reading a book, a proscribed book, on the ancient Jews, and he had thought often about the message. It had prompted him to look up the rest of Leviticus, which he thought rather bizarre and impractical, particularly its bias against prostitution. But the original passage had stayed with him over the years. *Is it coming to that point?* he wondered. He shivered as the last lines went through his mind again and he pondered the notion of whether they would be prophetic: *They that hate you shall reign over you; and ye shall flee when none pursueth you.*

0920 Hours
Vasto, Italy

The moaning in the bed across the small room from Sam was his first indication that he might have won his wager with Captain Sylvia Midgley.

Sam and Sylvia had left the other couples at the hotel bar at midnight, and Sam had walked Sylvia back to her quarters—another hotel leased by Eighth Army. When he came back to the Adriatica, he waved at the others still in the bar, and then headed to his room and fell hard asleep.

He wasn't sure if it was the bright sunlight or the moaning which woke him, but he shot up in his bed as though he were surprised to have slept until daylight. Compounding his bewilderment, when he looked cautiously over to Perkin, he saw that it wasn't his cousin in the other bed. It was Finley-Jones, and he was moaning in his sleep.

"Waller . . . Waller, wake up."

The Welshman opened one dark red eye and glared at Sam for a moment, then closed it as he said, "I'm sleeping in today."

"Do you need anything?"

"Your pillow, mate." Sam tossed it over, and Finley-Jones rolled over to put his back to the light, with Sam's pillow crammed over his head.

Sam had a long, soaking bath in steaming hot water, and it felt wonderful. It was, he thought, the most marvelous feeling he'd had since leaving the States. He went downstairs in search of breakfast and found Perkin and Helen at a small table in the hotel restaurant. Sam intended to leave them alone, but he was waved over to the table by Perkin.

Helen stood up and kissed Sam on the cheek, and said in a mock American accent that sounded like it came

from *Gone with the Wind*, "I'll see y'all tonight. Bye now."
She gave Perkin a stunning smile and walked out of the
restaurant.

"My God, Perkin, how do you do that?" Sam watched
as a dozen sets of male eyes followed the nurse out of the
hotel.

"Do what?" Perkin asked innocently as he poured
Sam a cup of tea from a pot on the table.

"You not only found the prettiest English-speaking
girl in all of Italy, you seduced her, found dates for your
friends, and have another date planned for yourself."

"That's not fair. You make it sound somehow shallow
and superficial."

"What'd I get wrong?" Sam asked with an anticipatory
smile.

"I have dates planned for *all of us*. By the way, yours
is strictly platonic. But of course, it probably would have
been even if you weren't married. Still, I give what I can
of my gift to others." Perkin smirked at his cousin, and
waved a waiter over.

"Yes, I hate to think of what you gave to Helen last
night." Sam remarked dryly. "So, what's your secret?"

Perkin laughed at the insult, ordered a breakfast for
Sam, and replied to his cousin, "I got this charm gene
from my mother's side. That's my theory, anyway."

"A charm gene from your mom's side? That's a new
one for me. So, as your theory goes—since our mothers
were identical twins—I suppose I got the charm gene as
well?"

"You might think so, Sam," Perkin lectured. "But
empirical evidence tells us otherwise. Besides, science
don't work that way. So, did you get the charm gene? No,
of course not . . . but it's somehow both cute and quite
pathetic that you think you did. Now, I'll say in your
defense that most pigs and some dogs genuinely seem

to like you, so you must have gotten *something*. No, the way my theory goes, I got an extra helpin' of Granberry, exponentially accelerated by Berger. You obviously got shorted on Granberry but got a big heapin' helpin' of Taft ... maybe two. Or three."

Over the course of a long breakfast, the two cousins exchanged insults and jokes and told stories of Texas and old comrades. Outside of the drive to the Adriatic, it was the most time that the cousins had spent alone together for weeks, and it was restorative for both their souls. Perkin seemed the most at ease that he'd been since the landings at Salerno, and Sam just seemed happy. It was the most incredible feeling to be away from the war, even if the distant thumps of artillery could be heard.

Finley-Jones came downstairs and limped over to the table. His eyes were bloodshot and he looked rather despondent, but he picked up when Perkin told him about their dates and the New Year's Eve party they were to attend.

"Regina, my girl from last night, can't go—she has duty this evening. What have you arranged?"

"Helen is bringing another nurse. A girl from your neck of the island."

"A Welsh girl?" Finley-Jones exclaimed with delight. "Do you know from where?"

"Glabrous Morning or something foreign sounding like that. Did you know that Sam's friend is from a town named Bourbon and Water?"

At first, it was too much information for an injured and hungover Finley-Jones to absorb—the throbbing pain in his foot nearly matched by the throbbing pain in his head. Ignoring the mangled rendition of Bourton-on-the-Water, the Welshman looked puzzled for a long moment, then a wide, if pained, smile broke on his face.

He laughed, "Glamorgan! It must be Glamorgan. That's my home county. Well, how fun!"

"So . . . Captain Jones, what do you have planned for us?" Perkin asked. "Are we to watch you get your earlobe shot off, or will it be your pecker today?"

"God forbid, old boy. I must say that near-certain dismemberment was on the agenda for today, but since I can't play, we'll be spectators. I'm taking you to an officer's rugby match—Wales versus England—and then some of our Indian cooks have a special surprise for you chaps as a late lunch."

**1530 Hours
Vasto, Italy**

"Good God Almighty! That's the hottest thing I've ever tasted!" Perkin took a deep drink of water, which only seemed to accelerate the effects of the vindaloo—a particularly spicy style of curry, served this time with mutton and potatoes.

"I think it's pretty damn good," Sam said. He had more of a taste for spicy food than Perkin. Neither of them were fans of mutton, but the spicy gravy would have hid the flavor of any meat. He accepted another pint of Welsh Bitter from a battered Welsh officer—the Welsh were providing the drinks as the losing team in the rugby match—and took a deep drink as well. He had never had British ale before, and Sam, who believed in all things American, grudgingly admitted to Finley-Jones that it might be the best beer he'd ever had.

"It's not a beer like you know it, old boy. It's a bitter. There's a difference. But thank you anyway." Finley-Jones was somewhat lugubrious. The pain in his foot seemed to be getting worse, not better, resulting in him being placed in a wheelchair; his planned vindaloo revenge on Sam for the jalapeno sausage had been a bust; and worst of all, the Welsh had been severely beaten by the English officers of Eighth Army. There had been a moment before the match when things had looked up for Finley-Jones when a plan to put Sam into the Welsh scrum as a Lieutenant Davis had been contemplated. Sam had been an offensive lineman on the Texas A&M football team, and his size might have made all the difference to the Welsh forwards. But the plan had to be scrapped when Perkin introduced Sam to Colonel Scrope, who wandered over from the English side for a pregame chat.

For his part, Sam regretted deeply the lost chance to play. He had only played rugby once before, during a demonstration match at College Station, and he had barely enough time to begin learning the differences between American football and rugby union rules before the match was called when a tornado and golf ball–sized hail ruined the afternoon. The touring British players, good fellows who seemed a little spooked by the Texas weather, called rugby "elegant violence," and as a spectator, Sam appreciated the greater speed of the game. As a player, he thought he preferred the strategy combined with the brutal violence of American ball.

As for the Indian food, he genuinely liked it, and it was always good to see Perkin suffer a little bit. Sam traditionally got the worst end of the insult wars, and seeing his cousin gasp for air with red, watery eyes and a bead of sweat across his forehead was a schadenfreude delight. "Try drinkin' some more water," Sam suggested helpfully, knowing that it would be less than helpful.

"Thanks," Perkin wheezed. When they had a moment alone at the table, and after Perkin had controlled the tears and the runny nose, Perkin said to Sam in a low voice, "We're leaving day after tomorrow."

Sam nodded, "OK. I thought we'd have a bit more time, though."

"Me too. Colonel Scrope said we're getting a new set of orders from Eighth Army, and, uh . . . we have a little detour on the road home."

Sam shrugged and said, "Oh well, those are the breaks. Have you told the boys?"

Perkin nodded, "Just after the rugby match. I've sent Kulis and Fratelli down to Foggia in one of the jeeps to draw some more ammo from the American detachment there."

"You didn't need to do that. We still have my ammo pouch with clips for the Garand, and I still have a bunch of stripper clips for the Johnson. Your Thompson wasn't fired at all."

Perkin looked his cousin in the eyes. "We shouldn't need 'em, but I'd hate to come up short."

Sam raised a questioning eyebrow. "I don't like the sound of this. What kind of little detour? How far will we be from the line anyway?"

Perkin thought for a moment, then he smiled mischievously and said, "Worst case, ten miles."

Sam shrugged again and started to say that he still thought the boys were being sent on a fool's errand, when a thought occurred to him and he looked at Perkin with growing alarm, "Oh no . . .Perkin . . . do you mean ten miles on the other side?'

1630 Hours
Orvieto, Italy

It was in fact a simple plan. Grossmann had donned the clothes of a workman and headed down to the Orvieto train station with Father Girelli. The priest slowly led the way, and Grossmann followed several hundred feet behind so that the association between the two would not be noted. Grossmann carried the identification papers of a dead parishioner of Girelli's, the black-and-white photograph showing an older man with darker hair, but perhaps it would be passable in the dim light of winter. Grossmann would join the crew of the evening Rome-bound train and would step out of the locomotive just before arriving in Rome. The priest had known the engineer since birth, and he had used this method several times to move Allied POWs south to Rome.

The priest was stiff as he moved about the house, but he told Grossmann that an afternoon walk to the train station and back was no serious matter. As the old man moved slowly and with care, he never looked back on his distant charge.

If he had done so, he might have seen Grossmann step aside with two German soldiers—the same corporal and private from the previous day. Grossmann had stopped, issued a rapid-fire order, and passed a small folded piece of paper. He then kept moving.

As Grossmann watched the beautiful Italian countryside move by while the ancient train chugged slowly southward on a secondary line—the primary lines being electrified and only operating sporadically—he thought back to Father Girelli and the two German soldiers. He had found the problem that had nagged him since last night. When he had been forced to come up with the excuse about his brother, he had said that his brother had died when *Hornet* was sunk at Midway. It didn't come to him until that morning that *Yorktown* was the American carrier sunk at Midway, and that *Hornet* was sunk at the Battle of Santa Cruz a year and a half later. *The dangers of improvisation*, he thought wryly.

He earnestly regretted the arrest order of Father Girelli that he gave to the two soldiers—surreptitiously written on the old man's stationary, no less. The orders passed to the sharp corporal specified that the Abwehr was to wait until after the New Year's celebrations were done and Sunday mass had passed. Grossmann was certain that Girelli had not caught the mistake, but he could not take the risk that the old man would not recount the story to someone else and then realize the lie. The priest was too smart and well informed for his own good. He had to be arrested.

As it was pursuant to his orders from Admiral Canaris, the old man would be silently arrested in the dead of night, taken to an Abwehr station, and interrogated. After he talked about what he knew of the Vatican escape network—and he would surely talk—he would likely be executed. Abwehr headquarters might make the decision to intern the old priest in a concentration camp, but most likely, he would just be shot. It was out of Grossmann's hands.

As Grossmann reflected that it was not his fault, the intense heat and the white flame of the firebox brought forth a vivid notion of hell in his mind, which was unnervingly noted but soon relegated to the shelf of superstition. However unlikely damnation was, the priest's death would be a shame. He had enjoyed the old man's company.

2340 Hours
Vasto, Italy

The Adriatica Hotel was hosting one of the many New Year's Eve parties in free Italy that evening. While it wasn't close to being the largest of the parties, even in Vasto, it may have been the most lively. Both rugby teams, Welsh and English, went to the Adriatica, and a contingent of brave nurses showed up as well. Local Italian women were allowed, even encouraged, to join the officers' party, while local Italian men were turned away at the door to the ballroom by two heavyset British sergeants earning a little extra pay for the evening.

Sylvia Midgley and Helen Langley led the contingent of nurses, and Sylvia greeted Sam with a knowing smile and a handshake that covertly passed a pound note and the whispered words, "I'm so happy for her." Their Welsh friend, Emily Jones, was greeted warmly by her simultaneously disappointed and delighted second cousin, Captain Waller Finley-Jones.

The good captain only made it until 2215 hours, whereupon he passed out from a less than positive interaction between his pain medication and the prodigious amount of alcohol he had consumed. Sam and a huge English rugby player named Aubrey lifted Finley-Jones, wheelchair and all, onto a banquet table. They thoughtfully chocked his wheels, and while several nurses draped him in a white tablecloth and graced his head with a laurel wreath made from mistletoe, Perkin propped a handmade sign under the sleeping officer's chin, which proclaimed "Toeless Jones, Caesar." An English officer later crossed out "Caesar" and replaced it with "Welsh Git," which provoked a brutal assault on the Englishman by Emily Jones, who led with her right. The surprised and stunned Englishman was slowly debating with himself over how to deal with the angry woman when Emily finished the debate with a head butt that broke the Englishman's nose. The two combatants later left the party hand in hand.

The rugby players knew an astonishing number of bawdy songs, most of which Sam had never heard before, some of which he didn't understand, and even others that were so descriptive that he found himself blushing in Sylvia's presence—until he learned she knew all the songs already. The words, and the enthusiasm which with they were sung, tickled Sam immensely, and the giant of a man laughed until tears flowed down his cheeks.

Perkin and Helen alternated dancing with sitting at a small table in a corner and holding hands while gazing into each other's eyes. Sam couldn't have been happier for Perkin. Emily was a sweet, beautiful girl with short curly brown hair, a pale English complexion with rose cheeks, and blue eyes as intense as Perkin's own—she was exactly what Perkin needed to get his mind off of other worries. While Sam knew that Gianina would always have a place in his cousin's heart, he also knew that his cousin was already falling for the English nurse—and she for him.

Italian waiters brought in a steady stream of food, paid for in pounds sterling by the rugby teams with a generous donation in dollars from Sam and Perkin. When they weren't serving food and drinks, the waiters rolled unconscious officers under the tables so they wouldn't be stepped on, and they endeavored to keep their guests from swinging on the ballroom's chandeliers.

The British soldiers were mostly beer drinkers and they brought an amazing array of beers and ales shipped from home. Sam and Perkin were treated to bitter and porters, stouts and lagers. An English infantry lieutenant, a beer aficionado, explained the different drinks to the Texans, and then made a drink of pale ale, topped with a stout. "We call it a 'black and tan,'" he explained.

Perkin nodded thoughtfully, and replied, "We do the same in Texas with our beer. We call it a 'black and redneck'—although those two words are usually only seen together in police reports."

The English officer blinked several times and said, "Indeed."

By and large, the party was good-natured, which was surprising to Sam considering that all the men and women present had been surrounded by violence for such a long time. There were a few altercations, which was natural as there were fewer women present than men, and different services, ranks, regions, and nationalities all competed with one another in every subject that mattered, from the women to sports teams.

One of the few prospective fights appeared likely to involve Perkin. An English subaltern billeted at the hotel joined the party—as many others had done—and after a few drinks became genuinely obnoxious. He became even more so with the discovery of the two Americans.

He tried to engage Sam first, and staggering past Sam and Sylvia's table, he glared at Sam and sneered, "A Yank, eh? Come here to learn how to fight?"

Sam stood up and, towering over the drunken officer, calmly said, "No, partner. I came here to have fun. Go up to the bar and try it for yourself. You might like it more than the alternative."

The British officer looked into Sam's eyes and decided not to ask what the alternative was. He turned about and headed back to the bar without another word to Sam.

Fifteen minutes later, he decided to try out the other American present. Sam had kept a distant eye on the drunken soldier, and when he weaved toward Perkin, Sam sat up alert. Both cousins had been in their share of fights growing up, and Sam knew from experience that the difference between them was that he would stop when the fight was clearly won. Perkin continued to punish his opponent until pulled off. In the rare occasion when he lost a fight, Perkin had fought until he was knocked unconscious or someone else intervened.

Given what Perkin had gone through lately, and the hardening that Sam had seen in his cousin's personality, he wasn't sure that Perkin wouldn't kill the other man. So he prepared to be the intervention force.

Sam needn't have worried. As Sam watched, the drunken officer staggered up to Perkin and Helen's table and evidently, judging by the reaction on Helen's face, said something incredibly coarse and offensive. Perkin leapt to his feet, instantly grabbed the other officer by the lapel of his uniform, and slapped him hard across the face with the back of his hand. The sound of the strike reverberated through the hotel's ballroom, and most of the party guests stopped their conversation and turned to watch.

The English officer tried an awkward haymaker punch at Perkin's head. Perkin ducked and avoided the blow altogether, and while the drunk was off-balance, Perkin grabbed the other officer's necktie by the knot and kicked his feet out from under him. As he began to drag the struggling officer to the door by his tie, he bellowed in a savage voice, "I don't care what you say about the rugby boys! They're my friends!" When they got to the outside exit, Perkin pulled the officer to his feet, slapped him twice again, and pushed him hard out the door backward down the hotel steps into the falling sleet.

To the attentive crowd, Perkin explained with a concealed look of mirth on his face that only Sam could see, "He said that the only thing he hated more than Americans was rugby players. I thought it was just rude to our hosts and not at all in the spirit of the evening."

Perkin held the door open for two rugby players, the English officer named Aubrey and the Welsh team captain, also named Jones, as they walked resolutely outside together. Without another glance at the door, Perkin joined a proud, beaming Helen at their table, and he winked across the room at Sam. Aubrey later swung by Sam's table and said with a wide grin, "If he didn't like

Yanks or rugby players before, I guess collectively we're a little less endeared to him now. Jolly good!"

The clock was winding down toward midnight, and the waiters began to distribute flutes of Italian sparkling wine, true champagne being hard to find. At seven minutes before the hour, a thin Welshman made it to the chandelier, hoisted up by two muscular forwards. They began to push the thinner man as he dangled from the chandelier, and he cried out as he swung over the crowd, "I play the wing for Wales!" As if that were their cue, on one of the returns of the chandelier, the two forwards each grabbed a handful of their friend's trousers and yanked his pants and underwear down to his ankles.

While the women screamed and peeked through their fingers and the men roared with laughter, the chandelier twisted around enough to give Sam and Sylvia a view of the wing's backside. Painted on his ass in red was a Welsh dragon across his cheeks, and the Welsh motto, *Cymru am byth*" was painted down each leg in the same paint.*

They both laughed until tears flowed again down Sam's cheeks and Sylvia was gasping for breath. As Sam laughed, he saw that Helen was hanging onto Perkin and they were both laughing hysterically as well. He would later reflect that it was weak humor, but gaiety had been out of the lives of so many in the room for so long that it seemed the funniest experience of their young lives.

It was then that the brigadier chose to arrive. He was preceded into the ballroom by a red-faced and snow-covered lieutenant colonel who hesitated only for a second before calling out in a command voice, "Ten-shun!" The officers, including Sam and Perkin, immediately snapped to attention, and the band quit playing.

The brigadier, who wore a white scarf wrapped around his neck, began to walk into the ballroom, but his entrance was marred by the fall of the wing from the chandelier,

---

* Wales Forever.

who came in for a hard belly landing on a backward glide slope. His head smacked hard onto the floor, and he bounced twice before laying unmoving at the brigadier's feet—the ass dragon glaring up at the English officer.

In the stunned and appalled silence, the brigadier calmly pulled a pipe from his pocket, and after tamping down the tobacco, he bent down and checked the pulse of the unconscious officer. Satisfied that he was still alive and not in mortal danger, the brigadier struck his match on the wing's whiskered cheek, stood, and surveyed the room as he lit his pipe.

He looked back at the lieutenant colonel with a glint of amusement in his eye, and in a normal conversational tone, he asked of the room in general, "Who's in charge here?"

Immediately, several people pointed at the recumbent Welshman at the brigadier's feet, and the senior officer looked back at the lieutenant colonel as if to say, "I told you so."

"Who's next in command, then?" the colonel asked. Almost unanimously, the grinning crowd now pointed to Caesar Finley-Jones whose head had drooped to his shoulder. His mouth was wide open and he was snoring loudly.

The brigadier grinned and said mostly to himself, "Men of Harlech. Splendid." He checked his watch and said to the colonel, "Oh dear. We're running short on time, Dacre."

"Yes, sir, we are."

The brigadier looked around and saw an Italian waiter holding a tray of filled champagne glasses, "Could I bother someone for a glass of champagne, please?"

Sam was closest to the waiter. He took two glasses of champagne and handed one to the brigadier and one to Lieutenant Colonel Dacre.

The brigadier took the glass and nodded to Sam. "Thank you, *Leftenant*. Glad to see an American here tonight." He walked quickly over to the table where Finley-Jones sat sleeping fitfully in his wheelchair. The English officer hopped effortlessly onto the table, laid down his pipe, then straightened out Finley-Jones's head and closed his mouth with a gentle nudge of his hand.

"Ladies and gentlemen, my name is Paynell. We were driving by and heard the celebrations. I thank you for letting me join your little party, and I promise not to ruin it by staying past midnight—I was a young man once myself, and I understand that nothing drains the life out of a party faster than an uninvited senior officer. If I could make a few observations before the clock begins to chime: This has been a tumultuous year, but one that has seen our fortunes turn irrevocably. I am optimistic that 1944 will be the year that we liberate this continent through the force of Allied arms and bring a permanent end to the evils of Nazism. It seems that we soldiers of his majesty and those of the American Republic are the sole force of light left on this planet, and I'm proud to say that light grows brighter with every passing day. Pray God that we are allowed to continue His work. Ladies and gentlemen, in this last minute of 1943, please raise your glasses. The King!"

All present drank to the health of the King, and then to honor Sam and Perkin, they drank to the health of President Roosevelt. As the minute grew short, the brigadier lifted his free arm and began to call out "Ten, nine, eight . . ."

Perkin drew Helen to him, wrapped her up in his arms, and, oblivious to all that was going around them, they kissed each other passionately, as if they would never again need another person in their life. Sam took the hand of Sylvia, and they kissed each other as friends. As

Brigadier Paynell dropped his arm and the band began to play "Auld Lang Syne," the crowd roared out "Happy New Year!" and Sam thought with a new optimism that this year would be better than the last.

Chapter Eight

January 2, 1944
1300 Hours
Guardialfiera, Italy

The good-byes on their departure from Vasto had been surprisingly difficult for everyone. The evening of New Year's Day, Captain Finley-Jones had been readmitted to the British Army hospital. He had been running a high temperature, and the nurses, Sam, and Perkin were severely reprimanded by the surgeon who had amputated his toe for not taking better care of their friend. The doctor told them that it was possible that Finley-Jones now had a staph infection that could result in the amputation of the soldier's foot. It was a somber group that said good-bye to their old comrade, who insisted that he was well enough to make the drive back to their own area of operations. The surgeon, a full colonel, won the argument.

Saying good-bye to the nurses had been difficult as well. Sam and Sylvia had spent New Year's Day riding at an Italian country estate outside of Vasto that the war had passed by unmolested. They were there as the guests of Brigadier Paynell—an officer on General Montgomery's staff. They learned from Paynell that Montgomery had turned over the command of Eighth Army two days before to Lieutenant General Sir Oliver Leese, and Paynell and select members of Montgomery's staff were preparing to follow him to England.

The day spent riding was one of the most enjoyable days that Sam had since joining the army. The stable was large and well maintained, and the Italian owner was as accommodating as a man who was afraid of having his livestock confiscated could be. Laughing at his own wit, Sam told Sylvia not to look a gift horse in the mouth— actually the second set of gift horses of the morning. When they arrived at the stables, a handler led out two horses for Sam and Sylvia. When the handler looked up at the English nurse and the American soldier, he turned without a word and led the two ponies back into the stables. The horses he brought back a few minutes later were two gray Percherons, both over seventeen hands.

The Italian family didn't have any western saddles, so Sam rode English—not his preferred style, but one with which he was familiar. The day had been one of the few sunny days and the temperatures had risen to the high forties. There was a brisk breeze blowing off the Gulf of Vasto, and both the riders and the horses seemed to get energy from the crisp, sunny day.

Perkin and Helen had spent the day together as well—ensconced in the Hotel Adriatica. They ventured downstairs for breakfast, and again for a late afternoon dinner. Perkin bought two bottles of a nice prewar Bordeaux from the hotel's wine cellar and some cheese and bread, and that tided over the infatuated couple for the rest of the evening.

Morning had come and Helen had duty at the hospital. Perkin had dropped her off at her hotel early in the morning, and returned an hour later to take her to work. Despite both armies having prohibitions against public displays of affection, Helen gave Perkin a long, lingering kiss on the steps of the hospital while tears flowed down her cheeks, and it was with a big lump in his throat that he put the jeep in gear and drove to the Eighth Army headquarters.

The enlisted soldiers were likewise sad to leave. Privates Fratelli and Kulis had enjoyed the hospitality of the British soldiers, and they were both delighted to spend some time in the American PX that they found at Foggia Airfield. Grousing nonstop on the unfairness of the disparity of treatment between airmen and riflemen, they bought souvenir lighters, cigars, and alcohol to take back to their friends in the Gun Club.

Sitting in the town square of the village of Guardialfiera—a hilltop town next to the Bifurna River—Sam wondered again why they were there. He had not had the opportunity to discuss much in private with Perkin, and all he knew was that Perkin had orders from the Eighth Army staff. Sam knew that it was an intelligence mission of some sort, but he had no inkling of what that mission might be.

Sam would have pulled Perkin aside in Guardialfiera, but as soon as they parked the jeeps, he took Private Kulis with him and they disappeared into the town heading toward a church. Several of the villagers came by to talk, and through Private Fratelli he learned that Guardialfiera had seen the German Army pursued through the area by the Canadian West Nova Scotia Regiment, but that the fighting in the village itself had not been severe.

It was in the small towns and villages of Italy that Sam began to get a better appreciation of the generosity and friendliness of the Italian people. Unlike Naples, which seemed to bring the worst out in everyone, the Italian countryside was peaceful and calm, and although there were hard times there as well, the people wished to show their appreciation to the Americans. He was reflecting on this appreciation as he took another bite of a cornetto, this time filled with butter and a preserve that he believed to be gooseberry. It had been the gift of the baker, who had brought out a dozen cornetti leftover from the morning. He had taken Sam's canteen into his shop to be filled with coffee, and when he returned, the baker had brought several sandwiches made of ham and a white cheese, which he insisted were a gift.

The baker stayed and chatted with Sam and Private Fratelli, and it was through the baker that Sam learned that the town's old stone bridge over the river had been used by Hannibal's army. It meant little to him, but he tucked the information away in order to tell Perkin.

The baker went back to work, and still Perkin and Kulis had not returned. Sam poured some of the strong, black coffee into canteen cups for himself and Private Fratelli, and they sipped at the hot, bitter drink and waited.

"Do you know what we're doing, sir?" Private Fratelli broke the silence.

"Not exactly, do you?" Sam thought that maybe Fratelli had been given a head's up on the mission by Private Kulis.

"No, sir. Eddie won't talk about it, but I think he knows."

Sam shrugged. "Spooks. Whatcha gonna do?"

Fratelli nodded and said resignedly, "Yes, sir. Whatcha gonna do." He looked around, and saw no sign of their missing two soldiers. "Well, actually, sir, I was thinking what we might do is check and see what's in those duffle bags."

When Perkin had returned to the hotel that morning, he had several British army packs, heavy sleeping bags, and three large and stuffed duffel bags in the jeep with him. When Sam asked him about it, he just said, "I'll tell you later." It was an answer that didn't sit well with Sam, so he nodded and said to Fratelli, "Damn good idea. Be quick about it."

The private hopped over the seat into the back of the jeep, opened the first duffel bag, and pulled out a heavy, white, down parka. It had a silk inner lining, and the hood was fur-trimmed. Fratelli peered down into the duffel bag and said to Sam, "There's more of 'em, sir."

With a sinking feeling, Sam said, "Go ahead. What's in the other duffels?"

Fratelli opened the second duffel bag, and it contained heavy white trousers and fur-lined gloves. The third duffel was opened and Fratelli pulled out the largest winter boot he'd ever seen. He leaned over the seat and held the boot up against the shoe on Sam's crossed leg. It was a perfect fit.

"I'm thinking that maybe this is yours, sir."

"Oh Lord, what's he gotten us into?" Sam asked of Fratelli.

The private grinned and shrugged, "Sir, I'm half afraid to guess 'cause I might be right. Winter camouflaged gear, new ammo stores. Looks like we're going to the mountains for the holidays—and we're going loaded for bear!"

1300 Hours
Guardialfiera, Italy

Perkin cursed at the delays, but they were inevitable. First was the tour of the Church of Santa Maria Assunta. Another beautiful ancient cathedral with a thousand-year history that normally would have fascinated Perkin, but today frustrated the officer in charge of a party that needed to get moving. As he learned, while the church had been destroyed several times by earthquakes, it was fortunate enough to have been rebuilt with a Holy Door—the explanation of which took nearly thirty minutes.

Coffee needed to be drunk with their host—a genial old priest—and gratitude expressed for the hospitality. Eventually, they were making another round of good-byes, and finally the party of three men had left the church.

The third man was about the same age as Perkin but shorter. He had black hair, a pale complexion, and was hard and fit. Like the soldiers, he wore a uniform, but his was of the Church, and when he spoke, his voice reflected the tones of distant County Cork.

"Perkin, Edwin, it's good to see you again!" Father Patrick Riley smiled with genuine pleasure.

Kulis beamed at the recognition, and Perkin smiled in return. "Same here, Pat. How's tricks?"

"I can't complain. Before I forget, my brother passes his regards. He doesn't say hello, mind you. He passes his regards. His division is moving, though—maybe you'll get to see him in the future." The brother in question was an officer in British military intelligence.

"I hope so. How's the good colonel doing?" Perkin had met Riley's brother, Lieutenant Colonel Russ, several months before near the heel of the Italian boot.

"It's depressing, Perkin. The stress is taking a terrible toll on him. He's aged ten years since I'd seen him last. Speaking of which, you look well—aside from the scars and the bruising, of course." Riley grinned to take the sting out of the words.

"That ain't all, Pat. I got some gray hairs as well." Perkin grinned back at the priest.

"Gray hairs, is it now? You'll need a Zimmer frame before long."

"I don't doubt it. Maybe two . . . what's a Zimmer frame?"

Before Perkin could find out what a Zimmer frame might be, they turned a corner and came up to the jeep. Sam had a concerned look on his face, which Perkin correctly interpreted as meaning they'd looked into the duffel bags.

"Vincent? How are you doing?"

"Good Father." Private Fratelli also beamed as if he'd seen an old comrade, which in a way the priest was. Perkin's team had inadvertently prevented the priest from being arrested by German intelligence.

"Pat, I'd like to introduce you to my cousin, Sam Taft. Sam, this is Father Patrick Riley."

Sam stepped out of the jeep, offered a hand, and said as they shook, "Good to meet you, Father. I've heard a lot about you."

The priest looked up at Sam, then over to Perkin, and back to Sam. "Nice to meet you as well. I see the family resemblance—but they seem to have fed you better, me boy. What on earth do you Texans live on?"

Sam laughed, "State pride, mostly. When that don't work, us lucky ones get fried trout and tamales, but usually not at the same sittin'."

"I'll remember that. As big as you are, do you play sports like rugby?"

"No, but I saw a Welsh wing take flight two nights ago. It was pretty memorable." Sam started laughing and then began to tell the story. He stopped awkwardly when he realized the priest might not find it as funny as he did, and Perkin stepped in to save his cousin.

"I'll finish the story as we go, Pat. But we need to be moving. I want to be up close to the line of departure by dark." Seeing the look on Sam and Fratelli's faces, he added, "It's not as bad as it sounds. Don't worry."

1400 Hours
Viterbo, Italy

The train had not taken Major Grossmann to Rome according to plan. The rail line had been commandeered for German military traffic, and the train was directed to a side track at Viterbo. Passengers en route to Rome were told that the train might resume its passage the next day—or in the week after that. Those that wanted to had been disembarked at the station in Viterbo, and those who wanted to chance it stayed on the crowded train.

The fireman had shrugged when Grossmann asked him how long he thought the delay might be. "The Germans do not inform us of their intentions, my friend. I've seen thirty minutes, and I've seen four days. We won't go today, I would guess, but who knows? But if we haven't been sent on by 1700, we won't go because of the curfew in Rome." He had shrugged again and grimaced as he said, "The only good thing about the Germans is that we engineers are no longer fined by the fascists for being late due to their needs. But don't worry, my friend—one day, the light will go green and we will be told to go."

On New Year's Eve, the driver and the fireman had shared their meager meals with Grossmann, and he had doled out precious American cigarettes in exchange. One of the train's crewmembers had produced a bottle of a sparkling wine, and they had walked thirty meters away from the train and drank it together under an oak tree. When Grossmann asked why they had left the warmth of the engine, he was told that they were strictly forbidden to drink on the train.

While the crew slept in cots in the train station, he had slept on a blanket on the hard steel floor of the locomotive. The residual heat from the firebox kept him quite warm, but the deck was hard and unyielding, and he slept poorly. He hated sleeping exposed like that, and every sound awoke him with a start. It was not a propitious way to start the New Year, he had decided.

New Year's Day brought no further progress toward Rome. The German authorities were still holding the rail lines for their own traffic—even the local lines as he was on now. He had been tempted many times to leave the train station and see Viterbo for himself. He had been told by the stationmaster that there was an ancient papal palace in the town, and that the Pope had moved his residence from Rome to Viterbo during the thirteenth century for a couple of decades. Judging by the restroom of the train station, Grossmann decided that the town had been in decline ever since.

He had opted not to sightsee, however tempting it might be to see the palace, because there were too many German soldiers about. There were even some onboard the train when it had stopped, but they had all found alternate transportation into the city. Grossmann was taking his role of a downed American pilot seriously, and he wanted to avoid contact with his fellow countrymen unless it was to his advantage.

Finally the train had been cleared to move. Slowly, the old steam engine pulled out of Viterbo and before long, Grossmann was in the countryside again. His plan now was to stay with the train into Rome, and he would get off as the train slowed before a curve leading to the Vatican City station. Grossmann's train would not stop there, but the driver said that it was the closest to the Vatican he could take him. The offer had been made for Grossmann to stay with the driver and his family, but it was apparent that the offer was a token offering only, and that the driver was hoping Grossmann would decline. He did.

He had no intention of staying with the driver. The man, while well-meaning enough, was boring companionship. Besides, Grossmann had decided that he would now go straight at the problem like a good American. He would see if he could get entrance to the Vatican today.

1500 Hours
Salcito, Italy

Perkin and Riley rode in the second jeep together. Kulis navigated while Fratelli drove the first jeep and Sam dozed.

"How have things been for you, Perkin? It looks like the stress is wearing on you as well, my friend."

"Well, Pat, it's been a bit of a roller coaster, I must admit." Perkin hesitated, then said, "Not long after I said good-bye to you in Castellabate, I met a girl in Naples. Her name was Gianina, and, well, she was . . . special. We'd been together for only a few weeks, but in that time, I came to believe that we'd be together forever. But, um . . . it didn't work out that way."

"What happened?

"This German intelligence officer . . . Grossmann . . . who I'll be briefing you on before your return to the Vatican, was one of two officers I know of who executed a terror bombing campaign in Naples against civilians. One of his targets was the main Neapolitan post office . . . and . . . Gianina was buying stamps when the building blew up. She and some seventy others were killed instantly."

The priest looked shocked. "I had been told that you knew who Grossmann was—that you could identify him. No one told me that you had a personal interest."

"I don't hide the fact, but I don't advertise it either. Quite honestly, I don't know how much Scrope and company know about me, and I don't really care."

"What did you do after her death?"

Perkin had forgotten that a discussion with Father Riley was a conversation of questions and answers. "I'm a soldier," Perkin said simply. "I buried her and was back at work before the day was over."

"So you haven't had the opportunity to mourn her death."

"No, I wouldn't say that, Father. It's an odd thing . . . life as a soldier. In the division, I'm surrounded by fifteen thousand of my closest friends, and yet even with Sam here, it can be a lonely profession sometimes. No, I've had plenty of time to think about Gianina."

"And what conclusions have you drawn? About her, about her death?"

"I concluded that she had done nothing that justified her death other than being born Italian, which seems to be justification enough for the Germans. It was a pointless death and I think that fact made it worse for me, and quite honestly, the grief was pretty bad at first. It was just hard even to breathe. You know, we're surrounded by death here—I've seen people die. I've killed people. But it's different when it's someone you love. It's numbing in a way that's hard to describe. But numb or not, lonely or not, soldiering keeps you busy. I had work to do, and I just kind of threw myself into it."

Perkin thought for a moment and said, "Anyway, throughout all this, I was thinking that life is largely over. That everyone I know and love is going to die in this war, and there isn't a goddamned thing I can do about it. My friends all thought I was nuts—I volunteered for a mission that couldn't be described as anything but suicidal." Perkin laughed softly, "But it wasn't. Obviously. My regimental commander told me once that he thought that I had both suicidal and homicidal tendencies. Then he tried to get me assigned to his staff. Kind of a mixed compliment, wouldn't you say?"

"Are you? Are you, Perkin? Suicidal and homicidal?" Riley asked the question with keen interest but not with evident judgment.

Perkin didn't answer right away. He gave the question some thought and said, "No. I mean, I'm not suicidal, but I think that maybe my time here is short, and that I need to do what I can to contribute while I'm here. If my contribution involves risking my life, I'm not afraid to do it, but having said that, I just ain't gonna toss it away. As for homicidal . . . well, it's an odd thing, you know, being critical of homicidal tendencies in war."

"It's not the killing, Perkin. It's the how and why that distinguishes right from wrong in a war."

"Do you think so? Is there a difference between the rifleman who kills an enemy one at a time, or the bomber who kills thirty? Maybe with your collar, it's different, but I think those lines are blurred for us."

"It may be, Perkin, I don't know. But I've been thinking that . . . this war must lead us to rethink humanity, and the role that wars play in civilization." Riley tapped his fist into the palm of his hand to emphasize his point. "We need to look at more than just the origins of a conflict, the incessant pathetic puling of statesmen about who's wrong and who's right. Don't get me wrong, that has a place, of course, but we also need to be cognizant about how that fight is conducted. And like Clemenceau's dictum that 'war is too important to be left to the generals,' well, the peace is too important to be left to the politicos. We have to do better than Kellogg-Briand, and the soldiers and the politicians just can't be trusted to make up the rules.

I firmly believe that God needs to be the central part of the equation."

"Why do you say that?" Perkin downshifted and followed the lead jeep as their road ended, and they turned left onto another highway.

"Because if we leave Him out, if there is no moral, Christian foundation underneath us, then war remains simply a matter of consequentialism—that an act's acceptable if the consequences are beneficial . . . like firebombing a city is justified if it ends the war a day earlier. I'm thinking that we can't allow sophistry like that to guide how the postwar world looks at conflict."

"I don't know . . . if you're the soldier whose life is saved by that firebombing, you might have different sensibilities on the subject, Patrick. Besides, I thought you Jesuits invented consequentialism—the ends justifying the means being a sort of Jesuit motto."

Riley grinned. "I must have missed that lesson. I don't remember being taught that in seminary." The jeep went over a large pothole, and Riley grabbed the window frame of the jeep to keep from being rocked out of the vehicle. "Goodness. That'll teach me to make light of the Society."

That lightened the moment, and the two men changed subjects has they drove into the foothills of the Abruzzi mountains. Even as the wind had been brisk on the coast that morning, the temperature continued to drop as the jeeps groaned with the uphill climb.

Periodically, they would pass through burned landscapes that told of battles. Scarred countryside and shelled villages were witnesses to skirmishes that were too small for names, but nonetheless still devastating for the noncombatants caught between the two armies. Still other villages bore no signs of conflict, and the people usually waved at the American jeeps as they passed through, although sometimes they just stared at the foreign soldiers.

As they progressed further north, closer to the amorphous line, they began to pass military units—the rear echelon soldiers of the small supply depots, military police, and administration. Several times they went through checkpoints and were simply waved through with casual salutes.

Perkin and Riley told each other of the lands they came from—the cool, wet, rocky shores of Ireland, and the hot, flat, sandy shores of South Texas. Both expressed genuine desires to visit the other's homelands. Perkin was captivated by Riley's description of the raw beauty of the Cliffs of Mohr and the Dingle Peninsula, and Riley was equally intrigued by Perkin's tales of the exotic animals of the coastal bend including the armadillo and the wild jackalope.

Perkin gave Riley the complete briefing on Douglas Grossmann. As he drove, the priest looked through the Grossmann file and committed the high school picture to memory.

"He looks a decent sort, doesn't he now?" Riley observed.

"Strange, isn't it? By all accounts, he's amiable and, naturally, a conversationalist. Those are the tools of his trade. He can manage accents better than most actors—in fact, he is an actor. He's playing a role, and if Scrope and the others are right, he'll be play acting a role when— if—you come across him. Maybe he'll be a British officer, held in custody since North Africa, or perhaps he can do a Kiwi accent. I'm guessing that he'll be an American or perhaps playing a Canadian soldier taken at Ortona. The accent's natural to him, and there'd be less chance for a screw-up."

Riley was silent for a long moment, then he asked, "What do I do with him if I find him?"

"Kill him."

"And just how would I do that?" Riley asked with a faint smile.

"You must keep stocks of poisoned holy water on hand for occasions like this."

"We don't drink the holy water, you know. Seriously . . . what do I do?"

"Go to the Swiss Guards and have him detained. I'm sure there's a dungeon in the Vatican somewhere."

The priest rolled his eyes and sighed, "You Proddies and your imaginations. We closed that a long time ago— and no, we didn't turn it into a nursery for the nuns' children or papal offspring." Riley waited until Perkin had quit laughing and he said, "Detention by the Swiss Guard was Colonel Scrope's suggestion. What would you think about a papal demarche of the Germans? Use this to embarrass them?"

"Well, the Germans don't seem to handle embarrassment well. If they're looking for an excuse to shut down the Pope, this could be it. So I wouldn't give them the chance. Do it quietly, and then turn him over to us when we liberate Rome. Just thinking aloud . . . it might be better to try to ascertain Grossmann's intentions. I think he'd want to follow your underground railway to its logical end, so let him take off and send word back to your brother through the Church network. By the time that Grossmann makes it to where we're headed now, we can have a team in place and snatch him."

"Is that what you'd do? Snatch him?"

"No, Pat. I'd kill him. Just like I killed his partner."

1650 Hours
Vatican City, Italy

Major Grossmann walked casually along the outside of Bernini's Colonnades. There was a wide white line painted on the ground between the two ends of the colonnades that provided the demarcation between the Italian Social Republic and Vatican City. Grossmann couldn't remember the line being there before, so he assumed that it was a new addition to Rome.

A two-man patrol of the Palatine Guards walked on the far side of the line. A two-man German patrol marched on the near side. They did not acknowledge one another. The contrast could not be more vivid to Grossmann—the Palatine Guards were militia formed by the Pope to help protect the Church's property in Italy. Although they carried Beretta submachine guns, they weren't soldiers. Their counterparts on the German side undoubtedly were.

Whenever it had been painted, it was clear that one side was papal territory and the other was German and Italian fascist. *On the far side*, he thought, *I'm safe. They can't grab me once I'm on Vatican grounds. On the other hand, if I bring attention to myself and I'm denied entrance, the patrol will just grab me when I leave Saint Peter's Square.*

Grossmann leaned against a column and lit a cigarette. When the German guards turned about and headed away from him, Grossmann simply walked over the line into Vatican territory. *Safe from the German patrol*, he thought with a grin.

He had been to the Vatican before, of course, but he had not crossed its boundary since being posted to Rome in 1942. Although the art and the architecture were literally breathtaking, churches in general left him uneasy, and Saint Peter's Basilica was the church of churches. He found the ostentatious displays of wealth distasteful, and every time he viewed the gold inlays in the ceilings, he fancied that perhaps that gold had been mined by Indian slaves in South America. It wasn't the slavery that bothered Grossmann so much as the hypocrisy.

The Church had been very critical of the Third Reich's new world order, Grossmann thought, but where did the wealth come from to build the Pope's palace and cathedral? The Reich controlled men and wealth through blood and iron; the Church through rite and superstition. Different approaches, but it was all about control, he mused as he walked through Saint Peter's Square, past the obelisk and up the stairs to the basilica. *Perhaps we are not so different*, he thought.

The Swiss Guards standing at the center entrance to Saint Peter's Basilica provided yet another contrast to the Palatine Guards and the Germans soldiers outside of Vatican City. They were dressed in their colorful renaissance uniforms, and they looked almost comical holding their halberds, but Grossmann knew that unlike the Palatine Guards, the Swiss Guards were not a militia. They were highly trained soldiers. Grossmann couldn't remember if they had always posted guards at Saint Peter's or whether the guards there now were new, but he decided to approach them in any case.

As he walked up to one of the two guards, a tall soldier with black hair under a black beret, he wondered if the Swiss Guards were like the guards at Buckingham Palace. *Will they even talk to me?* he thought.

"Excuse me, signore," he began in Italian. Grossmann looked over his shoulder and lowering his voice, he switched to English, "Do you speak English?"

"Yes, sir. How may I help you?" said the soldier with a Swiss Italian accent.

"Is there a place we could talk in private?" Grossmann asked.

"No, sir. How may I help you?" the guard asked again.

"Look, uh, I'm an American . . ." Grossmann was suddenly uncertain how to proceed.

"Yes?"

"I'm an American pilot, and I'm looking for help. For a place to stay."

The guard shot a significant glance at his counterpart across the entrance to Saint Peter's Basilica, who was watching the conversation but too far away to hear. "We are not allowed to help combatants of either side. Vatican City is neutral territory, and we have been directed to inform soldiers such as you that, regretfully, we can not give you entrance."

Grossmann shook his head in disbelief. "I need help. I risked coming here because I thought you could help me. Isn't there someone here I could talk to?"

"No, sir. You should go, sir."

"Look, a ship is allowed to pull into a neutral port and stay there for twenty-four hours in an emergency, why can't I stay here?"

"Are you a ship? Is this a port? No. Sir, I must respectfully ask you to leave." Suddenly, the Swiss Guard didn't seem so comical. His face had hardened.

Grossmann didn't want a confrontation—he thought that would be out of character—but he was uncertain about what to do next.

A low whistle came to him from his right. It was the other guard, who waved him over with a nod of his head. When Grossmann looked back at the first soldier, he had resumed his post, his face back into a neutral expression.

As Grossmann walked across the grand entrance to the basilica, the other soldier, also tall but with blond hair and blue eyes spoke to Grossmann in a Swiss German accent, "You are an Allied soldier?"

"Yes. An American pilot."

"We cannot help you." The soldier looked at Grossmann with kind eyes, but his words didn't convey kindness.

"Yeah. The other guard told me so." Grossmann said no more. He'd been called over for a reason and he wanted to find out what that was.

The guard looked around and made sure no one was in earshot, "Soldier, we cannot help you, but come back this time tomorrow, and I'll have someone here who can." Seemingly from nowhere, the soldier thrust a crumpled wad of lire into Grossmann's hand. "It's not enough for a room at a *pensione*, I'm afraid, but it'll buy you some food. Stay off the streets after 1900; there's a curfew."

Grossmann was speechless for a moment; then, remembering his role as a noble American pilot, he tried to hand the money back as he said, "No, thank you. I can't accept. I'll be back tomorrow."

The guard shook his head and said, "Sir, with respect, if you are to stay out of captivity, you have to be prepared to receive charity. Please don't worry about me, the Monsignor will pay me back."

1945 Hours
Rome, Italy

Grossmann had contemplated sleeping in a park in order to stay in character, but it had started to drizzle and he simply wasn't prepared for the cold and the wet—as he admitted to himself, there were evidently limits to method acting in the Grossmann School. Alternately cursing his weakness and silently praising his good fortune, he went to an apartment he kept near the Piazza Navona.

The doorman was on the Abwehr payroll. He had seen Grossmann come to the apartment under the strangest of conditions and he never asked questions. He didn't even raise an eyebrow when Grossmann emerged from the twilight wearing a workman's clothes. He would of course make a discreet phone call to someone in Grossmann's chain of command and report that he had gone to the apartment, but that was to be expected.

"Alfredo, have you seen Signorina Seliquini?" Grossmann maintained an adjacent apartment for Antoniette Bernardi—known to the doorman as Antoniette Seliquini. It was rented mostly for her discreet liaisons with targets for intelligence collection. They had not used the apartment for that purpose for some months, but Grossmann thought that he would ask.

"No, signore. I have not seen Miss Seliquini for ages."

Grossmann nodded, then said, "Of course. Alfredo, I haven't any food in my flat. Please send a boy to the restaurant and have him bring me my usual and a carafe of wine. It's after curfew, so give him a few more lire. Do we have hot water today?"

"Yes, signore. And I'll get a boy off to the restaurant right away."

"Tell him if he takes a bite of my food again, I'll take a belt to him."

"Yes, signore."

As Grossmann took the stairs to the third floor, he cursed himself again at his own weakness. That he had asked about Antoniette would be reported to Abwehr headquarters. It would be jotted down in a report that ultimately would make it to the disagreeable colonel's desk, and someday he would use Grossmann's weakness against him.

He had slid a small thread between the door and the sill before he left the week before. It was still there and in the same place—that didn't mean that his apartment hadn't been entered, it just meant that the perpetrator, if there was one, had been a professional. When he slid the key in and opened the door, he almost sighed with relief. He was home, if just for the night.

The apartment looked undisturbed, and after lying on his bed for a luxurious few minutes, he went to the bathroom and began to run a bath. His bones ached from the cold, and he hadn't bathed since being dropped off in the garlic field—what was it? Four or five days ago? It didn't matter. He was home and could relax for a bit.

Grossmann sat on the edge of the tub and let the hot water run over his fingers. The steam coming off the tub and the sound of the running water was almost hypnotic as he thought about the day's events. Who would he meet tomorrow? Would it be Monsignor O'Flaherty? He was daydreaming about shutting down the Monsignor's operation when he heard a knock at the door.

Grossmann turned off the water and answered the door. The boy had brought over the food and a carafe of wine from the restaurant across the street. Since the curfew had been instituted, they closed before 1900, but they were so desperate for cash that they reopened the kitchen for the boy. Grossmann tipped the boy and sent him on his way.

He looked at the bath, then smelled the food, and decided that the bath could wait. The water was too hot anyway. The boy had brought over one of his favorites—a simple pasta dish of pappardelle and ham. Despite being a peasant's meal, it was delicious. He put on a record—a collection of Vivaldi's cello concertos—poured himself a glass of wine, and then wolfed down the pasta. He grimaced from the taste of the wine. It had a slightly bitter aftertaste, but he drank it anyway—and poured himself another.

The steaming hot bath was divine. The radiators in the apartment building barely kept up with the cold, but the hot bath warmed Grossmann completely through. He poured himself another glass of wine, leaned back and listened to the music. Although not all of the album was uplifting, this particular concerto was, and Grossmann could feel his worries fading. He closed his eyes and focused on the music. First the cello, then a violin in the background, then the cello again—a competition between the two, and as written by Vivaldi, a competition that the cello clearly won.

As he imagined being at the concert and hearing the pure music in person, he thought he heard a click in the living room—the sound of the door opening. He listened for the noise again, didn't hear it, and dismissed the sound he heard as an imperfection in the album—besides, he was sure he had locked the door. Grossmann poured another glass of the wine—the carafe was nearly empty now—and he contemplated having the boy sent back for another. The wine was too good to pass up. It might be ages before he had another wine this good again, and Grossmann thought that perhaps he'd never felt this relaxed before. It was almost a magical feeling.

He closed his eyes again, and the music seemed more vivid than ever. Grossmann could hear the perfection in every note, and it was if he'd never heard music played so well before. Then he caught her scent—the slightest essence of flowers—and before he could open his eyes, she gently kissed his lips. A slow, lingering kiss that was every bit as perfect as the wine and the music.

"Douglas," she whispered. "I've missed you so." She kissed him again, and it was more moving and powerful than the first.

He opened his eyes, and there was Antoniette kneeling by the bathtub. Her face was alive with pleasure, and her eyes glowed with love and compassion.

"Oh, my love, I've missed you as well!" he sighed. "Are you really here?"

She stood up, and Grossmann noticed for the first time that she was naked. She leaned over to pour the remaining wine of the carafe into his glass, and she brushed his face with her breasts. Before he could touch her, she stepped into the tub, and eased herself into the hot water opposite him.

"I am so glad to see you, Doug. I missed you so much," said Antoniette in a soothing, hypnotic voice. She pouted very prettily, "I was so bored. Skiing was dreadful and I missed our work so." She lifted his foot from the water and placed it between her breasts as she began to rub the aches and the stress away. As he groaned involuntarily, she said with the most loving of smiles, "Tell me everything you've been doing. I want to hear it all."

2000 Hours
Sixteen Miles Southwest of Castel di Sangro, Italy

They were on the front line, but it was unlike any other front that Sam had seen. There was no shooting, little light discipline, and a very casual attitude toward the war. Although it made him nervous on one hand, the Canadian soldiers that they were with looked hard and professional on the other.

They were in a platoon command post that was little more than a makeshift lean-to reinforced by sand bags. Ongoing construction indicated the Canadians were working on reinforced breastworks, trenches, and bunkers capable of housing their soldiers. A platoon commander of the West Nova Scotia Regiment explained, "We're essentially in winter quarters here. We haven't heard a shot fired in anger for over two weeks now, and we don't expect any until the winter line is breached on either our left or our right. Straight ahead of us are the Abruzzi mountains of the Apennines—they're the tallest mountains south of the Alps, and the Eye-ties haven't developed them. Few roads, no rail. Just wilderness."

"What are the Germans doing?" Sam asked.

"Same as us. Digging into the rock and dirt, building bunkers, and so on. Their line is another dozen miles or so that way, and we both patrol in between. But it might as well be in Rome—we can't move heavy equipment up, and no infantry's going to break us loose in these mountains. We have to do that from our flanks on either side."

"Do you see any patrolling patterns?"

"Nope. Jerry's too good for a pattern, but we had a patrol pass through here yesterday." The Canadian lieutenant pointed to a place on a tabletop map. "That might give us at least two days before they return. Maybe more. Listen, no one's being aggressive up here. We've had patrols wave at each other as they pass within half a mile of one another on either side of a little cut in the mountains. No shots fired. If it makes no difference with the war, I'm fine with that."

Sam was surprised. His experience with the Germans had been anything other than live and let live.

"Where are you headed?" asked the Canadian officer.

"We're going about here." Perkin leaned forward past Sam, and pointed to the map.

"To that farmhouse?"

"Yes. You know it?"

"We do. It's the only thing on that little mountain—well it's not really little. It backs onto a big ridge that runs for at least ten miles northward before sloping to another ridge that evidently goes to Avezzano about thirty miles north of here. We stop in and check on the Gildardino family from time to time. Nice people. Even though it's on the German side of no-man's-land, it's more difficult to get to from the north, so I don't think that the Germans have checked in on them since the current lines stabilized." The lieutenant was curious why the Americans were interested in the Gildardino farm but was too polite to ask.

"Do we need to deconflict with your patrols over the next two days?" asked Perkin.

"No, sir. We weren't going along that route for a couple days. We can stay clear for a while, or I can put a squad in behind you for support if that would be better."

Perkin's heart warmed to the lieutenant. It was a tempting offer, but he didn't want to increase the Allied footprint any further in the vicinity of the Gildardino farm. He wasn't carrying any communications equipment and didn't want to borrow from the Canadians.

"No, thank you. We'd like to keep this low-key. How far in can we get with jeeps, or can we go all the way to the farmhouse?"

"Two weeks ago you could have gone all the way, but at their elevation, there's a lot of snow and ice there now, and it's a steep incline. You'll be a better judge when you get there, but right here," the lieutenant pointed to the map again, "is where their driveway up the mountain starts. There's a good spot to leave your jeeps. We won't bother 'em, but I can't speak for any stray Eye-ties that might be around. Anything else, sir?"

"No, and thank you for your hospitality. We should have our tents up, and we'll be out of your hair by daylight."

"I'll escort you through our checkpoints, sir, and we'll give you our challenge and password in the morning." The lieutenant turned to Sam. "Is that a government-issued rifle, Lieutenant Taft?"

"Yes and no. It's signed over to me, but not the weapon that I normally carry. Wanna look at it?"

The Canadian officer nodded, and Sam passed over the Johnson M1941. The Canadian examined it closely, and whipped it up to his cheek several times to check the sights and balance of the rifle. He handed it back to Sam with a rueful look on his face.

"That is a beautiful weapon, Lieutenant. I wish we had something like that. We're still issued with these old Lee-Enfields—no semi-automatics—and Brens for our light automatic."

Sam nodded seriously. "That Lee-Enfield's a nice rifle, and I know some of your best boys can almost keep up with the rate of semi-auto fire, but an American platoon armed with Garands can lay down a serious amount of lead." They talked more about weapons and tactics, and then Sam and Perkin headed back to their little encampment. The privates had set tents up in the lee of a small outcropping of rocks, and Father Riley had a good fire going. They ate the remainder of their sandwiches and Sam traded a large wedge from a wheel of cheese that he had bought from an Italian farmer to a Canadian sergeant for some excellent ham.

After a bite to eat and a shot of bourbon all around, Perkin told the party to turn in. Tomorrow would start early, he said.

Sam was sharing a tent with Perkin, and when they crawled into their sleeping bags, Sam said, "I ain't asked about our mission because I know it's classified. But I'd like a better understanding of what we're doing and why."

"I don't blame you, Bear. I'm sorry to have kept you in the dark, but we're dropping Patrick off with the Gildardino family tomorrow. They're now the southernmost link in a network the Vatican uses to move escaped POWs out of German territory. You know about Grossmann, right?"

Sam answered, "The American Kraut?"

"Yes. Allied intel believes that Grossmann is running an operation against this network, and their fear is that Grossmann's information will be used as a *casus belli* against the Pope—a pretext to take over the Vatican."

"Why would they do that?" Sam didn't see that there was much to be gained by a German occupation of Vatican City.

"Why invade Russia? Why declare war on the United States?" Perkin snorted, "It ain't like there's a lot of clarity of thought in Berlin this past decade or so. So we're sending Pat back to the Vatican to head off Grossmann and hopefully put him into detention until we get there."

"Do you think it'll work?"

"I don't have any idea. I'm not sure that Grossmann's even involved in penetrating the Vatican network—although the British certainly seem convinced, and it does make sense given his abilities," Perkin admitted. "But at another level, if we can get Pat back to Rome and he can facilitate getting our boys into safe houses or even back here, this little side-trip will be worthwhile."

Sam yawned, "All right. Just in and out, right? Nothing else? No booby-trapped rooms or flying Welshmen? Just in and out?"

"Well, I can't promise no more DiRenzo sisters, but other than that, Sam . . . nothing else. Just in and out."

Chapter Nine

January 3, 1944
0900 Hours
Gildardino Farm, Italy

They had left slightly before daylight in the dark gray light of a cloudy dawn. The Canadian lieutenant had been true to his word and had ridden with Perkin to a Canadian roadblock.

"Here you go, sir. Everything north of this point is no-man's-land until you get to Jerry's lines. If you run into a German burp gun, you've gone too far."

Perkin laughed, shook the Canadian's hand, and said, "Excellent advice. We'll be back through here later today if possible or two to three days at the most. Thanks for the hospitality."

Two West Nova Scotians moved a barrier out of the way, and Private Fratelli's jeep with Kulis and Father Riley pulled out first. The roadblock had been placed on a hilltop, so as Fratelli pulled out, he was going downhill on a rough country road—no pavement, only sparse gravel. Within a few yards, the jeep slid slightly before righting.

Perkin's jeep slid as well, and Perkin watched from behind as Private Fratelli shifted the four-wheel drive over to the low side of the transmission. It would slow their progress to little better than a walk, but it gave the jeep better traction on the icy slope. He did the same.

"Well, shit, Bear. It's gonna take us all day to get there."

Sam was hanging tightly to the windshield frame of the jeep with one hand and the bottom of his seat with the other. Without taking his eyes off the road he said, "You ought to let me drive."

Perkin laughed. "You've lived in South Texas all your life. You have no experience, like I have, in driving in either ice or on hills. I ain't tradin' spots."

"If God meant for me to drive on hills, he'd have given me some," Sam groused.

"See?" Perkin said triumphantly as the reached the bottom of the first hill. "Nothin' to worry about."

Sam laughed as the jeep slid slightly sideways on a patch of ice and Perkin swore as he turned into the slide. "Yeah, nothin' to worry about."

Progress was slow as they went up, down, around and through a small set of hills. The Gildardino farm was halfway up a mountain and deep into no-man's-land, but the only road leading to the farmhouse came from the south through a series of hills fronted to the west by an ice-cold stream. German patrols would have to cross the little river or come into the Allied side of no-man's-land to use the road or, as the Canadian officer explained, they could simply climb the backside of the mountain—a hard climb, but doable.

After two hours of a slow crawl, they reached an area at the base of the Gildardino Mountain where they decided to park the jeeps and continue on foot. The weather continued to worsen, and the road was getting progressively slicker with ice and sleet. Perkin's initial reconnaissance up the mountain road resulted in the jeep losing traction after only twenty yards, and the jeep slid harrowingly backward down the mountain and came to a hard stop against a boulder.

"OK, boys. We're on foot from here on out," Perkin said as he surveyed the damage to the jeep.

The jeeps were driven into a copse of trees just off the road, parked, and camouflaged. The privates brushed out the tracks as well as they could and hoped the wind would cover the rest. Sam slung his new Johnson rifle but wrapped the heavy Mauser and his Garand in two of the now-empty duffel bags, and covered them with tree boughs several yards away from the jeeps. He hated to leave either the jeeps or the weapons behind, but he saw no alternative.

When they returned to the road and began the trek up the mountain, Perkin spied a well-used path next to the road. A man's footprints were mixed into the mud and slush alongside those of a very large dog. Sam looked at the man's tracks and said, "I don't think they look like German boots. Doesn't look like they've been here very long, though. Ain't covered in snow or sleet yet."

The road was wickedly slick even though it looked as if it had been plowed recently, and the soldiers and the priest found it easier to follow the same track as the man had on the side of the road because it was uneven ground. Even so, it took a long time to work their way up the mountain. Hard frozen banks of snow had been built up along the outer walls of the switchbacks and turns and served as a railing of sorts. As Perkin leaned over one of the snow banks, he saw that the road dropped away quickly to a gully fifteen feet below, and he shuddered at the thought of a jeep sliding off the road.

"Sir!" Private Kulis hissed as he dropped to a crouch. "I saw somethin' comin' down the road." He pointed through a clearing in the trees to the road several hundred yards high above them as it curved up the mountainside.

"What'd ya see?" Perkin asked as he ran into the brush alongside the rode.

Kulis looked a little confused and said, "Sir, I don't know what it was. I'd hate to guess."

"This ain't school—I don't take points off for not knowing. Give me your best guess."

Kulis looked a little embarrassed as he said, "It looked like a damn big white dog's head, and it was movin' superfast down the mountain."

"So it's a dog runnin' down the mountain?" Perkin asked. A dog might be a problem if it belonged to German soldiers.

"Well, sir, he didn't look like he was runnin' or nothing. You know how a dog kind of lopes? Well, this one wasn't. It was movin' smoothly . . . I can't explain," he finished weakly.

Perkin looked up the mountain road and canted his head to listen. Something was moving down the mountain. He watched as Private Fratelli began to track a target with his BAR, and then Fratelli lowered his weapon with a huge grin on his face.

Almost faster than Perkin could comprehend, a sled on runners banked around a curve before them and whooshed past their kneeling position in the brush. Lying on the sled was a young man wearing skiing goggles and a look of absolute joy on his face. Sitting on the man's back was a massive Great Pyrenees whose trailing tongue and wild grin firmly suggested that the ride down the mountain was entirely for his benefit. Neither the man nor the dog noticed the soldiers on the roadside.

The party walked onto the road and watched as the sled disappeared around a turn, and Father Riley remarked, "Now, that is truly one of God's miracles."

Perkin was laughing at the image of the dog as he said, "How so, Father?"

The priest laughed back and said, "Only God can put a sled dog in the driver's seat."

1200 Hours
Gildardino Farm, Italy

The Gildardino farm was comprised of a large stone farmhouse with a barn and several outlying buildings. The house was built on a large open plateau about halfway up the mountain, and it had a beautiful view to the south, where the foothills of the Abruzzi lay before it, and a stunning snow-covered mountain view behind it.

The Gildardinos had obviously taken great pains with the landscaping, and it struck Sam as more of a resort than a working farm—until he caught the scent of cattle. There was no one working outside as far as he could see, but the snow was quite trampled, particularly where the road turned into the farm.

Sam and Perkin had decided to approach the farm cautiously, but Father Riley said, "Nonsense. They're friends. We walk to the door and knock like Christians."

So that is what they did. Kulis and Fratelli dropped back and stood watch while Sam, Perkin, and Father Riley walked to the front door of the house. As they drew closer, Sam looked at the building. It was quite large, and although it was built in a traditional Italian style, it looked like was built using modern tools. A half circle of the driveway went to the door, and their boots crunched on the ice as they walked over the frozen gravel.

Before they could knock, the door flew open and a middle-aged Italian woman in black work pants, a white shirt, boots, and a heavy white sweater ran out and beamed at Father Riley.

"Father! We were wondering when you'd come." Her English was flawless with just a trace of an Italian accent.

"Maria! I was wondering myself. So good to see you again! Allow me to introduce my friends. This is Captain Perkin Berger of the American Army. Lieutenant Sam Taft and Privates Vincent Fratelli and Edwin Kulis. They saved my hide a long time ago, and now God has seen fit to let them watch over me again."

Maria ushered the soldiers into the house and looked them over with a surprising kindness and grace. "You are most welcome in our house. When I saw the white uniforms, I thought the Germans had come again. Please come in." Turning back to Riley she said, "Luigi is in the barn. Lucia and Gemma are upstairs playing, and Angelo is supposed to be bringing in the cows with Scipio before the storm hits, but I heard him screaming down the mountain, so he's goofing off. Again. So, while you gentlemen take off your coats and overshoes, let me go get Luigi, and then I have a surprise for you."

As Sam looked around for signs of a storm, Riley explained, "Maria was my Italian tutor in Dublin before the war. Her late husband taught the language at the university, and she tutored on the side. She and her children came back here in '40 when Alessandro passed away—you boys should quit smoking right now—and she lives with her brother Luigi. They are both good friends of the Church."

Maria brought in Luigi. He was a big man—nearly as big as Sam—and he had a broad, genuine smile on his face as he shook hands with Father Riley and greeted the soldiers. He looked up at Sam with something like surprise on his face, shook his hand, and nodded to the other soldiers.

Luigi had been working in the barn and smelled of animals—a good honest smell that had Fratelli wrinkling his nose, but brought smiles to the faces of the Texans. Unlike his sister, he spoke little English, but he said with a shy smile, "Welcome! Welcome!"

Two young girls peeked over a railing and, seeing the American flag sewn on the sleeve of Fratelli's coat, came running down the stairs. "Mama, Mama! Americans! Americans!"

In English, Maria said, "Yes, girls. Americans. Now run upstairs and bring down our surprise please."

"Sì, Mama!" The girls turned and raced back up the stairs.

Perkin smiled as he heard the girls arguing about who got to bring down the surprise. His smile faded when he heard heavy footsteps upstairs, and he was reaching for his Thompson when he heard an Australian voice call out, "Oi! You blokes take it easy down there. We're coming down."

1245 Hours
Gildardino Farm, Italy

Two bottles of wine were opened, and the Americans and Father Riley had been left alone to hear the story of the two Australian soldiers. Angelo had returned with Scipio and Perkin could hear the huge dog barking in the snow-covered yard.

The senior of the two Australian officers was an artillery officer, a lieutenant named Fred Hardy, and he did all of the talking. Hardy had black hair and dark, sunken eyes that reflected a long period of uncertain meals, but were now alight at the prospect that his ordeal was nearly over. The other officer was a very young infantry lieutenant with brown hair named Jim Van Deventer— the lieutenant's eyes darted back and forth nervously.

"Jim and I didn't know each other when we were took on Crete," Hardy said. "What a bloody shambles that affair was. I hadn't been on the damn island for more than a week before I was took prisoner along with most of my battalion. Three years of service getting ready for war, and I'm surrendered after a week of fighting without my permission. Anyway, Jim and I were transferred from German control to the Italians, and ironically, we were tossed into a camp at Sulmona. Campo 78—"

"Sir, why do you say ironically?" Kulis interrupted.

"It's ironic because it's only about thirty miles or so from here. But we had to cover a distance from Brisbane to Sydney to get here. When the British crossed the Strait of Messina and began working their way up the peninsula, the prisoner camps in the south of Italy were closed and we were loaded up in cattle cars and moved up north. When you blokes landed and Italy switched sides, we were in Campo 19 in Bologna. Our Italian guards buggered off but they told us to wait until we were liberated. A Pom colonel ordered us to stay put, but some of us Diggers decided to light out anyway. The Germans were coming through the front gate whilst we were heading out the back." Hardy shook his head at the memory.

"Sir, sorry to interrupt again . . ." Kulis said.

"That's all right, mate. If you're taking us home, you can interrupt all you want."

"Thank you, sir. What's a Pom officer and what's a Digger?"

"Same language, different slang, Private Kulis. A Pom is what we call an Englishman in Australia. What's it stand for, Jim?" Without waiting for an answer from the young lieutenant, Hardy continued, "Prisoner of his majesty, I reckon. A Digger's an Aussie soldier. So we lit out, a handful of us Diggers, but some of the boys weren't able to cut it, and so we split up." Hardy looked unhappily at Perkin, the senior officer present, and explained, "It wasn't my decision, Captain. I don't know what happened to those men, but I suspect that they were picked up by the Italian police in the north or by the Gestapo."

"I'm not making any judgments, Fred. I'm just glad it worked out for you." Perkin understood the officer's unhappiness—Hardy was no doubt feeling guilt about leaving the others behind, and he was probably uncertain how it would be viewed by the service when he was repatriated.

"Thank you, sir. We had a former walloper with us—a policeman—the bloke who made the decision to split up. He said in a manhunt that the cops would assume we were on foot, and would begin their search in expanding circles from where the escape occurred. He said they would use a four-mile radius to start for the first hour, so we would have to do better than that. So we did. I chundered twice, I have to admit." He preempted Private Kulis and said, "Vomited—it'd been awhile since any of us had run anywhere. We ran parallel to the rail line for several miles, and then a train comes along and we hit the dirt to let it pass. It was a German train carrying tanks and artillery pieces down to your fight, I'd imagine. Open, flatbed cars. The cop says, 'Let's give it a go!' So we jumped on and crawled under a panzer. Slept through the night off and on, and crawled off when we stopped for some damn reason north of Rome."

"You said there was a third man with you—a former cop. What happened to him?" Perkin asked.

"He slipped under the train as we were climbing aboard. I don't know what happened to him . . . he didn't make a sound." his voice trailed off. Then he nodded and said, "A good cobber. We'd all been together since Campo 78."

"Sorry to hear that," Perkin said. "What happened next?"

"When we were in Campo 78, we were visited by an Irish priest—a fellow named O'Flaherty. He came to check on the conditions of the prisoners for the Vatican, and he stopped and chatted with the boys in my blockhouse. A nice gentleman and a real comfort to the Catholic men. Anyway, even though the Italian guards were escorting him, he looked at us before he left and said, 'When you lads get out of here, come see me. My name's O'Flaherty and I'm at the Vatican.' And then he winked at us, and I knew he meant if we ever escaped."

"How'd you come at the Vatican? How'd you approach it?" Perkin was fascinated by the story and thought that perhaps Hardy's story might mirror how Grossmann would approach the Vatican.

"We didn't come at it directly, sir. We found a small parish priest in northern Rome who was willing to help us. He put us up overnight, and then got us into the home of an Italian family. We stayed there for over a month until they reckoned it was safe to move. O'Flaherty came and visited twice. What a sharp bloke! I didn't ever talk directly to him in Campo 78—his time was taken up by the Catholic lads—but he remembered my face. Can you believe that? Out of hundreds of Diggers that he met with, he remembered my face and the names of the Catholic boys in my blockhouse. O'Flaherty wanted to keep us in place until the Allies took Rome, but Jim and I wanted to keep moving."

Perkin looked at Lieutenant Van Deventer. His eyes kept moving back and forth nervously, and Perkin realized that the lieutenant hadn't said a single word, not even during the introductions. "Why was that, Jim?"

Van Deventer's eyes focused on Perkin for a few seconds and then began shifting back and forth again among all the other faces. Hardy answered for him gently, "We wanted to keep moving out of Rome because the bombing was making Jim a little nervous. You see, Jim doesn't speak much. At all, actually. I don't know what happened to him on Crete, but the boys in the camp thought that concussion from a bomb blast scrambled things around up there. Some Jerry guard used that as an excuse to push him around pretty hard, so I took him under my wing. I don't think things are so scrambled, myself. He ain't feeble. He'll do what you ask him to—I reckon you'll talk when you've got something to say, hey, Jim?"

Van Deventer didn't answer, and Perkin asked, "How long to make it down here, Fred?"

"We left Rome in late October and stayed in two different churches and five different Italian homes between here and there. The priests would make the arrangements, and one day a milk or a hay wagon would pick us up early in the morning, get us into the countryside, and then we'd walk to the next stop from there. We slept outside a number of nights and snuck into garages or barns when we had the chance. Jim never oversleeps so I'd tell him we'd need to get up at 0500, and on the minute, he'd wake me up. That's how I know things are still working up there." Hardy grinned at Van Deventer and gave him a friendly shove, "Scrambled, my arse. We been here for three days and we were waiting for another Canadian patrol to come by and head out with them."

"How'd you get through German lines to here?" Perkin asked.

"I don't think there are many Krauts in the Apennines, mate. They're just caretakers in my reckoning. Just waiting for the spring offensives to start so they can begin retreating again." The last sentence was said with a satisfied grin. "The last priest, Father Carlo, walked us through the mountains himself from Avezzano. There is a trail over the backside of this brute that has apparently been used by the family for generations, but it's not intuitive. I doubt Jerry would ever find it."

"Where do you want to go from here? We can do two things for you. We can leave you with the Canucks or take you back to Fifth Army with us," Perkin said.

"Are there any Australian units in Italy that you know of?"

"I don't know of any. There's a Kiwi division in Eighth Army, but I think that most of your boys have gone home. Like I said, I don't know for sure."

"If we see any of the sheepshaggers, you can drop us off with them—we get along well with the Kiwis. Otherwise, take us back with you, mate. Then we'll figure out how to get home from there."

1630 Hours
Vatican City

Major Grossmann had slipped into Saint Peter's Square a half hour earlier than his appointed time. He wanted out of the apartment, and wanted some quiet time to himself to think—a near impossibility in Rome.

Grossmann found a bench and sat down. He was sure he'd definitely been set up the night before by Bernardi. *Probably set up. Well, maybe.* Although he wasn't certain, he thought she had used the same techniques on him as they'd used together on countless other targets. What he wasn't sure about the day after was whether he'd known that all along and allowed it to happen.

The narcotic that she must have used, mixed with the bath and the wine, was a standard tool for Grossmann and Bernardi, but the key element was desire. Desire to sleep with a beautiful woman. Desire to make oneself appear important. It didn't matter as Antoniette Bernardi was the best in the business in exploiting desire, and it was all the more fun for her if she was the center object of the desire—which she surely was when it came to Major Grossmann.

As he sat in the shadow of the palace of the Pope, he cursed and then asked himself again whether he'd allowed it to happen. He probably had, he thought, and then he realized that he would again. Then he dismissed the whole notion of being played so patently.

She had left before he had awakened that morning, and a note on the bedside said, *My darling, as I told you last night (you had so much to drink, do you remember?), my family and I are heading to Tuscany until the seventh. I'm afraid I have to leave without saying good-bye—Father is already furious, I am sure. All I can say is last night was magical. Simply magical. I had no idea that you felt that way about me, and I didn't know until then that I feel the same about you. I hope that in the sober light of day that you never change your mind! As for me, I can't wait to see you again. Good luck in whatever you are doing (you'll have to tell me all about it), and I'll be waiting for you when you get back. All my love, Toni.*

Grossmann wished that he had the note with him, but of course, he didn't bring it. But even with the morning's mental haze, he had memorized it. He had analyzed it line by line, and naturally she said all the things that he wanted to hear. Bernardi was a master at that, and no one knew it better than Grossmann.

And yet he thought, what if she meant the words? What if the look in her eyes was real? How would he be able to distinguish between Bernardi on the job and Bernardi in love? Wasn't it possible that she loved him? There was a real connection between them, he had told himself all morning. He had felt it—*it was a magical night*—and he couldn't be fooled. Not by his own agent. Could he?

"*Mein Gott,*" he muttered, and he looked at the cross atop the obelisk. It was time to go. Grossmann shivered and stood up. As he walked to the entrance to the basilica, he allowed himself one last thought on Antoniette Bernardi: *If she was on the job last night, who was she working for? Or did she do it just for fun?*

1645 Hours
Gildardino Farm, Italy

The decision had been made to stay overnight at the Gildardino farm. Mr. Gildardino had assured them that another storm was blowing in, and the sleet of the morning was nothing more than a prelude. He was right.

During the early afternoon, heavy snowflakes began to fall, and within an hour, an inch had accumulated. The winds coming off the mountaintop over two thousand feet above them picked up dramatically, and the whine of the wind was ceaseless.

Sam had gone out with Angelo and brought one Holstein milk cow, four Chianina heifers, and two steers of the same breed into the barn. Angelo spoke excellent English, and he explained that his uncle normally maintained a herd of nearly a hundred head of the Chianina cattle plus two milk cows. "It was a prize herd— the Chianina is the tenderest beef in the world, and we would sell to the best restaurants in Rome, Florence, and Venice for *bistecca alla fiorentina*. The Germans bought most of the herd last month. They paid in Reichmarks, of course, so we'll never actually be paid."

Sam was heartbroken for the family. It would take a long time to build the herd back. "Why didn't they take all of them, and your draft horses as well?" Sam asked.

"They took what they needed. If they need more, they'll come back." he said simply. "There's just not many Germans in the mountains. Besides, these soldiers are reservists from the North Sea. They're sons of fishermen and shopkeepers, and most of them had never seen a mountain before. They call themselves *Gebirgsmarine*— mountain navy—as a joke. They don't like to climb the hills. They don't like to herd cattle. We only see them from time to time, and they just leave us alone."

"Damn. You're gonna have to get a bull up here for them heifers."

"All these heifers will calve in the summer. That's why Uncle saved them. We'll miss the other milk cow, though. Still, we're better prepared for the coming months than most." Angelo shook his head sadly. "We'll get by off these steers for a while. We have a good stock of flour. We press our own oil and cider. We make our own wine and apple brandy. Uncle has a hen house and a brooder house that the Germans left alone—maybe they are afraid of chickens—and we have driven the pigs to the far side of the farm. We have a smokehouse here, but we hid the hams a long time ago. Mama let the Germans buy some sausage and smoked trout with their worthless money, but we kept the good stuff. I think they were homesick and they really wanted the fish most of all."

Mr. Gildardino came into the barn, and he smiled when he saw Sam spreading straw onto the floor of the barn with a pitchfork. He said something to Sam in Italian, and Angelo translated it: "Our guests have tried to help, but they're not farmers. I watched you bring in the cows, you've done this before?"

Sam laughed. "About a million times. I have a few of my own as well, Luigi. I'd rather be here working in the barn than runnin' around playin' soldier. What can I do, you want me to toss some hay into the manger from the loft?"

"Uncle says no, thank you. That's my job, then I need to check on the chickens."

"Is there anything I can do to help?"

"Uncle asks if you would mind milking?" Angelo and Mr. Gildardino both looked at Sam expectantly.

"Of course. Where's your bucket and the stool?" Sam kept a handful of dairy cows on his ranch. There was nothing he liked better than fresh milk, and his cows also provided enough milk for his hands and their families. Generally he didn't do the milking himself anymore—one of his ranch hands usually did, or sometimes one of their wives would pitch in and help. But it had been his job growing up.

Angelo pointed to the wall where a bucket was hanging from a nail. Sam saw that it was clean but walked outside and scrubbed the bucket with snow for good measure. When he came back into the farm, he noticed a set of shackles hanging on the same wall where the bucket had been. He picked the shackles up and turned to Luigi, raised his eyebrows and said, "Do I need these?" Shackles were sometimes used to keep an ornery cow from raising a hind leg and taking a poke at the milker.

Angelo grinned, "No. That's for the cow we sold the Germans."

Sam laughed at the thought, and sat down on the stool next to the cow. He stroked her side gently and said a few encouraging words, and then cleaned her teats with a wet towel that Luigi handed him. He gently punched the udder several times, then firmly pinched the base of two teats and rolled his fingers down, squeezed, and began to milk. Luigi watched over his shoulder, nodded approvingly, and then went to an old record player on a shelf. Surprising Sam, Luigi wound up the record player and it began to play a scratchy version of Puccini's *Tosca*.

Angelo grinned at Sam and said, "Uncle believes that Margherita, uh, *come si dice* ... Daisy gives more milk when he plays *Tosca*. So he plays the same opera over and over. Hope you don't mind. I've got to tend to the chickens. Ciao."

Without question, the cow, apparently named Daisy, relaxed and the milk began to flow. Sam had never been a fan of opera, but as he milked, he rested his cheek on Daisy's flank and listened to the music. Whether it was familiar smell of home or the unknown tenor singing of his love for Tosca in the aria *E Lucevan Le Stelle* Sam would never know. But the haunting music and the deep, powerful voice moved him unexpectedly, and a tear trickled down his cheek as he milked.

1700 Hours
Vatican City

True to his word, the blond Swiss Guard was back, standing by the entrance to Saint Peter's Basilica, although he was not wearing the ceremonial uniform of the Guard. He was wearing a decidedly more low-key black suit with a dark grey overcoat and fedora. Standing next to him was a smiling priest—a tall man with alert eyes and the crimson-trimmed robes of a monsignor.

The guard silently held his hand out when Grossmann approached, not as a handshake but as an indication to the priest of, "Here's the man I told you about." The guard didn't acknowledge Grossmann. He simply turned and walked away.

"Good afternoon," said the tall priest in a rich Irish brogue. "I'm Hugh O'Flaherty, and who might you be now?"

"A pleasure to meet you, Father." Grossmann knew that O'Flaherty was a monsignor, but he hadn't introduced himself as such. "I'm Lieutenant Doug Peabody."

"The pleasure's mine, Doug. Shall we take a little walk?"

O'Flaherty led Grossmann through an arch on the side of the basilica, past another set of Swiss Guards, and down a winding path to a garden adorned with statues of saints. O'Flaherty sat down on a stone bench, patted the seat next to him, and said, "What's on your mind, me boy?"

Grossmann collected his thoughts and began, "We were shot down north of Rome, and I lost the rest of my crew when I bailed out. I don't know what happened to 'em—maybe they've already made it to Rome." Grossmann allowed his jaw to twitch—a manly display of concern for his fellow airmen. "Anyway, I'm trying to work my way back to Allied lines. I was hoping to see if someone here could help." No pleas, no desperation—just bluff determination to get back in the fight—was the course that Grossmann had decided on.

"Son, there was a time when we helped in any manner possible, but his Holiness is coming under pressure from the least of the holy—"

"So you can't help me?" Grossmann interrupted.

"Not at all. What I was saying, me boy, is that we have to do this without the Pope knowing about it, God bless his soul. That's all." O'Flaherty had a twinkle in his eye. "Are you saying now that you don't want to stay until your forces liberate Rome?"

"Oh, no, Father. It's my duty to make it back." Grossmann made eye contact with O'Flaherty. "I couldn't live with myself if I stayed here while my friends are still flying missions."

"I understand, my son. I hear that occasionally from your countrymen, but I don't recommend it. I can put you up on papal property—in my apartment in the German college, for example." He smiled at Grossmann's raised eyebrow. "You'd be surprised to find where the allies of goodness and light can be found. Anyway, I can keep you here in Rome, possibly on a papal property or most likely in the city with like-minded friends."

"I appreciate the offer, Father. It is 'Father,' isn't it?"

"I answer to Hugh, Father, or Monsignor. Sometimes 'hey, you' to Americans." O'Flaherty said with a smile.

Grossmann returned the smile. It was difficult not to like O'Flaherty. His energy and enthusiasm for life radiated from him like a light. "I appreciate the offer, Monsignor, but I want to get back. I don't do any good taking up someone's food and space here in Rome."

"I respect that, me boy, but I'd advise you to reconsider. There's only a million Germans between here and where you want to go, and you're bound to be caught up in the fighting. Everyone believes the Allies will be here soon. I'd wait."

"Sir, in my opinion, and I'm just a flyboy, the Allies aren't going to be here anytime soon. Maybe summer. Do you ever help people like me get back to our lines, or do you know anyone who can?"

"Do you really believe that it'll be summer before Rome is liberated?"

"Yes, sir, I do. But again, I'm just a lieutenant. What do I know?" Grossmann shrugged. Actually, he believed that the Allies were undermanned and overmatched for the two-pronged strategy that they were taking. It'd be awhile before the first Allied tank rumbled past the Coliseum.

O'Flaherty looked troubled for a moment, and he said, "That'll ruin the golf season for another year. Never worry, me boy, even though it'll take some time, we'll figure a way south for you. Now tell me, do you play golf?"

1945 Hours
Gildardino Farm, Italy

"Ma'am, that was the best dinner that I've had since leaving Texas," said Private Kulis. Although he thought that after virtually every meal that didn't come from a can, it was a sincere sentiment. The soldiers had had the opportunity to eat plenty of Italian cuisine since arriving on its shore the previous September, but Italian food is regional. The area surrounding Naples was famous for seafood and pizza, neither of which had made much of an impact before the war on the life of the young rifleman from Rosebud. Equally foreign were the cream-based dishes found further north in Italy, and Kulis thought that the first course, ravioli stuffed with Scamorza cheese in a cream sauce, might in fact have been the best dish the soldier had ever had. But he wasn't sure as Luigi had fixed what he called bistecca alla fiorentina for the second course, which had melted in his mouth. Perhaps even better for Kulis than the steak and pasta, Mrs. Rinaldi—Maria's married name—had also baked nearly a dozen thin reddish brown loaves of bread with a crisp crust and she had slathered the slices in home-churned salted butter. Kulis couldn't possibly eat more, yet as he sat there feeling grotesquely full, he eyed the bread again and reached for a loaf.

Perkin watched his soldier with an amused air. The food was indeed fantastic, and he had thought the steaks were better than any that he'd ever had—even in Texas. Luigi had brought his guests over to the large open fireplace in the kitchen to explain the technique while he started an oak log fire. While Angelo had pumped the fire with a bellows until it was white-hot, Luigi explained that the steaks for bistecca alla fiorentina had to be aged properly—for at least a month—and that the fire had to be as hot as possible. "Four hundred and fifty degrees Celsius. No less."

The farmer had brushed each steak—a thick porterhouse—with a generous layer of fragrant olive oil, and then dropped a metal grate with upright legs over the fire. He flipped a small hourglass and then carefully laid the steaks on the grate. The result was an explosion of aroma that had Perkin salivating. As Private Kulis took a turn on the bellows, Maria handed her guests a glass of a full-bodied homemade wine that she called a *Montepulciano d'Abruzzo*. "It's a local wine with enough body to complement the beef. The grape is grown in these mountains."

When the hourglass emptied—Perkin estimated five or six minutes had passed—Luigi flipped the steaks and seasoned them with a coarse salt and white pepper. A bead of sweat had broken out across his forehead from the heat of the fire, and when he was done turning the steaks, he turned the hourglass as well. Another five or six minutes and the steaks were done and off the grill. Luigi poured a generous helping of the olive oil over the steaks and proclaimed, "This is the most famous steak in the world."

Perkin resolved to remember the process to tell Sam— he and Lieutenant Hardy were on watch, and generous portions were set aside for the two officers.

The dinner was eaten by the light of lanterns and candles, and the windows were blacked out by heavy curtains. The farmhouse was built on the ruins of the ancestral

Gildardino home and was in fact less than a decade old. At Maria's urging, it had been presciently built with electricity and running water in mind, but neither connection had ever been made. Maria explained that the promise of rural electrification had been made by the fascists but never delivered, and they were told it might not happen until after the war. Luigi followed the conversation pretty well and laughed as he noted in Italian, "I didn't have electricity for the first forty years of my life, and if I have to depend on the government, it looks like I won't have electricity for the last forty years either."

"If I go back to the farm after the war, there won't be electricity waitin' for me there, neither," observed Kulis.

Shocked, Private Fratelli looked at his friend in disbelief. "You don't have electricity at your house?"

"Oh, hell no. Pardon me, Father, ma'am. Old Roosevelt's got his goddamned, uh, I mean, sorry, we have the Rural Electrification Program, but before I left, only about 2 percent of Texas farms had electricity. Hope they get it soon, 'cause since I'm livin' the sweet life now, I don't wanna go back to no lights." Kulis explained to Maria as he reached for more bread, "I ruint my eyes reading in bed by candlelight. It'd sure be nice to have light at the flip of a switch."

"What about water?" Fratelli persisted. "What'd you do for water?"

"Same as they do here," Kulis explained. "Being a city boy, you probably didn't notice, but some of the gutters on this house go underground. They lead to a cistern, and they save the water from winter and spring rains in a big tank or a cavern-like thing underground, and then they pump the water up from there. Don't save the water from summer, though, or it'll go sour on ya. We had a couple bad years during the dust bowl where we had to watch what we used—dry years, you know."

"Oh dear," said Maria. "I've seen the pictures of the dust storms. They looked terrible—a big black cloud of dust about to consume one of your frontier towns. Will you really go back to that after the war?"

"No, ma'am. I doubt it, but to be honest, we never had it as bad as the Okies or them in Panhandle. Those to the north of us, I mean. No, ma'am, I think I'll keep soldierin' after the war."

Before Maria could say anything—she was still thinking about the dust bowl—Fratelli burst out, "What? You wanna stay a soldier? Are you crazy?"

Perkin intervened, "Why not, Vince? He's a great soldier. So are you. Both of you will be able to go to college with this new GI Bill that's being proposed. Go to school, get a degree, come back into the army as an officer. Why not?"

Fratelli laughed, "Why on earth would I want to be an officer, sir? I won't get to school again either—I'll go home and work with my pop in the shipyard. That's all I think about. And no, Father, I won't go into the priesthood, either."

Father Riley, who had obviously been about to propose that very course of action, instead asked, "Why not?"

"I had this talk with my mother and Father Bill a long time ago back in Jersey. I love the Church, but I love girls too. I don't wanna be a priest."

"Well, that is a hurdle to be sure. But the rewards are great, my son." He saw a lost cause in Fratelli, and turned to the other young man in the room. "How about you, Angelo?"

Angelo, who was between the ages of Kulis and Fratelli, smiled shyly and said, "I'm with Vincent, Father."

Before Father Riley could respond, Gemma, the older of the two girls, exclaimed, "I'll join, Father!" Then her sister, Lucia, jumped in, "I want to be a priest too!"

As Father Riley took a deep breath to explain the nuances of Catholic ordination, he was interrupted by Scipio's barking. The door opened, and a frigid blast of air and snow chilled the room almost instantly as Sam and Lieutenant Hardy hurried inside. Ice had formed on the eyebrows and eyelashes of both men, and they headed immediately to the large blazing fire in the kitchen to thaw out.

"There's no need to relieve us, Perk." Sam said, his teeth chattering. "No one's coming up the mountain in this."

Perkin opened the door and looked out into the darkness. It was unlike anything he'd seen before. In the dim light of the lantern he carried, he saw the wind blow the snow across the farmyard horizontally, and several tall Cypress trees were whipping wildly back and forth. Drifts were already building on the side of the house, and as Perkin stepped outside for a closer examination, he shivered violently. It was bitterly cold. He stepped back inside immediately, sat down at the table, and poured himself a glass of wine and lifted it to his hosts.

"Thank you, Maria, and thank you, Luigi, for such wonderful generosity and the best meal I can remember. Best of all . . . I don't know how you arranged it, but I've never seen a blizzard before. So if the war ends tomorrow, I can go home a happy man."

Chapter Ten

January 4, 1944
0600 Hours
Gildardino Farm, Italy

Perkin and Sam walked out of the Gildardino house at dawn and looked at the sparkling white landscape with wonder. The storm had left over a foot of snow, and the wind had built large drifts on the sides of the buildings. The sky was still gray and ominous, and Perkin had no way of knowing whether the current calm would last or whether it was a mere interlude between storms.

"This is the most snow I've ever seen," Sam said.

"I think so too. Wish we could stay a little while and try out skiing. Looks like fun."

"I've never skied, but I know it's a damn sight more fun than what we're headed for," Sam observed dryly.

Perkin nodded but said nothing. They were heading back to the division this day, and if they left now, they might be back by noon. The nearly idyllic mission was over, and the war would soon be a reality again. Even Perkin, who enjoyed soldiering, was depressed at the thought.

As if he were reading his cousin's mind, Sam said with a touch of humor in his voice, "Maybe we got snowed in. They'll never miss us for another day or two."

"No. We got to be going." Perkin had not heard the teasing tone and had made a firm decision.

More than anything else that had happened during the war, Perkin's delivery of his decision crystallized a growing understanding that Sam had of his cousin. Sam knew at that moment that the Perkin that he'd known all his life had changed. The old Perkin would have skipped school to go fishing or missed a college final to talk to a pretty girl—although he would have happily accepted whatever consequences might have come his way. *Not that there were many,* thought Sam. The old happy-go-lucky Perkin always took the risk. Always chose fun. And almost never paid the price. The old Perkin would have never rushed back into harm's way because of duty, because he didn't understand what duty truly was.

"Copy that. When do you want to pull out?"

"As soon as we've had breakfast, we'll start the hike down."

0715 Hours
Gildardino Farm, Italy

They stood at the end of the Gildardino drive where the road began its precipitous drop down the mountainside. They had already said good-bye to the family, and it was with genuine regret that they were leaving the warmth and hospitality of Maria and Luigi.

The youngest soldiers, Kulis and Fratelli, had convinced the officers that it was in everyone's best interests for them to sled down the hill. Kulis had sealed the deal with the argument, "We get the jeeps brushed off and the weapons loaded. By the time you come down, we'll be ready to leave."

Angelo had assured Perkin that the extra snow would in fact slow the sleds down, and that they would not be descending at anywhere near the speed of the day before. As he watched the three young men push off down the road, with rifles and packs on the backs of the soldiers and Scipio on Angelo's back again, Perkin was not sure that Angelo had been entirely truthful. There was a solid layer of ice on the road under the snow, and the sledders departed with a delighted scream and at a worrisome speed.

"Well, Pat," Perkin said as he offered his hand. "This is it. We'll look you up when we take Rome."

"Any idea when that'll be?" asked the priest.

"Well, General Clark said he meant to take it by Christmas. Looks like he forgot to mention it was Christmas of '44. You be careful now."

"I will, and same to you. I plan to be cautious, and like these boys' journey coming down," he nodded to the Australian officers, "it may be a few weeks until I get back. Actually, maybe a little longer than that. Even Angelo says it's not safe to pass through the mountains now—not until there's a thaw. A terrible hardship to be stranded in all this beauty to be sure." Father Riley smiled and offered his hand.

Perkin smiled in return, shook Patrick's hand, and began walking down the road, followed by the Australian officers. Sam stayed behind and offered his hand as well. "Good to finally meet you, Father. Take care."

"You too, Sam," and in a lower voice, Riley said, "Watch over Perkin. Keep him out of trouble."

Sam laughed, a deep belly laugh. "That seems to be my life mission. So long, Pat. See ya on the other side."

Perkin seemed to be deep in thought, so Sam walked alongside the two Australians and struck up a conversation with Lieutenant Hardy. It was inconsequential conversation—the usual give and take about the respective soldiering abilities of their two armies, and discussion of sports, weapons, women, and weather.

By the time they were near the base of the mountain and the jeeps, Sam's well of conversation had nearly run dry, but he remembered a comment that Perkin had made once and decided to run it by the Australians. "I've heard that there's a test of whether or not a country will be a good ally to the United States. Wanna take it?" Sam asked.

"Sure, mate. There's no better ally than an Australian."

"The first requirement is English as a first language. I reckon that rules out France and Mexico, and most of the northern states. How's Australia fare?"

"A bloody good song, mate," Hardy laughed at Sam's inadvertent pun. "Our English is so extraordinary, I understand his majesty has a bloke from down under teaching him how to speak, so I think we got that one covered."

"Excellent," Sam said. "It gets harder as we go. Here's the second requirement: the national drink has to be beer."

"You're joking, mate. Australia is home to the best beer in the world. We'd rather drink beer than shag, most of us would. If we can do both at the same time, it's nearly paradise."

Sam laughed, "I think you got your priorities backward, partner, but I think you definitely get another up-check."

"Well, I don't want there to be any question, Sam. Our beer's the best."

Sam raised a questioning eyebrow, "So you say . . . but we got a sayin' back home: you can put your boots in the oven, but that don't make 'em biscuits. The beer from

Shiner is world-famous—at least in Texas. But, I'll grant you this one too."

Although slightly upset that he didn't get Sam's acknowledgment of the superiority of Australian beer, Lieutenant Hardy was ready for the next question. "Give it to me, mate."

"OK, the third requirement is that you have to play a contact sport. Soccer don't count."

Hardy clenched his fist in mock triumph, "That proves we're worthy allies. Our national sport's rugby."

Sam was about to ask Hardy if he'd ever seen a flying wing when Lieutenant Van Deventer croaked out, "Aussie rules."

Sam and Hardy stopped dead in their tracks. Perkin, who had been deep in thought, also stopped and turned around.

"What's that, Jim?" Perkin asked softly.

"Aussie rules. National sport. Not rugby." The lieutenant's eyes focused sharply for a moment, then they started shifting back and forth again between the faces.

"Crikey, mate! Where'd that come from?" said Hardy.

It was then that they heard the first shouts.

0745 Hours
Gildardino Mountain, Italy

The first indication of trouble that they had was when Scipio came running past them without a glance and with his tail between his legs. Angelo wasn't far behind. He stopped briefly, his chest heaving, and gasped out, "Germans coming. Halftrack from there." He pointed northwest. "Kulis said to warn you. Not sure if they saw us."

There was a flurry of conversation as Sam and Lieutenant Hardy asked Angelo a sharp series of questions—numbers? Unknown. Distance? Less than a kilometer. More than one vehicle? No, but it looked it was pulling a haywagon.

Sam looked at Perkin and said, "They're coming to requisition fodder. The barn is filled with hay." It made sense. Despite the great sweeping mechanized campaigns of the *Wehrmacht*, the German Army was no more than a third motorized. Troops had occupied Poland and France the way that soldiers had done for centuries—by marching in on foot. Workhorses still moved the lighter artillery pieces and ammunition wagons, and like countless armies before them, the Germans had a difficult time feeding their animals so far from home.

Perkin nodded, "Shit. Angelo, get back up there. Tell your mama to clean all the dishes from us, but leave out those of your family. You saw us for the first time this morning when we approached the house looking to buy hams from you if they ask. You think we rode out the storm in the barn last night. We're going to try to lead them off. Good luck."

As Angelo resumed his run up the mountain, Perkin and the rest of the party began a dangerous sliding run down the mountain. Perkin's mind was racing as he led the group—he was debating between running away or engaging the German halftrack. If the Germans hadn't seen them, an ambush might be easy enough to pull off, but that would leave the German wreckage and bodies at the base of the Gildardino driveway. On the other hand, if they ran away, the Germans would see the tracks of the jeeps and follow the footprints up the mountain to the house. A resumption of the snow crystallized Perkin's decision.

"Start the jeeps! Start the jeeps!" Perkin shouted, but they were already coming up the mountain along the tree-lined road. A grim-faced Private Fratelli was in the lead jeep, followed by Private Kulis, who had a huge grin on his scarred face. "Sam with me. The others in Fratelli's jeep!"

Perkin saw that Kulis had already reclaimed the weapons they had left behind—a stroke of luck. A necessary stroke of luck if his plan was to work. Perkin tossed his Thompson to Lieutenant Hardy, who caught the weapon with one hand even while he pulled Lieutenant Van Deventer up from a fall on the ice with his other.

"We're gonna draw them off toward Canadian lines. When we round a bend, we're gonna whip around and ambush 'em and Bear's gonna take out their engine with that Mauser. Fratelli, take the lead. If something happens to us, keep moving to the Canucks."

Fratelli nodded and spun the jeep around. Perkin ran past Fratelli and looked back to see the two Australian officers jump into the back. Hardy was already exchanging the Thompson for Fratelli's Browning Automatic Rifle. Van Deventer hesitated, then picked the Thompson. He looked at Hardy, and then slid the bolt back to check if the weapon was charged.

Sam followed behind Perkin and moved to sit in the passenger seat of Kulis's jeep. Kulis had the Mauser lying across his lap, and Sam had to pick it up before he sat down. It was an unwieldy weapon—easily five feet long and unbelievably heavy. Sam opened the bolt—it was already loaded.

"I thought we might need this," Kulis said. "Can I shoot it?"

Ignoring the eager looked on Kulis's face, Perkin asked, "Eddie, what do we have?" Perkin could not yet see the German vehicle. The long driveway up the mountainside was flanked by trees all the way to the Gildardino farm, but at its base, the driveway came out of the trees and joined the dirt road running along the valley floor. Any minute now, the German halftrack might begin its turn onto the driveway.

"An old Model 11 *Zugkraftwagen*. The three-ton model. Looks like it's got a flatbed on it instead of a rear compartment, and it's pulling a flatbed wagon. I didn't see any soldiers, but they could be sitting behind the cab."

The halftrack that Kulis described was well known to the soldiers. It was one of the mechanical workhorses of the German army—very versatile, and it could go almost anywhere. A capable piece of machinery that was used mostly as a prime mover for artillery, it may have an MG-34 mounted, but its weakness was lack of armor. It was a tractor, not an armored personnel carrier. The Germans were looking for an early morning theft, not an assault.

"Change of plans!" Perkin shouted to Fratelli. Kulis pulled his jeep next to Fratelli, and Perkin told them what he intended to do.

0750 Hours
Rome, Italy

Major Grossmann awakened with a start. One of the men sleeping in the room was snoring loudly in starts and stops, and Grossmann, who had slept poorly to begin with, could not ignore the sound encroaching into his dreams anymore.

He had been dreaming about Antoniette, and he found that even as he and Monsignor O'Flaherty escaped the Vatican grounds through a little used gate, he thought of her all the time in his waking hours as well. Grossmann had still not made up his mind whether he was being played or not, and he was even less sure whether he minded if he was. Succumbing to his feelings about Antoniette

Bernardi reminded him of an old Irish Republican saying, "Once in, never out."

Grossmann raised himself onto an elbow and looked around the room. He was in a very large, tastefully decorated apartment in an expensive neighborhood. In the large living room were three mattresses on the floor, each with a sleeping Allied serviceman. The apartment's three bedrooms also housed another soldier each.

He had met them all the night before when O'Flaherty brought him to the apartment, which he was told would be his new home for at least a week, maybe more. There were two British soldiers, two American soldiers, and an Australian soldier. Grossmann had been nervous when he found out that he was to be stashed with other escapees, and he was profoundly grateful that there were no airmen in the apartment as he didn't relish a conversation about airframes or fellow aviators.

If there had been airmen in the group, he decided he would be taciturn and keep to himself, which meant that most of the information that he gathered would be passively collected. Since he had no such worries, he could be as gregarious as he wanted, and he thought that he'd get more information that way.

O'Flaherty had taken him through a winding set of roads, and he stopped at a small market on the way and picked up a bag of groceries, which were waiting for him. The grocer, he had explained, was a friend of the Church and was able to get the bread, meat, and wine from the black market without the limitations of ration cards.

The doorman at the apartment building smiled when he saw Monsignor O'Flaherty, and Grossmann was waved through without questions. They walked up a flight of stairs and down a dark hall before stopping at an ornately carved door, and O'Flaherty tapped "Shave and a Haircut" on the door and waited. A few seconds later, he was rewarded with "Two Bits"—or as Grossmann later mused, perhaps it was "Five Bob" as the person who unlocked the door was one of the British residents. O'Flaherty had a grin on his face as he walked in and said hello to the collection of men who obviously revered him.

"Hello, me boys! Allow me to introduce Lieutenant Douglas Peabody of the American air service. He comes from California, has an Italian mother, and speaks the local language almost as well as I do. The only fault that I've found with him is that he doesn't play golf, which is a malady that he shares with you all. Pray make him welcome." O'Flaherty then turned to Grossmann and said, "Doug, this will be your home until we can move you south. I wish it weren't so, but it may be a matter of weeks, not days, before we get you out of here safely. The boys will explain the rules to you. I have to be going, so good luck to you now!" He nodded to the rest of the men, and left.

As Grossmann lay on the mattress wondering if he would go stir crazy over the course of a week, the Australian officer across the room stirred, yawned, and sat up on his mattress. Grossmann caught his eye and pointed to the snoring American soldier, and made a slashing motion across his throat with his index finger.

The Australian grinned at Grossmann, stretched, and then stiffly walked over and knelt next to the sleeping man. He studied him for a second, walked back to his own mattress, and pulled a feather from his pillow. He knelt next to the sleeping man again and tickled his nose with the feather. The soldier slapped away at the imagined bug in his sleep and then rubbed his nose. The Australian did that several more times, and each time the sleeping man swatted back with more agitation. Unable to awaken the American with a tickled nose, the Australian dropped the small feather into the man's open mouth and then scampered back to his bed on the floor.

A scant second later, the sleeping man choked, gagged, and suddenly sat bolt upright as he tried to spit out the feather from the back of his throat. Both Grossmann and the Australian looked over in mock surprise, and Grossmann asked innocently, "Are you OK, Mac?"

The soldier didn't answer, just held up a hand to Grossmann like a base runner would to signal time to an umpire, and continued to gag loudly. The noise brought one of the British officers in from a bedroom, "What the bloody hell's wrong with him?" he asked.

With a wicked grin, the Australian replied, "I reckon one of those bloody black spiders hopped into Bobby's craw while he was sleeping. I've seen it happen before in the Outback. Sometimes a bloke gets bit on the tongue and they have to cut it out or it'll swell up so big he can't breathe."

Bobby looked at the Australian with concern, gagged again, and thrust his fingers to the back of his throat. After several gags and a dry heave, his fingers emerged holding the feather. It took Bobby nearly a minute to collect himself and to wipe his eyes dry, "Goddamn," he croaked. "I swallowed a feather."

Grossmann nodded sagely and said, "I've seen that happen too. Big snorers like yourself often suck in bugs and pillow feathers and such."

Bobby looked at him scornfully, "I don't snore."

The Australian shrugged and said, "Well I've heard worse, mate, but I reckon they could hear you next door at Gestapo headquarters."

"What's that?" Grossmann asked. The British officer had turned about and returned to bed.

"Didn't Hugh tell you?" the Australian asked with a wide grin. "We're next to the bloody Gestapo headquarters. He said they'd never reckon to look for us here."

"By God," Grossmann laughed and shook his head. "I bet they wouldn't."

0755 Hours
Gildardino Mountain, Italy

One of the jeeps was driven into the trees, but one was quickly parked across the Gildardino road. Sam unfolded the legs to the Mauser's tripod, propped the rifle on the hood of the jeep, laid out spare ammunition next to him, and waited.

Perkin put Fratelli on one side of the road, and the rest of the party on the other. He was careful to make sure that they wouldn't be in a crossfire, but he wanted to make sure no German soldiers escaped on the other side.

The halftrack came into view, and once the driver had the track aligned, he gunned the vehicle's engine to approach the slope of the mountain with some speed. The driver was terrified of going up the large mountain, even in as sure-footed a vehicle as the halftrack. So he paid less attention to his surroundings as he might have while he lined up with what he thought was the centerline of the road. It was as he was accelerating up the slope that he noticed the footprints and the tire tracks leading up the mountain driveway. It caused enough alarm for him to let off the accelerator slightly, and when he saw the American jeep blocking the road only fifty meters ahead of him, a jolt of adrenaline went through his body and he thought briefly that he would ram his way through the jeep. But as his foot began to push down again on the accelerator, what was behind the jeep truly caught his attention. It was the largest man he'd ever seen, holding the largest rifle possibly ever made—and it was pointing right at him. He slammed on the brakes, slid to a halt in the snow, and raised his quaking hands.

The soldier next to him did likewise—neither considered themselves combat soldiers—and the three soldiers huddling behind the cab did the same when the five men with weapons came running out of the woods.

Perkin walked around their prisoners, identified a corporal, and asked in English, "What are you doing here?"

The corporal was mute, but obviously terrified. Unlike the soldier in Ortona who had insulted Perkin only a few days before, this soldier no longer had any fight left in him. Perkin was about to ask the question in German when the driver—an older private—said in passable English, "We were sent to buy hay from the farm. He doesn't speak English."

"Where'd you learn to speak it?" Perkin asked.

"From English fishermen in the North Sea. We traded a lot before the war. We all worked together, except for him." The driver indicated the corporal.

"Where are you from?" Private Kulis asked. He disarmed the Germans of their bolt-action rifles and razor-sharp fisherman's knives, and then handed out cigarettes to the prisoners as Fratelli began to back the halftrack and the wagon down the hill.

"Norderney."

"Frisian Islands?"

"Yes!" Surprised, the German soldier asked, "You know of it?"

"Yeah, it was in a book I read. Have you read—"

"*The Riddle of the Sands*? No, but everyone knows of it. Did you know the English hanged the author?"

Perkin grabbed a downed tree limb and began to brush away their tracks. It wouldn't fool anyone who passed by in the next hour or so, but the falling snow and the brisk wind would level things out soon enough.

The German soldiers were set on the back of the halftrack, and Fratelli sat against the back of the cab and covered the Germans with his BAR—but there was little need. The soldiers seemed quite content to become prisoners and live to fish another day. Perkin placed one jeep in front and another jeep behind the halftrack and wagon, and they worked their way back to the Canadian lines.

When they were within a half mile of the Canadian command post, Perkin stopped the convoy and disembarked his prisoners. They looked nervously at one another and at Private Fratelli, who had glared at them rather than discuss literature. But they needn't have worried about being executed by their captors. Perkin sent Private Kulis ahead in a jeep with the Australian officers to warn the Canadians of their arrival and then cleared everyone away from the halftrack.

Sam walked fifty paces ahead of the halftrack, turned, and raised the Mauser to his shoulder. He pulled the rifle in as tightly as he could to his shoulder, braced himself, and fired an armor-piercing 13.2 mm round into the engine block of the halftrack. It was the hardest kick he'd ever felt from a weapon, and he fell in love with it immediately. The heavy projectile ripped through the thin metal body protecting the engine, went straight through the radiator, and buried itself deeply in the engine block. Through sheer kinetic force, the round tore through the running engine and ripped through two cylinders before coming to a rest.

Perkin had expected an explosion and was disappointed. However, while the crack of the rifle was still echoing through the mountains, the engine began to whine loudly and smoke began to pour out from under the vehicle's hood. Still the engine wouldn't die, and the whole halftrack began to shake as the engine became unbalanced. After an agonizing ten seconds where Sam began to reload the Mauser, the engine finally died with a terrible screech.

To Perkin, it looked just like he planned it. The German soldiers had missed their turnoff in the early morning light, got too close to the Canadian lines, and were captured because of the mistake. He hoped that would lessen the attention on the Gildardino family. The tracks in the snow could be problematic, but with the snow resuming and a strong wind, he hoped that the weather would soon erase the tracks.

While Sam decided against a second shot, replacing the Mauser with his M1941, Private Fratelli put the prisoners in column formation and ordered them to march with their hands on their heads. Ten minutes later, they were through the Canadian lines and enjoying a cup of coffee.

1600 Hours
1st Battalion Headquarters, Near Alife, Italy

The smile on Bill Spaulding's face told the story. The battalion had been off the line since they had departed over a week ago, and the division was getting some rest, hot food, and the chance to relax. Perkin hadn't seen Major Spaulding so at ease since before the start of the San Pietro battle nearly two months before.

"I can't tell you how glad I am to see you both. Hard to imagine—this is probably the longest we've gone without seeing each other for two years. I ain't sayin' I missed you boys, but welcome back."

Sam smiled in return and said, "Good to see you too, Bill. I'm going to check in with the company—Perkin can give you a briefing on what we've been up to this past week. If Ebbins doesn't make me the duty officer as soon as I check in, I'll be back around to balance out Perkin's report with the truth. See ya, Perk." He shook Bill's hand again, saluted, and walked out of the large tent into the cold.

"Where's Waller? Did you drop him off at regiment?" asked Spaulding.

"No, Waller got wounded by a grenade. It was the damnedest thing, really. We were in a house in Ortona that was booby-trapped. Sam and I had tripped one grenade in the room we were in, and Waller and Fratelli had tripped a grenade from the door they were opening. As near as we can tell, he caught a fragment from our grenade while he was runnin' from their grenade. He had the worst bad luck with them Brits—he should stay with us forever—that little fragment cut right through his boot and severed his big toe without touching any of the others, and then his blind date on New Year's Eve turned out to be his cousin, and then his foot got infected."

Spaulding soaked in all the information and asked, "His blind date was his cousin?"

"Yeah, and she left with another man—after beating the snot out of him . . . the new guy, not Waller."

"I swear. Don't that beat all?" Spaulding grinned, knowing that the story would all come out eventually. He pointed to a cot in the large tent serving as his headquarters. "That's yours, by the way."

"I get to sleep in the big tent? This may be the happiest day of my life. So, I met a girl, Sam rode a horse and got a new rifle, we saved two Australian officers, captured five prisoners, provided cover for some engineers that blew up a house, saw a flying dragon, dropped off a priest, confiscated a 13mm antitank rifle, and learned about mouseholing. Waller lost a toe, and Kulis and Fratelli are forever unwelcome in the village of . . . of . . . uh, shoot, I can't remember its name." Perkin stretched out on the cot and grinned up at Spaulding with his hands behind his head. "That's my report, any questions?"

"Oh . . . so an uneventful holiday? That's what you're saying?" Spaulding spit into a battered German helmet—a gift from Perkin—that he used as a spittoon.

"Yeah, pretty much. It was about par for the course. Except for the flying dragon—that was unexpected."

"I imagine it was. While I'd like to hear the flying dragon and . . . what was the other thing, mouseholing? Get to the important stuff—tell me about the girl."

"Her name's Helen. She's an English nurse—she's got kind of a naughty Hedy Lamarr look about her. It's a really great look . . ."

"Hedy Lamarr's not naughty enough for you?"

"Hmmm, let me think. No, not really. So, great looks, very smart, very sweet, English accent—we can't all be from Texas you know—likes jazz. What more can a guy ask for? I don't know when I'll get to see her again, but I hope to someday. So . . . what's happening here?"

Spaulding shrugged, "We're still in limbo. The division doesn't have orders, and we don't know what's coming next."

"Where's the smart money?"

"An army level attack across the Gustav Line, with us in reserve. That's where I'd bet my insufficient paycheck."

Perkin yawned—it had been an exhausting holiday. "So no talk about us taking the lead across the line?"

"Nope. None at all."

1800 Hours
Rome, Italy

The *persiane* shutters had been closed, the heavy blackout curtains had been tightly drawn, and the apartment settled in for the night.

Grossmann learned that this was the routine for the OTL Club, as the men called themselves—OTL standing for "on the lam." There was a mix of officers and enlisted men with the Australian being the senior man as a captain. When Grossmann asked why he wasn't in one of the bedrooms, he was told that they rotated in a two-day rotation and he would have a bedroom tomorrow. On the Australian's orders, they were on a first name basis, the chores were also rotated, and everyone took part. It was a very egalitarian arrangement, one that Grossmann was more open to as an American than he was as a *Wehrmacht* officer.

This had been Grossmann's night to cook, and he made a tolerable veal picatta out of a meat that he strongly suspected was horse. Even pounded thin, the mysterious meat was tough, but the dish was well received by the rest of the OTL Club—even if the one lemon Grossmann had to work with was desiccated and there were no capers in the apartment. Grossmann learned that on occasion, some of the women in O'Flaherty's organization would bring by groceries and stay to cook for the men, but the fare was otherwise generally unimpressive.

The day was passed in playing cards or chess, and Grossmann learned more about his apartment mates. Far and away, he liked the Australian captain the most. His name was Tim Mullen, and he was a former police officer who escaped from a prison camp in northern Italy after the Italian armistice. Over a game of chess, he told Grossmann a harrowing tale of escaping with other Australians and attempting to board a moving German supply train, only to lose his grip and nearly fall under the train's wheels. As he told it, he rolled down the grade, was knocked unconscious, and only awoke the next day when a farmer found him.

"I stayed with that farmer and his family for nearly a month before I could move again, and I've been making my way south ever since. I'm like you, Doug, I don't want to wait until next summer. I want to get down to our own lines and get back in the fight."

"I can't stay here another six or nine months without going crazy," Grossmann said truthfully. "I'm not sure that I can handle another day or two without getting into the fresh air. I might have to leave on my own if it comes to that."

"Don't worry, mate. Trust me, you can count on Hugh. He's never let anyone down. Besides, as I tell myself every night, I can handle Bobby's snoring a lot easier than being Jerry's prisoner—"

Bobby interjected from across the room, "I don't snore."

Mullen smiled and continued, "Hugh knows about the dangers of being cooped up, and he takes unnecessary risks to help us all. I wouldn't be surprised if once he gets you a set of proper papers he takes you for a stroll or two or even out to the symphony with him."

"What?" Grossmann was incredulous.

"Yeah, mate, he takes risks that make my hair stand up. I understand that he's taken one of the boys with him before to a concert or something. I can't even fathom why he'd take such a chance."

Grossmann took out a cigarette, tore it in two, and gave the other half to Mullen. As he lit the cigarettes, he asked, "How many boys is the Monsignor hiding, anyway? I'm going to get your queen in a moment, and there's not a damn thing you can do about it."

Mullen shrugged, "We'll see about that. I don't know for sure how many Hugh's hiding, but he has an associate, a Pom named May, who reckons that there's at least three thousand stashed in and around Rome, although mostly outside the city."

"An English priest?" Grossmann asked curiously.

"He ain't a priest, mate. The British maintain a diplomatic mission to the Holy See, and May's on the ambassador's staff. They say he's the ambassador's servant, but I reckon he's British intelligence—"

"You don't know that," Bobby interrupted again.

"No, you're right, Bobby. But I've been around enough Special Branch boys in my life to know one when I see it. Maybe he's just a butler as they say, but he's certainly well connected. Anyway, as I was about to say to Doug, May's a scrounger—he works the black market for everything we need, and he's got some dago on his payroll who'll make perfect identity papers for you. He's also a money man for Hugh."

"What do you mean, a money man?"

"The story goes that Hugh approached the Pommie ambassador, High Lord King Arsewell or whatever his bloody name is, and says, 'I got a church full of your blokes, can you help me out, mate?' And the ambassador refuses to help. Says he can't compromise his majesty's government or jeopardize his position with the Pope. Hugh can't believe what he's hearing and storms out of the ambassador's residence. A little while later, May pulls Hugh aside and hands him about twenty thousand pounds worth of lire. Says it's just a down payment from his majesty. And there's been a lot more since then from the Poms and from Uncle Sam as well. Anyway, May's kind of become Hugh's right-hand man."

"No shit. Wow. That's a lot of money." Grossmann was impressed.

"It is to you and me, mate. But it doesn't go far in feeding all these mouths in and about Rome." Mullen stared at the chessboard, and he shook his head and grinned, "You've right buggered my queen, mate."

"It's what I do in life," Grossmann grinned back. "I cook gourmet food out of horsemeat and bugger queens."

"Not a bad living. What'd you do before the war?" Mullen asked.

"There was a life before the war? I sold insurance, used cars, medical equipment . . . whatever I could. Life was hard. Maybe I'll stay in and fly after the war. I don't want to go back to sales."

"Wife? Kids?"

"Nope. You?" Grossmann wanted to move the discussion away from him. Policemen were experts at spotting liars, and he didn't want to undergo any unnecessary scrutiny.

"Yeah. I've been married for ten years and have a little boy waiting for me in Brisbane. He's seven now, and I haven't seen him for four years."

"That's damn hard luck." Grossmann glanced casually at his new friend's face to see if he teared up at the mention of his family, but he hadn't. Grossmann was glad—he didn't want to be cooped up with a bunch of weepy men.

"It is, mate. But I'll make it home. Speaking of bad luck, I'm about to do to your king what you did to my queen. Checkmate."

Chapter Eleven

January 15, 1944
0600 Hours
Victory Road, North of San Pietro, Italy

Sam shivered in the gray morning light as he jogged over to the heavy truck. It seemed that he could never get quite warm enough these days, but he thought that maybe it was the mission that had him shivering. He dismissed the notion that he was scared, and he tried to focus his thoughts.

After he had returned to the company nearly two weeks before, he had hoped that the division would remain in bivouac indefinitely. They had been working hard to integrate the new soldiers into the company, and the new officer. Second Lieutenant Frank McCarter had been transferred to a company in the 142nd that had lost all of its platoon leaders, and the 142nd didn't have enough officers with combat experience to balance out its companies. McCarter's replacement was another second lieutenant named Albert Norstad—a recent graduate of the army's infantry school.

The new soldiers were flowing into the division, but not at a rate fast enough to satisfy the needs. Although the division was not in combat, the recent battle for San Pietro had been costly, and training, disease, and ill fortune also took a constant toll on the rolls of the division. The division was only up to 70 percent strength, and about a third of those soldiers were replacements since San Pietro. Sam had heard it from another Aggie officer that the division's makeup was now less than 40 percent Texan. That would surely drop even more in the months to come, thought Sam, although the Texas flavor of the outfit remained. Some companies gave their new soldiers certificates to mail home announcing them to the world as an "Honorary Texan" for their service in the Texas Gun Club.

Captain Ronald Ebbins, the new Able Company commander, had neither the time nor inclination for morale-building frivolities. As Ebbins apparently saw it, unit cohesion achieved through punishment, screams, and coercion was the most effective—and like the approach of thousands of like-minded officers before him, that approach fell spectacularly short of the mark. As Lieutenant B. G. E. Beams dryly remarked to Sam, "When I was a cop, I noticed there are two kinds of bosses in the world—same in the police force as the army—you got shit screens and shit accelerators. And Old Ebbins is the fastest, most determined accelerant of shit I've witnessed across two careers. I wish I had one of my old phrenology textbooks, I'd study the shape of his skull to find out what's wrong with the son-of-a-bitch. B. G. E. stands for Bullshit Gets on Everything."

Among the many complaints that Sam received from the junior officers, the NCOs, and more than a few privates was that Ebbins punished at the drop of a hat. KP was his favorite punishment, and Private Froman claimed to have set the record for the most trivial infraction of the law as Ebbins saw it: Froman's fingernails were deemed dirty in a company-wide inspection that Ebbins held. The young butcher's son from Chicago complained vociferously to Sam and then made a valid argument: "So what if my hands are filthy, we're still working, you know, and so he sends me to the kitchen to cook food. That's army logic for you."

Sam gave Ebbins a great deal of thought upon his return. He'd had a long complicated history with Ebbins going back to South Texas, and, of course, there was the letter from Margaret detailing her encounter with Ebbins's father. Sam felt that Ebbins was clearly out of his league in command. He was abusive to be sure, but worse than that, he was incompetent and quite possibly a coward.

Sam could deal with bullies, and he was a good enough officer that he could mitigate the worst of Ebbins's impulses through redirection, or by taking the heat for a perceived infraction himself. It was just more army bullshit to Sam, and he could deal with it. But he had a hard time making allowances for Ebbins's shortcomings as a soldier that emerged during the training evolutions of the past couple weeks.

Ebbins had difficulty reading a tactical map and was extremely slow in preparing fire-support missions. Sam was very concerned that under pressure Ebbins might call fires onto his own position or, worse, those of his forward troops. Ebbins's approach in the training exercises had been to lead from the rear—a mixed blessing as the few times he ventured forward, he gave contradictory and confusing orders. As Sam had learned on Christmas Day, Ebbins lacked both the situational awareness and the imagination to successfully direct a fight from the rear, so by definition, any orders he issued would be ill informed and ill conceived.

There were other things that Sam noted: Ebbins hadn't fired his carbine since arriving in Italy. A small thing, perhaps—company commanders weren't expected to take the point—but one that mattered to Sam. He had always held Bill Spaulding up as the model company commander. Spaulding had fired his weapon in combat, and the battalion commander had recently joined Sam on the rifle range to hone his skills.

Another little thing nagged at Sam. Ebbins liked his comfort and had not hardened himself for the physical demands of the job. Whenever possible, he chose not to share in the hardships of his soldiers. He had soldiers from the headquarters platoon dig his foxholes, and they requisitioned a kerosene heater and a cot for his tent—although the company's soldiers were sleeping on the frozen ground. While he ordered company physical training—calisthenics and runs—he never led them himself.

Worst of all of Sam's suspicions was the nagging doubt that Ebbins was a coward. Everyone was afraid in combat. Sam knew that. He certainly was. Sometimes more than afraid. Only "terrified" could describe the sensation he'd felt while under artillery fire on Mount San Chirico back in September. But being terrified and petrified were two different things. The army made allowances for fear. Inaction when action was called for was unacceptable. Sam would watch Ebbins closely.

As bad as it was, Sam admitted it could have been worse. Ebbins's historical antipathy toward Sam had been partially replaced by reliance on Sam's expertise. Since Christmas, the bullying seldom extended to Sam—not that he would have cared much anyway. Sam's conflict with Ebbins was one that many seconds-in-command had felt throughout the countless centuries of warfare: he despised his commander and yet felt loyalty to him as well. It was an awkward schism: the desire to lean back and criticize, the schadenfreude exultation of watching Ebbins's little failures overlaid with the knowledge that he could do better—yet knowing that to take the low road and passively undermine Ebbins's authority would also undermine his own position as an officer and hasten the disintegration of the company. Although Sam didn't put it to himself in such a manner, his relationship with Ebbins became guided by his own professionalism, character, and integrity. Sam may have disliked the army as much as he detested Captain Ebbins, but he would still strive to be the best soldier and officer possible.

How Ebbins would perform in combat was on Sam's mind. The division was pulled out of bivouac and returned to the San Pietro area. Orders for breaching the Gustav Line had not arrived, but it was now becoming a distinct possibility with every passing day, and this forward movement of the division hinted that the happy days were coming to a close. But that wouldn't happen today.

The regiment was ordered to extend Allied lines to Mount Trocchio—a great hulking hill of rock that overlooked the no-man's-land between the two armies. By taking Trocchio, the Allies would be effectively reducing no-man's-land to a mile of open, flat, shattered valley, and it would reduce the ground that that assault force would have to cover when the order came to breach the German defensive line.

The 1st Battalion of the 141st Infantry Regiment was being held in reserve. The other two rifle battalions would get the day's dirty work, then the regiment would mark the territory as its own. The 143rd Infantry Regiment would move adjacent to the 141st and a new Allied line would be drawn on the maps following such events.

Perkin had told Sam that the forward movement would be a double-edged sword. It would make staging for the ultimate assault possible, but it would also bring the division back into the range of the German guns and place them under the all-seeing eye of the artillery observers on Monte Cassino. Sam, like every other Allied soldier in Fifth Army, was certain that the Germans would use the abbey on the mountainside as an observation post—secure in the knowledge that the Americans would be loathe to shell the ancient site. Perkin's main concern was that while the movement might tidy up an unimportant bulge in their lines, it also indicated to the German commanders that the time was drawing close.

Trucks were drawn up to haul the soldiers of the battalion forward if necessary, although the informed assessment was that they would not be. This was considered an easy evolution. Shermans from the 753rd Tank Battalion would make the assault, and the riflemen of the 141st would support the tanks. The Germans had already prepared their winter line, and the German soldiers on this side of no-man's-land were mere caretakers.

Sam shivered as he jogged over to a two-and-a-half-ton truck. Much to the chagrin of the truck driver, Captain Ebbins was sitting in the relative warmth of the cab smoking cigarettes. Sam hopped onto the running board, tapped on the window, and opened the door.

"Sir, you were looking for me?"

Ebbins looked impatient even though he had sent a messenger looking for Sam only a few minutes before. "Yeah. I want you to run over to battalion and see what's going on. They're only over that little rise there." Ebbins pointed to a small hill a few hundred yards away.

Sam studied his company commander briefly. Ebbins was a handsome man with carefully cultivated movie star looks, but he had deep, dark circles under his eyes. Eyes that he would not bring to look directly at Sam—they stayed focused on the truck's door. Sam surmised correctly that Ebbins was concerned about the company going forward but he didn't want to appear anxious by going to battalion himself.

Sam nodded. This wasn't the time to tell his company commander that there was nothing to worry about, or that if there was, he should go himself. It was just better to do what Ebbins asked. "Any message for Major Spaulding?"

Ebbins hesitated before answering. "No. I just want to see how things are progressing. Don't tell Spaulding that I sent you. Don't waste time talking to your cousin, either. I need you here."

As Sam jogged the distance to the battalion command post, he laughed to himself. He was being sent over to find out how things were going, but he gathered he wasn't supposed to say why he was there. Sam laughed again as he was going strictly to pass the time with Perkin and get a cup of coffee, although he would say hey to Bill if he got the chance.

0615 Hours
1st Battalion CP, North of San Pietro, Italy

"Howdy, Bear!" Perkin's face lit up at the sight of his cousin. He and Major Spaulding were sitting next to radio operator listening to the reports come in of the battle.

"Hey! Y'all got any hot coffee?"

"K-rats café," said Spaulding, who picked up a green army thermos and tossed it to Sam. As Sam poured some into his canteen cup, Spaulding asked, "How are things with y'all, Sam?"

"You know how it is, sir. We're hangin' on by a nose hair. Our position is precarious, we might not last 'til dawn. How 'bout y'all?"

"About the same. Maybe worse." Spaulding grinned and spit into his German helmet. "Did you come over to find out if we're winning?"

"Not officially. But are we?"

"We are. Tell Ronald he can relax. The attack is progressing just as we planned—the Shermans moved up, the Germans moved out. You break it, you buy it. Looks like we own this side of the river now."

A deep rumbling explosion echoed through the valley. It was a distinctly different sound from the heavy thumps of artillery that had been heard throughout the night.

Perkin nodded, "It's ours now. I'll bet you that was the Krauts blowing the bridge to San Angelo. That's good news."

"Why's that?" asked Sam.

"It means that not only have they permanently withdrawn to the other side of the winter line, but it means that the 141st and 143rd can start withdrawing from the river as well."

"But we just got to the river," Sam protested.

"Yeah, but they can see the whole valley from the abbey, so we can't have the entire division encamped down there. We'll have to leave pockets of soldiers out there and withdraw three or four miles at least. I would think that maybe the rear elements go back as far as San Vittore. We don't have to worry about the Germans crossing in force, but we have to worry about getting the crap shelled out of us on a daily basis."

Spaulding nodded in agreement. "We don't know where we're gonna toss our bedrolls tonight, but I'm sure we'll get a turn in the rotation patrolling the valley. There's a meeting today at division that Perk and I are going to—hope it's a big picture view with an idea of what our assignment's gonna be."

Sam said, "Let me know if you can. I gotta head back before the world comes to an end. Perk? Did you ever hear anything more from the Australians?"

Perkin smiled and said, "I did. Fred came by to see me yesterday. He says they're hopping a ride with the Royal Navy to Palestine, then getting on a cargo flight with stops in Arabia and India, and then catching another ship home to Australia. He said once he gets to India, he'd see about getting reassigned to another Australian unit in the Pacific. Says he's seen all he wants to of Europe. Jim's just going home."

"Any more . . .?"

"No. He ain't said nothing except for what we heard." Perkin stopped and thought for a second. "Although the subject matter wasn't particularly profound if I remember right, I'm privileged that the only words the poor fellow's spoken in two years was to us. I don't know what happened to him on Crete, but it must have been bad."

1300 Hours
36th Division HQ, Alife, Italy

The assembled officers sat in the schoolhouse, a borrowed building, and talked among themselves expectantly. The boss, Major General Walker, was going to tell them what was next for the Gun Club. Theories varied in the nuances, but most had heard the rumors that the Texas Division was going across the river.

The officers were all battalion and regimental officers. Commanders, operations, and intelligence officers, they would be the ones to put the plan together with the Old

Man's staff. They just needed to know what the mission was.

The door to the classroom opened and a young captain strode in, propped the door open, and said in a strong voice, "Stand by." The officers in the room stood up, and when the general walked through the door, and "Ten-hut" was called out, the room was already at attention.

Following General Walker into the room was a young lieutenant colonel, Fred Walker Jr., the division's operations officer and the general's son. Behind the two Walkers came a stocky, bull-necked colonel who took a seat in the front row, next to Lieutenant Colonel Walker.

"Good afternoon, gentlemen. Thank you for coming." Walker waited until everyone was seated and the room was silent. "I know that everyone came here with expectations that I would be telling you what's next for the division. I'm sorry I can't do that—I don't know myself. We have no orders beyond holding the territory we took this morning, so I'd like to address that. First of all, my congratulations to the 141st and 143rd Regimental Combat Teams, and the 753rd Tank Battalion. Your teams did a fine job, it went as well as could be expected, and casualties were low. Now, we can't be blind to where that places us. Our division is now, once again, toe-to-toe with the German Army. We command the center of the Fifth Army line, and on a map, we are in the middle of the sole lane leading to Rome. But there are a thousand variations of how General Clark might approach breaching the Gustav Line, and the 36th isn't in the best position to do so, no matter how it might look on a map."

Walker paced back and forth for a moment, then faced his officers again with a serious visage. "We don't have orders, but let's start thinking about what to do while we're waiting. First, I want to make sure our flanks are secure. Make sure we have established good communications with the British 46th Division on our left and the American 34th Division on our right. I want my respective regimental and battalion commanders to spend some time with their counterparts, and I want that coordination to be airtight. Deconflict patrolling so there are no incidents of friendly fire. Which leads me to my second point: I want aggressive patrolling in our territory up to the Rapido River. There are undoubtedly minefields emplaced, and we need to we know where those are. From our side of the river, let's establish where the Germans are on their side. They will aggressively defend that river; let's determine how. That means, third, we need to patrol on the German side of the river. I'm not holding any illusions about how difficult a task this is, but we need an assessment of the battlefield conditions and its defenses that is as complete as possible. Finally, I'm sending my engineers in to make an assessment and provide recommendations for the best places to cross. Again, I don't have any illusions—there are no good places to cross, but let's do our best to make the terrain work to our advantage. I wish I had more for you, but I promise to let you know as soon as I do . . . any questions for me?"

A gray-haired lieutenant colonel stood up—one of the division's new battalion commanders. "General," he said. "How do you see this unfolding?"

"I can't say. The recommendations that I made to Generals Keyes and Clark are for us to continue the work we started at San Pietro. Get up into the mountains to the east of Cassino, work our way up and above the abbey like we did on Mount Sammucro, and we force their flank. If the British do the same in the mountains on our left, the German position in the center will become untenable. They will have to withdraw from the winter line. It's slow, methodical, backbreaking work, but we've proven it can be done."

"Sir, have you heard any talk about us going up the middle?" The questioner this time was a regimental operations officer from the 142nd.

Walker didn't answer directly. He said, "Well . . . I've recommended against such a course of action. Gentlemen, let me tell you a story. The rolls were reversed for me at the Battle of the Marne in July 1918—I was a battalion commander with 1,200 soldiers defending against a German assault of 10,000, supported by the most intense artillery fires I've ever seen." Walker paused and looked at Perkin. "Captain Berger's father, another Captain Berger, was killed in that barrage." Looking back at the assembled officers, Walker's face hardened. "Despite that barrage; despite that this was our first battle, and the German units were veterans; despite the Marne being more fordable than the Rapido, and that it was summer and the water warm; despite their bravery and determination to cross that river, we slaughtered them in the most one-sided fight that's ever been. At the end of the day, not a single German soldier was still alive on our bank or not taken prisoner. I don't know of any successful river crossing of that nature—where the river itself is the main line of defense—in all of history."

1700 Hours
Teatro Reale dell'Opera, Rome, Italy

It had been the most boring two hours of Major Grossmann's life—except for the previous two weeks. The opera had started early with the permission of the German overlords of Rome—even showtimes were dictated by the occupiers.

As someone for whom security consciousness had been paramount for almost all of his adult life, he was appalled at the risks Monsignor O'Flaherty took on behalf of his Allied charges—although as Grossmann had learned, not all of his charges were Allies. He had more than a few German deserters, mostly Austrians, stashed around Rome, as well as Jews, Italian officers, Roman nobility—anyone who needed help.

This afternoon, although O'Flaherty was definitely on the Gestapo's watch list, the Monsignor was attending the opera. Not only attending the opera, but he had provided tickets for a half dozen escaped Allied servicemen as well. Granting that all of the servicemen who attended that night were at least proficient in Italian and had expertly crafted identification papers, Grossmann still thought it was an unnecessary risk—prompted by overconfidence and hubris.

He had never been an opera aficionado. Grossmann preferred the coarser humor and music of cabarets, and he vastly preferred Mozart's symphonies to his operas. Tonight he was being bombarded with the screeches and wails of *The Barber of Seville*, and he realized that there wasn't a single piece of music that touched him. Still, it was vastly preferable to sitting around the flat playing chess or cards and listening to the same stories in different accents. Had he been a real fugitive, he would have left the OTL Club a long time ago, preferring the risk to the boredom.

Oddly enough, he had thought many times, most of the others were completely happy with their circumstances. They seemed grateful to be both out of the war and out of a POW camp, and ennui was better than capture or death. The Australian officer was different. Captain Mullen shared Grossmann's desire to be on the road, and they had both pressed Monsignor O'Flaherty in the three times that they had seen him since Grossmann's arrival. Every time he would give them a winning smile and say, "Don't worry, me boys. Soon. Soon."

Grossmann had volunteered to do some courier services for the network, and after being quizzed by an Italian priest, it was decided that his Italian was good enough to pass all but the keenest of interrogations conducted by a native Italian. It was the best decision that he had made so far in the operation. He had already gleaned all that he could from his flat mates, but by becoming a courier, he learned many of the safe houses and more importantly, was able to develop a working model in his mind of who the key players were and how they channeled escapees and funds back and forth.

O'Flaherty was by far the single most important figure, both operationally and symbolically, in the Vatican escape network. He had established enough layers around himself that the Pope would survive close scrutiny should the Reich decide to shut down the network, but Grossmann had heard rumors that Pius XII was aware of O'Flaherty's actions, and in the best of papal traditions had chosen to ignore it until confronted with facts.

Grossmann had mixed feelings about O'Flaherty. Undoubtedly, O'Flaherty was violating the spirit and the letter of the neutrality of both the Vatican and Ireland, and as such was a de facto enemy of the Third Reich. Yet there was so much that was admirable about the man— not the least of which was his fearlessness and great humor. It would be with great sorrow that Grossmann would recommend his arrest—once O'Flaherty was gone, the network would surely cease functioning.

Finally the screeching opera was over. It hadn't been a complete waste. He had walked past the Royal Opera House many times without seeing the interior—although he wasn't sure if it was still called that as the Italian Royals had decidedly deserted the cause—and it was a truly magnificent building. Grossmann was down in the cheap seats on the floor, while O'Flaherty was now leaving one of the best boxes in the house.

It had been determined that they would not meet nor acknowledge one another. Grossmann was completely capable of making his way back to the OTL Clubhouse on his own, and he began to shuffle out with the rest of the audience. By the time that he reached the main exit of the building, the crowd had largely dispersed—it was better to leave in the crowd than to leave singly these days—and he caught a sight of O'Flaherty talking to several people in the lobby.

Grossmann would have to walk past the Monsignor on his way out, but he had no worries. O'Flaherty was the coolest man he thought he'd ever met, and he knew that the Monsignor would do nothing more than cast a twinkling eye at Grossmann if he even saw him. Then Grossmann did a double take as he caught a glimpse of a glossy pair of jackboots behind the priest. As he looked again, he saw a balding blond man wearing the black and red uniform of the SS strutting up to the monsignor. As they caught sight of the uniform, O'Flaherty's companions melted away and O'Flaherty turned to greet the German officer with a wide humorous smile. It was Lieutenant Colonel Herbert Kappler—the Rome Gestapo chief—and he had a black murderous look on his face.

2120 Hours
Teatro Reale dell'Opera, Rome, Italy

Grossmann stepped back behind a granite column and watched as Lieutenant Colonel Kappler walked up to Monsignor O'Flaherty. Grossmann was out of earshot and missed the conversation, but O'Flaherty never lost his smile and Kappler never looked human.

Grossmann knew Kappler, although not well. In early October, Grossmann had made his way to Gestapo headquarters—deliciously close to the OTL Clubhouse—and introduced himself after Kappler's posting to Rome. He had made the trip to offer his assistance and to brief Colonel Kappler on the capabilities of his Rome Abwehr office. Kappler was arrogant and dismissive, and Grossmann marked him as one of the many opportunists in the SS hierarchy. There were only two kinds of SS officers in Grossmann's opinion—fanatics and opportunistic fanatics. The meeting had ended with Kappler dismissing Grossmann with the words, "I expect you to share all your information while you remain in Rome. I'll see about getting your unit transferred out of my jurisdiction as there needs to be only one German intelligence office in this city."

Nothing ever came of it. Kappler didn't have the authority to make such a transfer, and Grossmann was certain that the SS officer had forgotten about it even as Grossmann walked through his office door. He had said so merely to establish a service pecking order. Naturally, Grossmann never shared any information with Kappler, and the SS man reciprocated in kind.

The conversation with Monsignor O'Flaherty concluded and the SS officer walked away, his face even darker and an angry aide in tow. O'Flaherty allowed the German to leave and waited until his staff car drove off. With a wide smile, the Monsignor walked out of the opera house and headed back to his apartment in the German college.

Grossmann had no idea what the conversation was about, but he suspected that Kappler threatened the priest with arrest. It was in his style of doing things. And judging by the reactions he saw, O'Flaherty had called the Gestapo chief's bluff. Grossmann thought it was a delicious ending to an otherwise dull evening.

There were still scores of people milling about—having a final chat with friends or a cigarette before making their way home. Grossmann started to walk away when he caught her scent.

He whipped around and there she was. Antoniette had disappointed smile on her face, as she said, "I was going to kiss you on the back of your neck. How did you know I was here?"

He was going to retort that some prey knows when it's in danger, but he couldn't. She looked so lovely, so happy to see him that he simply stood there with his mouth open. Seeing an amused look replace the disappointment on her face, he remembered himself and took her hand and kissed it.

"You have an aura about you, my dear. It's like . . . magic." It was true, he thought. *Well, maybe black magic.*

"What are you doing here? And where did you find that dreadful jacket? It really doesn't fit you." She was looking at him curiously. "Did you finish your mission?"

"No. I've been trapped in an apartment since I saw you—I just decided to go to the opera. Who are you with?"

"Papa. He's supposed to be getting my coat, but I think he went to find his mistress instead. You men." Changing the subject, she said, "If you can get out, why haven't you called on me? I've been home for over a week." She seemed genuinely uneasy as she asked the question.

"I haven't been out much, my dear. But if makes you feel better, I have thought about you every waking hour for the past two weeks."

"Just the hours? Not the minutes and the seconds?" She pouted for him, and Grossmann's heart skipped a beat.

"And the minutes and the seconds too, my dear. I think of you all the time." Grossmann said with genuine feeling.

"It does make me feel better." Looking around to see if anyone was watching, she leaned into him suddenly, pressing him back against the granite column with her body. She touched his cheek gently, her eyes glowing with pride and love, and pulled his lips down to hers.

After an exquisitely gentle kiss that was far too brief, she pulled back before they became an object of attention.

"Douglas? Why not meet me tomorrow at your apartment?"

"What time?"

2300 Hours
Able Company Encampment, Near San Vittore, Italy

The war had resumed. It wasn't close enough for concern, but the sounds of combat kept Sam awake in his tent. He didn't need to see the action to know what was going on. He could tell by the sound.

A fast-ripping machine gun told Sam that a German MG-42 was in action. It was a marvelous weapon, he thought regretfully. Fast, sharp, popping of rifles told him that American M-1 Garands were firing back. *Wait for it*, he thought, then the deep booms of artillery completed the rest of the story for him.

An American patrol of the 36th, probably from a sister company of the 141st, had been detected along the river. The first to fire had been the German defenders from their side of the river, the west bank, when an American tripped on a jingle wire, or perhaps set off a mine, or was just seen or heard by a sharp German sentry. But Sam thought the MG-42 was firing at noises, most likely, and the Americans fired back. Probably a mistake, but hard to say without being there. Firing back only confirmed their presence. The artillery would only go for a moment—just enough to send the patrol scurrying for home.

As he lay there in his pup tent listening to the sounds of war, his thoughts drifted to home. Sam could never keep straight the time difference between Italy and Texas, but it was early evening back home. His hands had wrapped it up for the day and were heading home to their wives and families—most of the younger men had been drafted or had enlisted, but there were still a few of the older, steadier men that kept the ranch running.

Some of the single men lived in an old bunkhouse on the ranch grounds, but those were the old ways, and his people mostly lived in Taft, Gregory, or Portland these days. Sam and Maggie paid a fair wage and it was good enough that his folks could afford to live off the ranch. A few of the wives of the ranch hands worked there as well. Old Lupe had been the ranch cook as long as he could remember, and other women helped Maggie in the house or with the calves.

His thoughts left the ranch, and he wondered what Maggie was doing at that moment. It was a Saturday night, so she might have headed into Portland to visit with her mother, or she might have gone over to Old Perkin and Anna's for dinner. Although it could get cold in January in Portland, the odds were pretty good that it was a nice cool evening. Old Perkin would have a fire going in the backyard, and they would be sitting on the bluff and listening to the waves roll in. The sun would be setting behind them, and Maggie would watch the dying rays of the sun sparkling off the water, or maybe she would watch a pelican diving for fish.

It was a hard image to get out of his mind because that was the life he desperately wanted. A hard day's work on the ranch, and then dinner and drinks with family. Watch the sun go down and the stars come out on the ranch, or head into town and feel the cool bay breeze on his face. Sam worried whether he'd even fit in back home after the war—he'd been in uniform for nearly five years, over three on active duty. Maggie was making it her home, her ranch, and Sam suspected in his heart that it might be difficult for her to give it back to him. On the other hand, they might both be in their thirties by the time the war was over, and if they were to have children, the sands were surely falling in the hourglass.

Sam was an optimist by nature, but even so, he worried about bringing children into a world like this. The world would be a better place if the Allies won, but would it necessarily be a safer world for his children? Would America find its own splendid isolation, or was America to be involved in the running of the world, as Perkin believed? If so, he didn't want any part of it.

2315 Hours
1st Battalion Headquarters, Near San Vittore, Italy

Several hundred yards away from the insomniac Sam, Perkin, Major Spaulding, and Private Kulis were discussing a reconnaissance plan for the next week. Orders had been given to the rifle companies to patrol in no-man's-land, and the divisional reconnaissance troop would venture into German territory.

On paper, it was a simple evolution. In truth though, the reality was much different. While the soldiers knew how to patrol and the terrain before them was not particularly complicated, the lack of terrain features made the patrols infinitely more difficult. The Liri Valley that the 141st occupied had been cleared of trees and other features that could provide cover and concealment. The narrow neck of the valley that the 36th held meant that the German enemy could concentrate its defenses. It was a very challenging environment.

As Perkin and Spaulding both knew, sometimes patrols brought back valuable information or even prisoners. Sometimes the patrols got lost, or shirked their duties, or simply found nothing. Sometimes, the patrols didn't return. The army looked on these losses as inevitable. Just as men would be sacrificed in, say, an assault on an enemy stronghold, so would men be sacrificed in the ceaseless battle to acquire information.

"Tomorrow, I want to see if I can talk to the locals about the river. Depth, current, the kind of thing that can't be told from an aerial map."

Spaulding nodded. It was all good—everything that Perkin proposed was correct and necessary. But he was still deeply troubled.

"Perk," he began. "What about what the Old Man was saying today? That there's never been a successful assault across a river where the river is the main line of defense. Is that true?"

Perkin looked at him and shrugged, "I don't know, Bill. I was thinkin' about it all day long. Obviously my family history's tied up in it, but like the Old Man said, on the winnin' side. Some win for the Bergers, huh? Well, let's see. The Battle of Fredericksburg ain't exactly what you're looking for, but it's illustrative of what the dangers are. Our regiment fought at that battle by the way, as the 1st Texas—again on the winnin' side." Perkin grinned, "Maybe it'll bring us luck. Anyway, in December of 1862, the year before Gettysburg, the Union Army tried to force a crossing of the . . . uh, which one was it? The Rappahannock River. They were en route to Richmond and thought they could slip past Lee's army there. I don't remember all the details, but they made a crossing of the

Rappahannock at the town and another one further down
the river, which was to be an envelopment of the town.
They did all the things that we'll have to do here: a cannon
barrage of the defenses, engineers bringing in pontoon
bridges, and then a crossing under fire."

"How'd they manage the bridges?" Private Kulis asked.

"It was tough, as you'd imagine. The pontoon bridges
were special boats that their engineers floated into place
and then lashed together. Then they came along and
dropped planking over the top of 'em to make a road
across the boats—all while under small arms and artillery
fire. Snipers worked the engineers over pretty severely, and
the Union had to send a party over in boats to clear the
snipers out of the waterfront area. Shitty job, but they did
it. So Burnside's troops made it across the river, but it was
the fight on the other side that undid them. Once them
Yankee boys crossed over, Union fires couldn't support
them anymore from the far bank without risk to their own
troops. Of course, that didn't apply to General Longstreet.
He had hundreds of guns behind fortifications in the city
and they poured canister and ball down on the damn
Yankees from behind a stone wall and ramparts at a place
called Marye's Heights. It was the one of the first real
massacres of the Civil War, and coming not long after
Sharpsburg, it's surprisin' that Lincoln stuck with it."

"What ended it, and what happened with the
envelopment?" Spaulding asked.

"The southern attack also failed. They were unable
to turn the Confederate flank and get behind 'em. The
casualties were pretty bad there, but not as bad as in the
town, even though that was meant to be a diversion.
But it became the main attack. So after two or three
days, where the Union Army was pinned on the ground,
under constant fire, they withdrew back across the river.
I understand it was terrible for them boys before they

withdrew. It was freezing, and they were pinned down throughout the nights, and our artillery just kept the fires goin' all night—I can't even begin to imagine how brutal it was."

Chapter Twelve

January 16, 1944
1600 Hours
36th Division HQ, Alife, Italy

The attending officers sat in stunned silence. The orders had come, and the division was going across. Alone.

General Walker had delivered the news to his reassembled battalion and regimental officers. He was unhappy and it showed on every line on his face. He had nothing but optimism in his words, but the tone of his voice and the profound sadness on his face betrayed his true feelings. The Old Man believed that the division was headed for a defeat, and his officers knew it.

"Are we just doing a demonstration, sir?" asked a battalion commander. A demonstration was like a feint—a show of force without the actual assault.

"No. We're to cross the river, establish a beachhead on the far bank, and open the path for the 1st Armored

Division to shoot north toward Rome with Frosinone as an initial objective."

Perkin sat in silence listening to the discussion. As a mere captain, it wasn't his place to interject, but Frosinone was more than thirty miles up Victory Road from Cassino. *What makes Fifth Army think we can gain thirty miles in a day or two when we've been fighting for yards the past four months?*

"What about our flanks, sir?" asked Colonel Robert Wranosky, the commander of the 141st.

"British 46th Division crosses the Garigliano a day before us to secure the mountains on the left of the Liri Valley. Once they're in the highlands, they can protect our flanks. On our right, the US 34th Division is doing a demonstration. It's hoped that will tie down German forces in the vicinity of Cassino and up in the hills toward Mount Cairo."

Hoped? Perkin thought.

"Are success of those operations a go–no-go criteria for us?" Wranosky asked.

It was a good question, Perkin thought. *If the British can't protect our left flank, is the assault cancelled?*

"No."

After a long pause in the silence of the room, Colonel Wranosky asked another question, "What about air and artillery, sir?"

"We're working out the details, but we'll precede the assault with a barrage unequalled so far in Italy. Maybe sixteen battalions' worth. Airpower is dependent on the weather, but they'll be in the game as well."

"Sir, I'd like to get a river crossing rehearsal for my troops and establish a relationship with the engineers that'll be working in my sector. How much time do we have to prepare? When's the assault?"

"Five days. Maybe four."

1630 Hours
Rome, Italy

Major Grossmann hurried along the sidewalk toward the TLC Clubhouse. He had spent the entire afternoon with Antoniette, and he knew that the other men would be worried. If Grossmann was picked up by the Nazis, their security would likely be compromised.

Not that it wasn't already. Grossmann, after spending a delightful time getting reacquainted with Antoniette, had drafted a long report to Abwehr Headquarters. Antoniette had actually fixed him a surprisingly good lunch while he worked on it. It detailed everything: the role of the Monsignor; the supporting committee he established to help; the transfer of funds from America, the British Empire, and wealthy Romans to cover expenses; the known safe houses; and the merchants who provided support as well. To be fair, he also noted that the Monsignor was acting in the traditional sense of charity, and that he was not encouraged to action by animus toward the Reich. That may not have been entirely true, but Grossmann felt that O'Flaherty's motives were mostly pure. He also noted that Pius XII was insulated from O'Flaherty's actions and while arrests of O'Flaherty and the other complicit Church officials would be damaging to the Pope, those actions did not necessarily constitute a *casus belli* in his opinion.

Grossmann was happier than he'd been for a long time. Somehow, quietly and unconsciously, he and Bernardi had become partners in every sense of the word. She proofread his report, and her outrage was genuine upon seeing some of the Italian names listed in it. "For shame," she had fumed. "This man is a fascist official, and he's helping the Allies?" In other ways that Grossmann couldn't describe, they had drawn closer together—not just physically, but spiritually. He was sure of it.

When he had said good-bye and told her that he might not see her again for a month or more, she had cried. In all of the honey-traps that he'd seen her execute, she had never dissolved into tears. It was this single act that convinced Grossmann her feelings were genuine— that he wasn't being played.

Once the report was complete, he had walked to the other Abwehr apartment maintained in the building— next to his own in fact—and he had left it on a table. He placed a call to his Abwehr office, went through a banal ritual of pretending to have called the wrong number, and then he and Antoniette walked to the Navona Piazza arm in arm. The Abwehr courier was already on the way, and his report was likely read by the time he'd finished a glass of wine with the beautiful girl. It was a lovely day to be a German spy in the Eternal City, he had thought with a smile.

As Grossmann hurried back to the OTL Club, he thought about the wonderful day and then turned his thoughts to the coming days. He would push the issue with Monsignor O'Flaherty. Tell him that he couldn't bear to be in the apartment for another week. No, he thought. He'd tell him that duty called and he had to return. O'Flaherty would appreciate that.

1700 Hours
Rome, Italy

"Where have you been, son?" Monsignor O'Flaherty asked Major Grossmann.

The Monsignor was at the apartment, dressed as a street sweeper—one of his favorite disguises. Evidently there had been a growing concern that Grossmann had been picked up by the Gestapo.

Grossmann hung his head and said, "I'm sorry, Hugh. I didn't mean for you to worry."

"Well?"

"I spent the day with a girl I met the first night that I was in Rome." Grossmann lifted his head up and smiled sheepishly, "No offense to these fellas, but I vastly preferred her company today to theirs."

"I don't question that, me boy." The tall Irishman thought for a moment, then said, "Doug, I came to tell you that I've got transportation arranged for you and Timothy for tomorrow. We'll get you out of Rome, and then it will be a slow journey to the Abruzzi mountains and your own lines. I have to be candid with you, me boy. Your language skills have come in very handy, and I've found that I've come to rely on you. If this young lady changes your mind about leaving . . . well, I'd be very happy, and I'd even say a prayer or two on her behalf."

Grossmann smiled and said, "Monsignor, thank you very much, but I have to go. I need to get back to my duties. Will you still say the prayers?"

"You know I will, my son."

They sat down at the kitchen table with Captain Mullen, and O'Flaherty outlined their escape from Rome. "We have a dairy truck that shuttles back and forth to inner Rome from the bottling plant east of the city. The truck, which has all the proper permits, has a false bottom in its bed. It normally runs daily, but it's been broken down these past few weeks so we haven't been able to use it. We'll get you set up in the compartment tomorrow morning, and by tomorrow night, you'll be out of the city. Mind, it won't be comfortable, but it's the safest route out of the city for Timothy, who doesn't speak the language as well as you, Doug."

Timothy didn't speak the language at all, Grossmann reflected. A week before, Grossmann had quietly argued that Mullen's lack of language skills disqualified him from embarking on this journey, but O'Flaherty had laughingly waved his concerns away. "He'll be fine in your hands, Douglas. And if not you, he's always in God's hands."

Once out of the city, friends of the Church would see that they were properly boarded on an eastbound train to the town of Avezzano. "It's safer to catch a train outside of Rome, me boys, particularly one that runs from one provincial area to another. The conductor is a friend of the Church, and he'll be expecting you."

They discussed the details further, then the Irishmen lowered his voice and said, "There's one last task for you, gentlemen. I need for you to carry a message out to your commanders."

Grossmann's ears picked up. *Is O'Flaherty going to ask us to pass on some intel? Maybe something about the defenses of Rome?*

"This is why I decided to let you move on, rather than insisting you stay. This message is urgent, and it needs to get to Mr. Churchill and it needs to get to Mr. Roosevelt. I know it's a tall order for a couple of young officers, but they need to hear it now. We can't wait until Rome is taken. For some time, we've known about the Germans' obsession with the Jews. I saw it meself in Czechoslovakia when I was there before the war, and we've all known what it's been like for those poor people in Germany. The Church is getting information from priests all throughout occupied Europe that Hitler is placing more and more of the resources of the German state to work in the round up, concentration, and extermination of the European Jewry."

"Extermination? Excuse me, what are you saying, Monsignor?" asked Mullen quietly.

"Me boy, our people in what used to be Poland report that the Germans have built a number of camps in that territory and throughout Eastern Europe—the former Yugoslavia, the Baltic States, the Ukraine. These camps have trainloads of people coming into them, but no one leaves, yet they aren't big enough to house all the people that are coming in."

"What happens to them?" asked Grossmann seriously. He was, of course, aware of the concentration camps. They had been in use in Germany almost immediately following Hitler's ascent to power. He had no illusions that life was hard in the SS-run camps, but what the priest was implying was far more than that.

"Son, we're getting reports that the Germans have established special camps for the extermination of the Jews. A step beyond their barbaric concentration camps. They are brought in by rail, in the most unimaginable conditions, then worked in labor camps until they are exhausted. Then they are murdered and the bodies cremated. When I say murdered, they started by shooting them in the early days of the war. Now they've become much more methodical . . ."

"What do you mean, sir?" Mullen was quiet. Serious. Angry.

"Captain Mullen, they've established huge gas chambers that hold hundreds, maybe thousands, at a time. The Jews are told that they're getting showers or being deloused, then the SS gasses them. The bodies are then burned. Polish priests are telling us that the smoke stacks of the crematoriums are pouring smoke around the clock. That the ash from the bodies falls like snow. That the stench is unbearable."

"Sir," Grossmann looked at O'Flaherty uncomprehendingly. "No offense, Monsignor, but I don't buy it.

How do you know that it's not some, say, Soviet propaganda? How do you know this is true?"

O'Flaherty looked at him compassionately but said nothing.

Captain Mullen answered for him. "It's through the confessional? German soldiers told you—told the priests—this through the confessional?"

There was a long silence, then O'Flaherty said, "Boys, let me say that I have every reason to believe it's true. It didn't come to us through one Polish or German priest, but through dozens of them. I want you to remember these names—they are the names of the camps that I know of in Poland—and take them back to your commanders: Auschwitz, Treblinka, Chelmno, and Sobibor—although the last three may have been closed by the Nazis." O'Flaherty had them repeat the names until they were memorized then he said in an uncharacteristically harsh voice, "My sources say it's almost certain that hundreds of thousands have already been killed in these camps—maybe more."

"More?" croaked Grossmann.

"Yes, Douglas . . . are you all right?"

"Yes, sir." Grossmann was stunned. As a very astute judge of character, he wasn't sure that O'Flaherty's tale was the truth, but he was dead-certain that the priest believed it himself. O'Flaherty had already demonstrated to Grossmann that not only did he have a formidable network of assistants, but that he inspired legions to risk their lives for him. These priests who fed the information back to Rome took great risks—they wouldn't have done so on the strength of rumors.

There was one other thing that bothered Grossmann. He was a member of the Nazi Party, but he wasn't a Nazi. He had joined to advance his career, but he didn't buy into the Aryan nonsense or the even dimmer mysticism of the fanatics. He really didn't care much for the Führer or the bombast of Nazism. But he knew members who did—and not just in the SS, but in the army as well. The anti-Semitism of the Nazis had never bothered him. He didn't have any Jewish friends, and he never personally witnessed any deportations, but the hatred of the Jews among some of his colleagues was staggering. But he couldn't imagine anyone, any German, doing these things, and yet, while his imagination and his intellect told him that such a horrible thing was inconceivable, in his heart, he suspected it was true.

2300 Hours
East Bank, Rapido River, North of San Angelo, Italy

Perkin was cold and tired, and was ready to head back to the battalion headquarters. He was on his first reconnaissance of the river and he was already disheartened beyond words. It would not be a report that he cared to bring back to Major Spaulding, who had seemed to age a decade that very afternoon. Spaulding, a soldier's soldier, was tough and unflinching, but he had left the general's briefing pessimistic and the burden of command had never weighed upon him as heavily as it did then.

Perkin and Private Kulis had joined a Baker Company detail that was escorting engineers to the river. The engineers knew the path to a proposed river crossing site, and were in fact leading the riflemen, who were there for protection. Several sites had already been covertly surveyed by the engineers, but none were ideal and few were even feasible. But the Old Man had orders, so the division had orders, and most of the soldiers were determined to make the best of it.

That was one of Perkin's objectives. Help the engineers find the best route, identify the enemy minefields and defensive dispositions. It was going to be a ball-buster, and there was little that they could do about it, but every little bit of knowledge helped.

There had been precious little light all night, but the sky was clear and starry—a tiny sliver of a moon gave enough light for the soldiers to see by. After leaving the relative safety of Mount Trocchio, the first thing that had struck Perkin was the terrain. The ground was relatively smooth and soft. Although the winter rains had been still for the past two weeks, most of the walk to the river was through an inch of mud. Several times Perkin stopped and pushed a finger down into the mud, and there was no resistance. An inch of mud to a walking man, but a quagmire to vehicles. It would get even worse with hundreds of men walking over the same path—there could only be a few pathways through the minefields. The Germans had spread tens of thousands of mines in the Mignano–San Pietro area. Initial reports from survey teams indicated the Gustav Line was far, far–worse, so the engineers would have little time to clear even a few lanes.

The Germans had done an efficient job of preparing the last thousand yards before the river. Beginning at the crest of a little hill, which sloped gradually down to the river, all manmade structures had been razed to the ground. Stone walls that had seen the passage of countless armies were leveled by German bulldozers, and trees had been felled and burned, along with any bushes that might provide cover. Oddly enough, several vineyards were spared, but Perkin suspected that those that they passed were heavily mined.

It was the mud that his subconscious kept coming back to. Finally, he had turned to the engineer, a major named Bellingham, and whispered, "Why's it muddy? It ain't rained here for two weeks."

"The Germans control a dam upriver. They've diverted water from the dam and flooded our side of the river valley. We'll have to bring Marston mats in for the tanks to use, or they'll bog down sure as shit."

Then Perkin realized what was bothering him. "How do we get the bridging equipment and the boats down to the river by truck?"

"We don't. We carry it."

"Are you kidding me? That's over a mile from the assembly areas to the water."

"I know."

When they had gotten closer to the water, they came to a lane that was marked off by a white tape. Following the engineers' lead, Perkin had dropped on all fours and began probing the ground ahead of him with his trench knife. The tape delineated lanes that had been swept of mines, but the engineer had whispered that the Germans were coming in and re-sowing mines, or they sometimes moved the tape.

Sure enough, a line of Schu mines had been detected by the knives when they drew within fifteen yards of the riverbank, and it was slow, methodical work clearing the wooden box mines from the mud. Even when they had reached the bank, the engineers continued the demining until they reached the water's edge.

The banks, which had been mined as well, were steep with a drop of nearly six feet to a small step of ground before the water. Perkin had slid slowly and silently over the bank, where he had knelt by the water's edge. There was a small thin layer of ice right along the water, but not extending into the river. It was moving far too fast for freezing, but as Perkin felt the water, it was ice-cold to the touch.

As Perkin knelt in the dark, he wondered how he was going to present his intelligence to Major Spaulding. The difficulties were already apparent to him, and that was based on a quick survey. It might be better looking in the daylight, but that didn't matter, as the crossing would be conducted in the dark. Any attempt to carry the boats and bridging materials across the valley in the light would be suicidal. It would have to be a night crossing.

Perkin could see the dark shape of the far bank across the water, and wondered how close to a German position they might be—although the engineer had told him that there were no bunkers immediately in front of the proposed landing site. They were further inland.

The engineers had been carrying a rubber pneumatic boat, and Major Bellingham asked Perkin in a nearly silent whisper if he wanted to cross the river with him. His heart pounding, Perkin joined the engineer, and he nearly gasped from the cold as he stepped into the water before sliding into the boat. As Private Kulis pushed them away from the shore, they were immediately swept downstream. Even though the river was only thirty or forty feet across, Perkin felt that they were going downstream four or five yards for every yard they progressed laterally.

"We have to wade back to the crossing site. Don't walk on the bank. It's mined," whispered Major Bellingham.

In freezing water that was waist deep, they waded back to the crossing. With shaking hands, they checked for mines on the German bank and then climbed cautiously to the top. Perkin peered over the rim of the bank to the plain beyond. There was nothing in his limited line of sight, and except for the noisy river behind them and an occasional thump of artillery in the mountains, the battlefield was quiet.

After five minutes of examining the far bank, the engineer whispered with chattering teeth, "I got what I needed. Let's go."

During the long cold walk back to Mount Trocchio, Perkin asked, "What'd you find?"

"We got a crossing site that meets our minimum requirements. We can put out several pontoon bridges there—footbridges—and when you fellows debouch into the valley . . . well, once we've got a lodgment on the far side, we'll bring up the Bailey bridges. You won't have tanks over there until that's done."

"How long will that take, sir?" Perkin asked.

"That depends on the infantry. We don't build the Baileys under fire. You have to clear out the Germans first."

"Says who?" Perkin asked incredulously.

"Says the army, Captain." The engineer was sympathetic, but the Bailey bridge construction would take at least eight to ten hours. It couldn't be done under fire, and it couldn't be done at night without lights. At least, it hadn't been yet.

"That's a pretty tall order, sir."

"This whole operation's a pretty tall order."

Chapter Thirteen

January 19, 1944
1600 Hours
1st Battalion Headquarters, Near San
Vittore, Italy

The briefing had been scheduled, then pushed back, and then pushed back again. To Major Spaulding's great frustration, information kept coming in from higher echelon that was confusing or contradictory, and he wanted to make sure that instructions that he gave to his company officers was as correct as possible.

Finally, he gave up. The briefing would go forward, just like the attack, in the best manner possible. If there were significant changes to the plan, the information would be disseminated later.

Perkin walked into the shattered barn that was serving as the briefing room with Major Spaulding. Private Kulis had arranged the maps on a large easel, and the attending officers took a seat in the wooden manger or simply stood.

When Spaulding waved everyone to their seats and had the collective attention of all in the barn, he cleared his throat and said, "Afternoon, gentlemen. Sorry to keep all y'all waiting. My intelligence officer, Captain Berger, is going to kick us off with the big picture, and then we'll follow that up with what we know of company assignments. Perk . . ."

"Thank you, sir. Good afternoon, gentlemen, Aggies. As Major Spaulding said, I'm going to cover the fundamentals of our crossing of the Rapido River, and then I'll give you the intelligence lay-down of the battlefield. First, we head to the assembly areas tonight, and leave the line of departure tomorrow night at 2000. Our objective is to cross the Rapido River, establish a lodgment on the west bank, and provide enough cover for the engineers to complete bridging of the river. Once the bridges are established, the 1st Armored Division will pass through our lines en route Rome, with Frosinone as their initial objective. In other words, this is the assault to breach the Gustav Line and put the German forces on their southern front into retreat. There are no other established defensive lines between here and Rome, although they've started a new line a few miles back, so once we're through in force, the Germans will necessarily retreat to Rome or further north."

Perkin paused and took a sip of coffee. He had the rapt attention of all who were present including Sam, who was standing in the back. "The 36th has this mission. We will have limited access to all available artillery—about sixteen battalions' worth—plus two engineering companies for the assault. The 142nd Regiment is being held in corps reserve and will not be available for the crossing, although may be used to exploit any openings we create. The two assault regiments are therefore the 143rd and ours, the 141st. We will cross the river at two main points:

in the 143rd's sector south of Sant'Angelo, and in our sector north of Sant'Angelo. When we cross the river, we will envelop Sant'Angelo and eliminate all German defenders there. We believe that the town has been evacuated, so civilian casualties are not a concern."

Perkin paused to show on a map where the crossing sites would be. While at the easel, he said, "The British 46th Division is crossing the Garigliano River in X Corps's sector and will protect our left flank—the Garigliano is what the Rapido is called after the confluence with the Liri River. It's critical that their attack succeed; otherwise we'll be exposed to fires on our left from artillery and mobile ground forces hiding in the foothills. Here, on our right flank, on our far right, the Free French Forces have been pushing hard into German territory in the mountains north of the town of Cassino. On our near right, the US 34th Division will conduct a demonstration to fix forces in the mountains to our right. We go up the center in a frontal assault," he added needlessly.

"Each regiment," Perkin continued, "will have to carry both their assault craft and the initial bridging equipment from the bridge and boat depot behind Mount Trocchio to the crossing site. Engineers will help with that, but we'll be doing most of the heavy lifting. Trucks and tracked vehicles can pass through, but the land has been flooded by the Germans and is too soft to support much traffic until the engineers get Marston mats down to the river sites. Don't count on the trucks to ferry either soldiers, the wounded, or equipment down."

Major Spaulding turned around and face his assembled officers. "I wish to God it wasn't true, but it is. Doctrine calls for trucks to carry the boats to the river, and then they are soldier-lifted no more than a distance of fifty yards. We'll have to carry them over a mile—in the mud—plus carrying weapons and ammo."

After an appalled silence, Perkin nodded, hesitated briefly, and resumed the briefing, "Each regiment will have a total of about sixty boats available to support their crossing. About half will be heavy rubber pneumatic boats. The other half are heavy wooden boats. I can't get any information on how many troops they carry, but I'm told they're pretty damn heavy—about four hundred pounds. Convey to your boys that we'll have only the bare minimum of boats. We'll lose some of those boats through attrition—artillery fire, small arms fire—but we can't lose any to stupidity. They have to watch what they're doing. When they get to the river it's going to be hard to get the boats in the water without them crashing into each other or floating downstream. The first crew over will go downstream maybe a long ways before getting to the other side. I know because in a small boat two nights before, my boat went thirty or forty yards. The crews will need to wade them back and get the boats going in a rope-pulled ferry. We should be able to get a company across quickly this way . . . except for the other part: the enemy."

Perkin stopped for another drink of coffee. He hadn't had more than three hours sleep per night since learning of the mission, and he wouldn't get much this evening either. He cleared his thoughts and resumed, "Here's the enemy disposition, and the reports of our reconnaissance teams. We're facing the German XIV Panzer Corps, which we believe is comprised of six divisions. Directly opposing us in this crossing is the 15th Panzer Grenadier Division. They're a veteran division, and we've faced them in Salerno before. We know that the Germans are exceptionally good at defense, and they've prepared a mini-Maginot line through Cassino. Except unlike the Maginot line, there's no way to go around it other than by sea. So we're going through it. They've had since September to prepare these defenses, and they've conscripted thousands of Italian men into slave labor battalions to make the Gustav Line ready. As we approach the Rapido, we will encounter tens, no, hundreds of thousands of mines. We won't have time to clear them all, so we're channeled into narrow lanes that have been partially cleared. A naval officer once told me that there's a synergism between mines and coastal artillery. For them to defeat the artillery, it's best to approach the shore in a zigzag movement. For them to beat the mines, it's best to go straight in. Mines and artillery work well together at sea, and I'm thinking that's gonna be our problem here. When the artillery fires begin, we'll be tempted to run laterally outside of our lanes. If we do, we'll run straight into minefields. If we run forward along our taped off lanes, we'll inevitably bottleneck and bunch up, and the artillery will be . . . severe. I don't want to overly dramatize this, but Jerry has to be aware of our approach lanes, and don't think that they don't have every square meter of this valley pre-registered for artillery."

Perkin looked out at the pinched white faces before him. Sam's brow was deeply furrowed and Perkin knew that Sam was worried about keeping his troops alive. Captain Ebbins's eyes were wide and his adam's apple went up and down several times as he swallowed hard. It was just as evident that his concern was keeping himself alive.

"When we get to the river, the banks are mined. The engineers have done the best they can, but mine casualties are going to be a fact of this operation. By the way, we've discovered Schu mines, Bouncing Betties, and Tellers. * We'll also encounter the front line German outliers. There are some concrete pillboxes set in the far bank, not directly at our crossing sites, but they'll be able to range

---

*Schu mines were small antipersonnel mines contained in a wooden box that was difficult for metal detectors to find. S-mines, or Bouncing Betties, were antipersonnel mines with two charges. A small squib charge blew the main charge and payload upward out of the mine casing, which in turn detonated seconds later, throwing hundreds of metal balls outward. Teller mines were heavy antitank, antivehicle mines.

our approach. We've also discovered several prepared sites for machine guns—shallow, sandbag-protected pits—that they'll man after the initial barrage lifts. Then there's the river. I can only guess how fast it is, maybe five knots or better, but, hey, the Eye-ties named it the Rapido for a reason. And it's cold—it originates in snow melt only about fifteen miles from here. Don't let your boys try to swim across. If they don't drown in the current, they'll die of hypothermia shortly thereafter—or at least be pretty damned uncomfortable. The river itself is ten feet at its deepest, so there is no fording this river anywhere in the central valley. When we cross the river, the far bank is mined as well, and both banks are steep—six or more feet. That means we have little room for the engineers to build footbridges, and they'll have to bring in bulldozers to shape the banks for the Baileys—maybe. Can't get a straight answer on that one."

An engineering officer from the 111th Engineering Battalion stood up and spoke. "Let me try, Captain Berger. Ideally, we'd want to set the Bailey bridge down a little for stability, so they'd want to grade the approach to the bridge. I looked at the 141st crossing site last night, and I think that it's flat enough on both banks that . . . in layman's terms, we just lay the bridge across the banks to support our immediate needs. It's not how it's done by the book, but, well . . . I think if we don't get the bridges up and across in short order to allow for armor support, um . . . things could be problematic on the far bank. So, I'm willing to try an unconventional approach."

Perkin thanked the engineer and said, "Coming off the river, like a trench fighter in the Great War, we're going over the top. Immediately, we will encounter concertina wire, and lots of it. Not the friendly old 'bob wahr' that Mr. Glidden envisioned for our farms back home. This is multiple lines of razor wire. These wires are booby-trapped with grenades, so tell your boys to be careful—not that it will matter much in the dark. Then we come to more mines, very likely tens of thousands more. Understand that it's not going to be one continuous belt of mines across the valley floor, but fields that are carefully laid according to the German calculus of what our most likely line of advance will be. They'll have their own ingress–egress routes through both the wire and the minefields, but even though we've talked to all the Italian men left on this side of the valley, none of them worked on the Gustav defenses. We had so little time to prepare for this assault that we have no appreciable mine charts for the German side of the valley to share."

"I don't understand, Berger. Isn't that your job?" The speaker was Captain Ebbins.

Perkin's jaw twitched, and for a second his anger showed. He knew that the assault teams needed better information than he could give them, but it just wasn't possible. "You're right, of course, Captain Ebbins. But in the past two nights, seven of our last eight recon teams have either failed to return or lost their boats to enemy fire approaching the river. The one team that made it over spent four hours in a minefield twenty feet from the river before returning before dawn." Perkin smiled a humorless smile and said, "You know, it's almost as if we're not welcome over there."

Amid a smattering of laughter, Ebbins stood up angrily. "Stop making excuses!" he snarled. "It'll be your fault—"

"That's enough!" Major Spaulding interjected. As always, he appeared calm, but Perkin could see the anger in his eyes. "We ain't going down this road, boys. If we knew to the inch where every mine was laid, this would still be a tough nut to crack. Cap'n Ebbins, you should know that Cap'n Berger led the one team that made it to the other side. Now, I can't spare any company commanders, but don't tempt me to have you lead the recon tonight!"

Ebbins closed his mouth abruptly, quickly regained his composure, and nodded to Major Spaulding. He sat down without another glance at Perkin.

After an awkward silence, Perkin resumed the briefing, "Behind the minefields, aerial reconnaissance and prisoner debriefings are telling us that the Germans have arrayed the most extensive defenses we've encountered yet in the war, and that they're building a new line a few miles back, called the 'Hitler Line.' That ain't our worry yet, so what do these Gustav defenses look like? The distances vary from the river because the river ain't straight, but ranging from seventy to a few hundred yards back the Germans have built extensive trenches. The first trench that we'll encounter is an antitank trench, and they'll also try to channel our vehicular passage into kill zones with dragon's teeth and hedgehogs.[†] The kill zones will be served by Pak-40 antitank guns, supplemented by panzer grenadiers with their new Panzerfaust—their bazooka. Shortly behind those, or, in some places, integrated with the antitank trenches are World War One–style firing trenches with concrete and steel pillboxes providing interlocking fires. They've built into this maze of trenches underground bunkers for ammo and troops. Each of these bunkers can house at least a squad of soldiers—complete with bunks and all the niceties of home. In any case, they should be adequate protection from our artillery. Feeding into the lateral trenches are communication trenches similar to the Great War, allowing for resupply and the forward movement of reserves to the prepared fighting positions. Behind the trenches are

---

† Dragon's teeth were reinforced concrete pyramids or cones designed to block or slow down tanks and other vehicles. The spaces between the concrete blocks were usually mined for good measure. Hedgehogs were heavy iron beams that were cross-welded such that they resembled a child's jack. The most iconic image of the hedgehogs is the anti-landing obstacles placed in the surf and water's edge at Normandy.

prepared mortar pits, and behind those are nebelwerfer launch pads. They've created caves or adits by blasting into the mountain bases, and they'll wheel the nebelwerfers out of the adit, fire a six round volley, then pull them back into the mountain for reloading and concealment from our aerial spotters. Further beyond that, and up into the mountains, are the prepared artillery positions. As we saw from the captured German positions on the Barbara Line, they use caves, either natural or manmade, to conceal the artillery. We know that they've got 75 and 88mm stuff in close, with the heavier pieces further back from the line, and we should see the eighty-eights being used as antitank and antiair. We've also identified further north the use of ground-mounted Panzer turrets, and it's possible that they've been able to successfully conceal them from our view here as well."

Perkin paused to take a breath. His briefing was about over, and he felt terrible for the reaction that he saw in the soldiers before him. Tough men who in many cases he'd known for years. Everyone was taking this mission seriously, and he could see the heavy burden resting on the shoulders of all these leaders.

"Excuse me, Cap'n." B. G. E. Beams spoke from the back of the barn. "What's the deal with the abbey on the hill?"

"Do you mean, are they using it for observation?" Perkin asked. When Beams nodded, he said, "I don't know. I talked to a priest who was familiar with the monastery; he said that you can see for miles in any direction. He also said that the abbot wouldn't consent to it being used for military purposes, but in my opinion, that ain't likely to slow down the Germans. Doctrinally, the Germans use a camouflaged point midway up a hill or mountain to place artillery spotters, but they'd be hard-pressed not to want the comfort and security of that fortress up there."

Speaking for every single man there, Beams said, "They're in it." Then speaking for himself, he added, "I can feel their eyes on me every time I take a shit in the valley. B. G. E. stands for Bad Guys Watching me crap."

The barn erupted in laughter, and Perkin saw the first smiles for days. "I think that's B. G. W. isn't it?" Perkin asked with a grin on his face.

"How the fuck should I know, sir? I'm just a dumbass Aggie—we didn't have time for spelling in the Corps." Beams took a couple of bows when Sam and two other officers from Texas A&M started whistling and applauding.

With a nod from Perkin that he was done, Major Spaulding took the center stage. "Boys, we've got a lot to do to get ready for tomorrow. I don't know yet what formation we'll advance in. That decision's coming from division. As soon as I know, you'll know. We're going to cover company missions now. Understand that these are subject to change when we receive our final orders. Hopefully today. Maybe tomorrow."

2350 Hours
1st Battalion Assembly Area, Mount Trocchio, Italy

The motor pool had made a two-and-a-half-ton truck available to Major Spaulding to use as a mobile command post of sorts. It had no heat, no communications, in fact, no accommodations of any sort other than a heavy flap that dropped from its canvas top to below the tailgate of the truck. The heavy flap had been augmented by a couple of army blankets hanging from a cord stretched across the back of the truck, giving it a modest protection against escaping light.

Sam found Perkin and Bill Spaulding sitting on the bed of the truck, legs crossed, looking at a map of the battlefield by the light of a lantern. As he climbed into the back of the truck, careful not to let any light out, he sighed with relief as he left the confusion of outside behind.

The battalion had mostly completed its movement to the assembly area behind the protection of Mount Trocchio. The movement had begun at dark, and there were still straggling soldiers trying to catch up and find their units. No one was certain that they were in the right place, no communications between echelons had yet been established, and the runners that had been sent out between headquarters seldom found their intended targets—even when they did, they had a hard time finding their way back.

Sam wasn't a runner, per se, but he had volunteered to head to battalion and report the company's progress to Major Spaulding. It should have been Captain Ebbins's job, but Ebbins had taken Spaulding's threat of a recon patrol seriously and had decided to manage the company's affairs quietly, away from a higher echelon. Sam had wandered around as lost as anyone else until in the light of a distant star shell he spied Private Kulis, who showed him the way to battalion headquarters.

"How's tricks, boys?" he asked as he sat next to Perkin. Judging by their reactions, tricks weren't going well.

"The British 46th has called off its attack," Perkin said quietly.

"Whaddya mean, called it off?"

Major Spaulding answered, "After a day of dick dancing around, they crossed the Garigliano without much resistance but failed to drive the Germans out of the mountains on the south side of the Liri valley. Said they weren't trained for that kind of work. They gave it a halfhearted try, then called it a day. I don't get it. They've been fighting in these mountains since we got here in September. What kind of bullshit is that?" Spaulding spit contemptuously into his German helmet spittoon. "Our left flank is wide open."

Sam scratched an itch on the back of his hand with the stubble on his chin. "OK. How long does that postpone us? When do they resume?"

Perkin spread his hands out, "They don't resume. Leastways not so it helps us. We go tomorrow. Rain or shine, exposed flank or not."

"Naw, y'all are all wrong. General Walker wouldn't do that." Sam shook his head, puzzled. He didn't consider himself an expert strategist by any means, but it was such a violation of sound military principles that he couldn't conceive of the order coming from the division's commanding general—a man he respected deeply. A man everyone in the division respected deeply.

"No, he wouldn't, Bear. But this ain't his call." Perkin said, "It's comin' from higher up."

"Oh." Sam said, and as he studied a stain on his trousers, he repeated, "Oh."

Spaulding stood up and said, "I gotta stretch my legs. Able getting bedded down, Sam?"

"Yeah. We're gonna make the best of it tonight and try and get some sleep. I gotta head back and check on things."

As Spaulding crawled over the tailgate, Sam looked up and studied Perkin's face. He looked so terribly tired and worn that Sam almost teared up. Instead he offered a faint smile and said, "Well, that'll liven things up a little bit don't you think?"

"I think it might, Sam." Perkin hung his head, "I'm so sorry that I talked you into this all that time ago. This is all my—"

"No. This was my idea, remember? Anyway, let's not get ahead of ourselves here. If any unit in the army can pull this off, it's us." Sam took a deep breath, and pushed back his actual thoughts. "Do you remember what that old sergeant told us in Brownwood about problems?"

Perkin thought for a moment. "Which old sergeant? You mean Sergeant Grant? No. What he'd say?"

"He said there are two kinds of problems in the world. The first is those that you can fix. So ya fix 'em and don't worry about 'em. Then there are those you cain't do nothin' about. Since you can't fix 'em, it don't make sense to worry." Sam got up, and put his hand on Perkin's shoulder and gave it a squeeze. "I ain't worried, Bubba. We'll be OK. Get some sleep, dream of Helen, and I'll see you in the morning."

Chapter Fourteen

January 20, 1944
0800 Hours
Able Company Assembly Area, Mount Trocchio,
Italy

Sam walked through the company's assembly area and talked to the soldiers. He wanted to share a few words with old comrades, soldiers that he had fought with before. Their steadiness comforted him, as his apparent calm steadied them. Stories were shared about the battles at Paestum, San Chirico, Mount Lungo, and its sisters, Rotondo and Sammucro, and San Pietro. Several times Sam felt himself wondering how to get his soldiers out of this coming battle, but he knew that he couldn't. He felt the need to protect the old-timers, some of whom were still teenagers, yet he knew that the veterans were the key to success.

He made a point to spend time with the new replacements, whether they were in his platoon or not.

Some had joined the company within the last week and were sincerely dazed and confused. And terrified. Sam comforted them as best he could. He told them to stay with the veterans, to do what the Texans did, and to remember their training. With each of the replacement soldiers, Sam personally looked over their weapons, their ammunition pouches, made sure that each man had fresh water in his canteens. He talked about hometowns, girlfriends, wives, children—whatever was on the minds of the new men. But there was only one thing on their minds—the battle— and most of the newcomers couldn't bring themselves to talk of the fight to come. A few of the replacements surprised Sam, though. They were young, bright men who asked intelligent questions about their squads, tactics, and communications. Sam knew instinctively that they would become good soldiers. He hoped they survived the battle.

Most of the soldiers were quiet and reflective before Sam engaged them. They cleaned their weapons, sharpened their bayonets, wrote letters home to parents or wives, smoked cigarettes, and waited. Some looked up and smiled as he walked by; others didn't acknowledge him but looked off into the distance.

Sam was pleased to see that his NCOs were doing the same as him. Talking, cheering, steadying the men. Sam and his platoon sergeant, Bill Kenton, crossed paths several times as they made their rounds through the squads. Each time Kenton said, "They're looking good, sir. We're good to go."

Sam had inherited Sergeant Kenton from Perkin, and Kenton had inherited the Mauser antitank rifle from Sam. He was a monstrously large man, almost as tall and heavy as Sam, with closely cropped red hair under his helmet. He was one of the best sergeants that Sam had known since being in the army, and he felt extraordinarily blessed that Kenton was with his platoon. If anything happened to Sam, Kenton would take care of the men and would continue in command.

As he passed by a soldier for the second time, Sam realized that he had talked to all of his men, and had talked to many of his favorites throughout the company. Looking around, he thought that he had talked to everyone he needed to. Except for Captain Ebbins. He was nowhere to be found.

Sam sought out Master Sergeant Bob Hawkins—the company top sergeant. Hawkins was an old campaigner himself, and Sam had known him since coming to the battalion years before. Hawkins had likewise talked to the new soldiers, but he had focused his time on the noncommissioned officers, particularly the new corporals and the young sergeants. He told them all how lucky they were to be there that day, that they were making history, and that they would forever remember leading men into battle. He had picked most of these men to be leaders, and he was justifiably proud of what they had accomplished since being in Italy, but he wanted to make sure that they didn't forget what they were chosen to do on this particular day.

Hawkins had lit up a cigarette and was enjoying it by himself. Sam was going to leave him be, solitude being hard to come by, but Hawkins saw Sam and walked over to him.

"Good morning, Lieutenant. What a fine army day, isn't it?" Hawkins said with a grin. Unlike some Sam had talked to, Hawkins' good mood wasn't forced. He was doing what he enjoyed most in life.

"It's certainly a fine army day," Sam noted as he looked around. The sky was overcast, but it wasn't raining, thankfully. The air was ripe with the smell of unwashed men and perpetually damp clothes and canvas.

"Knock, knock!" said the sergeant unexpectedly.

"Who's there?" Sam replied with a grin.

"Orange."

"Orange who?"

"Orange you gonna ask me where the boss is?" Hawkins said with a wicked grin.

"I'm not sure that I want to know," Sam said truthfully.

"Let me try again, sir. Knock, knock!"

"Who's there?" Sam said a little more warily this time.

"Ronald."

Sam looked around to see if any of the men were listening. They weren't so he replied, "Ronald who?"

"That ain't the right question, Lieutenant. It's 'Ronald where?' and the answer is, 'That son-of-a-bitch's at sick call.' I mean . . . the captain's at sick call, sir. Were you aware of that?"

"No, I wasn't," Sam answered. His heart sank at the news. Even though Captain Ebbins wasn't a popular officer, it wouldn't do much for the morale of the company to learn that their commanding officer was possibly shirking his duties.

"Strange. He said to refer any issues to you. Guess he didn't have the balls to tell you himself. I mean . . . he must've forgot. Anyway, the only issue I have to refer to you is a shitbird for a company—"

Sam cut off Hawkins. "No. That's enough. Leave it be, Top. I'm sure the cap'n will be back soon. If he ain't . . . well, let's just plan on Sergeant Kenton running my platoon. I'll want you with me."

Unchastened, Hawkins grinned again. "Yes, sir. My plan as well. Glad you agree with me." Hawkins lit another cigarette and said, "None of the boys requested sick call this morning. Not even Froman, which is good. You know why?"

Sam smiled in anticipation. He knew there was a setup coming. "Because he's an expert marksman?"

"Hell no, sir. Because he'd be in a lot of trouble. I understand that Major Spaulding, God bless him, asked for the list of soldiers who went to sick call today, and told the battalion surgeon to have any officers trying to get out of combat on medical grounds report directly to Spaulding himself. I guess Captain Ebbins must have missed that directive."

"There was something on paper?" Sam shook his head, knowing what was coming.

"Yes, sir. I got it right here," Sergeant Hawkins tapped his jacket pocket. "Shoot. Now that you mention it, the captain was in such a hurry to see the doc this morning that I must have forgotten to show it to him."

The sergeant had such a complete look of innocence about him that Sam had to laugh. "Top—"

"Sir," interrupted the master sergeant. "I been around this man's army for all of my adult life. My job's not just to train the boys, but to train you young officers as well—and I done a good job with you. You're a good platoon commander, and you'll be a good company commander if you live through this week. I watched you pump the boys up this morning, and that's all I need from you until the battle starts. So until then, sir, you go deal with battalion, and I got things here. Now, Cap'n Ebbins, begging your pardon, sir," Hawkins' face got hard, "is like a mean, stray dog. He ain't trainable, and he won't look you in the eye, and when ya ain't watching, he'll bite you from behind. As a Christian, I'm ashamed to say so, but I pray to God the surgeon finds somethin' wrong with him."

0900 Hours
1st Battalion Headquarters, Mount Trocchio,
Italy

Sergeant Hawkins's prayers weren't answered. The battalion surgeon found Captain Ebbins medically fit for duty, and in accordance with Major Spaulding's directive, the surgeon sent Captain Ebbins to report to his battalion commander. On his own initiative, the doctor sent a runner with a note for his boss, so that by the time Captain Ebbins reported to battalion headquarters, Major Spaulding was white with fury.

The battalion's operations officer and Perkin were kicked out of the truck, and while the ops officer used the opportunity to go relieve himself, Perkin hung back to eavesdrop.

In an ice-cold voice dripping with distain, Spaulding said, "Tell me why you think you're too ill to participate in today's attack."

"I'm not. I saw the doctor for trench foot . . . I wanted to make sure that I was good to go. That I wouldn't slow the company down," Ebbins smoothly said. "Thankfully, he said that my trench foot wasn't too bad."

"That's odd, because he told me that your trench foot's nonexistent, Captain. He told me that there's no apparent problem whatsoever. How do you explain that?" After a long silence Major Spaulding continued, "Do you want to know what else he told me?"

Perkin couldn't hear the answer—an artillery burst only four hundred yards away caught his attention. Then he heard Spaulding say, "He told me that you requested a declaration that you're medically unfit for combat. Well, it may be true that you're unfit, but it's not because of bad feet. If I relieve you, it'll be for cowardice, is that what you're looking for?"

"No, sir."The smoothness was gone from Ebbins voice. It'd been replaced by a mixture of anxiety and desperation.

"Captain Ebbins, I've had my concerns about your performance since you assumed command of Able Company. I've been willing to give you the benefit of the doubt because you've not been in combat previously, and you've only been in command for less than sixty days. It's a damn hard job, I know that, and I felt you deserved a grace period to grow into it. Well, your grace period is up. My patience has ended. You'll pull yourself together, return to your company, and begin doing, right goddamned now, what you should have been doing all along! Leading men. You're gonna take your soldiers into combat with your head held high, and even if you're shitting your pants every thirty seconds, you're going to at least pretend that you know what you're doing and that you're confident of success. Those soldiers are looking to you to set the example of how to lead and fight, not to duck and run. The army doesn't have any more time to waste on you, Ronald. If you don't master combat leadership today, you're through in my battalion! Are we clear?"

Perkin couldn't hear Ebbins's answer, but he'd had enough ass-chewings in his own career to know when they were wrapping up. He walked quickly away from the truck, and after a few paces, he did an about face and began to mosey back to the command post. When Ebbins jumped down from the back of the truck, it looked like Perkin was just walking up.

Ebbins's face was drained completely of blood and he looked at Perkin with glassy eyes.

"Hey, Ronald. Good luck today," Perkin said sincerely.

There was no answer from Captain Ebbins, and as Perkin climbed into the back of the truck he watched Ebbins walk away. His head was down and his shoulders slumped forward. He looked defeated.

Spaulding looked up at Perkin. "I assume you eaves-dropped. Was I too hard on him?"

"Why would you say such a thing about me?" Perkin said in a wounded voice.

"Cause you're a spook and a busybody, that's why." Spaulding's anger with Ebbins was quickly ebbing, and he started reviewing his draft order for the movement of the battalion.

"Busybody? That's a hurtful thing to say. I'd argue with you, but I'm too tired. Besides, I *was* eavesdropping." Perkin shrugged, "I don't know, Bill. It's gonna be a tough battle for him to pop his cherry on, but I'd cut him loose if you're anything less than delighted after tonight. I just don't think he's cut out for the infantry."

Spaulding nodded and said, "Quite honestly, I thought about relieving him on the spot and appointing you acting commander of Able Company, but I can't let him off that easily. I hope I didn't make a mistake." Spaulding moved on to more pressing issues, "When ops gets back, let's go over the crossing plan one more time ..."

1400 Hours
1st Battalion Headquarters, Mount Trocchio, Italy

"All right, gentlemen. This is it. Your last set of marching orders." Major Spaulding stood before a blackboard propped up on a stack of heavy wooden beams—the blackboard was easier to follow than a map, although they would go over those again as well.

Spaulding paused to watch a low level flight of P-40s scream overhead, then he pointed at a dotted line running across German-held territory on the west side of the Rapido River. "This is Phase Line India Red, where we will be tomorrow morning." As Spaulding spoke, he looked at Perkin and rolled his eyes. At an earlier regimental meeting, Colonel Wranosky had offered Perkin the honor of naming the phase line with the proviso that the first codeword started with "I" and the second word with the letter "R." Perkin was aggrieved that his suggestion of "Itchy Rectum" was not given due consideration.

"The 143rd will be south of Sant'Angelo; we will be north. In our sector, there are two battalions crossing tonight. Us and 3rd Battalion. Second Battalion is being held in regimental reserve. Facing the river, 3rd Battalion crosses to our right at the S Bend, which means we cross closest to Sant'Angelo. Within our battalion area of operation, Able Company deploys on our right. Baker in the middle, and Charlie to the left. We are not holding a rifle company in reserve. Our job is to penetrate German defenses to a depth of 1,000 to 1,500 yards—India Red. We eliminate all direct and indirect fires within that zone, the key to which are the German defenses in Sant'Angelo. That little village is on a bluff over the Rapido, and gives the Germans great visibility up and down the river. Once the village is cleared, we'll reduce machine gun and mortar fire on the banks from the village and eliminate their closest artillery spotters. If we do all of this, the engineers should have enough breathing room to construct the Baileys. Once the Baileys are across, the 1st Armored Division, supported by the 91st Reconnaissance Squadron and the 142nd RCT flow through us. Any questions?"

Captain Ebbins stood up, and Perkin held his breath, waiting for another explosion. He was surprised when Ebbins asked, "Yes, sir. Where will the battalion CP be located, and when you do anticipate it'll be operational?"

"Good question, Ron," Spaulding said. "Battalion headquarters will not cross until a beachhead is firmly established. My CP will be behind Baker Company's crossing site until Colonel Wranosky orders it forward. That doesn't mean that I won't be going forward during the course of the crossing to see conditions for myself, but send your runners here." Spaulding pointed to the blackboard. "As to when—my staff and I will depart the assembly areas for the bridging and boat depots when you do at 1800. At 1900, I'm going forward as the lead elements of the companies depart the depots, and I'll have my CP established about the time the barrage begins at 1930. As soon as it lifts at 2000 hours, we cross."

1635 Hours
West of Avezzano, Italy

The day had started out well for Major Grossmann. He and Captain Mullen had slept at the home of a railway worker, and after a generous breakfast, the smiling man had seen them personally onto the train—another small regional train that would cover the fifty miles between the cities at an average speed of less than twenty miles per hour.

They had taken two seats together, and according to plan, Grossmann took the outer seat in case there was a talkative neighbor. Mullen pulled his hat down over his eyes to feign sleep, and off they went.

It seemed that the train stopped at every little town between Rome and Avezzano, and their neighbors seemed to come and go, yet thankfully, there was no social chitchat directed at Grossmann or his sleeping companion.

They were less than fifteen miles from Avezzano, and the train had no more local stops to make, when it began to slow down in the smaller mountains ringing the Abruzzi range. The train came to a halt just inside a tunnel cutting through a mountain ridge. Surprising even Grossmann, who had considerable experience in Italian eccentricities, the passengers began to disembark.

"What's going on, mate?" Mullen whispered.

Grossmann put his hand on Mullen's arm to quiet him and then asked the same question of an elderly Italian women. After helping her to her feet and listening to a voluminous reply that included the extensive use of her hands, Grossmann returned to Mullen in the now empty car.

"The engineer's grandmother lives down the hill and he always stops on the way to Avezzano to check on her. He used to stop closer to her house, but since the war started he parks in the tunnel so us flyboys aren't tempted. The old lady said no one cares whether the train is late to Avezzano, and so, we have about an hour to kill."

The Australian officer laughed. "Well, I don't think I've ever heard of anything like that, but it's good to take care of your grandmother I suppose. One of mine was a real sweetheart, she was, and she'd always make us kids a nice cream-filled Lamington." Seeing the puzzled look on Grossmann's face, he said, "It's a Queensland dessert— two sponge cakes dipped in chocolate with coconut and cream in between. Yeah, she was a sweetheart, but my other grandmother was a right old hag. She hopped off the boat from Ireland at sixteen, was preggers the next day, and never looked back. When I was a little kid and running around her house in Brisbane, she'd scream at me and my brothers, 'Fer fuck's sake, Timmy, shut the fuck up!' And then she'd take a belt to us. Oh, she was a hard one."

Grossmann laughed at the image. He couldn't see either his American grandmother or his German grandmother cursing or taking a belt to him. "Come on. Let's get a smoke."

"Sounds good, mate. Let's just move away from the crowd though."

Grossmann could see light at the far end of the tunnel, so he pulled on Mullen's arm and they set off in that direction. The tunnel was several hundred yards long and both officers stumbled a few times in the dark, but they were rewarded at the far end of the tunnel by both solitude and an amazing view.

The tracks exited the tunnel directly onto a bridge that spanned a gorge over two hundred feet deep before going into another mountain tunnel. Mullen started to walk out onto the bridge, shook his head, and came back. He pointed to a utility platform at the side of the tracks, and as he headed for it, he said, "I've had enough tough luck on train tracks this year; maybe I'll just stand over here and enjoy the view."

They lit their cigarettes and enjoyed the silence and the country scene. Mullen was the first to break the spell. As he leaned against the railing of the platform, he asked, "Doug, what are your thoughts about what the Monsignor said about the Jews? Do you reckon Hugh had it right?"

"I don't know, Tim. I've thought a lot about it, and I don't see Hugh lying, do you?" Grossmann said honestly. "But the Germans aren't savages—I just have a hard time believing them capable of something like that. I'll bet you it's Soviet propaganda."

"You don't know 'em like I do, mate. I saw their atrocities in Africa, and then again, when I was sent to Cyprus. One of my mates that I escaped with—a bloke named Jim—had already surrendered and one of their sergeants almost beat his brain in with a rifle butt. Truly ruined a nice boy. Never said a word after that." Mullen inhaled deeply and said, "I hope he got out. I'll tell you what though. I joined the police force in order to protect those who couldn't fend for themselves. I despise bullies, and the Germans have taken bullying to a whole new height. I swear to you, Doug, I'll make it my life's mission to carry that information out to my government. I don't know that Australia's got much juice in the world right now, but I promise you, I'll make sure we do the right thing."

The Australian officer was so earnest that Grossmann could feel his moral outrage, and he knew that Mullen would indeed make it his life's mission to bring these crimes to light. It sickened him too, but he was still an Abwehr officer, and he knew that the alleged activity in these camps wasn't a secret that should be let out. At least not yet.

The train blew a long blast on its whistle, and Captain Mullen turned toward the tunnel entrance. Grossmann drew his arm back sharply, and with all of his strength, he hit Mullen hard in the throat with the base of his hand. The blow crushed the Australian's larynx, and Captain Mullen dropped to his knees and grabbed his throat trying to breath. He looked up at Grossmann with fear and confusion in his eyes, and as Grossmann struggled to lift Mullen to his feet and pull him toward the platform's railing, Mullen heard Grossmann's voice in an apologetic whisper, "You deserve to know why. My name's Doug Grossmann. I'm a German officer. Sorry, Tim."

1745 Hours
1st Battalion Assembly Area, Mount Trocchio, Italy

Perkin felt a nervousness that he'd never felt before. It was worse than even the landing at Paestum, which had been his initiation into the brotherhood of war. Noting his nervousness, he said to himself, *Maybe I just know better now*. The Germans certainly had to be aware that something was afoot by now. Airpower, mostly P-40s and A-20s, had been bombing and strafing targets of opportunity all day, and the increasing level of patrolling must have been noticed by the German defenders.

Certainly the Germans had not been still all day either. Mount Trocchio offered excellent protection from observation from the German lines, but the sight of any movement on the mountain itself was instantly met by artillery fires. Artillery was also directed sporadically throughout the day at unseen targets on the far side of the mountain from the Germans—usually without much effect. On the other hand, reflected Perkin, if the Germans were aware that two infantry regiments were now huddled behind Trocchio, German artillery would be leveling Trocchio to try and get them.

A Presbyterian chaplain, who knew Perkin from the battalion staff, had been praying with several soldiers, and passing by spied Perkin. "Captain, would you like to pray?"

"I've been doing nothing but for the past three hours, Chaplain. Is there a passage that comes to mind that you can think of about our particular situation?"

The chaplain, an older lieutenant, said, "Psalms 23? 'Yea, though—'"

"I know that one." Perkin interrupted with a smile. "I've said it so many times in my mind today that I'm beginning to think I was the original author in a previous life."

The chaplain knew Perkin and therefore wasn't shocked, but he said, "That's bordering on sacrilege at so many different levels, Perkin. How about Galatians 6:9: 'Let us not become weary in doing good; for in due season we shall reap, if we faint not.'"

"That's a great one because I am as weary as all get out, and I almost fainted about fifty times today. I hadn't heard that before. What are your thoughts on—"

Perkin was interrupted when Major Spaulding and Sam joined them. "Sorry, Chaplain, would you pardon us, please?" Major Spaulding asked.

The chaplain was on the verge of an interdenominational joke about needing a priest for that kind of work, but he nodded and joined some passing soldiers instead.

"He was about to set me up with the Almighty. What's more important than my salvation?" Perkin asked of Sam.

"Considering the amount of thought you've given it over the years, evidently just about everything," Sam said dryly.

"That hurts. What's up?"

Major Spaulding pulled three paper coffee cups out of his pocket, and passed them around. "I can't go into battle without a roister, but I wanted to keep this one to ourselves. We'll have to keep it down though. Anyway, we've been together since the beginning, so . . . well, anyway, pour 'em out, Sam."

Sam took his flask out—a battered silver flask with an engraved naked lady on it, a late Christmas gift from Perkin, who found it in Vasto—and poured a healthy shot into each cup. The officers assumed the roistering posture with their cups held together with their wrist bent strangely outward.

"To God," they said together. They lifted the cups to their ears, listened to the bourbon momentarily and then returned the cups to their starting position.

"To country," and the cups repeated the odd passage.

"To Texas!" and again, the cups went back and forth without a drink.

"Perkin, would you do the honors?" Spaulding asked. The last toast was always improvised and different.

"Yes, sir. To friends and family." Perkin said with a touch of emotion.

"To friends and family," they all repeated. Then, more subdued than usual, they finished the toast with a rolling "Roiiiiiisssssster!" and then threw back their drinks.

Feeling the bourbon burn down their throats, the emotional moment passed, and they grinned at each other.

Spaulding said, "Come on, Perk. We gotta go. Sam, good luck. Keep 'em moving. I'll see ya down at the river." He shook Sam's hand, and without waiting for Perkin, he strode off to supervise the march.

"I gotta go too," Sam said.

"Well the party's usually livelier that way. But I guess I'll go as well." As they walked to the boat dump, Perkin asked, "How's Ron got the platoons laid out?"

"We proceed in column by platoon. B. G. E. leads the way with his platoon. Two-Bit is second across. We're third in the gate, followed by Ronald crossing the Delaware. Norstad and the weapons platoon cross on order. I should've been first, but Ronald wouldn't hear of it." He offered his hand and said, "Be careful out there, Bubba."

"You too, Bear. I'll see ya at the river or on the other side. So long."

1815 Hours
Avezzano, Italy

Grossmann sat cross-legged on a folding cot. It was more comfortable than the chair in the priest's office, and he didn't wish to enter the nave and sit on a pew.

The priest at the Avezzano church was a pleasant man, eager to please and full of bombast about fighting the Germans. Grossmann didn't mind that so much as he minded the priest's unnecessary concerns for security.

He felt like he was on the other side of the world from Monsignor O'Flaherty.

The priest had been very concerned that Grossmann had been seen when the engineer delivered him to the church. Seen by whom, the priest didn't say. But security was obviously paramount, and the priest insisted that Grossmann stay in the church office and not leave. Friends of the Church would help the priest with food and drinks for Grossmann, and he had plenty of novels for him to read, but he would not budge, not even when Grossmann explained the latitude he had in Rome.

The priest was likely nervous in all ventures in life. He was that sort, Grossmann decided, and he was definitely spooked when he learned from the train's engineer that there had been two Allied soldiers, but one had wandered off and missed the train at the mountain pass. That the other soldier might be arrested, or worse, show up unannounced at his church was definitely cause for concern.

Grossmann hoped that Father Carlo's penchant for security would prompt the priest to accelerate his departure to the next way station, but the priest had told him that there was only one more stop—a mountain farmhouse. It was in the middle of no-man's-land between the warring armies, and the only safe passage was a two-day hike through the mountains—except it wasn't safe in the current weather.

"We have to wait until there's a thaw. I got two men through a couple of weeks ago, and it was nearly the death of me. It would be suicide to attempt it now," the priest said.

"When will there be a thaw?" Grossmann asked.

The priest spread his hands out, pursed his lips and shrugged. "Who can say? It's in God's hands. Last year, it wasn't until March, but the year before the passage was clear in January."

Dear God, not March, thought Grossmann.

1815 Hours
1st Battalion Boat Dump, Mount Trocchio,
Italy

Although Perkin trailed Major Spaulding by less than a minute to the boat depot, he found his battalion major already engaged in a hot conversation with an unhappy engineering lieutenant.

"I swear to you, sir. We just found this as your lead company arrived."

"What's up?" Perkin asked as he joined Major Spaulding.

"The engineers say at least half our boats are perforated and may not float." Spaulding kicked the ground in frustration. "The lieutenant thinks that that a lucky airburst in the last hour or so shredded the boats with shrapnel."

"Lieutenant, what's the half number based on?" Perkin asked.

"Just a Mark One, Mod One Eyeball sir. We haven't had time to assess them. There's some thirty boats or so that are damaged by my guess—just based on how they were stacked."

"Lieutenant, here's what you're gonna do," Perkin looked at Major Spaulding, who nodded. "We're gonna set up a quick triage on these boats. Get a flashlight on the ground, put a boat over it, and if no light shines through, pass it off to an assault team. If a little light shines through, set it over yonder, and we'll pass it to a later assault team. Maybe the footbridges will be up and we won't have to use 'em. The really bad ones go over there."

The lieutenant started to say something, looked at the face of Major Spaulding in the dim light, and changed his mind. He ran off motioning to two sergeants, issued some rapid-fire orders, and Perkin was gratified to see them nod vigorously.

In short order, several "triage" stations were established with a private laying on the ground holding a flashlight and an assault team holding the boat over him. The damage was as extensive as the lieutenant feared. Some of the boats were completely unusable, and they were tossed in a growing pile. As the number of destroyed boats grew, the commander of Charlie Company made a command decision and started accepting boats with partial damage.

Able Company was next in line. While Captain Ebbins insisted on undamaged boats, his protests were ignored, and Able and Baker companies followed the lead of Charlie Company. Each unit would depart with about half the anticipated number of boats and many of the boats they would use were already compromised to a degree.

"Well, we knew it wouldn't go according to plan. Glad we got the foul-up early on," Perkin said as he watched the soldiers line up in column formation by platoons. Some soldiers were in teams of four and they carried the small rubber boats by a rope attached to gunwale. Other soldiers found themselves assigned to the heavy wooden boats. Twelve-man teams were required to lift and move the four-hundred-pound boats, and in addition to carrying their share of the boat, each man carried his rifle and another forty pounds of ammunition, water, and emergency rations.

"Your assumin' we're only allocated one foul-up. Let's hope so. Come on," Spaulding said, and they walked to the line of departure to wish the first teams good luck.

They were joined by their regimental command-er, Colonel Wranosky, at a point at the southern end of Mount Trocchio. In the dim twilight, Perkin and Wranosky jumped on the hood of a jeep and looked back at the boat and bridge depot. It was unlike any sight that either had ever seen before. Thousands of men from two regiments were moving about—it looked like chaos, but Perkin knew the soldiers were generally being shepherded with purpose—and his throat tightened. He looked over to Colonel Wranosky, and tears were silently streaming down his face.

As the historian in Perkin wondered to himself whether a river crossing like this had been attempted by the American Army since Fredericksburg, the soldier in Perkin felt awestruck and privileged to be a part of it. Even if he had severe doubts about the wisdom of the operation, it was a sight he would never forget.

1925 Hours
South of Mount Trocchio, Italy

Sam had a far narrower sense of history than did his cousin, but he still felt shorted somewhat by the commencement of their march to the river. He didn't know what to expect, but part of him thought that there should have been dramatic orders to march, and drums and fifes at a minimum. Instead, the officer directing the march at the line of departure gave an anticlimactic "Move out! Good luck!" to each of the platoons as they set off. The officer and several assistants were making sure that each platoon departed as a group, and he was separating their crossing of the line to ensure the units didn't bunch up on the march to the river.

Even with the best of intentions and schedules, things didn't go as smoothly as planned. The need to keep the noise minimized—surprise was still a possibility—and the darkness led to stragglers in each and every platoon. Some soldiers ran to catch up with their squads, others waited and departed with the next unit to cross the line.

The platoons were lead by engineers and scouts. Most of the soldiers had not covered the ground between Mount Trocchio and the Rapido River before, and they would have gotten easily lost in the confusion. It was relatively straightforward in the daylight but difficult at night. Adding to the confusion, a cold, heavy fog set in, and Sam heard several soldiers swearing under their breaths as they became disoriented and stumbled in the dark. It was easier on a starry night, as a soldier could generally fix on a star or discern a horizon, but in the heavy fog, it was more akin to marching blindfolded.

Sam was part of a team carrying a heavy wooden boat, and he was mirrored on the other side by Sergeant Kenton. As big as the two men were, and with ten other soldiers lifting the boat, Sam's arms were still tiring. *If it's hard on me,* he thought, *what about the soldiers who are eighty or ninety pounds lighter than me, but still carrying the same weight?* To Sam's left, the 143rd Regiment was marching to its crossing site. They had farther to go than Sam's regiment, and he felt for the soldiers who had to cover all that ground.

At its base, Mount Trocchio was an oval-shaped mountain, which rose to a rocky peak over what was otherwise gently rolling valley floor. Able Company's path to the river took them around the southern base of Mount Trocchio, and then onto a north–south gravel road that skirted the far side of Mount Trocchio from the assembly area. The platoon would stay on the road for about one thousand yards, then break sharply to the left, come over a rise, and then march the final thousand yards to the river. All told, the boats would have to be carried at least a mile and a half.

Very quickly, Captain Ebbins lost command and control of his company. The scout that led Lieutenant Beams's platoon to the landing site was confident in his ability to follow the landmarks, and Lieutenant Beams set a fast pace down the road. The second guide, leading Lieutenant Hoar and his platoon, was less confident and soon became disoriented in the fog. As is frequently the case of traveling in the dark, the distance walked was perceived to be longer than the distance actually traveled, and Hoar's platoon turned off the road before Beams's platoon, the first platoon on the march, had done so.

By the time Sam's platoon and the headquarters element had covered seven hundred of the thousand yards of the road march, they seemed completely isolated— Hoar's platoon was to the left and behind them, and Beams was now several hundred yards ahead of them. Third Battalion would later move to the right of Able Company, but it had not yet passed the line of departure.

"Halt!" A muted shout from Captain Ebbins came from behind, and Sam repeated the command. His arms ached from carrying the boat, and several groans could heard from the soldiers.

"What?" Sam hissed into the dark behind him, and he heard running footsteps along the road.

"We missed our turn!" Ebbins was nearly screaming.

Sam swore to himself. They weren't lost—yet. "Richards! Get back here." This was to the engineer scout leading the platoon.

As the soldier came running back, Sam said in a low voice to Captain Ebbins, "No, sir. No, sir! We've got several hundred more paces."

"No, we missed our turn. I thought I caught a glimpse of Hoar's platoon to our left. I knew we'd gone too far!" Ebbins turned on the young guide. "Where's the second platoon?"

Calmly, and in a midwestern accent, the young corporal said, "I don't know, sir, but we ain't at our turn yet. It's still another 250 to 300 yards ahead of us."

"Bullshit! You got us lost! And you lost contact with 2nd Platoon! Goddamn it!" Swearing to himself, Ebbins paced back and forth, and then said, "We turn here, and we'll catch up to the other platoon."

"Ron . . . this ground isn't cleared. It's not our surveyed path—"

"Shut up! You're wrong, Taft. Move it!" Without waiting, Captain Ebbins wheeled and began walking to the back of the column.

So much for "follow me," thought Sam. He shrugged and said to his platoon, "Well, here we go boys. Column left, march! Come on, quit complaining. You heard the cap'n, we're almost there."

Behind Sam, he could hear the NCOs encouraging the troops as he had done, and Sam called out for his guide, "Richards? Richards?" but the soldier had evidently decided that the platoon was on its own. Swearing, Sam called out to a soldier at the front of his boat—a veteran of all the battles since landing at Paestum, "Martinez, get up front. Lead us down to the river."

A whispered "Yes, sir," and then the burden of the boat increased on the remaining soldiers as Private Martinez ran forward in the dark. Over a course equal to several football fields, Martinez would bravely run forward several steps and then call back to the lead boat crew, "Smooth ground." Or, "Watch your step." Even with Martinez's help, the going was much harder once the platoon left the road. Involuntary curses drifted back to Sam as soldiers slipped in the mud or tripped over rocks even as they marched up a hill and above the fog. Sam thought about halting the platoon for a rest—his heart was pounding, and despite the cold wind, he was sweating profusely—but he thought he could see stars emerging as they rose above the fog. He would press on.

Abruptly, the terrain shifted. They had been carrying the boats up an incline, which crested and began to slope back downhill. They were now on the final slope down to the river. It was the incline that convinced Sam they had turned too early. Their pre-mission briefing indicated that hill flattened out about where they were supposed to turn. *We're in Baker Company's sector*, he thought, *but at least we're headed to the river. We'll figure it out at the water.*

Distant thumps and the first roar of artillery overhead caused the platoon to duck as a man. Even the veteran soldiers, who knew the artillery wasn't coming close, still flinched in the darkness. The far bank of the Rapido River began to light up as the rounds, scores of them, began to explode. The flashes were both above and below the fog layer, and the lights underneath the fog reminded Sam of lighting across the sky in a thunderhead. It was strangely mesmerizing, and all the soldiers hesitated briefly to watch.

"Keep moving!" urged Sam, and obligingly, the boat crew began moving again—with their eyes locked onto the show of a lifetime only eight hundred yards before them.

It was easier going than a few minutes before. They were going downhill and the ground had lost its rocky cover. It was then that Sam noted that they were on the edge of a vineyard—the gnarled vines were visible to his left. In another flash of light, he saw another vineyard to his right. The platoon was passing along a gap between the fields. With a sinking heart, Sam remembered what Perkin had said about the vineyards. He opened his mouth and shouted, "Halt!" but his warning was drowned out by the sound of the Shue mine detonation when Private Martinez became the company's first casualty of the battle.

1955 Hours
1st Battalion Command Post, East of the
Rapido River, Italy

On the same hill, but several hundred yards away, the sound of the exploding mine was lost among in the crescendo of artillery strikes on the far side of the river. The establishment of the battalion headquarters east of the river was nearly complete, insofar as the battalion commander was present at his designated site. Communications, both up and down echelon, would take some time to establish, but linesmen were already busy running wires to the company crossing sites. Wires would then be run across the river and to the provisional company command posts. Walkie-talkie and handi-talkie radios were deployed of course, but few of the Texans had empirical faith in radio communications.

The command post was a hastily converted pigsty. The smell was nearly overwhelming and the sty had been extensively booby-trapped with grenades, but neither would prove to be a deterrent. The pigs had long been commandeered by the German army, and an engineering team working in the daylight had disarmed the sty.

It was a low stone hut for the pigs with rough planking for a roof. The pigsty would provide some protection from distant rifle fire and artillery fragmentation, but it offered no protection from a direct or near-hit. Soldiers were busily digging slit trenches and reinforcing the stone walls with sandbags. Camouflage netting was draped over the little building with the hope that the building would be unnoticed in daylight, and machine guns were brought up in the unlikely event of a German crossing of the river.

All that remained of the farm was the pigsty, a decision perhaps made by droll German pioneers, as the house and the large outlying buildings had been bulldozed in November. Despite the odiferous accommodations, the farm was ideally placed for the battalion's commander. It was on the western slope of the hill and looked down over the distant river and, far to the left, the village of Sant'Angelo. It was also roughly midway between the division and regimental headquarters at Mount Trocchio and the river.

"All of the companies should be in place by now," remarked Major Navarro, the battalion executive officer, to Major Spaulding.

"Yeah," was the terse reply. The waiting was nearly unbearable for the officers on the hillside. The Allied barrage was magnificent—the largest barrage the soldiers had seen close-up. The sound of the explosions rolled outward like thunder, and brief white flashes showed that the barrage was moving slowly westward away from the river—a rolling barrage that would crater the earth for some thousands of yards, but probably do little to the fortified Germans soldiers other than force them into bunkers until the barrage lifted.

The German artillery began their response. Unsure of what was happening, a significant portion of the initial fires were counter-battery—attempts to strike at the Allied artillery tubes. But the counter-battery fires quickly diminished as calls for artillery support began flooding the German divisional and corps artillery fire control centers. Allied troops had been spotted in force along the river, north and south of Sant'Angelo.

German rounds began impacting on preregistered sites in the 1st Battalion sector. The roadways were targeted, as were the routes that German intelligence assessed to be most likely. As Perkin had predicted, soldiers scattered on either side of the surveyed routes and into minefields. Boats were dropped as soldiers hit the ground, and shrapnel from artillery began to perforate the hulls of the boats as well as the soldiers' bodies. Several strikes ahead and to the left of the battalion command center had several new staff soldiers scrambling to deepen their new foxholes, although the veteran soldiers didn't move.

"Those are right on top of the Baker Company route," Perkin said.

Spaulding nodded but said nothing.

The signal to begin the assault was sent out over the 1st Battalion command net, but no replies were received. It didn't matter. The companies would begin their hot work with or without the signal. At 2000 sharp, the assault across the river began.

Major Spaulding scanned the river with his binoculars, looking for signs that the assault was underway. It was difficult to make sense of the battle, even with the elevation of the farm. What is called the fog of war was compounded by actual fog, and at first, the officers on the hill saw no indications that the attack had begun.

"Where are they?" muttered Spaulding.

"Come on, come on," repeated Perkin as he bounced on his feet anxiously.

A bright white flare climbed rapidly toward the sky to their right, and several sets of binoculars trained toward the area. It was at the Able Company crossing area, and finally, the battalion staff sensed that fighting was underway.

"Muzzle flashes," Perkin said. "Good old Able Company." Then the sound of rifle fire came to them, but there was something wrong. "There ain't enough. I don't think they're all there, sir."

Then the sky lit up as the German defenders began firing flares along the several miles of battlefront, and German artillery began pumping star shells into the sky. The light turned the battlefield into a shadowy, smoky haze that offered little illumination on the progress of the battle.

"Where's Charlie and Baker? I don't see much going on down there."

The battle had been underway for less than fifteen minutes, but it was apparent that things weren't moving according to plan. There should have been a huge volume of fire coming from the American side, but there wasn't much evidence that the assault forces had made it to the river.

The minutes passed agonizingly slowly without any evidence that the battalion was crossing in force. There was rifle fire across the entirety of the battalion front, but it was not of sufficient volume. It became obvious to the battalion staff that movement had ground to a halt.

"XO! I want you to check on Charlie Company. Get 'em moving. Ops, you've got Baker. Perk, check on Able Company." Spaulding pulled Perk aside and said in an intense voice, "Use your best judgment. I don't want you to relieve Ebbins, but if you think he's shy at all, you have my authority to do so. Get them across! It only gets harder the more we wait. Report to me as soon as you know something."

2035 Hours
1st Platoon Able Company, East of the Rapido River, Italy

It was unknown how far the platoon had penetrated the minefield before Private Martinez became a casualty, but it was obvious that the platoon had mines on every side.

The first thing that Sam had done after forward movement had stopped was to call for a medic for the wounded Martinez, and then have soldiers look for mines directly under the boat. They had found one. Sam had them probe again, and when they found no more, they gratefully set down the heavy boat.

The mine that the soldiers found virtually under their feet was a Teller antitank mine. Evidently the German pioneers assumed that equipment would be moved up to the river between the vineyards, and had planted both antitank and antipersonnel mines.

Martinez was in great pain, but he would live. Sam didn't know whether the doctors would be able to save his foot though. Perkin had told Sam once that low charge mines made more sense than powerful mines—wounded soldiers had to be carried off the field by at least two more men taking three soldiers out of the fight. *For Martinez, he was out of the fight for good*, thought Sam.

Sam had heard nothing from Ebbins, so he gave the command to begin working backward out of the minefield. As they had no idea how far toward the river the field extended, Sam thought it was best to work back to the road, and see if they could acquire their originally intended route. They were already a more than a half hour late for the crossing, and Sam knew it might take hours to get out of the minefield. *What a goat-rope*, he thought.

2057 Hours
East of the Rapido River, Italy

The road was choked with soldiers still heading for their crossing sites. Soldiers struggled under the weight of boats and of the bridging equipment, and the muddy roads became slicker with the passage of each soldier. The need for silence was gone and NCOs shouted directions to their soldiers over the din of the artillery. As the lights flashed through the valley with an odd strobe-like effect, the scene was of surreal chaos.

Perkin drove his jeep alongside the road. He moved slowly as he was driving without the benefit of headlights—even blackout lights were too risky. But there was enough ambient light now from fires burning on Mount Trocchio and on both sides of the river that he was able to see well enough.

The American artillery had ceased fire. Perkin had heard from a friend on the regimental staff that there was a shortage of ammunition in theater, and that after the initial barrage, the gunners were directed to be parsimonious with their shells.

The Germans didn't seem to have the same issue. German fires continued unabated, and they continued to shell the river crossing sites, Mount Trocchio, and seemingly random spots in the valley. *It will get worse tomorrow,* thought Perkin, as daylight would give the German artillery spotters on Monte Cassino a huge advantage over the poor souls trapped in the valley.

All of the traffic on the road that Perkin had encountered so far was headed toward the crossing sites. The wounded had not yet begun to trickle back, nor had engineers carrying equipment begun to make round trips. In the sudden light of a star shell, Perkin saw a soldier walking against the flow of traffic, and he slammed on the brakes to avoid hitting him. It was Captain Ebbins.

"Ron! Captain Ebbins!" Perk called out.

Ebbins looked at him but didn't answer at first. He squinted in the darkness, unsure of who was calling his name, then he said, "Oh, it's you, Perkin."

In the entire time that they had known each other, Perkin could not recall Ebbins ever calling him by anything other than his last name or Pickin' Boogers.

"Where's the company, Ron? Where are you going?"

"First platoon's up that hill. They're stuck in a minefield. I . . . it's my fault." Ebbins was close to tears—Perkin could hear it in his voice. "I was . . . I was heading to the crossing site to see what I could do there."

"Well, you're heading the wrong way, but hop in. I'm going there myself." Perkin watched as Ebbins hesitated and then climbed into the jeep.

"Are you coming to relieve me?"

From Ebbins's flat, emotionless, monotone, it wasn't clear to Perkin what answer he wanted to hear. "Are you still in the fight, Ron?"

"I don't . . . yes. Yes," he said more resolutely.

"Then I'm just here to give you a ride to the crossing, but ya gotta pull it together, Ron. This whole thing is pretty shaky and the boys will need you to be clear-headed."

Unexpectedly, Ebbins whined, "You made me look like an idiot in front of Colonel Wranosky, you know. With the combat infantryman's badge. Why'd you do that?"

Perkin was seldom surprised, but he didn't expect this conversation. "It was payback for screwing with the Jap officers."

"Why do you care about the Jap officers?"

"I don't like bullies Ron. That's why."

"I'm not much of a bully today. I'm scared shitless."

Perkin had seen a movie once where a Rasputin-like villain hypnotized his victims. Ebbins sounded like one of them—distant and barely conscious. "We all are. Hold it together for the boys." Perkin repeated. He wasn't sure where the conversation was headed, but he wasn't surprised to find out that Captain Ebbins equated bullying with courage.

There was silence for several minutes as they edged along the side of the road, then Ebbins asked in a stronger voice, "What's the news of the other companies?"

"They're having trouble, too. Charlie and Baker got runners to us just as I was leaving. Baker had an entire platoon wiped out by a single shell before they even got to the river. Charlie Company doesn't have a single soldier across. The Germans have got the river registered, so their artillery's giving the engineers fits with the bridging equipment. There ain't any footbridges over the river yet, and the boats are getting shot up pretty bad."

Perkin had questioned the wisdom of telling Ebbins the hard facts, but if he was going to break down, Perkin wanted it sooner rather than later. He was prepared to relieve Ebbins, but he had thought about Spaulding's emphasis to do it only if necessary. Perkin looked over at Ebbins. In the flashes of light coming from the battlefield, Perkin saw that Ebbins kept his eyes forward, straining in the darkness—he looked neither left nor right. Ebbins chest was moving up and down rapidly, and Perkin was concerned that the other officer might hyperventilate and pass out, but he didn't.

Perkin pulled off the road. An MP was in place directing traffic and he told them that they were about to cross into 3rd Battalion's sector. "Able company should be straight to the river," he said.

"Have you directed anyone that way?" Ebbins asked. It was the most coherent that he'd sounded since being picked up by Perkin.

"Yes, sir. A platoon of infantry and some engineers. Y'all better walk from here. If you get outside the tape, you're dick dancin' in the minefield."

Perkin parked the jeep out of the way, grabbed his Thompson, and said, "Let's go." As Ebbins climbed slowly out of the jeep, Perkin looked at him and said, "Ron? Where's your carbine?"

Ebbins looked back into the jeep, then said, "I don't know."

The thought occurred to Perkin that Ebbins had likely dropped his M-1 Carbine in the minefield and ran out of terror. *That's definitely not the army-preferred method to egress a minefield*, thought Perkin dryly. *Well, the son-of-a-bitch is here now. Better get some work out of him.*

"You'll be able to find one at the crossing," Perkin said. "Let's get moving."

2135 Hours
Able Company Crossing Site, East Bank Rapido River, Italy

The thought of chaos remained with Perkin as they jogged down the gentle slope to the river. A tangle of wrecked bridging equipment greeted them while they were still fifty yards from the water. Craters all around them indicated that the area had been shelled heavily.

A soldier emerged from shadows. He was limping, using his rifle for a crutch, and an arm was wrapped in a bloody sling under his coat. "Thank God you're here, sir."

The words were spoken to Perkin, but Captain Ebbins assumed they were for him. Ebbins replied, "I got here as fast as I could, Corporal Evans." Encouraged by the welcome, he strode off to the riverbank to see the crossing for himself.

"We don't even have a Corporal Evans to mistake me for. That's the funniest damn thing that's happened all day—I gotta remember to tell Eddie." Private Pfadenhauer laughed. The soldier had been in Perkin's platoon when he was in Able Company, and was now assigned to B. G. E. Beams's platoon.

"He'll get a kick out it, that's for sure. Bring me up to date, Howie."

"Yes, sir. We got sighted as we were coming down the slope, and we got pinned down for a while by an MG-42. It was taken out during the barrage. At 2000, no one else was here, so Lieutenant Beams launches the assault. We had a hell of a time controlling the boats in that fuckin' river, sir. We had a rope tied to the end of the wood boat and it whipped the boat down the river so fast that we was out of rope before the boat was halfway across. Finally some replacement kid volunteers to swim across with a rope tied around his waist. I never seen anyone swim so fast. So he pulls a couple guys over in a raft and then they set up a little ferry."

Private Pfadenhauer was shaking uncontrollably, and Perkin opened Pfadenhauer's coat and looked at his wounds in the battlefield light. He noticed for the first time that the young soldier was soaked. "My arm's broke and sliced open, and I think my ankle is sprained if not broke as well. Lieutenant Beams sent me back on the ferry. Then I slipped on that fuckin' riverbank and rolled into the fuckin' river. One of those goddamned engineers pulled me out—"

"I'd think that you'd be grateful to 'em."

"He pulled me out before I could catch my rifle, and I had to jump back in to get it. Besides, do you see any of 'em now?"

Perkin looked at the river and while he saw some men struggling with a rope, there was no bridging effort underway. "Where are they?" he asked.

"They dug foxholes in that damn holler there. Said they'd wait until the fires lift."

"Where are your officers? What have they been doing about it?" Perkin looked for the Able Company officers but didn't see any.

"Lieutenant Beams is gone, sir. I reckon him and the platoon are at the phase line or maybe they've already captured Hitler. We crossed thinkin' everyone was behind us, and he just kept going. He called out, 'B. G. E. stands for 'Beams Goes to Europe,' and then he was gone—that guy has style, sir. Lieutenant Hoar and them arrived about ten minutes or so before you did, but he don't know what's going on yet. He just jumped into the crossing. Where's Lieutenant Bear?"

"They were guided into a minefield, and they're digging their way out now."

"Goddamn. This is a terrible place," and, daring greatly, he added, "Perk."

Perkin smiled, put his hand on the private's good shoulder, and agreed. "At this very moment, I believe it's the worst place in the world, Roscoe. Now, if you can handle a little chore on your way to an aid station, take my jeep and find Major Spaulding at the battalion CP, and tell him I'm helpin' out Cap'n Ebbins here. Have him send Eddie to fetch me if he needs something."

2205 Hours
Able Company Crossing Site, East Bank Rapido River, Italy

The entire platoon was finally out of the minefield but not without cost. One soldier detonated a mine as he was trying to remove the fuse. It killed him instantly and wounded four others. Compounding their difficulties, two more boats were perforated.

Sam was pushing the platoon at as fast a pace as possible, but the soldiers were tired. Most hadn't had any sleep for thirty-six hours—some even longer than that. Although they were superbly conditioned and tough, the ordeal in the minefield had been disheartening, and the heavy boats were rubbing raw blisters into their hands.

The platoon had run into Private Pfadenhauer as he was making his way to the battalion CP. He gave Sam the same update as he had Perkin, and when Master Sergeant Hawkins overheard that Captain Ebbins was at the crossing site, he whispered to Sam, "The bastard might want his carbine back. He dropped it in his haste to see more combat."

When the platoon was crossing over the crest and beginning the march to the river, Sam was gratified to see glimpses of white tape on either side of what was now a well-traveled lane. They delineated a mine-free path, and the muddy footprints at least hinted at safety from the mines.

From the crest, Sam could get a sense of the battlefield. Third Battalion was heavily engaged on his right, but he didn't see any signs that they had yet crossed. Tracer rounds were being used by some of the German machine guns on the far side, and the burning phosphorous tips on the rounds showed Sam how exquisitely defended the river was. Interlocking machine gunfire came from several hundred yards behind the river and pinned down the Texans, as the German artillery threw shell after shell along the river.

Directly in front of Sam was Able's crossing, and the far bank here looked as inactive as in front of 3rd Battalion. *If it's true that Beams is on the other side*, thought Sam, *he's one lonely son-of-a-bitch tonight.*

He looked to his left, and both Baker and Charlie companies were engaged, but once again, it looked like all the American firing was on the near bank. Far to his left, Sam couldn't see much except for the occasional flare, but it sounded like the 143rd Regimental Combat Team was taking a pounding as well. As he said a silent prayer for his fellow Texans, Sam asked himself, *Is it possible this attack has already failed?*

Putting such notions out of his mind, Sam halted the platoon when they were still three hundred yards short of the crossing. "Y'all stay here!" he called out, and there was no argument from anyone in the platoon.

The first person he saw was Perkin, who was arguing with another officer just a short distance away. Sam headed to them, and when he arrived, he saw Perkin as angry as he'd ever seen him before.

"Listen to me, goddamn it!" he shouted into the face of a short lean officer. "The boats won't do it—they're all shot up. We need to get the footbridges over."

"And I'm telling you, Captain, that it does us no good if we lose these bridges and the men to set them up. And I'll tell you something else as well: I don't take orders from you!" The shorter man was just as angry as Perkin.

"What's going on, Perk?" Sam asked.

"Able has lost all boats, save what you brought. We gotta get a footbridge across, or we're done. Beams is done. The engineers are over yonder." Perkin pointed to an unorganized collection of foxholes thirty yards in the distance where a number of heads could be seen poking out and watching the argument with great interest.

"Where's Captain Ebbins?" Sam asked.

"He and a couple boys ran up river to see if we can cross with the 143rd at one of their sites. To see if their engineers have more balls than ours."

The engineering officer started to walk away, but Sam grabbed him by the jacket and pulled him back roughly. "We ain't done yet. Perk, what's your status here?"

Understanding the question, Perkin said, "I represent Major Spaulding. Ebbins is in command, and I'm here to help out where needed."

Sam nodded, and said, "OK. I'm in command of Able Company until Captain Ebbins returns. How about you give me a turn with this asshole, and if I can't get him to see the light, we'll bring in Major Spaulding."

The engineered sneered at Sam, "Your threats don't bother me. I'll do what's in the best interests of my soldiers, and you can go to hell!"

Perkin shook his head and shrugged, "Good luck, Sam. I'll see how Hoar's doing and then we'll get ready to cross." He glared at the engineer and said, "I'll find you later," then he wheeled away and jogged to the river.

Turning to the engineer, Sam asked, "What's your name, and why are your men sitting on their asses?"

"I don't have to answer—"

Sam's short patience came to an end. With a sigh of disgust, he pushed the officer out of his way. The man tripped over a wooden beam lying on the ground and landed hard on his side. As the engineer struggled to catch his breath, acting on impulse, Sam kicked the engineer hard in the stomach. Sam turned back to the platoon and he whistled loudly and said, "Kenton! Fratelli! Get over here on the double!"

The two men broke from the platoon and ran to Sam. In a loud voice that could be heard by both his platoon and the engineers, he ordered, "Fratelli, kill anyone who as much as points a rifle in my direction. Bill, be ready to help me get these assholes out of their hiding spots."

Sam stomped over to the foxholes, and called out, "Who's senior NCO here?"

A soldier climbed out of his foxhole and walked up to Sam, "I am. Sergeant Martin."

"Martin, can you get these men working on the footbridges?"

"Not unless my lieutenant orders me to. How dare you—"

Sam took a step toward the sergeant and the sergeant's complaint died off. In truth, he nearly hit the sergeant out of frustration, but he needed to find a way short of violence to compel the men to work. Sam decided if necessary, he'd work his way through the entire body of engineers until he found one willing to help, and he reached over to the sergeant's arm, dug his fingers into the chevrons, and ripped them from his jacket. As Sam contemptuously pushed the sergeant out of his way, he asked, "Who's next in command?" Silence. "Who's next?" Sam bellowed again in a voice loud enough to be heard at the river over the artillery.

"I am, sir." A soldier ten yards from Sam, hidden by the shadows, jumped out of his foxhole and ran over to Sam. "Sergeant Dunnigan."

"Come with me, Sergeant." Sam grabbed the man by the sleeve and pulled him along as he jogged to the riverbank. After a few steps, Sam let go of the engineer, and they ran together to the riverbank.

The scene at the river was grim. The heavy artillery fires had shifted down river for the moment, but there was a mortar in the distance that continued to blindly lob rounds in the vicinity of the crossing. Fog and smoke drifted through the crossing site, and the disarray at the bank was seen only in the dim light reflected off the clouds over the burning battlefield.

The bodies of four soldiers had been pulled to the upper bank and were laid out neatly next to each other. Sam looked at the faces of the dead in the flashes of light from a distant flare—they were men that he'd known for years. Two were from Beams's platoon and one came from Lieutenant Hoar's platoon. The fourth man, he didn't know.

"Is he one of yours?" Sam asked.

"No, sir. He came floating down the river earlier from 3rd Battalion's sector. We pulled him out, but he'd drowned." Sergeant Dunnigan shivered.

Sam pointed to the soldiers of the 2nd Platoon who were struggling with one of the heavy boats. "What do you see over there?"

"I see your men puttin' that boat into the water, sir," the soldier said simply.

"I reckon that boat's holed already, but they're still gonna try. Do you know why?"

"Orders," Dunnigan answered.

"It's more than that, Sergeant. We have a team on the far bank. They've done their duty, they crossed the river, and they've moved inland. As far as I know, in the eight hundred men of this battalion, they're the only ones who've done their job tonight." Sam pointed to a distant flash of light, and he tilted his head. "Can you hear that weapon firing right now?"

"Yes, sir."

"What's it sound like to you?"

"It sounds like a BAR, sir. It ain't German."

"No, it's not German. It's one of ours, and when I say ours, I mean *ours*—from this company. Now, I don't know if we're gonna be able to do all the things that we want to with this assault, but what I know for certain is that unless we get across the river and link up with that platoon, they'll all be dead by tomorrow. I know that as certain as I know the sun'll come up in the morning. Now, you look at those boats. Do you think we can cross on those?"

Sergeant Dunnigan looked at the shredded wooden boats, and the deflated rubber rafts that were strewn about. He shook his head, "No, sir. You can't."

"But you see those riflemen trying anyway?"

"Yes, sir."

"Do you know why now, Sergeant?"

"Yes, sir."

"OK, Dunnigan. What's it gonna be?"

"I'll get my men, sir. We'll try putting a pontoon footbridge over there." He pointed to his left.

"God bless you."

Chapter Fifteen

January 21, 1944
0200 Hours
1st Battalion Command Post, East of the
Rapido River, Italy

Major Spaulding couldn't stand the smell of the pigsty any longer. He had only been inside for a few minutes, but there were no communications coming in anyway. Virtually every wire that had been laid over the course of the battle had been cut by one cause or another—German artillery or a careless GI. It really didn't matter why to Spaulding.

He breathed deeply of the air, but it wasn't fresh. It reeked of chemicals, smoke, and dirt. The artillery fire never ceased, and Spaulding estimated that between the two sides, at least fifty thousand rounds had already been fired. How anyone was left alive in the valley was beyond him. Spaulding saw a trail of lights climbing up to the sky in the distance behind Sant'Angelo. A few seconds later he heard the faint *whoosh, whoosh, whoosh, whoosh, whoosh, whoosh* of the Nebelwerfer rocket launcher and then the scream of the rounds as they tipped over toward their targets. Spaulding couldn't see the impact—they landed in the 143rd's sector.

"Perk, let's saddle up. XO, let Wranosky know that we've gone forward to check on things ourselves."

"You got it, Boss."

Perkin drove the jeep, and they backtracked to the road and headed south first. Again, the road was choked with soldiers moving back and forth. A long line of walking wounded were moving toward the battalion aid stations in the rear, or were simply heading back to the assembly areas behind Mount Trocchio. Other soldiers moved forward to the fighting, many of them wounded as well—back to the companies and the crossing sites.

They passed heavy trucks carrying the Bailey bridging equipment, and Perkin knew that they would not be used this evening. *They might as well turn back now,* he thought.

They turned down the cleared lane leading to Charlie Company, and as they crested the hill, Perkin's heart sank. It was a repeat of what he'd seen at Able Company's site, only worse. Twisted, wrecked bridging equipment had not even made it to the crossing site, and the path was littered with perforated boats. Judging from the look of things, the company had been brought through a minefield.

They stopped the jeep several hundred yards from the site and approached it by foot. The soldiers of Charlie Company were taking fire from all along their frontage, and it was apparent that they had dug into fighting positions and were no longer attempting to cross.

Major Spaulding and Perkin passed a mortar team that was working at a feverish pace, and they were lobbing rounds toward Sant'Angelo, but neither Perkin nor Major Spaulding could see where the rounds landed.

When they got to a line of trenches, an officer spied them and came running out. It was the company commander—a captain named Wilson. As they knelt, Captain Wilson shook hands with Major Spaulding and Perkin. He ignored Perkin's observation that if only they had a Rawlings in the battalion they could put a sports team together, and said, "Wish I had good news for you, sir."

"How bad?"

"We still don't have anyone across. All our boats and bridges are destroyed. The engineers are trying to jury-rig something, but . . . well, we'll see. My casualties are eleven dead, including two officers, and over forty wounded, including my other two officers, and several missing. I hope they turn up, but they might have been swept away in the water. If we get a bridge up and running, I could get maybe two small platoons over."

Spaulding took a deep breath and blew it out. There was literally nothing he could do to help this company. "OK. You do what you gotta do. We still go if we get a way across. Keep the CP informed. I'm heading to Able, then Baker, and should be back at the CP in an hour or so."

As they walked back to the jeep, Spaulding said in a low voice to Perkin, "This attack is gonna fail, Perk. I can't see any way that we can succeed. If the other two rifle companies are this bad, I must be running close to 25 percent casualties already. Shoot, I'll be sending the battalion cooks and the chaplain across next. It'll be light in about five hours, and if we haven't pushed inland at least a thousand yards or so by dawn, we'll have to withdraw back to Trocchio. As far as I can tell, Beams has had the greatest penetration north of Sant' Angelo, and no one's heard from him for six hours."

"That's because he's probably already liberated Rome." Perkin grinned, but the grin died quickly. "I hope them boys are OK."

"Me too."

They heard the whoosh of more Nebelwerfers, and they turned to watch the burning rockets and the smoky trails—visible even in the darkness. It was a much more extensive attack this time, and they saw the trails of what appeared to be a score of rockets. Although it looked as if the launch site were the same, the angle of the lights was different—rather than crossing the sky, these appeared to be heading straight up. The rockets were coming their way.

0200 Hours
Able Company Crossing Site, East Bank Rapido River, Italy

The casualties continued to climb, and little progress was made. The engineers had begun a pontoon bridge not unlike the bridges at Fredericksburg eighty years before. Rafts were lashed together, and an attempt was made to extend them across the Rapido River, but the current was too strong. Every attempt was met with failure, but the engineers were trying and dying next to the riflemen.

Colonel Wranosky had come to the crossing site to see for himself how the battle progressed. He gave Sergeant Dunnigan a battlefield commission, and he had sent the other engineering officer and his sergeant back to the assembly area in disgrace. He truly sympathized with their sentiments, but now was not the time to be sentimental.

Colonel Wranosky, Captain Ebbins, and Sam knelt on the edge of the bank and watched the engineers in the flashing lights with intense interest. They were going to try again, and this was the last attempt to put a pontoon bridge across. They had agreed with the engineers that if this failed, they would be forced to look at other options. A burst of heavy machine gunfire upriver and the distinctive sound of mortar rounds landing in the 3rd Battalion's sector reinforced their sense of urgency.

Lieutenant Dunnigan appeared doubtful. He pulled Sam aside, not yet comfortable talking officer to officer with captains and colonels, and said, "This is our best shot. We got these boats lashed together as tightly as we can. One of your boys volunteered to swim the river, and he'll pull our barges across, then we'll throw planking down on top of the boats for your troops to walk on. You'll need to get everyone across as quickly as possible 'cause I don't think this will hold for too long."

Sam had his doubts about the wisdom of moving a body of soldiers across unless they had a guaranteed means to bring them back, but there was no question that they would do it. Colonel Wranosky had made it clear that he intended to get his regiment across, and *he* was prepared to die trying. He expected no less from his men or the engineers.

Despite Dunnigan's words, Sam was heartened by this bridge. It looked more rigid than the other attempts, and he thought that perhaps this time they might actually have a pontoon lash-up that would hold in the current. He could see, however, that not all of the engineer's boats were seaworthy—every remaining boat of the company had been perforated in an artillery strike at midnight—so the engineers were forced to use leaking, perforated boats as placeholders. It was the only way they could cover the thirty-foot distance across the river.

The volunteer swimmer was a veteran soldier from Wyoming—a machine gunner from the weapons platoon. Amid hoots and catcalls, he stripped completely naked, turned, and faced his fellow soldiers in a Charles Atlas pose before diving into the water with a rope tied around his waist. The soldier was indeed a strong swimmer and he made it across the Rapido without being pushed too far downstream. He worked his way back to the crossing site hunched over, trying unsuccessfully to minimize the effects of the cold wind on his wet naked body. Sam was in awe of the soldier—the water was near freezing and the wind was biting—as he sat naked on the opposite bank, planted his feet in the mud, and began to pull the line of rafts across.

Sam heard the whoosh of Nebelwerfers and looked up to the sky to see if he could find the smoke trail, but he couldn't. As he listened to the whine of the incoming munitions, his veteran's ear judged that they would be close but not on their position. Sam returned his attention to the bridging effort. It looked as if the soldier on the far bank would not be strong enough to pull the boats over, that he would not be able to counteract the strong current, but he found a iron stake that he been used by Lieutenant Beams during his crossing hours earlier. The soldier wrapped two loops of rope around the stake, and pulled and tightened the line as he worked the boats across.

The rounds from the Nebelwerfer came down with a loud explosion. Sam could see an intense white fire burning several hundred yards down the river, and he imagined he heard screams from across the battlefield. The fires must have illuminated American soldiers because shortly after the Nebelwerfers struck, a rapid-fire MG-42 opened up.

Wranosky swore and stood up to see if he could identify who was on the receiving end. Realizing that Charlie Company was probably being struck, he hung his head and said in a low voice to Sam, "God help me, I hoped they would land in the 143rd's sector."

Sam had stood as well. He put his hand on his regimental commander's shoulder and gave it a short squeeze before turning back to his soldiers. He whistled loudly and called out, "First Platoon on me! We go over in single file." He had said the words out of custom, and then Sam shook his head in disgust—there was no way to cross other than single file.

Without hesitation, a soldier had dropped into the rafts and was sliding planks of wood through the gunwale ropes—the boats were deployed with their bows to the current and the planks were placed athwartships over the gunwales. The boats that had some perforation sunk perilously low as they took the soldier's weight, but the bridge held. After a frantic effort, the soldier and two helpers crossed the Rapido River over the pontoon bridge, and the naked volunteer ran back across to the east bank, dry clothes, and a round of applause from grinning soldiers.

"Don't come over yet," called one of the engineers from the far bank, and he walked back to the east bank with his arms held outward for balance. Sam hadn't noticed it in the dark, but it had been Lieutenant Dunnigan laying the planks across the pontoons.

Dunnigan scampered up the riverbank, waved one of his soldiers over, and told him what was needed. As the private ran off to grab supplies, the new lieutenant nodded at the infantry officers and explained, "We need to secure the other end better. It won't hold on that spike, and a man can't hold it for long."

A few minutes later, the private came running back with three steel fence posts and a heavy post driver in his arms.

"There aren't any trees on the other side to anchor to, so we'll use fence posts for now. No sense in anything permanent. We'll be finished building a steel catwalk in the next couple hours. Be ready though, driving these posts will be noisy."

"Got it, let's be quick then so we can get our boys across before the shelling starts," Colonel Wranosky said.

Dunnigan nodded to the soldier, who hesitated and then started across with his load. The stability of the bridge was precarious, and the soldier froze twice in his tracks as he was crossing the pontoon bridge. When he was across, he handed the post driver to the other soldier on the far side, placed the fence post where he wanted it and nodded. The soldier slid the heavy iron driver over the fence post and listened. When he heard the boom of heavy artillery, he lifted the driver and brought it down hard on the fencepost. The post went two inches into the riverbank. The soldier waited for another boom, and drove the post in deeper and deeper still.

"Look!" An engineer pointed at the river.

Several bodies, victims of the mortar attack against 3rd Battalion, had floated down the river and were lodged against the pontoon bridge. They were wedged against a raft that was slowly leaking air, and the pressure of the bodies pushed by the river was sliding the raft out of line. Still, it looked like the bridge would hold.

"One of 'em's alive!" an engineer exclaimed.

A wounded soldier in the water had come to a stop against the bridge, and had desperately clutched one of the bridge's mooring lines. He was too weak to climb out, and the force of the water was pulling him under the bridge. But the soldier wouldn't let go.

Understanding what was at stake, Lieutenant Dunnigan ran onto the bridge and tried to pull the man's hand from the rope, but it was locked tight around the line in a death grip. Dunnigan's weight leaning over the bridge's side and the drag of the bodies in the water put a tremendous strain on the bridge, and suddenly the sole stake holding the bridge slid silently out of the mud, freeing the mooring lines from the bank. Before the engineers on the bank could grab the ropes, the far end of the bridge whipped downstream. With a scream,

Dunnigan went headfirst into the swirling water, and he and most of the boats disappeared into the darkness, never to be seen again.

0220 Hours
Charlie Company Crossing Site, East Bank
Rapido River, Italy

Perkin had never been under Nebelwerfer attack before. He had heard the unnerving scream of the rockets from a distance but had never been on the receiving end of an attack. Major Spaulding had, however, and he grabbed Perkin, and together they sprinted to one of the Charlie Company trenches. They slid in to the crowded trench just as the rounds began to impact.

By this point in the day, every soldier was already a veteran survivor of multiple artillery and mortar barrage. But those attacks had been different—the munitions used then were high explosive and in addition to the explosive effect, the metal casings of the shells fragmented on detonation into white-hot shrapnel.

The Nebelwerfer also fired high explosive rounds, but that was not the payload in this attack. At least three dozen incendiary rounds rained down on both sides of the river crossing, spreading hundreds of liters of burning oil across thousands of square feet of battlefield. Adding to the noise and confusion, Shue mines emplaced on the far riverbank exploded in sympathetic detonation.

A handful of engineers surveying the damaged bridging at the river crossing were engulfed in the burning oil—some jumped into the river and were swept away. Others died where they stood. None lived through the attack.

In all the scenes of violence and indifference to humanity that Perkin had witnessed in the war, this was the worst. He had thought that the chemical warfare used in the First World War was the most obscene method yet invented for taking life—until now. It was murder, plain and simple. Sadistic, horrific murder.

As a German machine gun opened up from the outer defenses of Sant'Angelo, Perkin swore that if he were ever given the chance, he'd pay back the Nebelwerfer crews for what they'd just done.

0340 Hours
Able Company Crossing Site, East Bank Rapido River, Italy

The chaplain was a different man than the one Perkin spoke to only the day before. He had spent the entire night praying with soldiers, comforting those who were wounded in mind and body. As he told Perkin, he would never be the same again.

The chaplain had joined Spaulding and Perkin at the Charlie Company crossing site, and accompanied them to visit the other companies. He had more work to do with Charlie Company, he told the battalion command, but Spaulding had said that he had to tend to all of his flock—other soldiers needed him as well.

A steel footbridge would be across the terrible river in minutes, and barring another unforeseen calamity, Spaulding intended to send what was left of Able and Baker companies across. He'd had a long discussion with Colonel Wranosky, who was adamant that the crossing continue if possible. Wranosky wanted a beachhead, even a small one, on the other side of the river to support the increasingly remote possibility that the division would be able to get a Bailey Bridge across. Perkin had heard Spaulding arguing with his regimental commander clearly and logically. Four or five platoons, he said, would not be able to hold the beachhead during the daylight hours when the Germans were certain to counterattack, nor could such a small force accomplish the reduction of the German defenses at Sant'Angelo by themselves. If the remainder of the regiment could not cross, what was left of Baker and Able companies would be wasted in a futile attack.

Wranosky had an explosive temperament, and he was unused to subordinates arguing with him, but he listened carefully to Spaulding's arguments, then replied, "If we don't take and hold ground on the west bank, we come back and do this all again tomorrow night. We need to control at least a section of both sides in order for there to be even a glimmer of hope of getting armor across. The attack goes. When they've penetrated to the phase line, you'll move your command post west of the river, and you'll support the flow of forces through your beachhead. But not until then. Clear?"

"Yes, sir." Spaulding had said without further argument. He told Perkin later that there was an element of truth in what Wranosky said. Of course it was desirable to have a beachhead on the far bank, but only if they were able to maintain communication and resupply of the forward companies. Otherwise, Spaulding said, he was afraid they'd just be sacrificed.

The chaplain had called the assault platoons together for a prayer while they waited for the engineers to finish the bridge. As Perkin waited for the last soldiers to kneel and the chaplain to begin, a phrase used by Colonel Wranosky was nagging at Perkin. The colonel had said if we were to have "even a glimmer of hope," and it had Perkin thinking of the night he'd had drinks with Sam, Jimmy Cardosi, and Waller Finley-Jones at the hotel in Santa Croce del Sannio. Perkin had then described such a venture as they were now embarking on as a forlorn hope—the forlorn hope being the lead element in a suicidal assault against a defended castle or defensive line with the promise of promotion and glory if one lived.

Perkin was thinking about the forlorn hope, and the historical examples where the forlorn hope succeeded. It wasn't a comforting thought, as few examples came to mind. Meanwhile, the chaplain was giving an impromptu sermon, and the words drifted in and out of Perkin's conscious thoughts as he fretted about the assault. But a passage caught his attention and he began to listen to the words of the Bible as recited by the chaplain from memory.

And as he talked with them, behold, there came up the champion, the Philistine of Gath, Goliath by name, out of the armies of the Philistines, and spake according to the same words: and David heard them.

And all the men of Israel, when they saw the man, fled from him, and were sore afraid.

And the men of Israel said, Have ye seen this man that is come up? surely to defy Israel is he come up: and it shall be, that the man who killeth him, the king will enrich him with great riches, and will give him his daughter, and make his father's house free in Israel.

I'm not the only one thinking of a forlorn hope today, thought Perkin as he listened to the passage from I Samuel. *Great riches and a king's daughter must have been the Biblical equivalent of promotion and glory*. The chaplain continued the passage, stopping occasionally to make a point.

And when the words were heard which David spake, they rehearsed them before Saul: and he sent for him.

And David said to Saul, Let no man's heart fail because of him; thy servant will go and fight with this Philistine.

And Saul said to David, Thou art not able to go against this Philistine to fight with him: for thou art but a youth, and he a man of war from his youth.

"We are like David. Not surprisingly, the Germans are the Philistines, and perhaps like Goliath, they believe they're invincible. But Goliath wasn't invincible, was he?" When the soldiers shook their heads, the chaplain said, "No, because God was on David's side."

And he took his staff in his hand, and chose him five smooth stones out of the brook, and put them in a shepherd's bag which he had, even in a scrip; and his sling was in his hand: and he drew near to the Philistine.

And the Philistine came on and drew near unto David; and the man that bare the shield went before him.

And when the Philistine looked about, and saw David, he disdained him: for he was but a youth, and ruddy, and of a fair countenance.

And the Philistine said unto David, Am I a dog, that thou comest to me with staves? And the Philistine cursed David by his gods.

And the Philistine said to David, Come to me, and I will give thy flesh unto the fowls of the air, and to the beasts of the field.

Then said David to the Philistine, Thou comest to me with a sword, and with a spear, and with a shield: but I come to thee in the name of the Lord of hosts, the God of the armies of Israel, whom thou hast defied.

This day will the Lord deliver thee into mine hand; and I will smite thee, and take thine head from thee; and I will give the carcasses of the host of the Philistines this day unto the fowls of the air, and to the wild beasts of the earth; that all the earth may know that there is a God in Israel.

And all this assembly shall know that the Lord saveth not with sword and spear: for the battle is the Lord's, and he will give you into our hands.

And it came to pass, when the Philistine arose, and came, and drew nigh to meet David, that David hastened, and ran toward the army to meet the Philistine.

And David put his hand in his bag, and took thence a stone, and slang it, and smote the Philistine in his forehead, that the stone sunk into his forehead; and he fell upon his face to the earth.

The chaplain concluded the passage with the observation, "I love the ending in this one, boys!" He was about to make a more profound conclusion to his mini-sermon, but was interrupted by a soldier from Baker Company.

"Excuse me, sir, why did David need five stones?"

"You want to know why, if God was on his side, did he draw five stones?" When the soldier nodded, the chaplain said, "It is not a sign of diminished faith. David proved his faith by going forth against the terrible Philistine, Goliath. I think that what the Bible is telling us is while there's no substitute for faith, a little preparation also goes a long way. Army chaplains have always said, 'Pray like it all depends on God. Work like it all depends on you,' and in the end, you can have faith that you'll succeed. And, men, through this terrible night, as we strive for God and country, it's faith that holds us together."

0345 Hours
Able Company Crossing Site, East Bank Rapido River, Italy

Sam sat some distance away, not listening to the sermon. He'd prayed nearly nonstop during every lull in the activity, and instead of a sermon, he wanted a few minutes to himself.

He absentmindedly opened a can of C Rations. It was a can of the familiar beef hash, and he ate it without even tasting the food. His thoughts were on home again, and he wondered if he would live through the day to see Margaret and the ranch once more.

The army psychologists told the soldiers that it was best not to dwell on home at times like these, but Sam couldn't help himself. He wanted a clear, untarnished image of Maggie in his mind before they crossed the river—he wanted to have her in his heart and soul once more in case he died this day.

He pulled a letter from her from his pocket and opened the envelope—he knew he wasn't supposed to carry personal items like this with him, but he didn't care. The letter had arrived after their return from Ortona, and it was a mundane letter. There was absolutely nothing important or earth-shattering in its pages, but he desperately wanted to read it again. It was too dark, and even with the flashes of light from the fires and the combat surrounding him, he could only make out a word or two before it went dark again.

It didn't matter so much, as he had every word, every sentence memorized. He could picture the sweater she described that she was going to give her mother for Christmas, as well as the spinning reel she bought for Old Perkin. Sam grinned in the dark—the old man would never use it, as he was strictly a baitcaster man. As Christmas had come and gone since her letter had been mailed, Sam wondered if she'd badgered Old Perkin into taking her fishing. He'd have to use the reel then, Sam supposed.

He went to the last page and ran his fingertips over the letter. Margaret had ended the letter with a kiss and he could feel the outline of her lipstick on the page. Sam lifted the letter to his nose and breathed in. She had sprayed the letter with Joy, and Sam imagined he could smell the French flowers that had gone into the perfume. He had almost told her several times over the year that the perfume was far too expensive to be sprayed on a letter, but he was grateful that he hadn't. Although she had worn many different perfumes since he'd known her, the smell of Joy was so closely associated in his mind with Margaret's scent that it seemed briefly for a second as if she were there.

But she wasn't. Margaret was in Texas. Sam was in Italy, and the war came back to him in a rush. The ceaseless pounding of the artillery, the cries of the wounded, the smell of death over Joy. Sam had no more illusions about this fight. It was clear that the division had taken a terrible beating since nightfall, and he was hoping that sanity would prevail and the assault would not continue.

It was time. Sam sighed, put the letter away, and stood up. He knew that if the engineers completed the bridge, the company would go. He didn't see much point in it now, but they would go. And he would go too.

0400 Hours
Able Company Crossing Site, East Bank
Rapido River, Italy

"Hey, Bubba."

"Hey, Bear."

They stood together some hundred yards from the crossing site. The sermon had ended and both of them were preparing to go. The word was that this time the bridge would work, and it seemed as if the stars had finally aligned to make it so. The engineers had welded together a steel footbridge made of parts from four other destroyed bridges. Most importantly, the artillery had shifted elsewhere—other crossing sites that were still being actively pursued.

Soldiers from Able and Baker companies had cleared paths on the eastern slope to Able's crossing, and here Major Spaulding intended to cross the majority of his battalion. Able Company would cross first and head inland. Baker would cross next and move to their left. The notion of reaching the phase line was being discarded, even if no commander would say so. It was tacitly understood that all they would be able to achieve initially was to carve out and hold a small beachhead. If other units could use the little footbridge, they would fan out from there.

Sam had already handed Perkin a letter addressed to Margaret, and was carrying one from his cousin addressed to Old Perkin. There was little left to do but shake hands.

Private Kulis walked up to them and offered his hand to Sam as well. "Good luck, sir. We'll see y'all in a little while."

"Thanks, Eddie," and as Kulis turned to go, Sam said in jest to Perkin, "If you see Ebbins running, shoot the son-of-a-bitch for me, would you?"

"Does he have to be running?" Perkin asked. He saw Major Spaulding waving them over, "Take care, Sam."

"You too, Bubba."

The bridge was ready. It wasn't much of a bridge—a catwalk of foot-wide plates of steel and no handrails—but it would have to do. Sam's platoon would cross first, followed by Hoar's platoon and the weapons platoon. Two undermanned platoons from Baker Company would cross next—they had already lost their company commander and an entire platoon the night before in their march to the river.

Sam looked to Ebbins, who stared uncomprehendingly back at him, so he looked at Spaulding, who nodded.

"Follow me!"

Sam slid down the four-foot bank and stepped onto the bridge. It bounced as he moved over the water, but it held. As soon as he was to the west bank, he jumped to the left of the bridge and turned to help the others.

A squad leader led his team over after Sam, and they moved cautiously up the west bank. Without hesitation, Able Company made its first incursion into German held territory in eight hours. When the rest of his platoon made it over, Sam relinquished his position to Lieutenant Hoar.

The first obstacle was a double layer of concertina wire. It had been methodically laid out in an orderly fashion weeks ago by the German pioneers and Italian laborers, but now it was a ragged mess. The Allied barrage had torn gaps in the wire in many places, and many of the German rounds fell short as well, tearing further gaps in the wire. More than that, Sam could see a trail through a breach in the wire, and Sam assumed that it had been made by Beams's platoon when it passed through.

Sam moved the platoons through the wire by squads and then quietly deployed his soldiers in a skirmish line, but they only advanced a few yards and waited. Sam wanted to make sure that the company and the platoons from Baker Company had the chance to cross the bridge before the battalion advance came to the attention of the defenders. Most soldiers immediately dropped and started probing for mines in front of them. *So far, so good*, Sam thought.

Shortly, he was tapped on the shoulder by Hoar, as he deployed his platoon to Sam's left. A few minutes later and Baker Company was across and moving to Hoar's left. Following behind the riflemen were engineers and linesmen to spread the spider's webs of phone lines from the battalion CP to the forward companies.

Sam was joined by Captain Ebbins, and the skirmish line began its advance. The German fire seemed concentrated on the 143rd's sector, and the flares and flashes were distant but provided enough light to walk by. The plan was to advance to the point of making contact, and then the hard work would begin. Just like the landings at Salerno, the soldiers would charge forward and begin to methodically eliminate the German defenses. They had received very limited rifle fire during the night, which suggested to Sam that the Germans were content to let the Americans come to them. There wasn't any need to send soldiers forward, because their artillery and machine gunfire had been so effective. *So good,* he thought ruefully, *the Germans probably hadn't even called up reserves to the Gustav Line.*

That didn't mean, however, that the Germans hadn't sent patrols forward during the course of the night to assessment the nature and progress of the assault, and they had undoubtedly sent troops forward to deal with Beams—there had been no sound of American fire in front of them for over two hours. But the question on Sam's mind was how far forward were the Germans deployed now?

The first fifty yards went without incident, and silently and cautiously, Sam continued the advance. Then things began to happen quickly. A soldier on Sam's left, in Hoar's area, stepped on a mine. A loud crack, a white flash of light, and screaming overcame the pounding of the artillery throughout the valley, and signaled quite clearly to the Germans that another crossing of the river was underway.

0515 Hours
1st Battalion Command Post, East of the Rapido River, Italy

Listening to the distant combat was the hardest part.

Major Spaulding and Perkin paced back and forth in front of the pigsty that served as their command post and communications center. Listening and pacing was about all they could do.

Shortly after the mine detonation, the German defenders turned their full attention to the Able crossing site. For the first time since the initial assault the night before at 2000 hours, German artillery initiated a sustained barrage on the Able crossing, and within the first five minutes, the new bridge was collapsed from the combined fires of dozens of guns. Not surprisingly, the telephone lines connecting the company to the friendly world were severed by the barrage.

Able and Baker companies, representing the majority of 1st Battalion's combat power were across the river and cut off. Allied fire missions in support of the isolated soldiers were problematic at best as Major Spaulding didn't know the exact disposition of his companies at the start of the barrage and had no way of knowing whether they had advanced or retreated since coming under fire.

The best that the division could offer was counter-battery fire—an attempt to knock out the German artillery and mortars that were firing on the American crossings. It was difficult to do at the best of times, but nearly impossible at night with the smoke and fog hanging over the battlefield.

"Bill, let me swim the river and bring 'em back," Perkin said anxiously.

Before Major Spaulding could reply, they heard the whine of a jeep's engine as it came up the hill. "Who's this?" Spaulding asked. On this morning, the use of a jeep most likely meant a senior officer.

It was Colonel Wranosky and Brigadier General William Wilbur, the assistant commander of the division. Perkin had met Wilbur several times before. He found him to be mercurial, tenacious, and tough.

"Good morning, gentlemen," said Spaulding and Perkin in unison as they came to attention and saluted. It was a custom normally dispensed with on the battlefield, but they were in the near darkness and out of the range of enemy sniper fire. Besides, Wilbur was a general officer and been awarded the Medal of Honor for heroism in Morocco in November 1942—the only soldier of their acquaintance so honored.

Wilbur and Wranosky returned the salutes, and Wranosky said, "Get your XO and Ops, Bill. We need to talk about what's next."

Wilber sat on the fender of the jeep, and the other men formed a semicircle around him. He accepted a cup of coffee poured from a thermos by Private Kulis, cleared his throat, and said, "Let me give you a rundown on how the team's doing, then I'll issue orders. To be blunt, the attack has failed across the entire front. As it stands right now, instead of two regiments with a lodgment on the west bank of the Rapido River, and Fifth Army rolling onward to Rome, we have two partial battalions fighting for their lives—the 1st of the 141st, and the 1st of the 143rd. All other efforts to cross were defeated. I'm giving the order to the regimental commanders to prepare to withdraw all forces east of the Rapido back to the assembly areas. I want you out of here by daybreak and behind Mount Trocchio. We need to reorganize and regroup before continuing the attack tomorrow night."

Wilbur held his hand up to forestall the protests, "Higher command, and I mean II Corps and Fifth Army, don't understand what's going on up here. They were warned by the Old Man, chose to ignore his warning, and they still haven't figured out that a single division isn't going to crack this nut. I'm hearing from friends on II Corps staff that General Keyes doesn't think we've tried hard enough and will formally order the resumption of the attack as soon as possible. I have no doubt that General Walker will attempt to dissuade them from that course of action, but we need to be ready to execute those orders."

Perkin felt like he'd been kicked in the chest by a war horse. *Not tried hard enough? A resumption of the attack?*

"Sir?" Perkin asked, "Resume the attack with what? There's every possibility that the two battalions across are already near combat ineffective. The battalions on this shore aren't any better. We went through all the boats and bridges last night—who do we send over and what do they cross with?"

"It's Berger, right?" asked the general.

"Yes, sir."

"Captain Berger, those are exactly the words that I expect the division commander will express to the corps commander when he comes calling later today. If he doesn't, I sure as hell will. But we're soldiers. We'll press our case and try to convey the realities on the ground here to men who haven't been in combat in twenty-five years, but if we are ordered to attack, we will salute smartly and try our best to comply with those orders."

"Colonel Wranosky." Spaulding cleared his throat. "I don't mean to put you on the spot with General Wilbur here, but I'm formally asking to withdraw my battalion from the west bank of the river. They'll be picked off over the course of the day, and as Perkin said, won't have much fight left in 'em when we cross again later . . . today? Tonight?"

General Wilbur answered for Colonel Wranosky. "Son, General Walker has said no withdrawals. We need that shallow beachhead that your boys have given us. We're going to attempt a Bailey crossing regardless of conditions, and we need to control the far bank as deeply as possible. And truth be told, I don't know that we can get them back before daylight. If we have a battalion massed at the water's edge and waiting for a boat, they'll be massacred come sun-up. They need to dig in and gut it out until we can relieve them."

0530 Hours
Able Company Command Post, West Bank Rapido River, Italy

The company had pushed its way over three hundred yards from the river before the advance ran into heavy machine gunfire. In the darkness, Sam couldn't see the German positions clearly, but he assumed that they'd come up against the steel pillboxes that they'd been told about. Sam had sent a squad forward and crawling in the dirt, and they had come within seventy-five yards of the machine gun nests before being forced to withdraw. Several more soldiers were now dead, and almost everyone in the squad was wounded.

Without being told, the remaining soldiers of the company had made a decision to dig in, and that's what everyone was doing. Sam had made sure that he had a reasonable line of communication with Baker Company, and without waiting for Captain Ebbins, Sam and Master Sergeant Hawkins had begun coordinating the placement of the machine guns and mortars with Lieutenant Norstad of the weapons platoon.

A few minutes later as Sam was busily scraping out a slit trench with his helmet and bayonet—a few soldiers had brought entrenching tools and Sam was waiting for a turn—he was joined by a breathless Captain Ebbins

"Sam, we gotta get out of here." Ebbins said urgently.

"Sir, you should start digging a foxhole."

"I'm telling you Taft, we need to withdraw." Captain Ebbins's voice rose from emotion and several soldiers turned around to hear the exchange.

Sam couldn't see the soldiers in the dark, but he knew they were listening. Sam had a lot of sympathy for Captain Ebbins's position, but he said, "Cap'n, if we withdraw, we have to retake this ground again tomorrow night. And if we pull back, we're leaving Baker Company just hanging out there all alone. We're at least protecting their right flank."

"I don't give a shit about—," Ebbins started to shout, but he quieted down when Sam grabbed his forearm. "I mean, we have to do what's right for ourselves."

"Sir, what we have to do is follow orders. We've heard nothing from battalion since we came over but we knew we'd have to brace for a rough day, and, well . . . we'll just have to do it. We'll be OK." Sam kept his voice low but tried to sound reassuring. He didn't remotely believe that they'd be OK, but he meant what he said about Baker Company. "If we form a pocket with Baker and dig in, we can take what they give us. If we can hold on, we'll be relieved tonight."

Ebbins didn't say anything, and Sam assumed that he was mustering the courage to order a withdrawal on his own. Sam was pretty sure that Lieutenant Hoar had told him the same thing, so it would all be entirely on Ebbins's shoulders if the company retreated to the river.

"Can you promise me that, Sam?" Ebbins asked in a low voice.

"No, Ron. I can't. But just like we won't abandon Baker, they won't abandon us. They'll try again tonight."

0555 Hours
Able Company Crossing Site, East Bank Rapido River, Italy

They had driven down in a jeep to the crossing site to look the battlefield over once more.

"I should have gone over with them. Goddamn it, and then I'd be in a position to—" Spaulding's voice was thick with self-recrimination.

"To what?" Perkin replied. He felt the same guilt. "Having you here or having you there won't make a lick of difference in the outcome, Bill." Perkin spat. His mouth was dry and bitter from the smoke. "But I know what you mean."

The sky was turning gray. It would be dawn before long. The terrible long night was coming to a close, but the fighting wasn't over.

"I can't even get the word to them that they've got to hold on until we resume the assault."

"Let me go. I'll swim it, pass the word, and be back before you know it."

"No."

"Bill, really, I can be there and back before sun up. I don't mind swimmin' and runnin' around naked; I do it all the time."

"No. Let's load up and work the staff side of the problem. That's how we can really help. We've got to get the boats and bridges lined up, and I'll cross Charlie Company first thing right here." Major Spaulding started walking toward the jeep—one hundred yards further back, with a sleeping Private Kulis at the wheel.

"Bill, please just let me—" Perkin stopped as he heard the whistle of an incoming round. "Get down!"

Both officers dropped to the ground and held their helmets to their head as the heavy mortar round landed twenty yards away and detonated in the churned mud of the crossing site. The blast wave ripped over them, and the high explosive charge threw shards of white-hot metal in all directions.

Perkin's ears were ringing and he felt a searing pain in his side and his shoulder. He reached back frantically to try to pull the burning metal from his side. Amid shouts from Major Spaulding, he buried his face in the mud as more rounds began to fall, so he heard rather than saw the jeep wheel up to their position.

"Come on, let's go!" Private Kulis yelled at the officers. "Let's go!"

Perkin sprang to his feet, adrenaline overriding the pain and the terror, and he saw Spaulding already on his feet, looking at the ground. "Let's go!" Perkin screamed.

"I'm looking for my finger!" Spaulding screamed back.

"Get in the goddamned jeep!" Kulis screamed at the two officers as a round landing sixty yards away peppered the jeep with spent steel fragments—the sound reminiscent of hail on a tin roof and loud enough to catch everyone's attention.

As the two officers piled in the jeep, Kulis gunned the vehicle and sped away from the crossing site. When he crested the hill, he slid the jeep to a halt and looked at the two officers. Both were breathing hard and covered in mud. Both were bleeding, but in different places. Perkin and Major Spaulding also looked at each other, and they started laughing. It was the laughter of men who were hurt, but recognized the absurdity of their situation—the laughter of men still young enough to appreciate these things.

"Let's have a look at you gentlemen," said Kulis calmly in what he believed to be a doctor's tone of voice.

He looked over Major Spaulding first. When Spaulding dove to the ground, he had fallen with his head directly toward the blast. A fragment had torn through his left hand and had come to a halt in his helmet. The shell fragment was still there but his index finger was gone down to the knuckle. Blood was pouring out over the white end of the bone.

This wasn't Kulis's first field dressing and he expertly wrapped up the major's shaking hand and cheerfully noted, "First Captain Jones's toe, and now your finger." He turned to Perkin and said, "Just your ordinary *in extremis* wounds, don't you think, Captain?"

Perkin was shaking violently himself; the laughter had passed. He looked at Private Kulis, slightly confused, then a slow grin spread through the pain, "Pretty good, Eddie. I like it."

Spaulding took back his wrapped hand, and as Kulis gingerly helped Perkin out of his equipment and his jacket, Spaulding asked, "What the hell are y'all talking about?"

Perkin answered, "It was a good play on words. In extremis means 'to the farthest reaches.' Like your fingers and toes—extremities. But it also means 'on the edge of death,' I think. Get it? An ordinary in extremis wound? I really like—oh Jesus, be careful."

Major Spaulding wasn't paying attention. He was looking over Perkin's wounds and he whistled, "We need to get you to an aid station now, Perk."

Perkin tried to lift his arm to look at his ribs, but his shoulder wound hurt abominably.

"Does it look bad? I can't see it, but it hurts like hell."

"I can see a couple ribs here, buddy, and you're bleedin' like a stuck pig. It sliced through your side like a carving knife. An inch or two over and it might have gone into your belly. Kulis is gonna dump some sulfa powder on that, then we're gonna wrap you up. I can't clearly see what's goin' on with your shoulder, but it look's like there's a lump of somethin' over your shoulder blade. I'm guessing a small piece of shrapnel kind of slid under the skin here and is restin' in the meat there." Spaulding held his bandaged hand a few inches away from the other to show the distance the fragment traveled.

Kulis wrapped Perkin up as best he could with gauze taken from Perkin's first aid kit. There was no mention of morphine from either man. As Kulis climbed behind the wheel again, Spaulding said, "Kulis, drop me off at the battalion CP and take Captain Berger to the aid station at Trocchio."

"Yes, sir."

Perkin started to protest, but Spaulding held his finger—his good index finger—up to silence him. "Not a word, Perk. Those are orders. Eddie gets you to the aid station. Understood?"

"Yes, sir. Understood."

0650 Hours
Battalion Boat Dump, Mount Trocchio

"This ain't a good idea, sir." Private Kulis generally saw eye to eye with what his captain described as a "winter rules" approach to following orders. If it made sense to do, he was all in favor of positive action whether it was proscribed or not. But this was not a good idea, and he said so again.

"Eddie, I ain't asking you to go, just drive me down there." Perkin had spied a small two-man raft that had been abandoned on the roadside. He had made Kulis stop, and he checked the raft for bullet holes and there were none. This raft would float.

"Sir, I'd rather go than you. You can't even pick the goddamned raft up let alone paddle it with your shoulder."

"I'll make it work. I just need to get across and check on 'em."

"Sir, you have orders, and I heard 'em, to report to an aid station. You're still bleeding and you need to get stitches." Private Kulis was beginning to weaken. He had friends and comrades on the other side as well.

"Major Spaulding neglected to say *when* I had to go to the aid station. I'll do that as soon as I get back. I won't bleed out before then."

Kulis looked at Perkin, and swore as he put the jeep into gear. As they headed back one more time to the crossing site, they passed a long line of soldiers from the 3rd Battalion—the final redeployment of the first failed attack across the Rapido River.

These soldiers looked worse than Perkin felt, and his heart went out to his fellow Texans. Many were more seriously wounded than he was, and even those without outward wounds looked terrible. They were covered in mud, grease, and their comrade's blood, and their deeply sunken eyes had a vacant, glassy look of defeat.

The engineers were busy lighting smudge pots all over the eastern side of the river, and the chemical mortar teams were throwing smoke rounds all over the far battlefield. The bowl of the valley was filling with smoke and even though it was now light, visibility was limited to fifty yards or less.

The artillery was still pounding the battlefield, but it was difficult to tell what area was being hit. It seemed that the greatest concentration of fire was on the far bank. Sam and the boys of Able Company were surely under fire, as were the troops still on the far bank in the 143rd's sector.

They stopped the jeep at the familiar spot, and Perkin saw the crossing site for the first time in daylight. It was unlike anything he'd seen in his experience as a soldier. Not a single bush or shrub remained. The ground was completely pockmarked from hundreds of artillery and mortar rounds and scores of haphazardly dug foxholes. The battalion had seen to the collection of the bodies of all the dead, but in the darkness, one lone body had been missed. The soldier was on the bank of the river a dozen yards from where the footbridge once served, and he lay draped over the bank with one arm and leg over the side as if he were sleeping.

Equipment lay everywhere. Packs had been discarded. Bandoliers containing clips for the M-1s were strewn about, although it looked as if someone had begun to collect rifles—five Garands were stacked neatly at the abandoned site, bayonets pointing to the sky, and Perkin was reminded of pictures that he'd seen of Civil War encampments.

In all the debris, Perkin found what he was looking for—a paddle for the raft. He tried, but he couldn't bend over to pick it up, so he knelt on a knee and picked the paddle up with his good right arm. He had to use the paddle to push himself upright. The motion did not go unnoticed by Kulis who said, "You can't row—paddle— with your shoulder, Perk."

"I can, I can," said Perkin, but he knew he couldn't. He could no longer move his left arm because of the swelling in his shoulder. He tried practicing with the butt of the paddle tucked under his chin, but he knew that the Rapido River could not be crossed with only one working arm. He would be swept hundreds of yards downstream before making it across, if he made it across at all. "Goddamn it!"

"I'll go." Kulis started pulling the raft to the river bank.

"No." Perkin said. "I can't let you do that."

"Jesus Christ, sir. If it was important enough for you to go, it's good enough for me. Right?"

"No, Eddie." Perkin hung his head. "I just wanted to go check on Bear and the boys."

"You think I don't know that, sir? That's all I want to do as well. Let me take those ammo pouches there to 'em, and I'll have one of the boys follow me back to the river and we can leave the raft with them."

Perkin thought for a moment, and said, "You can row me over, and then come back."

"No, sir. I'm sorry, but you're too big. You gotta be close to 200 pounds, and I weigh about 125. I just can't do it. Let me go. I'll cross, run up to the company, and be back in fifteen minutes."

There was truth in what Kulis said. With both of them in the raft together, the odds were good that they'd capsized before making it across. Against his better judgment, Perkin said, "Let's do it."

0710 Hours
Able Company Crossing Site, West Bank
Rapido River, Italy

The crossing of the river was the most harrowing experience of Private Kulis's young life. He hadn't shared with Captain Berger the pertinent information that he couldn't swim very well. He thought of the one time that someone had tried to teach him, and it wasn't an encouraging success. During the Dust Bowl when the family farm briefly had water in their pond after a heavy storm, his father had taken Kulis and his brothers to the pond and tossed them in one after another. After a lot of flailing and swallowing of muddy water, the boys all made it to the bank of the pond. "Now you know how to swim," his father had told the boys.

The Rapido River had pushed him downstream just as he knew it would, and the flat-bottomed raft had a tendency to point in whatever direction the river wanted it to go. Still, he made it across and dragged the boat back upriver to the crossing site. Because of the minefields, he wanted to make sure that he went inland from the same starting point as the company.

Kulis hadn't gone more than fifteen yards from the shore before the waving Captain Berger was lost in the smoke. He had a dry tickle in the back of his throat from all the concealment measures the army was throwing out, and he had a hard time resisting the urge to cough.

He walked slowly westward, pausing every few feet to listen. Not that it mattered much—the valley was as noisy as any battlefield that he'd experienced. The artillery never seemed to stop. He paused once at the body of a soldier and looked at the man's face. The soldier was a friend of his from Beams's platoon. They had known each other since Camp Bowie in Texas, and all the dead man could talk about then was cars, women, and how he hated the army. But he'd been a good soldier, and had been promoted to corporal at San Pietro. Kulis was profoundly sad at his passing.

Private Kulis resumed his movement inland and continued to pause to listen. He heard a man sobbing in the smoke and the fog, and Kulis decided to leave the man alone. *No sense embarrassing the fellow*, he thought. But the man was coming toward him, and there was no escaping a meeting.

It was Captain Ebbins, and he came stumbling out of the smoke like the loser in a prize match, except instead of blood, his cheeks were streaked with tears and snot was running down his upper lip. Ebbins saw Kulis and stopped for a moment, then continued his lurching walk to the river.

"Cap'n Ebbins!" Kulis hissed at him. "Where's the company?"

The officer turned partially backward and waved dismissively inland. "They're all dead," he said and he pushed past Kulis, wiping his nose on his sleeve as he went.

Kulis ran backward, got in front of Ebbins, and pushed him to a halt with his rifle. The officer tried halfheartedly to grab the weapon, but Kulis coolly stepped back. Kulis said in a calm voice, "Cap'n, I'm Private Kulis of the battalion staff. I'm a runner from Major Spaulding." That wasn't strictly true of course, but Kulis knew enough of the history between Ebbins and the cousins to know not to mention Captain Berger.

"Get out of my way, Jew-kiss or whatever your name is."

Ebbins tried to push past Kulis again, but Kulis was quicker this time and stayed ahead of Ebbins.

"Sir, where's the company?"

"I told ya, they're dead."

Kulis looked at the officer's eyes, and he knew Ebbins was lying. "I don't believe you, Cap'n. Where are they?"

"Back there." Ebbins waved his arm again.

"Why aren't you with 'em, sir? Come on, I'll head back with you." Kulis put his hand on Captain Ebbins's shoulder and kindly tried to turn him around.

Whipping Kulis's arm off of him, Ebbins's eyes narrowed and he suddenly asked, "How'd you get over? You aren't wet. Where's your boat?"

"I came over on the footbridge in Charlie sector, sir," Kulis lied.

Being a teenager, Kulis was an accomplished liar, but Ebbins shook his head and a grin slowly spread across his face. It was a mean, hard grin—a smile of ill-intentions. Ebbins said, "Now, I don't believe *you*, Private. Where's your boat?"

Ebbins took a step closer to Private Kulis, who stepped back, keeping the same distance between them.

Kulis nodded back to the river crossing, and Ebbins said, "At our crossing?"

"Yes, sir."

Satisfied that the teenaged soldier posed no threat to him, Ebbins stepped back and said, "I gotta get back to battalion. Let Taft know I'll be right back." Ebbins stepped backward again until he was just a shadowy figure in the smoke. "You won't tell on me now, will you boy?"

As the young soldier from Rosebud slowly lifted his heavy Garand, he replied with a greatly amused look on his scarred face, "I promise I won't say a word, Cap'n."

0715 Hours
Able Company Command Post, West Bank Rapido
River, Italy

When daylight came, Sam abandoned his helmet-dug slit trench and moved to a shell hole nearby. The thought had occurred to him that if a shell could hit there once, it could hit there again. *But maybe it's like lightning*, he thought hopefully.

Everyone was either dug in or a casualty. It was just that simple. Once the Germans determined roughly where the Texans were, they responded with grazing fire across the landscape. They didn't need to see through the smoke, and only well-dug holes would protect the soldiers.

Still, although the company was definitely receiving more than it gave, in a moment of clear air, Sergeant Kenton fired the heavy German antitank rifle into a steel pillbox from three hundred yards out. Sam couldn't tell what happened, but they hadn't received any more fire from that particular site. Private Froman, one of Sam's snipers, also took out an MG-42 gunner and its loader, and the mortarmen behind Sam were able to generally keep the Germans' heads down. Sam was under no illusions though. There was no need for the panzer grenadiers to take unusual risks—artillery would kill most of the Texans, and when they got bored with that, the Germans would send in armor to finish them off.

The machine guns took a short break from firing on Able Company and focused on Baker Company, and Sam was about to spring out of his hole and check on the men when he heard a low whistle behind him. When Sam turned around, he heard Kulis say, "Coming in," and then he heard the pounding of feet as the rifleman slid into the shell hole with him.

"Eddie, what are you doing here?" Sam looked back to see if there was anyone coming behind Private Kulis. There wasn't.

"I'm running, sir. How y'all?" Private Kulis had a pretty good idea of how things were going. He'd passed several dead soldiers lying on the path, and many more wounded soldiers crawling to the rear.

Sam smiled the first genuine smile of the day, "Same as usual. Tell Major Spaulding we're hangin' on by a nose hair. Our situation's precarious. The usual shit. What's Perkin up to?"

"He's waiting for me on the river bank, sir. He's a little banged up, and I was ordered by Major Spaulding to get him to an aid station." At the alarmed looked on Sam's face, Kulis said, "Oh, he'll be OK, sir . . . if he don't bleed out."

"What are you doing here then? Do you have orders? Do you want me to call over Captain Ebbins?"

"Oh, well, as to Ebbins, I passed him on the path, sir. He's, uh, moved on. Permanently—it's your company, now." Kulis beamed whole-heartedly.

Not understanding, Sam smiled in return, "Thanks for telling me. My first command. Well, it ain't gonna last too long, I'm afraid. Any orders from battalion?"

"Yes, sir. Look, uh . . ." Suddenly Kulis's eyes filled with tears. Embarrassed, he looked away. "Uh . . . General Wilbur says all units east of the river are to dig in and wait. They're puttin' together another assault."

"Oh." Sam thought for a moment and shrugged. "I didn't need for you to come tell me that, Eddie. I figured that one out on my own. Tell Spaulding not to risk you for stuff like that."

"Oh, he didn't, sir." Kulis's rare tears had passed and he grinned. Suddenly he looked like the seventeen-year-old boy he was. "Perk and I just wanted to check on y'all."

Sam was deeply touched and very irritated at the same time. He couldn't believe that Perkin would risk another man's life for something so trivial. His own life certainly, but someone else's? Sam knew Perkin better than anyone, and he must have been hurt pretty badly if he didn't cross over himself.

"Perk, eh? You mean Captain Berger?"

Kulis grinned and shrugged. "I told him I'd be back in fifteen minutes, so I gotta go, sir. Any message for Perk or for Major Spaulding?"

"Tell Major Spaulding that we can't hold until nightfall. We're running low on ammo and my casualties are close to 50 percent. We've had no contact with Beams. There's no more firing ahead of us, so I assume that he's surrendered or been wiped out—if he ain't in Rome. No stoppin' an Aggie. Look, tell Bill we can probably make it until 1000 or noon or so but we're losing too many men, and I'm gonna have to shorten my lines. Shrink the pocket. If the Krauts send in armor, we're done for. Tell him we got a bazooka but only two rockets. The rest fell in the river."

"Yes, sir. Anything else?"

"Tell Perk that I am, and always have been, a better fisherman. That's all. Thanks for coming, Eddie."

He offered his hand to the private, who shook it and said, "Say hey to Fratelli for me if you see him. Good luck, Bear."

Private Kulis slid off the ammunition belts and before Sam knew it, he was gone in the smoke.

0730 Hours
Able Company Crossing Site, East Bank
Rapido River, Italy

Perkin had taken refuge in a nearby foxhole. He'd been pacing back and forth in front of the river for ten minutes before the thought occurred to him that German snipers might be infiltrating to the river to kill engineers. He had heard two nearby rifle shots earlier, soon after Kulis left, and he was afraid that the young soldier had crossed into a firefight. But there had been no more firing that close to the bank and no shouting or other indications of a skirmish.

Guilt wasn't an emotion that Perkin was overly familiar with, so when it came, the guilt was nearly overwhelming. He shouldn't have sent Kulis, and he knew it. He let the emotions—his fear for Sam and his friends—cloud his judgment.

Anxiety and pain were also at work on the young captain. Each minute that passed seemed like ten, and only by regularly checking his watch was he able to keep an accurate notion of how long Kulis had been gone. The anxiety had Perkin jumping on the balls of his feet in the foxhole until the pain and fatigue forced him to stop. He took stock of his injuries, and the shrapnel wound on his side was going to be a problem. The bandages that Kulis had put in place a little more than an hour earlier were completely soaked with blood and beginning to pull away from the wound. The saturated bandages were now dripping like a leaky faucet, and his legs were cold and wet from the blood.

It was the shoulder that worried him long-term. He knew that the shrapnel under his skin would have to be removed, and it was likely that the surgeons would want to do it immediately. *On the other hand*, he thought, *there's a long line outside of medical today.*

Through the smoke, he saw a shadowy shape materialize on the far bank. It was Kulis. Perkin had a hard time pulling himself from the foxhole, and then an even harder time getting to his feet. He steadied himself upright, and then slinging his Thompson over his good shoulder, he tried a jog to the river. It was too tiring, and he dropped down to a walk.

Private Kulis was hauling the raft upstream when the soldiers heard the distant whoosh of Nebelwerfers. Perkin looked to horizon and saw flashes of light ahead and to the right—maybe coming from the base of the mountain underneath the abbey. He followed the trails and realized again that the rockets were inbound.

Kulis came to the same conclusion. He screamed, "Incoming!" at Perkin, and he disappeared back in the smoke. Perkin, charged now with adrenaline, ran back to the foxhole and slid in just as the first rounds began to drop.

They were high explosive rounds, not incendiary, and the ground shook from the detonations. They were not on top of the Able Company site, but further downriver. After a terrifying minute, Perkin lifted his head up and saw a vast cloud of gray smoke and dust drifting to the south as the explosions echoed through the valley. The riverbank was even more devastated, but as far as Perkin could tell, there was no one left to be hurt.

Once again, he climbed out of the hole and made his way toward the river. Kulis emerged again from the engineer's smoke with a wide grin on his face and a large wave to Perkin over his head. The smile disappeared when he got to the riverbank. The raft was gone.

With dismay, both Perkin and Kulis looked downstream, but the raft, which had slid into the river during the Nebelwerfer barrage, was long gone from view.

Kulis looked at Perkin calmly and called across the river, "I'll go join the boys now, sir. Lieutenant Bear said to tell you he was a better fisherman than you."

"No! Swim for it." There was no way that Perkin was going to allow Kulis to return to the company. He wasn't going to have the young man's likely death on his conscience.

Kulis looked doubtfully at the water. "I can't swim, sir. Not so you could recognize it in any case."

"Hang on, Eddie. Let me think." Perkin walked along the riverbank and spied the sunken footbridge twenty yards downstream. On opposite riverbanks, he and Kulis walked in parallel to where the bridge once stood.

The bridge was still anchored to the bank on Perkin's side, but it disappeared into the dark swirling waters of the Rapido after just a few feet.

"Let me see how far across it goes." Perkin said as Kulis watched curiously from the far shore.

Perkin laid down his Thompson and stepped gingerly on the foot-wide plates. The bridge didn't move so he edged further along, and again found that it was holding firm. He contemplated walking out along the catwalk into the water, but the bridge had been put across without handrails. He'd have a high center of gravity on a sloping surface and with a fast moving current around his feet. Perkin figured that he'd go about five feet or less before he fell into the river. That left him with two choices—straddle the beam and work his way out into the current sitting, or jump into the water and hold onto the bridge for support.

It didn't seem that one option was better than the other, so he eased himself into the water, gasping from the cold. Even close to the shore, the current was strong and pushed him back against the bridge.

"Run upstream twenty yards, get back as far as you can, then run and dive into the river. Swim toward the far bank, and I'll catch you as you go by. Hurry!" He tried to shout the instructions, but the shock of the water had taken his breath away.

Kulis hesitated, nodded, and threw his Garand across the river. It didn't make it. Neither did his helmet, which landed with a splash ten feet from the shore. He looked nervously at the receding ripples, steeled himself and ran upriver twenty yards. Kulis slid his glasses into his pocket while Perkin looked at the distance and said, "Five more yards, then do it. Go!"

As Kulis ran the last few yards, Perkin eased further out in the river. By the time he was ten feet from the shore, the water was over his head and he floated along the wreckage of the bridge—the force of the water pinning him against it. He was weakening quickly, and despite the pain, he was forced to use his left arm to hold on. At least the submerged bridge was stable—it was anchored well on the east bank—but if Perkin went much more, he would risk being pulled under the bridge. He couldn't hold on much longer. "Now!" he gasped.

With a mixed look of utter terror and grim determination, Private Kulis ran the three feet to the water's edge and leapt into the river. It wasn't a dive, his jump carried no forward momentum once he hit the water, and Perkin knew with a sick heart that Kulis would pass him by no farther than ten feet from the west bank.

Perkin slid further out into the river, the bridge still holding. Kulis went under, breached the surface with a shriek, and he struck out toward the east bank with a flailing hybrid stroke of his own devising that belonged somewhere in the aquatic realm between the crawl and a dog paddle. He was moving rapidly, but only downstream, and Perkin screamed, "Swim, goddamn it!" and the private flailed harder.

Perkin was well past midstream and he came to the end of the submerged wrecked footbridge. He looked back for Kulis, and he wasn't there. Desperate, Perkin leaned as far out as he could into the stream and flung his good arm out, grasping blindly under the water, and unexpectedly he had Kulis by the collar. He screamed in pain as the exertion and stress of holding the soldier in the current ground the shrapnel through more skin and muscle until the sharp, twisted piece of metal lay resting on the bone of his shoulder blade.

Perkin pulled Kulis to him, and with his right arm pulled the young man halfway out of the water. Kulis flung his arms over the bridge, gasped for air, blinked hard to clear the water from his eyes, and laughed as though he'd been on a carnival ride, "Whoa Jesus, Cap'n. What a hoot!"

0755 Hours
1st Battalion Command Post, East of the Rapido River, Italy

Kulis gunned the jeep as it headed up the hill toward the pigsty. He looked at Captain Berger in the passenger seat with concern. The captain's eyes were not open, and Kulis didn't know whether he was sleeping, unconscious, or dead, but he had a message to deliver first.

Kulis had been able to get Perkin pulled from the water, and he ran flat out to get the jeep and bring it to the riverbank to pick up the officer for the second time that morning. Kulis had stripped the winter coat off the stiff body of the dead soldier on the riverbank and draped it over the captain before setting off, but it wouldn't be enough, Kulis knew.

Kulis recounted to Perkin as they drove what Sam had told him, and Perkin had ordered that they return to the battalion first. The young private hadn't thought that was a good idea—Captain Berger was very pale and shaking so severely that Kulis was afraid that the captain might not make it without immediate help. But he understood why, and he followed orders.

Captain Berger wasn't the only one shaking. Kulis tried blowing into his hands as he steered the jeep with his left knee, but it made no difference. The cold winter wind was whipping though his wet uniform as he drove, and as his teeth chattered, he repeated over and over as he shook violently, "Oh, Jesus. Oh, Jesus!"

Major Spaulding was pacing back and forth in conversation with Colonel Wranosky when the jeep arrived. When the officers saw the jeep pull up to the pigsty, they walked over still in conversation. It wasn't until they were within a few yards that they saw Perkin was unconscious and that both of the soldiers in the jeep were dripping wet.

"What happened? Why didn't you get him to the aid station?" Spaulding asked as he checked Perkin's throat for a pulse.

"We're headin' there next, sir. I have a report to make, Major." Kulis said through his chattering teeth. He looked at the two officers and felt uncomfortable under their scrutiny. "I crossed the river—"

"You did what?" Spaulding looked at the young soldier in astonishment.

"Yes, sir. We found a raft that still floated, and I thought I'd cross while the light was dim and the smoke still thick. Cap'n Ebbins is dead. Lieutenant Taft is in command."

"Did you talk to Lieutenant Taft, Private?" Colonel Wranosky asked.

"Yes, sir. They're dug in less than three hundred yards from the river alongside Baker Company." Kulis walked over to a map on a table, and after studying it for a moment, he said, "The lines run about here through here. Don't know how Baker's deployed. Casualties—" Kulis went through a spasm of shaking and had to restart the sentence. "Casualties are high. More than 50 percent. Several dead. They can't advance, and will be forced to . . . what was it he said? Shrink the pocket pretty quickly. If the Germans bring up armor, they're done for. Lieutenant Taft says he can hold on until 1000 or so if things continue as they are, then . . . well, that's about as long as he thinks they can hold. Sir, can you give them the order to withdraw?"

Colonel Wranosky looked sadly at the scrawny, shaking soldier. He walked to his own jeep and came back with a green woolen blanket and draped it around Kulis's shoulders. He didn't answer the private's question, but instead asked, "What happened next?"

Kulis explained about the Nebelwerfer barrage and the lost boat. He was staring at the ground when he recounted the submerged bridge and so he missed the horrified look exchanged between the two officers. When he was done, he asked again, "Can they withdraw?"

Major Spaulding answered, "Our orders are to hold onto that far pocket. There won't be any withdrawal, Private Kulis. But we'll get back over as soon as we can."

There was something in the way that Spaulding answered—a bitter finality in his voice—that told Kulis that the two officers before him had already fought and lost the battle over withdrawing from the far side of the Rapido River. He also knew that any relief of the battalion and his friends in the company would be too late.

0915 Hours
Able Company Command Post, West Bank Rapido
River, Italy

They had been under a sustained barrage for over an hour. Unknown to Able and Baker companies, they were the only American units still remaining on the far bank—all others had withdrawn or been destroyed—and German artillery was being brought to bear on the remnants.

There was nowhere to go. Soldiers fled and were gunned down, or died from the barrage. Some made it to the river, only to find that there was no way across other than swimming. Some swam and made it. Others were swept away by the fierce current. More than a couple of soldiers made it to the river only to return to their units after taking a long final drink of the cold water.

Sam had no time for such luxuries. He had moved across the Able Company lines several times to talk to the soldiers and do a head count of the survivors. There were very few of them left whole. Master Sergeant Hawkins was dead. He'd been doing the same as Sam—moving through the smoke and checking on the soldiers when a gust of wind exposed him. The German gunner fired over a hundred rounds into his body before seeking out another target.

Vince Fratelli, one of the honorary Texans from the north, was also dead. His fire with the BAR had been so effective that the German company commander facing them had called in artillery directly on his spot. Fratelli and two squad mates were killed by the same shell. His death left Sam speechless—they had been through so much together that he had come to believe that Fratelli was indestructible.

There were no other officers left on the line—Norstad was dead. Hoar was wounded in the stomach and would

likely die soon, but Sam had him evacuated toward
the river in any case. Sergeant Kenton was the senior
noncommissioned officer left in the fight, so Sam gave
him one platoon, while he ran his own, but it mattered
little as there were no men left to man more than a few
squads in any case.

A few of the men seemed shell-shocked—or battle
fatigued as the army was calling it. Some were rolled up
tight in foxholes and wouldn't talk or even acknowledge
him. Some had broke and run; others were crying and
flinched whenever they heard an inbound round. One
phenomenon that Sam found interesting was the number
of men that he found asleep in their foxhole. He wouldn't
have thought it possible to sleep under such conditions,
but one old gray-haired corporal who had been with the
division in the First World War told Sam that it was a
reaction to a sustained barrage. "I don't know why it
happens, sir, but it does." The soldiers were shaken awake,
and Sam moved on.

Many more of the soldiers were fighting mad. Their
hatred of the Germans sustained them, and Sam was glad
to see that these soldiers were still alert. They would fight
to the end. Some of the replacement soldiers had not
fired their weapons though, and Sam stayed with them
and made them fire a complete clip in the direction of
the Germans. Perhaps, he thought, they'd have fewer
hesitations when the counter-attack actually began.

The wounds that he saw ranged from superficial to
shocking. Most of the soldiers had cuts on their hands
and faces—inexplicable wounds that, in many cases, the
soldiers were unaware they had. Other wounds were far
more serious, and Sam sent them to a collection point that
he'd established halfway to the river, but he had no faith
that they'd be evacuated before dying. Only one of the
company's original medics was still alive and unwounded,

and he worked nonstop to bandage up those who could still fight and tend to those who were done.

Sam himself was miraculously untouched. Other than his medic, he'd spent more time than any other soldier moving out in the open, yet he had no more than a scrape or two on his hands.

After a final barrage from a Nebelwerfer battery, the artillery stopped. It was only a matter of time, Sam knew, before they were counterattacked. *Panzers will come in and finish them off*, he thought, and he patted a soldier on the back and ran, crouched, back to his shell hole.

There it was. The squeal of armor. There were no antitank weapons left—Sam had moved the bazooka team forward to try to take out a bunker with a rocket, but the team had not returned and the fire from the bunker had not abated. Sam looked behind him one last time. *Perkin must be wounded bad or he'd be here*, Sam thought, and he said a quick prayer for his cousin. There were no reinforcements, and there would be no reinforcements. The remnant of the company was alone and defenseless. The end was just minutes away now.

Sam pulled Margaret's letter from his pocket, opened the envelope, and breathed in her perfume. It was so sad, Sam thought, that they'd not have the life together that they wanted, but it was out of his hands now. There was nothing to do but wait, so he breathed in her scent again and thought of her.

1510 Hours
Regimental Aid Station, Mount Trocchio

Perkin awakened with a start. He'd had a nightmare about being at the Charlie Company crossing site, but instead of Charlie Company being hit by the Nebelwerfers, it was Able Company. In his dream, the burning fuel landed on Sam.

It was a dream that he knew was a dream, and yet he couldn't wake himself up. Sam continued to burn and Perkin couldn't put out the flames or still the screaming of his cousin. But it wasn't Sam who was screaming. It was another soldier in the aid station, and one medic was holding him to his cot, while another administered a dose of morphine.

It took a long time for consciousness to return, and the best that Perkin could do was muster a foggy sense of activity all around him. Slowly his focus came back, and he realized he was in a large tent with dozens of other soldiers. He tried to sit up, couldn't, and tried again.

A medic saw him struggling, knelt beside his cot, and said, "Take it easy, Captain. We're about out of whole blood so we just finished topping you off with plasma. You need to rest before we think of letting you get up."

Shaking his head to clear it, Perkin asked, "How'd I get here? I wasn't hurt that bad."

The medic shrugged, "Well, sir, that's a bit of a judgment call. So, let's see . . . we put about forty stitches in your side—I got to do that, so if you're unhappy with your scar, come see me to complain. And we dug a little hunk of tin roofin' outta your shoulder and stitched that up, and you had a touch of hypothermia from your little wintertime swim outing. Honestly, sir, you're lucky to be alive."

Perkin soaked in the information, then asked again, "How'd I get here? I don't remember."

The medic stood up, "That colonel, the regiment guy, carried you in himself. Told the doc to look after you personally. Doc said, 'Of course I will,' and when the colonel left, I took care of you. No offense, but the doc can't play favorites."

Perkin nodded, "Any word on the fight? Do you know what's happening with the 1st of the 141st?"

"Is that his outfit?"

"Whose?"

"Sam's," said the medic. "You shout in your sleep. Who's he? A buddy?"

"Cousin. Any word on the battalion?"

As a soldier in a cot next to Perkin's spoke up, the medic walked away, "I been here since before you came in, Cap'n, but the word is that there ain't been any American fire from the far side since this morning. Sorry."

"Do you know if they withdrew?"

The soldier started to say that he didn't think so, but after seeing the look on Perkin's face said, "I couldn't say, sir. It's hard to follow the battle from here."

Perkin lay in his cot and stared at the ceiling. He couldn't believe that Sam was gone—that he was killed or taken prisoner. A wave of nausea swept over him, and he rolled onto his good side. He forced himself to his feet, staggered outside, and vomited. Immediately he felt better, but the sight before him was appalling. Hundreds of soldiers were milling about outside the field hospital— some had been treated and moved outside of the tents to make room for others. Many more soldiers were still waiting to be seen by the surgeons.

It seemed unconscionable to take up a cot when many men worse than he still hadn't been treated, and Perkin was ashamed that he'd been given preferential treatment. He spat to clear his mouth and returned to the inside of the tent. For the first time, he noted the smell—unwashed men, feces and urine, vomit and blood. He couldn't stay there.

He caught the eye of the medic and said, "Where's my uniform? My stuff?"

The medic replied, "You shouldn't go anywhere, Cap'n, but your jacket, that brown sweater, and your shirt are gone. There's a supply sergeant outside who'll set you up. I set your boots under your cot, sir, so no one would take 'em, and your locket's in there. That's a great painting by the way." The medic wagged his finger at Perkin, "Cap'n, we need to get some penicillin in you as a prophylactic measure. No tellin' what's in that river water these days. Don't leave without it. Do you understand, sir?"

Perkin nodded, grabbed his boots, and walked stiffly out of the tent into the cold, smoke, and haze.

1630 Hours
36th Division Command Post, Mount Trocchio, Italy

The light was already dying as the sun dropped below the mountains to the west. Perkin walked around looking for the battalion headquarters, but his heart honestly wasn't in it. Sam was likely dead, as were so many of his friends from the company.

Without being aware of it, he wandered into the divisional headquarters compound. MPs moved to steer him away, but they recognized Perkin from his days as the reconnaissance troop commander and he was allowed through.

Still, there was no purpose to his journey. He was just walking in order to walk. He wasn't yet clear in thought, he was just moving. He passed a trailer and heard shouted words, which caught his attention. He slowed to try and make sense of the anger that he heard, but the words were muffled.

The door to the trailer slammed open and two angry officers stormed out. Perkin saw that one of the officers was Brigadier General Wilbur, the assistant division commander. He did not know the other man but he saw two stars on his coat as he walked by.

Wilbur watched as the other man climbed into his jeep and was driven away. With an angry shake of his head, he turned about and saw Perkin standing there watching.

"Berger? That you? Are you OK?"

"Yes, sir . . . sir? I've just gotten out of the aid station. I'm a bit behind the times. Are we launching another attack?"

General Wilbur walked over to Perkin, looked at his pinched white face and noted the arm in a sling, and said, "General Walker and I were just discussing that with General Keyes. He just drove off. He thinks that we've inflicted a real beating on the Germans, and that their morale is low. Says it should take one more push to do it, and he and Clark want to know why we haven't already launched the second assault."

"Are you serious, sir? Do they know what happened last night?" Perkin was incredulous.

"They're not honest enough to understand, son. You'd have thought that they'd have enough military education— shit, enough common sense—not to send two regiments across a river like that against a corps in defense. It's gonna take weeks, if not months, to cross this river, and a damn sight more firepower than two under-strength regiments to do it. And a damn sight more tactical imagination than these clowns have shown!"

"Then why'd they do it, sir? Why destroy this division for nothing?" Perkin was getting angry—a slow, burning, inextinguishable anger.

"Berger, that's the million dollar question. I asked Keyes myself why we're not doing this properly, and the answer I got was that Clark ordered it. Shit. I know that," Wilbur said bitterly. "But I'll tell you something, son.

There's something else to it, but these jokers won't say what. They just have that shit-eating look on their face that they know a secret, and that secret's better than sliced bread."

Perkin thought for a moment, and for some reason the image of Jimmy Cardosi came to his mind. There was something there, but Perkin couldn't figure it out. He still wasn't thinking clearly, but he thought that it'd come to him later.

"Son, after I take a leak and get a cup of coffee, I'm heading out to the 141st headquarters to see if I can help. Do you want to ride along?"

"Yes, sir. I'd appreciate it very much. I'm completely lost."

Chapter Sixteen

January 23, 1944
1100 Hours
Mount Trocchio, Italy

The remains of the castle would have normally fascinated Perkin, as he would have walked through the ruins imagining the medieval defenses, the view from the ramparts, or merely what it was like to live in those times. Italy to a historian was like a laboratory to a scientist, and normally, he would have delighted in the experience.

He sat alone with his back against a stone wall. Perkin was cold, unbelievably stiff and sore, and as he admitted to himself only, probably a little feverish. *Maybe more than a little*, he thought. He hadn't slept since the aid station two days before. Another attack had been launched and had failed.

The 1st Battalion didn't cross this time—there were few whole soldiers left to send over—but Perkin had been busy helping Major Spaulding prepare to send the tattered remains of the companies over if ordered. Instead, the 2nd and 3rd Battalions had attempted to cross with precisely the same results as the night before. They were slaughtered.

It was the same story in the 143rd's sector, as the Texans there attempted another crossing and failed. The last regiment of the division was released from corps reserve during the night, and was told to cross on the orders of General Keyes. Of course, the boats and the bridges didn't exist any longer for the 142nd to use, and in response to the division commander's resistance, the order to cross was rescinded. Various schemes were suggested by higher headquarters—new lines were drawn on the maps—and each successive plan was less realistic than the last. It was inescapable that the combat power of the division had been greatly reduced. The initial muster indicated that there were over two thousand casualties— the simple fact was that the division had been destroyed.

A temporary truce had come and gone. The Germans had allowed American medics to cross, and German and American medics worked side by side to help the wounded and to prepare the dead, but there was not enough time. Perkin had talked to every medic who had crossed in the hope of finding some information about what had happened to Sam. A medic who had once been in Able Company crossed over and walked through the 141st battlefield on the far side. He knew Lieutenant Taft, and through the tears, he told Perkin he didn't find Sam's body, although he found the bodies of far too many of his other friends.

The lack of news about Sam couldn't lift his spirits. The absence of a body on a battlefield only meant that a whole body wasn't found. Perkin had now seen too many soldiers vaporized in artillery strikes to have much faith in the medic's news.

Perkin peered through the rifle's scope once again, and he followed the curving river from Cassino in the north to the mountains of the south. There was no sign of life on the battlefield—no hint that Sam had survived.

As each minute passed, Perkin grew angrier. The thought that Sam had been murdered preyed on his mind, and his mood grew darker and darker. General Clark was to blame, he knew. Perkin had braced himself for the possibility of Sam's death—they were infantrymen in the most murderous war in history after all. But he could not reconcile himself to the thought that Sam's death would be meaningless. That he would be wasted in a senseless frontal assault that achieved nothing. Nothing.

Some day, he thought, *there has to be a reckoning for what happened on this river.*

Perkin hung his head and sighed, and the sigh became a sob. He wiped away a tear before it could freeze, and he clutched his locket from Gianina and said a prayer for Sam. He had to go. There was nothing that could be done from here, and there was so much more work left to be done in the valley. Perkin tried to stand up. He couldn't at first try, so he laid down the rifle and rolled gingerly to his stomach, and pushed himself with his good arm to his knees.

Perkin groaned from the fatigue and the despair and the pain, but he got one foot planted, picked up the rifle, and was pulling himself to his feet when a staff car far below him emerged out of the smoke.

Another general come to assess the carnage, he thought bitterly. Perkin stood, then leaned tiredly against the stone wall of the castle. While he rested from his exertion, he brought the rifle's scope up to his eye to watch. Through the smoke and fog of the morning, Perkin saw a tall, arrogant-looking officer emerge from the car. Even without the distant glint of silver stars, he knew who the officer was. It was General Clark, and Perkin assumed he'd come to order another assault. He shivered from the fever, and then his whole body began to tremble with a building rage and hatred.

More than the German grenadiers, more than the enemy artillery or their spotters in the brooding abbey on the mountain, more than the swift freezing river or the mud or the minefields, the man in his crosshairs was responsible for the slaughter of his friends and Sam. He had given the order to cross the river—against all sound military principles—not once, but twice.

Murder, thought Perkin. *He's come to murder more of us. Well, General, the day of reckoning has arrived.*

1110 Hours
Mount Trocchio, Italy

Corporal Kulis would have run up Mount Trocchio, but he was exhausted—so his progress was better defined as more of a rapid trudge than a run. He had spent the last two days as a runner for Major Spaulding, and even though the battalion had not crossed again, that it wouldn't cross had not been clearly predetermined.

As far as intelligence work went, there wasn't much to do. Kulis had sat in on an interrogation of one of the very few captured German soldiers, and the information that they had gathered was disheartening at the very least. The Germans had been unaware for the first day that a serious attack was even underway. Their assessment was that the Texans were merely conducting a demonstration, and consequently, the German commanders had not even bothered to call up reserves to the winter line. The German soldier said—and Kulis had no reason to doubt his word—that the German casualties were very light, and almost all resulting from artillery fires.

Kulis had been promoted by Colonel Wranosky, which he thought was far preferable to the ass-chewing he got from Major Spaulding. The major had expressed his displeasure fluently and at some length, and Kulis knew that Captain Berger had received the officer version of the same wire-brushing that he received, but as Captain Berger had dryly remarked afterward, both of them came out of the experience wiser men.

Kulis had been sent to find Captain Berger by Spaulding, who wanted help preparing the plans to move the battalion away from Mount Trocchio and back to the vicinity of San Pietro. Captain Berger was going to be appointed to the command of Able Company, although he didn't yet know it. Kulis was headed back to the infantry as well, and he'd been told that he was going to help rebuild and retrain the new company.

Kulis spied Captain Berger leaning against the stone wall of the castle and looking down on the American encampment below. Kulis watched as the tall officer had difficulty controlling the Springfield with one good arm, and he saw with some concern that Perkin was struggling to pull his arm out of his sling.

"Cap'n!" Kulis called out, and Perkin's head jerked up with a guilty start.

Perkin lowered the rifle and tried unsuccessfully to slide his wounded arm back into the sling. His face was flushed and he was sweating even though he was only wearing a jacket over his uniform shirt.

Kulis ran the last few steps, and caught the Springfield before Perkin dropped it. "Hey, sir! Great news! I just heard it and had to come up here!"

Perkin stared at him and blinked hard trying to clear his thoughts. "What's good news, Eddie?"

Kulis looked at the taller soldier with some concern and came to a command decision, "Sir, I need to get you back to the doc's. You don't look so good. My grandma used to check our temperature by seein' how far down our doo-dads dropped—but in deference to your rank, I think I'll use the modern method." He reached up and put his palm on Perkin's head. "Aw Jesus, Cap'n. You're runnin' a hell of a fever."

"I forgot to get my shot. General Clark—" Perkin said.

"Should be shot as well, if you ask me," Kulis said. "Come on, sir, throw your good arm over my shoulder, and I'll tell you all the news on the way down."

"What news, Eddie?"

"We landed VI Corps at Anzio yesterday!"

"Anzio?"

"Yes, sir. About, I dunno, thirty miles or so south of Rome. If they get moving, they can cut off the Kraut's lines of communications between here and Rome, and we might even be able to make a breakout."

They moved carefully down the time-worn path from the ancient castle to the base of the mountain while Perkin digested the news. "That's why we had to launch our assault three days ago," Perkin said. "We fix the Krauts here, and they can't reinforce to the Rome area."

"Maybe. Would have been nice to know though, wouldn't it?"

Perkin sighed. It would have been good to know why they were being asked to sacrifice themselves. "What other news, Eddie? I swear, I gotta take a nap soon. I'm beat." Perkin was leaning more heavily on the corporal, and Kulis could feel the other man's legs trembling.

"Just a second, sir, and we're through." Kulis steered Perkin to his jeep, and after helping Perkin ease into a seat, he covered the shivering officer with a blanket. "Now, sir. I've saved the best news for last—sorry I didn't tell you earlier, but I wanted to get you off the mountain first."

"I'm off the mountain now; what is it?" Perkin leaned back and closed his eyes. He yawned, desperately tired.

"Stay awake, Perk. You'll wanna hear this. I was just over with the division intel bubbas listening to the radio intercepts about Anzio, and they picked up an interesting conversation. Some Kraut MPs were reportin' to their headquarters that several prisoners from the 141st Infantry had escaped—and that two of the escapees were 195 centimeters tall and weighed about 100 kilograms or more . . ." Perkin did a rapid conversion and sat upright in the jeep, his fatigue gone. "One was an NCO with red hair, the other an officer with blonde hair. A third escapee was an officer, 175 centimeters, 75 kilograms, older with black hair and a—quote, unquote—belligerent attitude. Seems they killed a guard in their escape, and the Jerries are out for blood. It's gotta be Sergeant Kenton, Lieutenant Beams, and—"

"Sam!" Perkin shook Kulis's hand and laughed. He leaned back, closed his eyes again, and smiled to himself. He knew exactly where Sam was heading.

Epilogue

February 14, 1944
1100 Hours
Avezzano, Italy

The priest walked to his office, a younger man in tow. He never would have thought that it would be God's calling to him to move Allied prisoners out of the Germans' reach, but there he was doing it—he was small and had never been tough, yet his calling gave him strength. And the truth was that he found he enjoyed the task very much. If he wasn't a man of God—a middle-aged man of God—as he told himself, he would be doing what these young soldiers were doing. Fighting evil by opposing Hitler and his minions on the battlefield. Well, he would oppose Germany in his own way.

Father Carlo had facilitated the movement of many prisoners, and he had been told that two more would be arriving one by one in the week ahead. Although they had escaped together with the man currently with him, the decision had been made to separate the escapees because, as the priest had been told, the soldiers stood out together. Certainly, this man would stand out in any situation—the priest couldn't remember meeting anyone quite so large.

He had to make room for the incoming men, and he hoped that they were interesting. Some of the escaped prisoners were hard men. They had no purpose left in their lives other than to return to the fight. The priest understood and appreciated that even if the conversation was lacking. Others, like the two men he was about to introduce, were quite enjoyable.

One had been in the church for at least three weeks. The one with him had just arrived in the town a few days before and had been housed with a sympathetic family. Tomorrow, he would lead them through the Abruzzi Mountains, and God would see them through that hardship together.

The priest knocked on the office door, unlocked it, and entered. The other man, the smaller of the two Americans, was sitting on the floor reading a mystery novel that the priest had lent him. He leapt to his feet and looked at the much larger man behind the priest with concern.

"It's all right. Don't worry," the priest said in his heavily accented English. "Douglas Peabody, meet Sam Taft."

Author's Note

The story of Monsignor O'Flaherty is one of the little known sideshows of the war. Like Major Grossmann, I'm amazed at the risks this brave man took to help others. Even after being warned by the German ambassador that the Gestapo was aware of his activities and that he would be arrested if they continued, O'Flaherty frequently left the confines of Vatican City dressed as a Swiss Guard, a street cleaner, a trolley operator, or a *nun* in order to help his charges.

Some of the great pearls of this little slice of Vatican history were used in this novel. American and British escapees did go to the Rome opera, and one of O'Flaherty's chosen safe houses was near the Rome Gestapo Headquarters. To say the least, his relationship with Colonel Kappler, the Gestapo Chief in Rome, was complicated. It appears that Kappler had issued orders for O'Flaherty's arrest and possibly his assassination, yet during his post-war incarceration, one of Kappler's few visitors at the Italian military prison at Gaeta was Monsignor O'Flaherty, who converted Kappler to Catholicism.

At the same time that the Monsignor was risking his life to help escaped Allied servicemen and the Jewish population of Rome, the Texans of the 36th were ordered into their Forlorn Hope on the Rapido River—and it was this story that got me interested in the saga of the Texas Gun Club in the first place.

I was in South Korea for a planning conference a year or two before I retired from the navy, and during a luncheon, I found myself seated with a US Army colonel. We started talking about Texas and soldiers, and over the course of lunch, he told me the story of the 36th Division at the Rapido River.

As I sat there listening to this story, it occurred to me that there I was—a former Guardsman, a college history major, a Texan, *and* I'd been stationed in Italy only twenty miles or so from the battlefield—yet I didn't know the story of the Texas Division at the Rapido River. I'd even been to the rebuilt abbey, looked over the Liri Valley and the river, and thought about the Americans who fought and died on a battlefield under my very eyes. I (modestly) thought that if I hadn't heard of the Rapido battle, then probably most other people hadn't either. By the end of lunch, I was already planning this book, and of course to get to the Rapido, I found I had a couple of other stories to tell first. Looks like I have a few more stories left to tell as well.

Several historians have written of the political pressures bearing on Mark Clark to show progress in Italy. The campaign to date had been a long, hard slog up the peninsula, and had run out of steam when the Allies came up against very formidable defenses built by a military that was exceptionally good at defense. Anzio was a clever plan, poorly executed, designed to further that progress and bypass those formidable defenses.

The fiasco at the Rapido River was described at the time as the worst disaster to befall the American military since Pearl Harbor. The casualties were initially estimated at over two thousand killed, wounded, and missing—a number that dropped over time to 1,681.

I've read defenses and criticisms of Clark's decision to send the 36th across by itself. The criticism to me seems self-evident: inadequate time to plan and prepare, lack of resources such as boats and bridges, unprotected flanks, too few assault troops, etc. Basically, all the criticisms inherent in this book. Timing is the interesting part of the critique from my perspective. I've had the pleasure of working closely with today's army—and while the army culture is distinctly different from that of the navy, I'll say without reservation, that the US Army can plan the bejesus out of crossing the street better than anyone, let alone a main line of resistance. It's simply mind-boggling that so little time was given to the soldiers that had to execute this plan, and so little attention was given to the division commander's reservations, particularly since it was known months in advance that Fifth Army would have to cross the winter line on the way to Rome.

The defense of Clark, which the army maintained during a postwar Congressional inquiry, is that the assault was an acceptable risk that was needed to draw down forces from Rome and away from Anzio. That inquiry originated from a meeting of officers, all University of Texas graduates, who met in a barn after the Rapido River and resolved to see that justice was done. The Congressional inquiry exonerated Clark, agreeing that the crossing was an acceptable risk.

Major General Fred Walker, who was held in high esteem by Clark before the battle, was damaged goods afterward. He expected to be made the scapegoat for the affair, but Clark waited until after Rome fell before sending Walker stateside to run the Infantry School. The regimental commanders were relieved despite one of them receiving the Distinguished Service Cross for his efforts that night. Congressional Medal of Honor-winner Brigadier General Wilbur was marked for relief by Clark—mostly likely because he made his feelings about higher echelon known in a characteristically direct manner. So were Walker's sons, Fred Walker Jr. (the division G-3) and Charlie Walker (the general's aide), on the grounds that Clark felt having the men in the division was bad for morale.

Fred Walker Jr, later wrote a defense of the division and of his father, where he noted that it ultimately took a four division corps-level assault following months of preparation combined with a simultaneous attack on both German flanks to successfully force the crossing of the Rapido River in the same manner that the 36th attempted. As Colonel Walker noted, "Even this massive effort barely succeeded, and it is hardly surprising, therefore, that two regiments could not accomplish the same task with a hasty attack in January."[*]

As with the story of Church intrigue, on the military side of this novel, I tried to use several of the little pearls of history where I could—the Canadian mouseholing in Ortona and the demolition of the house, for example. One of Major Spaulding's real life counterparts was Major David Frazier, who commanded a battalion in the 143rd. Despite orders to hold his position, he withdrew his battalion to avoid annihilation. He went back the next night and had several fingers shot off, and all the officers on his battalion staff were killed or wounded. The real Able Company was led into a minefield but made it across the river, and a lone platoon of Able advanced farther into German-held territory than any other unit that I could find—no doubt they had a real life B. G. E. Beams. The 1st Battalion's story is largely accurate as presented here, but far, far worse in the details than I could ever begin to describe it.

I have readers who are interested in the weaponry, and two new weapons were debuted in this book. I had the

---

[*] "Mission Impossible at Cassino: The First Assault Across the Rapido River Near Cassino in World War II, January 1944." A copy of this defense was given to me by Colonel Fred Walker Jr., in July 2008.

pleasure of firing an M1941 Johnson many years ago, and it is a truly fine rifle. The Denton County museum has a rare 1918 Mauser antitank rifle on display, and it is an unbelievably massive rifle that was no doubt taken out of service due to smashed shoulders. I would have loved to let Kulis fire it, but I was afraid the kick would kill his whole family.

Following the failed assault across the Rapido River, the division was rebuilt even while it remained on the line and in combat in the vicinity of the town of Cassino. Ultimately the division would be withdrawn from the Liri Valley, and landed at Anzio to help shore up that troubled operation. General Walker would be redeemed as the 36th ultimately gave the keys to Rome to Fifth Army . . . but that is another story.

—CDR Mark Bowlin, USN (Ret.)
Irbil, Iraq
November 2011

Victory Road: A Texas Gun Club Novel
2011 Winner, Gold Medal Award, Military Writers
Society of America

The Texas Gun Club
2010 Winner, Gold Medal Award, Military Writers
Society of America

Order your signed copy at www.MarkBowlin.org.

About the Author

Commander Mark Bowlin, USN (Ret.) is a somewhat opinionated former naval intelligence officer who believes that the Dallas Cowboys will eventually win another Super Bowl, that Texas is truly God's country, and that good Texas barbeque and a cold beer is superior to champagne and caviar in every respect.

Mark was a soldier in the Texas National Guard before being commissioned as an ensign in the United States Navy. Mark has lived in Wales, Japan, and Italy and served in a variety of billets ashore and afloat in the United States and overseas. His awards include the Legion of Merit and Defense Meritorious Service Medal among other personal, unit, and campaign awards.

He is the award-winnng author of *The Texas Gun Club* and *Victory Road*. This is his third novel in the Texas Gun Club series.